C000016097

THE QU

THE QUIET EARTH

By the same author

THE HERB GATHERERS
THE EGYPTIAN YEARS
THE SUN WORSHIPPERS
TIME OF THE WOLF

ELIZABETH HARRIS

The Quiet Earth

HarperCollins*Publishers*

HarperCollins*Publishers*
77–85 Fulham Palace Road,
Hammersmith, London W6 8JB

Published by HarperCollins*Publishers* 1995
1 3 5 7 9 8 6 4 2

Copyright © Elizabeth Harris 1995

The Author asserts the moral right to
be identified as the author of this work

A catalogue record for this book is
available from the British Library

ISBN 0 00 225014 4

Set in Palatino

Printed in Great Britain by
HarperCollinsManufacturing Glasgow

All rights reserved. No part of this publication may be
reproduced, stored in a retrieval system, or transmitted,
in any form or by any means, electronic, mechanical,
photocopying, recording or otherwise, without the prior
permission of the publishers.

For Richard, with love;
this is where you came in

Song of the French Crusaders

Comptes ni ducs ni les rois couronnés
Ne se pouront la mort dérober:
Car, quand ils ont grands trésors amassés,
Plus il leur faut partir à grand regret.
Mieux leur valût les employer à bien:
Car, quand ils sont en terre ensevelis,
Ne leur sert plus ni château ni cité.

12th Century, anon.

No count, no duke, no crownèd king,
Can ere avoid death's mortal sting:
For if in life great wealth he gain,
When left behind, 'tis all in vain.
Better on good his treasures rain;
For once his bones are wrapped in earth,
Castle and city have no worth.

Translation
Richard Stuart-Pennink

BOOK ONE

Prelude
TODAY

If we're going to save the world, Nina thought, I shall need a new stapler.

For the ninth time she'd had to stop to extract a misfired staple. The huge stack of papers Mark had dumped on her desk hardly seemed to have diminished at all, and she felt like hurling the lot out of the window.

She wondered, as she often did, why she'd spent the past year working so hard for so little. As always, the thought was followed by the attendant doubt: am I cut out for this?

Mark's a saint, no question that he's the right one for the job, she reflected, getting the stapler to work again and proceeding with the endless task of fixing together promotional literature. Did *anyone* actually read it, or did the somewhat amateurish look make them chuck it, unread, into the nearest bin? Possibly even the bold banner heading EARTHWORKS put them off – anything green, Nina had concluded, made people switch off, since it revived their guilt over not recycling enough paper and not trying hard enough to make their kids turn out unnecessary lights.

I'm going to have to put *my* light on, she realized. It's a wild extravagance, I know, but I can't see.

She worked on for another half hour, and gradually the repetitive task dulled her irritation.

Glancing at her watch as she put the last papers on to the pile, she saw it was six o'clock. Knocking-off time, even if you *did* work for a man who didn't count hours, only results. And there weren't many of those.

She stood up, eyes skimming the literature she'd just finished collating. The top sheet was Mark's latest attempt to arouse public concern over a waste tip being proposed by the council, for which a substantial acreage of ancient woodland would have to be sacrificed. She read through his beautifully written prose – really, he ought to write poetry, he uses words quite magically – then turned the page to look at her own mundane contribution, which was a list of recycling points, alerting attention to a new one right beside the supermarket car park. She'd been rather proud of 'Drop as you Shop!', although slightly worried that people would read it the wrong way and agree that, yes, shopping was a bugger, wasn't it? So exhausting!

Bryn had submitted an article on boot fairs. Mark had queried the relevance to conservation, to which Bryn had replied, 'Of course it's relevant! We constantly harangue them to recycle glass, paper, aluminium, and God knows what else. Why not recycle chairs and ironing boards? It all helps save resources!'

Bryn was the sort of man who could casually drop words like 'harangue' into everyday conversation without sounding precious. But then he had read philosophy at university. If he wasn't so kind-hearted and entertaining, Nina could have got quite irritated with Bryn.

Mark was still hard at it – she could see him at his desk in the next-door room. *He* hadn't put his light on. However, he was working at the word processor,

4

so perhaps he reckoned he was already using enough electricity. The word processor had been a major expense, taking virtually all their reserve capital, but it had certainly improved efficiency. Mark was the only one who knew how to use it, but he'd promised to teach Nina, 'when I've got a morning'. Nina wondered which would come first, learning word processing or her old-age pension.

She went into Mark's room.

'Are you coming down the pub?' She tried to say it casually, as if it didn't matter if he said yes or no. He'll say no, she thought, observing the back of his head as he bent over the keyboard, he's so absorbed it's taking him a while to register the question.

He turned round, smiling at her apologetically. 'Is it six already?'

'Nearly five past. Bryn's just gone.'

'No, I won't, thanks, Nina. I want to get this finished, then I can get on with the falcon report first thing tomorrow.'

He went into an elaborate explanation of all he still had to do, adding somewhat lamely that he'd look in at the pub on his way home and see if they were still there.

'Okay.' She managed a smile. 'Maybe see you later, then.'

I won't, she thought as she zipped up her jacket – it was raining – and went out into the evening air. I won't see you because you'll still be here at midnight, and when you finally call it a day the pub'll be long closed, glasses washed up and landlord sound asleep.

She dragged her bike out of the shelter and set off down the hill. The chain slipped – it was a boot fair bike, a 'recycled cycle', Bryn called it – and her foot caught on the pedal, wrenching her knee. 'Sod it!'

she yelled, then, in case Mark heard and happened to glance out of the window – which was unlikely, as with her departure from his office she might as well have stepped off the planet – she gave a cheery wave to disguise the anger.

Never mind, she told herself. Bryn's in the pub, I'll have a couple of drinks with him then go home and fix myself something nice for supper. Bryn was good company and rarely talked shop out of working hours. Unlike Mark, who rarely talked anything else.

But Mark had kissed her, under the mistletoe at the party they'd thrown in the Earthworks office at Christmas. They'd invited everyone who'd helped in any way during the year, from shopkeepers who'd let them put up posters to university staff who'd listened to what they had to say and promoted the organization among their students. Everyone had bought a bottle – some of the wealthier guests had bought several – and the majority of them had got slightly drunk. Including, uncharacteristically, Mark.

He'd found her in the tiny kitchen; she'd been making a cup of coffee for a short and bumptious man from the university's archaeology department who'd fallen over on the steps. He was singing 'Nellie Dean', and his rendition, besides being un-seasonal, was also ferociously tuneless.

Mark came up behind her and put his arms round her waist, turning her so that she was facing him. He said, 'Happy Christmas, Nina, who lights up my days.' Then he pulled her out into the hall, where the mistletoe hung from the light, and, holding her face in a gentle hand, closed his mouth to hers.

Nobody had kissed her like that before. Somehow – she'd never worked out quite how – he managed to combine a supreme tenderness with the promise

6

of deep passion. She hadn't wanted to let him go, and ever since she'd been waiting for him to do it again.

Freewheeling down the hill into the town centre, she asked herself if she really wanted to go to the pub if Mark wasn't going to be there. Wouldn't it be better to go straight home than sit watching the door opening all evening to admit people who weren't him?

Home. Ha!

She started pedalling, turning down the road that led to the pub. No, *anything* was better than a long evening at home, on a night when she already felt low.

She reflected on how misleading was the word home when used in the context of her tiny flat in someone else's house. Living room with a dining table in the corner, inadequate kitchen, bedroom in which the double bed – entirely redundant, she thought bitterly – took up far too much of the mean amount of space. And she shared what her landlady laughingly referred to as 'my utility' – nothing more than an unreliable old twin tub that Mrs Noah probably threw out and a rickety drying rack – with the woman who had the flat on the floor above.

She'd loved it, at first. It had symbolized her quiet revolt, her long-postponed flight away from the parental home in which the atmosphere veered wildly, as it had always done, between indifference amounting almost to neglect and total dependence dressed up as concern. Her father, she suspected, had made alternative arrangements – he'd spent much of his working life abroad, and only came home when he'd run out of excuses not to. Her two elder brothers had long been off fending for themselves, leaving her mother more or less alone in the big empty house.

Nina's conscience had fought to keep her there, the dutiful daughter, but a strong voice of self-preservation had countered, 'Get out! Go away while you still can!'

And she had.

Her flat had been loveliest of all two years ago, during the months – all three and a quarter of them – of her affair with Prosper Delgardo. He was handsome, romantic, and, to a relatively inexperienced woman of twenty-four, quite irresistible, once she'd got over his absurd name. Delgardo he obviously couldn't help – his father was Colombian. Or Argentinian. Anyway, somewhere in the lower half of the American continent. And the Prosper had been the choice of his mother; she was quite a Shakespeare buff, and had named him after the old magic-maker in *The Tempest*. Nina's mother, who wasn't a Shakespeare buff at all, referred to him as 'Save and Prosper'.

He told her once her eyes were too expressive to be blue, too lovely to be grey. She hadn't realized it was a quotation, although began to suspect it might be when he added that the hair that lay along her back was yellow like ripe corn; it wasn't, she had to admit, the way people actually talked.

She never told him she was pregnant. She might have done – it was a point she frequently pondered – only he wasn't there to be told, having left suddenly one weekend when she'd thought he was going to Cheltenham, leaving her a note that said, *Darling Nina, Couldn't bear to see you so had to write – my father has suggested we meet up in Rio for a month or two and has sent the ticket, so off I go!!!* (The studied jauntiness of his tone had hurt almost more than the words.) *It's been fun – you're a great gal. Love, P.*

I'm a great gal, she thought numbly. Oh, good.

He never wrote, not even a postcard of Sugar Loaf Mountain, or whatever it was called. In the bitter mornings as she threw up in the chilly bathroom, she hoped fervently he'd fallen off it.

It was bad luck to be pregnant. Apart from anything else, they'd only made love on three occasions and just once had it lived up to its name, as far as she was concerned; the other couple of times had been less like lovemaking, more like some sort of endurance test. But, unfortunately, the lovemaking experience had come first, and she'd entered into each of the repeat performances in the eager but vain hope that it would be like that again.

She didn't tell her friends, her family or even her doctor, discovering the truth via a home testing kit. She didn't even go to the doctor once she knew; she wondered afterwards if she'd known there was no need. She'd never really *felt* pregnant; she'd had the symptoms all right – nausea, overwhelming fatigue, bloatedness – but she'd never believed, deep in her heart, that the outcome of it all would be a living child.

It was just as well. Twelve and a half weeks after Prosper's last endurance test, her hopeless pregnancy had ended in a miscarriage.

For some time she'd felt nothing at all. No relief, no regret, nothing. The months went by with no desire for companionship, even, and certainly not for any close relationship – too dangerous! was her instinctive reaction. At the time when the baby should have been born – she'd worked it out carefully, for some reason – she had a strange, disturbing dream. She was lying in bed, but not her own bed nor any hospital bed. No bed, in fact, of nowadays, but what felt like a straw-filled mattress, with clean, soft woollen blankets and something made of fur spread over

her. She was quite sure she experienced a birth, although, of course, when she woke up, she hadn't.
But in the dream, she'd felt pain, felt tears, clung
with all her might to the arms of a shadowy figure
robed in black.

Afterwards – not immediately, but two or three
days later – the guilt began. Perhaps – probably – it
came about because in her dream, just for a moment,
she'd held in her arms a warm, living baby.

I killed it, she thought. I didn't want it, I didn't take
care of myself, I hardly acknowledged it existed.

And I lost it.

It was a realization that was very hard to live with.

* * *

Bryn was standing at the bar, a couple of inches
down his first pint. He acknowledged her arrival by
asking the landlord for a half of bitter.

'Mark not with you?'

She made an elaborate show of searching her
pockets. 'Nope.'

Bryn gave her a sympathetic glance. She occasionally worried that the Christmas kiss hadn't gone
entirely unobserved. 'Let's go and sit by the fire.' He
took her elbow. 'I need a warm. And a rollie.'

They sat down on a bench in front of the hearth,
and she watched as Bryn took out tobacco and papers
and neatly rolled himself a cigarette, lighting it and
inhaling with obvious pleasure.

In the Earthworks office, they observed a rule of
No Smoking and No Excess Heat. Consequently Nina
was always cold by six o'clock, unless it was summer,
and Bryn was always cold and nicotine-desperate. It
was, she thought, a tribute to their belief in Mark that
they followed his dictates so faithfully.

'Peter the Piss-Head's coming in later,' Bryn remarked.

'Who?'

'You know, your pal from the archaeology faculty. The song-bird.'

'Ah. Is this a piece of news to gladden my heart?' She hadn't much time for people who got so drunk that they made a nuisance of themselves – after Mark had finished kissing her at that Christmas party and she'd given Peter his coffee, Peter had been sick over the bumper of someone's car. Her faith in the sobering powers of coffee had been drastically diminished.

'Peter's okay. You shouldn't judge him on the strength of one misdemeanour.'

'No, I suppose I shouldn't.'

Bryn laughed. 'Once more, with feeling!'

She smiled. 'What's he meeting you for?'

'Us. He's supervising a dig up at that old monastery place – the one by Symond's Yat?' – she nodded – 'and he needs helpers. He's a flatterer, the way he phrased it was, "I want *intelligent* help, Bryn, people in the know like you lot, people who won't bash their spades through eight hundred years of precious history and who won't keep asking, who was Symond? Was he a monk?"'

'He's Peter the Elitist Piss-Head,' she observed.

'Don't be like that. He's right, you should know that. Enthusiastic amateurs do more harm than good.'

'All right. So, assuming we're going to give him our professional intelligent help, when does he want us?'

'That's what he's coming to talk about. I said I was interested, and that I'd ask you and Mark to be here too.' He looked at her ruefully. 'Fifty per cent's not bad.'

'Mark said he'd look in if he gets finished,' she said loyally.

Bryn made a sound expressing disbelief. 'Sure. Still, even if he had come, he'd probably have said sorry but he couldn't spare the time.'

'He works harder than you and me put together! He –'

'I know.' Bryn put his hand on her knee.

Taking his interruption as a kindly way of saying, shut up, she stopped.

The ensuing awkward silence was broken by Peter's arrival. Bryn waved across at him, and he redeemed himself marginally in Nina's eyes by smiling back in a friendly way and instantly asking what they'd have to drink.

'I've explained to Nina what this is about,' Bryn said.

'And you're both willing to help?' Peter looked eager.

'I am,' Bryn said.

Nina hesitated. On the one hand there was her instinctive dislike of Peter – even if he *had* just bought her a drink, she couldn't deny it. On the other hand, she'd had a fascination with the past ever since some distant relative had given her a book called *Boys and Girls of History* for her eighth birthday, and opportunities like this one didn't crop up every day. She'd joined Earthworks in the hope that she'd get involved in the fight to preserve old buildings and similar fascinating and important tasks; so far, opportunities for that hadn't cropped up at all.

She said, 'Me too.'

'Great!' Peter beamed from one to the other. 'Let me put you in the picture briefly. We're excavating what we think is a small monastery, maximum maybe ten inmates, dating from the twelfth or thirteenth century, although it appears from the remains that the monastery was built on top of an earlier settlement. One suggestion is that this was an ancient sacred site – you know, prehistoric worship, possibly a place of power.'

Bryn nodded knowledgeably. Nina, a shiver of excitement running through her, thought now wasn't the moment to ask, what's a place of power? She could talk to Mark about it.

'It's a simple settlement – chapel, dormitory block, kitchen and refectory, built around a courtyard. Oh, and what appears to be an infirmary.' He caught Nina's eye. 'We're assuming that because it has a big fireplace. Not a cooking hearth, like in the kitchen, but a recognizable fireplace. If you were a monk, you endured the seasonal temperature, whatever that was, unless you were sick.'

A bit like the Earthworks office, she thought.

'How much have you uncovered?' Bryn asked.

'We've got the full layout now, but we've not yet begun to go in deep. What's caught our attention at the moment is a graveyard. It's outside the walls of the monastery, on a little corner of flat ground behind the track, at the foot of the hillside. Do you know,' – he leaned forward, eyes alight with excitement, and Nina, warming to his enthusiasm, felt herself forgiving him his Christmas faux-pas – 'these monks, they must have still retained some fragment of heathen belief, because they were interred with grave goods.' He sat back, watching their reaction.

Nina, who didn't at first see the significance, felt she was letting him down. But Bryn – she recalled he'd studied ancient history as well as philosophy – was more rewarding.

'Is that right!' he exclaimed. 'That's fascinating. What sort of things have you found?'

'In the first grave we opened, the skeleton was holding some sort of agricultural implement – a scythe, we think – and at his feet they'd carefully placed a mattock and something that looked like a small spade. In the second, the hands were clasped around a pectoral cross, and at the feet were what we assume to be candlesticks, made out of pottery.'

She was picturing the bodies, lying in the ground clutching on to whatever the people who buried them had considered to be important to them. She said, 'A gardener and a priest.'

Bryn began to say something, but Peter interrupted him. 'Exactly!' he said. 'That's just what we think.'

'The Egyptians did it, didn't they?' she asked him. 'Pharaohs' tombs might have been full of luxury items, but ordinary people got buried with the tools of their trade.'

'Not only the Egyptians,' Bryn said. 'Until Christianity changed the rules, it was the done thing among most civilizations.'

'Why should Christian monks adopt a pre-Christian ritual?' Nina asked. 'If the monastery dated from the twelfth century –'

'Twelfth or thirteenth,' Peter said.

'– it's not as if they were newly converted, and still retaining much of their old ways. Is it?'

Peter shook his head. 'No. Christianity had been the country's religion for at least five hundred years, since Augustine landed at the end of the sixth century.'

'Perhaps they belonged to a new religion, one that revived the old beliefs,' she said vaguely. 'Some sort of –'

'There *were* no other religions, at least not till Henry broke from Rome,' Bryn said. 'There was hardly any

14

heresy in England till Wycliffe, in the late fourteenth century. Our ancestors were a conventional lot, spiritually. Isn't that interesting?'

Nina and Peter nodded dutifully.

'Come and see for yourselves,' Peter said. 'What are you doing on Saturday?'

* * *

Peter picked them up in the university minibus, and for the duration of the journey they sat uncomfortably jammed up against the rest of his workforce, trying to prevent boxes full of equipment falling over every time they went round a bend. There were five of them, Nina noticed, discounting Peter, Bryn and herself.

'Gus'll be working with Nina, Bryn and me in the graveyard,' Peter said over his shoulder. 'This is Gus, sitting by me.' He nodded towards the bearded man in the passenger seat. 'You four are getting on with the refectory. Right?'

Four people sitting along the back seat echoed obediently, 'Right.' Nina glanced at them, and one of the women smiled at her.

'Nice day for it, isn't it?' the woman said encouragingly.

'Lovely,' Nina agreed.

'You couldn't persuade Mark to join us, then?' Peter said.

Bryn laughed shortly, and Nina, thinking he was going to make some disparaging remark, was about to leap to Mark's defence. But Bryn said, 'He's up on Yat Rock today, talking to the chap who's watching the falcons. There's a breeding pair nesting in the rock face, and the bird protection lot have organized a round-the-clock vigil to stop vandals stealing the eggs or destroying the nest. He said he'd come and find us when he was through.'

'Did he?' The words were out before she could stop them, and she could have kicked herself for the eagerness in her voice.

Bryn leaned across and patted her hand. 'That's what he *said*,' he murmured. He shrugged his shoulders, as if to say, but you know Mark.

She turned away, looking out of the window to hide her face from his sympathetic smile. Yes, I do, she thought. So shall I spend the whole day hoping he'll turn up, which he probably won't, or shall I throw myself into enjoying being with Bryn and the others so that if he does come, it'll be a nice surprise?

I don't care, she told herself firmly. Whatever I do, it's not going to influence whether he joins us or not. So I might as well put him out of my mind and get on with it.

By the time Peter was backing the minibus into a parking space down by the river, she'd almost convinced herself.

They shared out the equipment, then Peter led the way down to a track that ran along by the water.

'We can't park any closer,' he explained, 'there's only a path, and anyway it soon gets too steep for vehicles.'

Nina, already finding her load heavy, thought that sounded ominous.

Bryn fell into step beside her. 'You can do it,' he said encouragingly. 'Just think, if you'd been a medieval monk, you'd have had to lug all your day-to-day necessities up there.'

'Where are we headed for?' she asked.

'There.' He pointed to where the track branched, one path weaving away up the hillside. 'The monastery's on the summit.'

'Bloody hell!'

He grinned. 'Quite.'

'Why don't they leave all this stuff up there? It would save us an awful lot of effort.'

'And where would they put it? Lock it safely away in a hypothetical garden shed, I suppose? Don't be daft, Nina – you can't leave anything lying around nowadays unless it's bolted down.'

She wanted to argue the point further – she hated it when he made her feel she'd missed something obvious – but already they were beginning the climb, and she needed all her breath for walking.

'Nearly there!' Peter called out some time later. 'Keep your eyes down, folks, and don't turn round till you're at the top.'

She wondered why, but when she finally reached the outer ruined wall and stood panting beside him, she understood. Taking hold of her shoulders, he spun her round to look back down into the valley.

The view was breathtaking.

In the foreground, the steep track wound through small saplings and bushes, disappearing in places beneath the thick spring foliage. Further down, the brilliant green meadow sloped gently towards the river, which surged by in a great sweeping bow. Symond's Yat stood up sheer in the background, like some Neolithic watchtower guarding the valley.

For an instant it seemed that the view was familiar, that this was a place she knew well. But it's not, she thought, I've never been up here before. What a place to spend your life.

Peter was relieving them all of their burdens, sorting the boxes out and putting some on the path and some inside the low walls.

'Refectory party, in here,' he ordered. 'D'you two want to have a look?' He glanced at Nina and Bryn, who went in through the gateway to join him. 'Infirmary there,' he pointed to a small room, three of whose walls were only an inch or two above the ground. 'There's the fireplace I was telling you about, on that side wall. Chapel across there,' – he indicated a better-preserved construction, built against the hillside which, she thought, had probably protected it – 'refectory, working and sleeping quarters over there on the other side of the central courtyard.'

'It's tiny,' she said. 'And so well-hidden – you can't see it from below. Nor when you're up close, not till you're almost inside the gateway.'

'It would have been a bit more visible when the walls were the full height,' Bryn remarked.

'Not much more,' Peter said. 'There are a lot of trees and shrubs out there, and it's ancient growth. I would think that this place was even better-camouflaged then than it is now.'

'Why?' Nina asked.

Peter looked at her. 'Your guess is as good as mine.'

She felt a shiver of – what? she wondered. Apprehension? No. She wasn't afraid, just excited. Then Peter leapt over the wall and picked up his rucksack, calling to her and Bryn to follow him, and the moment passed.

'This,' Peter said, 'is the graveyard.'

She stood at his side, slowly looking round. It wasn't obviously a graveyard – there were no headstones, no statues, no flowering shrubs. It was just a small sheltered area of grass, a natural hollow protected on three sides by the encircling hillside and on the fourth, open side, giving a wonderful view down the valley.

In one corner, two neat rectangular trenches had been dug, the freshly-turned soil looking red in the sunlight. A robin sat on the top of one mound, a worm in its beak.

Peter said softly – as if he didn't want to disturb the silence – 'That's the grave where we found the garden implements, on the left. The other one had the candlesticks and the cross.'

'Can we look?' Nina asked.

'Yes, but there's nothing to see. We've taken the skeletons and the grave goods down to the university's lab.'

She stared at him. 'You've *what?*'

'We're examining them,' he said patiently, as if explaining to a child. 'We can't do a thorough job up here, you know!'

She felt wildly angry. 'But this is where they were buried! Other people – their friends, their fellow-monks, *I* don't know – put them here, with ceremonies, with these grave goods you keep going on about, in accordance with their own beliefs, whatever they were. You can't just come along and dig them up!'

Peter was smiling. How can you smile! she wanted to shout. Don't you *see?*

Bryn said quietly, 'Steady on, Nina. You don't want him to . . .'

She didn't listen. 'How would you like it, if someone came along centuries after your death and dug you up? Spread your bones on a slab and poked about among them?'

'This is what archaeologists do,' Peter said patronizingly. She could tell, both from his tone and from his expression, that he was equally furious. 'Didn't you know?'

Her anger went as quickly as it had come, and she

19

felt foolish. Her face burning, she turned away. She heard Bryn mutter something, then Peter said in a carrying voice, 'Too emotional, women. Probably the wrong time of the month, or some other modern excuse for their congenital irrationality.'

She felt her eyes fill with tears, and hastily wiped them away. It's not him upsetting me, she realized, he's just crass. It's – she couldn't put it into words, even to herself. Wandering across to the violated grave, she looked down into it.

It's you, she said to whomever it was whose spirit hovered in the warm air. I'm crying for you.

And that, she thought as she got a tissue out of her pocket and blew her nose, really *is* irrational.

I'll have to apologize to Peter. Oh, damn.

He and Bryn were standing by a pegged rectangle in the grass, and Gus, who had come to join them, was gently lifting off strips of turf, rolling them up and placing them a few feet away. Bryn glanced up and smiled; Peter ignored her.

The apology stuck in her throat. Wordlessly she went to stand beside Bryn, waiting to see what would happen next.

They spent the whole day slowly digging out the rectangle and painstakingly sifting every trowelful of soil through a fine-meshed sieve. They found no-thing.

Resuming work after a brief stop for lunch – they'd all brought picnics of varying complexity – Nina wondered what made Peter so certain this was a grave and not just a rectangle of soil. She wasn't going to ask him – she'd exchanged a few words with him, but the antipathy was too strong for more – so she whispered to Bryn, 'Are you sure we're not wasting our time?'

'It's a grave all right,' he whispered back. 'They've surveyed the whole area, and marked out the places where the soil's been disturbed.'

'How can they tell? It was hundreds of years ago!'

He tapped the side of his nose with a muddy finger. 'They have their ways,' he said darkly.

'You mean . . .'

'They push a long tube down and bring up a sample of the layers. Apparently to an experienced eye – or, probably, an experienced eye plus a computer – it's child's play.'

'Hm.' She wasn't convinced.

The sadness returned as they delved deeper into the ground. She felt almost disgusted with herself, that she was being a party to the desecration, and wondered if she should announce she wasn't going to go on with it.

I wish Mark was here, she thought. I could talk to him, and he wouldn't give me that look men like Peter give you, as if they're mentally patting you on the head and telling you not to be silly. Not to be *emotional*. Whatever's wrong with being emotional, for God's sake? Look where the world's got since we came to the brilliant decision that emotions were not to be trusted, and we had to prove everything through logic.

Her mind flashed back to the image of a skeleton lying on a laboratory table.

Crawling back from the open trench, she put down her trowel and walked away. I can't, she thought. If Peter's right – and he probably is, damn him – and there is a body in there, I don't want to be the one who uncovers it. I'd be involved then, even more than I am already.

Mark, why aren't you here? You'd understand, even if I couldn't explain. She smiled, thinking of all the times he'd sat listening to her inarticulate attempts

21

to put her feelings into words, waiting patiently till she'd ground to a halt, then supplying whatever it was she'd been trying to say. Was he telepathic, or just very sensitive? Was there much difference?

She strolled over to the open side of the graveyard, walking along the path until Yat Rock came into view. Concentrating on him, over there with the falcons, she sent him a silent message.

'If you've given up work, Nina,' Peter's voice rang out in the stillness, 'perhaps you'd like to make yourself useful and pour us all a mug of tea.'

She was tempted to say, pour your own sodding tea.

But she didn't.

There was no excuse for not getting back to work after they'd drained the thermos. She sat herself down with her back to the grave and stuck to sifting soil that the others had dug out; it was the lesser of the two evils. We've found nothing all day, she reasoned, with any luck that'll continue.

When the sun was beginning to set and it seemed likely Peter was about to call it a day, there came a shout from the grave. It was Bryn's voice, and he sounded wild with excitement.

Spinning round, her heart sinking, she stayed where she was and watched.

The three of them were kneeling, backsides in the air, heads down below the surface. Their voices were muffled, and someone – Gus, she thought – was laughing.

Then they emerged into the light: Peter was holding a bone.

'What is it?' she asked. Her mouth was dry. Surely it was too small to be human? Perhaps it was from a rabbit? A badger? But not buried so deep . . .

'Seal this into one of those plastic bags,' Peter ordered her. Reluctantly she took it from him; it seemed to send a jolt through her, as if it were emitting some sort of force. As if – the thought amazed her – it wanted to make sure she noticed it. As if it or *something* did. Cringing from it, she held it at arm's length while she placed it carefully in the bag.

They were back down the hole, and their voices floating up to her were excited. Avid, almost. She had a sudden unwelcome picture of hounds round a fox.

A lot of time seemed to pass. The voices were falling silent. One by one – Bryn first, then Gus, and finally Peter – they pulled back from the grave. She stared at them as they sat there on the grass, trying to read their faces. Nobody was laughing now. Peter wore an insincere smile, Gus was expressionless, Bryn looked ashamed.

'What is it?' she whispered. No-one answered. 'What have you found?' she said, her voice rising.

Still they didn't respond.

She leapt to her feet, racing across to the trench. She thought she heard Bryn say, 'Nina, don't . . .' but she took no notice.

She stood on the lip of the grave and looked down.

The first little bone must somehow have become detached. There, in a framework of stones, surrounded by the carefully-removed earth, lay the rest of the body. A round skull, eye sockets huge and dark. The vertebrae, and, sticking up in an arch, the ribs. Arms and legs.

A complete skeleton. Tiny, tucked away in the earth like a child in its cot.

And, even to Nina's inexperienced eyes, a child no more than a few days old.

The others were speaking quietly, the dismay

apparent in their voices. Peter was saying something about monks traditionally looking after travellers, postulating that perhaps some woman going unexpectedly into labour while on the road had sought the help of the infirmarer. Bryn was muttering, 'A baby. I didn't think we'd find a baby.'

Gus had turned his back and lighted a cigarette.

Why is it so shocking? Nina wondered. We were digging out a grave after all – what did we expect to find but a skeleton?

But it's so little. It's not some monk, dead at the end of his natural span. It's a baby. And so pathetic, down there. To die before you've even lived is tragic.

For the second time that day she felt tears in her eyes. So that they shouldn't see, she moved away, out of the hollow and on to the path.

Someone was coming up the track from the valley. Coming closer, his panting breath audible as he hurried up the last few steps.

'I decided to come,' he said, noticing her, 'even if it is a bit late. I thought I could have a look, anyway, see what you've all been doing, then when you wrap up we can go . . .'

He was up on the path now, only a couple of paces from her. Close enough to see her face.

His smile faded. 'Nina, what's the matter?'

Stumbling towards him, she fell against him. After the briefest of pauses, she felt his arms go round her. As his gentle hands rubbed her back, he murmured in her ear, 'It's all right. Nina, don't.'

Even through the relief of having him there she managed to think, isn't that just like him? Wouldn't anyone else be embarrassed and say awkwardly, come on, old girl, pull yourself together! in a suitably bracing tone.

Only Mark would simply stand and hold me.

PART ONE

Aidan

Spring 1209

One

The body lay on its side in the muddy shallows, washed up by the racing current into a backwater of relative calm. Now and then a surging wave hurtling down the wild swollen river would send out powerful ripples, making the legs bob up and down as if in some vaguely remembered dance step. The hood of the cloak was caught fast on a tree root, holding the body as securely as a boat's painter.

Aidan had been instructed by Ranald not to show his face until he had a full basket of allium leaves for Benedict's potions. Had he not been so eager to get back to the relative warmth of the hermitage, he would have missed the human flotsam. The spring had been cold and wet – so wet that the Wye was running higher than ever before in living memory – and Benedict's precious leaves were being correspondingly slow to emerge from the shelter of the earth; Aidan had collected all those within easy reach, and to fill his basket he had to hitch up his robe and scramble down to where a light carpeting of leaves grew close by the river.

Icy water was oozing up through the mud, soaking his leather sandals. He muttered a curse, but under his breath – it was unlikely that Simon could hear, since he was a distance away and still suffering from catarrh-induced deafness, but if he did, he'd tell Ranald. And curses, even mild ones, earned you penances, such as being left to keep vigil by the altar when everyone else was snoring in their cells.

I've enough now, Aidan thought, that's a basket full, or it will be if I shake them up. Straightening, he put his hand in the basket and ruffled up the bright green leaves, bruising them sufficiently to release the pungent, garlicky smell. His stomach growled and saliva rushed into his mouth: the thought of the midday meal urging him on, he lifted the basket on to the grass above him and grabbed hold of the thin branch of a wispy shrub, dragging himself up the slippery bank.

The branch gave way and he fell back, the brief sharp pain as his shoulder hit a stone inflamed by the sound of Simon hooting with laughter.

'Heavier than you thought you were, eh, boy?' he chortled, voice thick with mucus. The laugh became a cough, and Aidan watched in alarm as Simon doubled over, his face the colour of mulberries.

'Are you all right?' he shouted, trying again to get up the bank and once more falling back.

'*NO!*' Simon spluttered between coughs. 'Fetch me the flask! I'm choking to death!'

Splashing through the shallows, searching for a stronger handhold, Aidan ran under a slight overhang. And tripped over the outstretched arm of the body.

After a few moments, the shock subsided enough to let him draw breath.

'Simon! *SIMON!*'

No answer. He could still hear Simon coughing, although it no longer sounded as life-threatening as it had. Bending down, Aidan took the still pale face in his hands, wiping the mud away from the mouth, probing the nostrils with a gentle finger. There was no response, and he could feel no movement of breath on his hands. Would I, though? he wondered frantically. My hands are so cold I doubt if I'd feel a mallet falling on them.

Do I pull him out of the water? Get him on dry land? But should I even try to move him? If he has broken bones, would I only make his injuries worse?

He ran his fingers lightly over the limbs, trying to make out any interruption in the line of the bones. The heavy sodden clothing made the task difficult, and the youth's utter immobility gradually killed Aidan's unreasoning hope. He's dead, he thought. The poor wretch is dead.

Touching the neck under the curve of the jaw, he could feel no pulse. Since it no longer mattered whether there were any broken limbs to cripple, he bent down, got his shoulder into the youth's belly, and lifted him from the water.

'Aidan? What have you got there?' Simon's face, blessedly returned to its usual shade of cherubic pink, loomed above him.

'A body,' Aidan said shortly. He heard Simon gasp, and saw his lips move in muttered prayer. 'Can you help me please, Simon? I'm sorry I couldn't come to your aid – I was looking for a place to climb the bank when I came across this poor soul.'

Simon seemed to shake himself out of his temporary state of shock. 'Oh, think nothing of it,' he said magnanimously. 'It was only a momentary inconvenience.' Aidan, head down as he bent under the corpse's weight, smiled briefly: for all his bossy ways and his tendency to tell tales, Simon wasn't a bad sort. And it took fortitude to dismiss the sort of bone-shaking cough that racked through him every winter

– and every spring and autumn, come to that – as a momentary inconvenience.

Between them, Aidan pushing and Simon pulling, they hauled the body up the bank. As they paused to catch their breath, Aidan glanced up at the steep path back to the hermitage.

'We'll need help,' he said flatly. 'I'll take it – him – as far as I can. You go on ahead, and send a couple of the others down to relieve me when I can't carry him any further.'

'Very well.' Simon looked anxious. 'Will you manage, boy? You're a strong young man, I know, but . . .'

'I'll manage.' I've no choice, Aidan thought.

'Give me your basket.' Simon stretched out his hand. 'I can take that as well as my own.'

'It's over there.' Aidan indicated with his head. 'Carry it carefully, it took me a long time to gather those leaves. And I got my sandals wet.'

Simon stared at him, his face working as if he were fighting some emotion. 'Aidan, what if you had not climbed down to the water's edge?'

The body would eventually have drifted off and the fishes of the open sea would have had a good meal, Aidan thought. But he was aware of Simon's deep fervour, and the horror with which he regarded the thought of a man going to meet his Maker without the benefit of prayer and ritual, and without the comfort of leaving his earthly body in a marked grave in hallowed ground.

'It would have been bad, yes,' he said soberly. 'Perhaps the good Lord guided me.'

Slowly Simon nodded. 'Undoubtedly He did,' he agreed. 'We must ask Ranald to give thanks.'

We might have been more heartfelt in our thanks had the good Lord guided me rather more hastily,

Aidan reflected. Then he pushed the irreverence from his mind and, beginning to recite what he could recollect of the prayers for the recently dead, slowly he started on the long climb stretching in front of him.

He realized very quickly that he was not as fit as he'd imagined. I'm barely fit at all, he thought, shifting the corpse on to his other shoulder and trying to shrug the cramp out of the side which had been bearing the load. That's what comes of a long winter cooped up inside, the only exercise chopping wood and stirring Benedict's concoctions for him. Too much time spent on our knees, not enough out in God's world, using our muscles in the ways He intended.

He intended for you a life of contemplation, snapped his conscience.

I can contemplate just as well – better, even – when I'm out in the open, living as a man is meant to live, he answered.

That wasn't what you said when you entered the hermitage, his conscience argued back. You said you wanted peace, wanted to be alone with God, united with Him in the tranquillity of a small devout community where . . .

I know what I said! Aidan arrested the memory – some things you just had to stop yourself thinking about. Bad enough that they surfaced in your dreams, where you had no power to prevent them so that, before the release of rising into wakefulness, you'd already been reminded of all you were trying to forget.

Arms tightening round the corpse's thighs, he resumed his climb. I *do* want to be here, he thought more calmly. I belong here. I'm happier here than I ever was outside. I couldn't manage life in the world

31

– it was the right decision to retreat from it. I'm only out of sorts now because it's spring, the sap is rising and the earth is green and beautiful.

He resolved to renew his pleas to Ranald to be allowed to take over from the ancient and arthritic Titus the task of sheep herd.

It had taken four of them to manhandle the corpse the last hundred paces up to the hermitage. The path became a narrow rocky track, more suited to goats than to humans – most of the community found it difficult enough even when not burdened with a heavy, awkward load.

Ranald, alerted by Simon to what was about to enter his domain, went out to meet the party and had the sense to take with him a blanket.

'Wrap the young man in this,' he said, 'and two of you hold each end.' He glanced at the four of them, Aidan, Mattheus, Benedict and Elias. Aidan was just thinking what compassion he had – 'the young man', he'd said, not 'the body' or 'it' – when he felt a touch on his sleeve.

'I will take your place, Aidan,' Ranald said. 'You look exhausted. You may go and rest a while.'

Fighting his urge to go on being involved – it was me that found him! – Aidan bowed to Ranald and thanked him. Then, the sudden relief from the burden of the body giving him the strange sensation that he was levitating, he went on up the path. As he opened the heavy wooden door in the hermitage's thick walls, every muscle in his body began to scream its protest.

* * *

Ranald must have given orders that Aidan be allowed to sleep. When he opened his eyes, the spring day was

32

nearly over and the corners of his cell were already shadowy.

His first thought was, I'm hungry.

He was more than hungry – he'd been hungry down by the river, and that had been in the early morning. He'd missed dinner, which the community took at noon, and if he didn't hurry he'd miss supper as well.

Ranald had thought of that, too. For a man who ate so sparingly himself, Aidan reflected, who refused the meat, eggs and milk that sustained the rest of them and existed on a limited diet of bread, vegetables and fish, Ranald always tried to ensure that his little community consumed enough to keep up their health and strength. Mattheus must have been detailed to save something more substantial than the usual supper fare of bread soaked in gravy; with a flourish, he set before Aidan a platter of mutton stew, flavoured with carrots and onions. He'd even heated it up.

'Ranald said you were to have this,' he said, grinning. 'I kept it safe for you – the cat's put a paw in it once or twice, but I took the lump of meat out of her mouth and returned it to the dish.'

'She doesn't like mutton,' Aidan said equably, his mouth full. 'Thank you, Mattheus. Now shut up and let me eat in peace!'

Slapping him playfully on the sore muscles of his arm, Mattheus returned to his kitchen.

Aidan bolted his stew, partly because he was starving but mainly because he was impatient to discover what had become of the body. They wouldn't think of interring it before tomorrow at the earliest, he thought, it'll be in the chapel, with someone kneeling beside it in prayer. In the morning, probably, Ranald'll order the ritual for the dead. Then we'll bury the body in our own graveyard.

33

There were six graves there already. The community had occupied its lonely, lofty site for less than ten years, but it was an exacting life, intolerant of all but the hardy. The tough winter just passed had taken two of them: the gardener Hubert had been ancient, at least by Aidan's standards, but the neurotic Paul, who used to hear voices in the chapel and talk aloud to God, had only been a few years older than himself. His death had come as no great surprise; his devotion had taken an extreme form, and the fasts he had imposed upon himself, from which Ranald's voice of reason had been unable to deter him, had left him a thin, pale wreck of a man who fell a ready victim to a late autumn fever.

Six of us buried out there, Aidan thought, wiping his platter with a chunk of Mattheus's rough rye manchet and cramming the soggy bread into his mouth. Now, there'll be an outsider among us.

Wiping the grease off his face and on to his sleeve, he hurried out of the small refectory and ran across the courtyard to the chapel.

He paused outside, adopting what Ranald referred to as a suitable demeanour, then went in, closing the door behind him. As he'd expected, the body lay on a trestle table at the top of the chapel's narrow nave; Ranald stood in front of the altar, his back to the corpse, and from his posture, Aidan guessed he was in prayer. Kneeling on the floor beside the body was Titus, whose calm expression gave no clue as to what he must be suffering; chronic inflammation in the knees, Aidan reflected, would make kneeling on a stone floor exquisitely painful. If ever a man were made for a life of patient devotion, it was Titus.

He moved silently to stand at Titus's side. Touching his sleeve, he bent down and whispered, 'Would you like me to relieve you?'

34

Titus opened his eyes and gave Aidan a brief smile. 'Not yet, my boy. I have not kept vigil long, and I have prayers I wish to say for the soul of our poor young man here. However, I should be most happy if you would care to join me.'

Maybe it'll ease his aching knees to have some company, Aidan thought. Not that he's giving any sign of being in pain. He made himself as comfortable as he could, which involved finding two areas of stone whose downward curves matched the bony outcrops in his knees. Settling, he closed his eyes and set his mind off down the tranquil, peaceful paths already occupied by Titus.

Some faint sound an unguessable time later made him open his eyes. The chapel was dark, the only spots of light given by two candles on the altar. Ranald must have lit them; looking round, for Ranald was no longer standing in front of the altar, Aidan saw him on the opposite side of the corpse. He, too, was kneeling.

The candles were made of tallow, extracted from the suet of Titus's sheep. The chapel smelt strongly of the fold.

What was the sound? A spot of grease from the candle, falling on the altar? It had been of that quiet level. Soft, and sort of . . .

As Aidan raked his mind for a suitable description, the sound came again. And it didn't come from the altar. It came from the table where the body lay.

He leapt up. Hands on either side of the table steadying it, he leaned down and stared. And, as if waiting for this moment, the dead youth moved his forefinger again.

The face was still corpse-pale, and whoever had tended the body hadn't managed to remove very much of the mud from the features or from the short

35

bobbed hair. Dye from the soaked felt hat had run down on to the forehead, giving the flesh a faint blue tinge. The tunic had been laced tightly up to the throat, and the short cloak was wrapped round the body and tucked in on either side. The youth looked so *dead* that Aidan was beginning to think the movement was mere illusion, brought about by the darkness and his own fatigue.

But he hadn't just seen it, he'd *heard* it.

Hardly breathing, he waited.

This time, the whole hand moved. And then, with a sort of snort, the youth opened his mouth and vomited out a copious amount of the river Wye.

Before he could draw in breath and choke on the slimy green mess, Aidan turned the head to one side. Under his hands, the cheeks felt very slightly warm.

Aidan said in amazement, 'He's alive!'

There was no response from Ranald or from Titus. Deep in prayer, they hadn't registered Aidan's voice. And, accustomed to speaking quietly when in chapel, he'd barely said the words aloud.

Alive. It's a miracle!

Joyfully, for who but God could have brought this about, Aidan filled his lungs and shouted, 'He's alive!'

Titus, shocked, stumbled up, only to slump down again. Dazed, he repeated over and over again, 'Alive! Thank the Lord!'

Ranald, practically, was instantly at Aidan's side, capable hands hurrying to help prop up the youth. 'We must warm him,' he said. 'Aidan, you and I shall carry him, Titus – Titus! Come along, we need you! – Titus will open the doors for us.'

'Where? What shall . . .'

'The infirmary, Titus,' Ranald said patiently. 'The one place that is always warm.' He glanced at Aidan, who saw a fleeting ruefulness in the older man's features. Ranald did not allow the rest of them to complain about the privations inherent in their chosen life – you accepted poverty of your own free will, he would remind them, and remember the words of Jesus on the subject of the rich! – and learning that he, too, suffered from the cold was somehow comforting. It made him seem more human. As human as the rest of them.

With Titus going ahead like a herald, Ranald and Aidan bore the youth the short distance across the courtyard and along the covered way to the infirmary. Benedict, alerted by Titus, was standing by the open door to usher them in. He wasted no time on exclamations, instead pointing to a narrow bed by the hearth. Simon was reclining on it, his cough sufficiently worsened by the day's exertions to permit him a night in the warmth of the infirmary, but at Benedict's gesture he got out of the way, moving to another bed.

'Put him here,' Benedict said. Bending down, he removed the round hat and began to rub the muddy hair with a linen rag. 'We'll soon have him dry.'

Benedict's fire was red-hot and glowing, and Aidan felt his fingertips tingle as, for the first time in months, they became really warm. He watched as Benedict began to remove the youth's clothing, first the cloak, then the tunic, undoing the laces and removing the cords which attached the padded woollen hose to it. Before taking off the drawers, he covered the boy with a blanket. Aidan smiled: modesty was a way of life in the community, and Benedict obviously wasn't going to abandon it, even when someone had just returned from the dead. Wrapping the covering tightly round the hips and the legs, Benedict glanced over his shoulder, spotted Ranald and said, 'Rub him with this. It'll help get the chill out of him.'

Returning to the tunic, he lifted the boy sufficiently to remove his arms from the sleeves and slip the garment from under him. The shirt came off next, and beneath it the youth was wearing an additional undergarment. It seemed to be made of strips of fine linen, bound round his chest like . . . like swaddling clothes, Aidan thought, an image of the infant Jesus before his eyes.

'Wet through, right down to his skin,' Benedict tutted, catching at one end of the linen and, with Aidan supporting the boy, unwrapping it and winding it round his hand as if he were balling wool.

Aidan, standing right by the boy, was the first to see his naked chest. The skin was pale and smooth, and as the linen slowly came off, revealed as being quite hairless. So young, Aidan thought, to be . . .

He didn't think any more. Not in any logical way, although his mind was filled with random delight. For another layer of linen had just been wound away, and in front of his eyes were a woman's breasts. Beautiful, they were beautiful – although marked with red stripes where the linen bands had been, the flesh was creamy-white and wonderfully curved, the nipples rosy, with perfectly circular aureoles. I've never seen breasts before, not in real life, he mused – there was a painting in the priest's house in my village of the Madonna, and you could see one of her breasts because she was suckling Our Lord. But her breast didn't look like these . . .

'Dear sweet God!' someone said.

Before Benedict or Ranald could stop him – before he could stop himself – Aidan's hand stretched out. Fingers trembling, he put them to the woman's left breast. The skin felt like – he had no word to describe it. He touched the nipple, and watched in fascination as it stiffened and grew erect.

Horrified, he pulled his hand back. Stuffing both fists into the opposite sleeves of his habit, he felt his face grow as fiery red as Benedict's glowing coals. Nobody seemed to have noticed – thank God, Ranald and Benedict were staring open-mouthed at each other, and Simon, unable to see what had caused the exclamation, was asking plaintively, 'What *is* the matter?'

Ranald reacted first. Pulling the blanket off Simon's bed, he threw it across the woman's naked chest. 'Simon must go back to his cell,' he ordered. 'I am sorry, Simon, but despite your cough you will have to endure a night of the usual cold. Benedict shall give you an extra dose of horehound. Aidan, you must leave, too.'

Aidan turned to scurry away – with luck, Ranald would miss his burning face.

But the voice said softly, 'Aidan?'

He froze. Then made himself turn round. 'Yes, Ranald?'

For a moment the dark blue eyes bored into his. He was about to confess – anything was better than this suspense! – when Ranald whispered, 'Not a word, Aidan. Not a word.'

'Yes. I mean, no.'

He ran out of the infirmary so fast that his sleeve caught on the latch and he had to reverse to release himself. As the door was closed behind him, he heard Ranald say quietly to Benedict, 'Thirty-five years old, infirmarer, and your first female patient.'

He couldn't have sworn to it, but he thought he heard Benedict answer, 'Aye. And she'll set the fox among the chickens, mark my words.'

Two

Aidan knew the secret hadn't escaped through any word from him.

He'd been so terrified that some chance remark would arouse the interest of the others that for a day or two he hardly spoke at all, which in itself his companions seemed to find suspicious.

He knew Ranald wouldn't have talked: it was up to him as the community's leader to maintain discipline and calm, so that his small flock could the better devote their hearts and minds to God. Revealing the nature of the person lying in the infirmary would hardly help them do *that*.

And it couldn't have been Benedict. The infirmarer was better at keeping secrets than any of them save perhaps Ranald. It had to be that way, Aidan reflected, concentrating hard and forcing the image of the first naked woman he'd ever seen right to the back of his mind, for how else could they trust him with the minor and sometimes embarrassing ailments that beset men living as they did? He smiled in recollection at poor young Elias's joy when, finally having plucked up the courage to confront Benedict with his haemorrhoids, the infirmarer's little pot of catmint ointment had brought almost instant relief. Now haemorrhoids were something to be avoided; Aidan was glad he hadn't been born studious and introspective like Elias, who'd acquired his affliction from months of sitting on a cold stone bench copying manuscripts. I persuaded him to go to Benedict, Aidan thought. He confided in me that day I found him sobbing outside the privy.

He quelled the small glow of pleasure that the recollection gave him: pride in yourself was a sin, men were merely the humble instruments of God's will. Not Aidan, not Benedict, but God had cured Elias's piles.

If it wasn't Ranald, Benedict or me, Aidan thought, the leak could only have come from Simon. But he saw nothing! At the most, he knew that a dead body had miraculously come back to life, and that something extraordinary – extraordinary enough to arouse the exclamation, 'Dear sweet God!' from a devout man not given to blasphemy – had been revealed when the revived body was unclothed. But that could have been anything! A wound, a scar, the first signs of some dreadful illness – Aidan said a swift fervent prayer of thankfulness that it hadn't been that – or even some valuable personal possession.

Surely it could only have been a long shot that had made Simon hit upon the right answer. If indeed it had been Simon. Whoever it was, the rumour had spread and the secret was out: in the darkness of the chapel, two mornings after the body had been brought into the community, Aidan heard someone whisper, 'There's a woman in the infirmary.'

During the day he observed the reactions of his companions, and the next morning, outside the walls cutting hazel wands to make hurdles for Titus, he summarized his observations. Ranald, always slightly aloof, was showing no sign of knowing the secret was secret no more. Benedict only appeared briefly for the offices – whenever he was required for intensive nursing of a patient, Ranald gave him dispensation and he was permitted to leave the chapel after the opening prayers. As might be expected, he looked preoccupied.

Perhaps she's suffered a relapse, Aidan thought. And he wondered why he should be so distressed at the idea.

Mattheus and Simon could be seen from time to time in quiet conversation. Like two wives gossiping at the well, Aidan thought, then berated himself for being malicious. You don't *know* that's what they're talking about, he told himself, it could be anything. Simon's cough is still bothering him – perhaps he's asking Mattheus to boil extra onions for him at the midday meal.

It was possible that Titus hadn't heard the rumour as, like Benedict, he was more often absent from the community than present. Especially when he had young lambs to care for – the bitter winter just past and the cold spring had affected animal as well as plant life and lambing had been late this year. Titus was still having to hand-feed four sickly lambs whose dams had died. If I am permitted to take over his job, Aidan thought, will I also acquire his remarkable touch?

He wondered what Elias was making of the whispered news. Does he even know what a woman is? Aidan wondered. He must have a past – must have been born of woman, perhaps had sisters and other female relatives – but it's as if he didn't exist before he came to the hermitage. As if his life began when he entered our walls, and all he has ever done or aspires to do is to copy manuscripts and paint beautiful illustrations.

Finally, he examined his own reaction. And abruptly stopped: again, like a shocking dream repeating itself the next night, he saw his hand stretch out to that vulnerable, exposed breast. Reach out and touch. In his fingertips was the memory of that soft, soft skin.

STOP.

As the full shame of what he had done rose up to confront him, he abandoned his work, hurried in through the gate and ran across the yard to the chapel. How could I have done such a thing? he asked himself. Already having acknowledged that he was guilty of the sin of lust – which he was storing away to confess to Ranald when he was brave enough – now he realized that the wrong he had done that pathetic unknown woman went deeper. She is our guest, he thought as he closed the chapel door behind him, she was in dire need and the Lord brought her to us for aid. He trusted us, had faith in us to care for her. And I, oh, what did I do? I touched her, abused her, assaulted her when she lay defence-less.

The sin was magnifying in his mind. Trying to force his chaotic thoughts into a true and sincere repentance, instead he found to his horror that his body was responding to the picture he couldn't get out of his head. I have forsworn womankind, he thought with silent intensity, I have chosen a life of celibacy.

So you have, mocked his conscience. But has it chosen you?

He supplied the next question himself: if not, have I any right to be here?

Rocked to his depths, he saw his past flash by. The miserable hunger that was his earliest memory, a grinding ache in his empty belly as he whimpered in the icy darkness for comfort that didn't come. The pain of the growing child forced to watch a loved mother work herself into the ground in return for the sort of scraps rich men fed to their livestock. The insecurity of not knowing where your next meal would come from. If it would come at all.

He closed off what had happened next, when he'd begun to turn from boy into young man.

Afterwards I came here, he thought. And Ranald took me in.

This is where I belong. The only home I've ever known.

The possibility that he didn't belong there, that he would have to leave and go back into the terrible world outside, wasn't to be borne.

He fell to his knees and tried to pray, for forgiveness for his sin and for reassurance that everything would be all right.

But the words would not come.

After supper that night, Ranald signalled to them to remain in the refectory. Moving from his place at table to the wooden lectern, the swish of his black robe was the only sound: the little community seemed to be holding its breath. Aidan felt nervous sweat on his brow.

Ranald stood with his hands either side of the lectern, long fingers smoothing the wood. He had made it himself, and the carved figures of the eagle and the spirit reflected his enduring dualist beliefs – the strange, other God, he had told them, fashioned four beings, a lion, a bee-eater, an eagle and a spirit, and the true God took from him the eagle and the spirit and with them made the good things of the world.

Ranald told them many stories. Stories of Satan's

fall from heaven, cast out for the sin of pride and taking with him in his plunging flight the captive angels whom he imprisoned in the bodies of men and women, so that they wept to find their sexless purity destroyed. Stories of Adam and Eve in paradise, where Eve was deceived by the serpent that Satan made, creeping from the reedbed to impregnate her with his tail.

Stories, too, of men and women striving for the ideal life – 'to be perfect', was his phrase – and giving up all that was base and evil. Daring to be different, and suffering persecution because of it. Fleeing from their homes, seeking tolerance in other lands, only to discover that men were the same everywhere.

Welcoming their questions, Ranald had tried to enlarge on his beliefs, but Aidan hadn't understood. He wasn't sure he understood now, for Ranald said that God was wholly good, and since nothing in the world was wholly good, nothing in the world was made by God. Nothing is wholly good? he'd wanted to protest. What of the dawn, when the stars fade before the coming of the light? What of the rich red sunsets over the Welsh mountains? What of bird-song, mother love, laughter, friendship?

But Ranald was wise, as wise as he was understanding. It was not in him to force his own beliefs on to others. Let us all love God in our own way, he would say, let us live together in harmony, respecting one another's right to work out his faith as he sees fit. Let us have tolerance here, in our own community, for it may be the only place on earth that it exists.

That was why they loved him. Why I love him, too, Aidan thought, coming out of his reverie. And why it is hurting so much that I have failed not only God but Ranald.

Making himself lift his eyes, he stared straight at Ranald and waited to hear what he was going to say.

Ranald had apparently come to the sensible decision that if the secret was out, refusing to acknowledge it would do more harm than good. Without preamble he said, 'It may have come to your notice, brothers, that the youth Aidan discovered in the river is not what he seems.' Aidan watched as the blue eyes flicked briefly to Simon, whose face quickly purpled. Just as I'd suspected, Aidan thought. Although how he saw her from where he was, I don't know. 'Whilst Benedict was tending to him,' Ranald was saying, 'it became apparent that he was not a young man but a young woman, for some reason dressed in the apparel of a squire.' A wealthy squire at that, Aidan thought, remembering the hose. Only rich families bought the more luxurious padded variety – young men grew so fast that mostly they had to put up with the cheaper sort, far less comfortable for a long day in the saddle. 'The lady is still unconscious,' Ranald went on, 'and, despite Benedict's devoted care,' – Benedict bowed his head modestly – 'remains gravely ill.'

Benedict got to his feet. 'If I may, Ranald?' he said. 'I don't like to leave her alone for long.'

Ranald nodded. As Benedict left, he resumed. 'Until we are able to question the lady, we shall not know her identity, for she bears no papers nor other distinguishing effects. We must assume that somewhere a husband, or a child, or parents are grieving for her, thinking her dead, and we must pray that they be comforted, just as we pray that she may be restored to health.' He paused, his eyes roaming the room and studying each of the five faces in turn. His glance resting on Aidan, he said, 'Whoever she is, lady or peasant, married woman or maiden, we will

46

treat her with respect.' Aidan dropped his head. 'There will be no gossip: the only time you speak of her shall be when you pray for her recovery.'

Aidan made himself look up again. Ranald was no longer looking at him – his eyes were closed and he was murmuring the Paternoster.

Although they didn't speak of her and nobody except Benedict and Ranald ever saw her, the woman dominated the community's consciousness. She was mentioned every time they prayed, and sometimes Ranald would give a brief bulletin: 'She still sleeps,' or, 'She has been muttering,' or, 'Benedict reports she is restless.' Once, 'Her fever is very high and it has caused convulsions.'

Aidan guessed she was suffering from some infection, no doubt contracted from her immersion in the Wye; if it wasn't the cold, he thought, then it'd be some noxious humour in the water, or in the mists that float above it. He developed a constant awareness of her, manifesting itself in a sort of prickling on his skin; observing the others, he thought they probably felt it, too.

Some of his companions would go to the infirmary door, silently handing Benedict posies of wild flowers or inappropriate offerings such as a small brown hen's egg, (Mattheus) and an illuminated letter 'J' (Elias, when he was asked what 'J' stood for, said, 'Jesus, of course!' looking at Simon, who'd posed the question, as if he were daft).

Aidan would have liked to take her a gift. But his troubled conscience wouldn't let him: he hadn't yet made his confession, and, instead of the penance Ranald would have imposed, he was administering his own punishment by not allowing himself within ten paces of her.

Benedict became increasingly tetchy, the constant anxiety showing in his face; the hollow cheeks and the dark semicircles under his eyes revealed how much sleep he was forgoing in the battle to save his patient's life. Once Aidan had the sudden thought, perhaps she was meant to die! Perhaps she's done wrong, and God made her fall in the river, and we're interfering with His will by trying to save her!

The thought was disturbing and painful. He felt a stab of instinctive superstitious terror at the thought of going against God's will, accompanied by a sense of disappointment in God that He should punish a young woman so severely, whatever she'd done.

As quickly, he was calm again. As if God's very hand were smoothing his brow, he knew that he was wrong. That a loving God didn't go throwing people in rivers to drown, and that He had arranged for Aidan to find her and pull her out before it was too late. With that knowledge came the certainty that she would get better: had Ranald not forbidden talk of her, so sure was he that he'd have gone straight away to tell the others.

His prophecy didn't seem to be in any hurry to come about. Over the next two weeks, the woman showed little if any improvement, lying in her shadow world, turning, twitching, muttering, inter-mittently running a fever which refused to respond to any of Benedict's nostrums.

Ranald suggested that Benedict have a rest, volun-teering his own and the others' services to watch over the patient. He must be worried about the in-firmarer, Aidan thought, to propose such a thing when to date he's been at pains to keep us away from her. Benedict rejected the proposal, so Ranald changed it into an order. Starting that night, they would all take a turn at sitting in vigil in the infirmary, allowing Benedict some much-needed sleep.

'But I should be –' the infirmarer protested.

'What if someone else becomes sick?' Ranald countered. 'Your diligence has been exemplary, Benedict, and no-one could have worked harder to save a fellow being. However, you have other responsibilities, too. If one of us needs your skills, what good can you do him if you are exhausted?'

The logic of the argument was irrefutable. Aidan watched several expressions race across Benedict's open face – truculence, anger, resignation, and, perhaps, a tinge of relief – and then he said, 'Very well. But I am to be called the *instant* there is any change!' He glowered at Ranald, as if Ranald had specifically said he wouldn't be.

'Of course,' Ranald said mildly. 'Go and settle your charge for the night, and in an hour I shall relieve you. Tomorrow night –' his glance ran round the community – 'the duty shall be Mattheus's, the next night Simon's. Titus I shall not call on, for on many nights he stays with his lambs. That leaves Aidan and Elias, who shall follow after Simon.'

Four nights away, Aidan thought. Unless the miracle happens within four days, I shall have to spend the night in the infirmary by her side. Or tell Ranald the reason why I can't.

Both options making him feel equally sick, he tried to pray for help. Again, the words would not come.

Ranald's rota didn't have a chance to begin operating. The morning after he had taken his turn sitting vigil, Benedict, Simon and Mattheus awoke with fevers of their own. Aidan was summoned by Ranald to the infirmary to assist, and he stood nervously on the threshold until Benedict snapped at him to come in and close the door, or was it his intention to let *all* the warm air out?

Trying to measure out medicines with trembling hands and reddened eyes in a flushed, sweaty face, Benedict said, 'I can't say what it is, Ranald.' Picking up his superior's unspoken thought, he added, 'No, I doubt it's anything we've caught from her.' He glanced at the sleeping woman, his expression indulgent and kind. 'Poor lass, if I were going to get ill with whatever ails her, I'd surely have fallen sick before now. Mattheus hasn't been anywhere near her, and nor has Simon, save for a short while that first night.'

Aidan, concentrating on keeping his eyes anywhere but on the woman in her bed by the hearth, saw Benedict knock over a flagon. Stepping forward, he stood it up again, catching up a rag to mop up the spilled syrupy liquid.

'Let me help,' he offered.

Benedict turned to him and said, 'Thank you, boy,' an indication of how ill he was feeling: Aidan knew that normally he regarded his infirmary and everything in it as his own personal property, considering the others far too clumsy to be allowed to interfere. 'This is white horehound and lungwort syrup, for Simon's cough. Pour some out into this smaller bottle –' He handed it to Aidan, '– and Simon can keep it at his bedside and dose himself as necessary.' He put the flagon back in its place. 'Now, symptoms of this malady are sore throat, for which we will gargle with an infusion of this –' he produced a small box of dried selfheal flowers, '– and headache, for which you shall make us all some linden tea.' He held a double handful of white lime flowers under Aidan's nose; they had a pleasant, sweet smell. 'Make it strong, boy, it'll help us sleep.'

His energy abruptly coming to an end, Benedict sank down on the bench, and would have fallen off it had Aidan not grabbed his shoulder.

'Take him to his cell, Aidan,' Ranald said. 'Then come back and make up those remedies.'

'But I –' Aidan began. Working as Benedict's assistant was one thing. Doing it all by himself was quite different.

'Do as I say!'

Aidan supported the infirmarer across the courtyard and along the dormitory corridor, finding the appropriate cell and settling him down as comfortably as he could. Benedict seemed to fall instantly asleep.

Back in the infirmary, Ranald seemed to be in a more reasonable mood. 'I'm sorry, Aidan, I omitted to say I'd help you with the medicaments,' he said. He checked swiftly through Benedict's supplies. 'We seem to have plenty of everything.' He added ominously, 'Just as well.'

The next day, Elias went down with the fever. Ranald ordered Titus to remain out in his sheep herd's hut, dispatching Aidan to help him take with him sufficient supplies for several days. 'He has not been much among us,' Ranald explained to Aidan, 'and is unlikely to succumb. If you and I fall sick . . .' He left the sentence unfinished.

Aidan, relying heavily on the support of his superior's calm authority and broad back, didn't dare think what would happen if Ranald were to succumb to the malady. The pair of them were busy from morning to night, Ranald tending the still-unconscious woman and making up the more potent medicines, Aidan brewing endless teas and infusions; his feet hurrying to and fro between dormitory and infirmary must, he thought, have worn a groove across the yard.

When Mattheus, Simon and Benedict were beginning to recover and Elias's fever had just turned,
Ranald fell ill. The earlier patients were not well
enough to leave their beds – Aidan was now produc-
ing mug after mug of rosehip tea, Benedict's sover-
eign fare for convalescents – and it was no use expecting help from them. Aidan struggled on alone, resist-
ing summoning Titus, for the old man, despite the
hardiness acquired from years of the outdoor life,
could surely not escape the illness that had felled his
younger companions.

All except Aidan.

He sat in the last of the day's light, trying to say the
evening office to himself. His mind kept wandering:
he thought of his patients over in the dormitory, now
fractious and demanding like overtired children.
Tomorrow he'd try to get them up from their beds, he
decided, even if only to sit outside in the fresh air for
a while. Maybe the day would be sunny. His mind
turned to Ranald, and he glanced across at the long
form lying asleep in the bed by the door. Ranald was
more unwell than the others had been – perhaps
because before he'd fallen ill he'd worn himself out
caring for his companions – and Aidan was concerned for him. I'll speak to Benedict in the morning.
If he's well enough, he'd better come and look at
Ranald himself.

The responsibility weighed heavy.

In the gathering gloom, he felt his eyelids droop.
Mustn't sleep, not yet. Got to take round the jug,
make sure they've got fresh water to drink. Benedict
says you must keep taking in liquids after a fever. Got
to . . .

He was aware of dozing off. Not quite asleep, he
thought it'd be all right to relax for a few minutes.

When he awoke, it was fully dark.

He leapt to his feet. Lighting a candle, he ran to Ranald, putting a nervous hand to the forehead. Not too hot, thank God. I'll sponge his face, make sure he's well covered, then I'll –

'Could I please have some water?'

The sound was a croak and the words almost unintelligible, as if the speaker had forgotten how to form them.

Nevertheless, the voice was irrefutably female.

Frozen, Aidan remained bent over Ranald's bed.

'Please?'

The inert body he'd abused so vilely – the unconfessed sin hung ever more heavy on him with each day – was no longer inert. The young boy he'd fished out of the water – whose life he'd saved – had turned into a young woman. She'd almost slipped away through death's door, but Benedict had held on to her, and gradually she had come back to them.

Now she was there, her spirit returned to her body – her *female* body. Of all ironies, Aidan thought bitterly, the only person to hear her supplicant voice is the man who shouldn't be allowed anywhere near her. Who, but for this mysterious and ill-timed sickness, would never have set eyes on her again.

'For pity's sake!' The voice was shaking now, as if she were near tears.

It's up to me, Aidan realized. I'm no longer punishing myself by pretending she doesn't exist, I'm punishing her.

It's up to me.

He picked up the jug of water, poured a small measure into a mug – 'Little and often,' Benedict had said, 'because when you've been ill, your belly cannot take too much at a time. Make sure they're not too greedy!' – and walked over to the bed by the hearth.

She was staring up at him, eyes huge in the deep circles surrounding them. Her pale face was framed by hair as dry and spiky as straw, and her lips were deeply cracked. Not letting himself think of what she was – of those naked breasts he'd seen so briefly yet found impossible to forget – he slid his hand behind her head, lifting her so that she could drink. Then he held the cup to her mouth.

She drew in the water, slurping like an animal. 'Steady, steady,' he said softly, 'don't choke, now,' removing the mug after she'd taken only a few gulps. She tried to lift her hand to put it back to her lips, but she was too weak; her arm falling back on to the bed touched him deeply. He let her lie, gasping, for a little while, then lifted her again and let her drink some more.

After some time, she closed her eyes. Turning away from him, she curled up. Her breathing deepened, and he realized she'd fallen asleep.

He stood up, quietly rinsing and drying the mug. He put it back in its place next to the jug, wiping up a few stray drops of water.

His mind in shock, he couldn't think.

He sat down again to resume his vigil. Slowly, so slowly, the world turned, and a faint light began to grow in the eastern sky.

He thought absently, another day's beginning.

Three

When it was fully light, Aidan built up the fire and stood for a few moments over each of his two patients: prompted both by the pale sleeping face of Ranald and by the feelings that ran through him as he looked down on the woman, swiftly followed by the familiar kick administered by his conscience, he disciplined his mind and said the morning office. The sound of his own quiet voice repeating the old words was strangely calming: standing there in the peaceful silence, for the first time in two days he no longer felt afraid. I want to stay here, he thought as he finished his prayers. If it's possible. If it's *right*. If not . . .

If not, his inner voice answered, you will go. And survive.

He let out the breath he'd been holding in and went back to work. Filling the jug, he went across to the dormitory corridor to check on the others. To his great relief, Benedict was not only awake but half sitting, punching at the hay-stuffed pillow supporting his back.

'Where have you been, boy?' he greeted Aidan, the familiar impatience back in his tone. 'You –'

Catching sight of Aidan's face, he stopped. 'I

forgot, there's only you to look after all of us, isn't there? How is Ranald this morning?'

'He's still asleep.' Aidan poured a mug of water and handed it to Benedict. 'He feels cooler than he did last night.'

'Ah, but fevers always run hotter in the evening. It doesn't necessarily mean he's getting better.'

'Oh.'

He noticed Benedict's eyes on him. The infirmarer said kindly, 'He's strong, you know. He'll be all right. And I shall help you today – I've lain here quite long enough.'

Throwing off his covers, he put his feet to the floor, wincing as the bare soles touched the cold stone.

Aidan pushed him back. 'Not yet,' he said. Then, seeing the resolve in Benedict's face, 'Think how much longer you'll have to lie here if you get up too soon and suffer a relapse! I'll have to run around looking after you for ever!'

It was the right tone to have taken: with a sigh, Benedict lay down again. Aidan held back what he'd been going to say about the woman; if I tell him now, he thought, he'll struggle over to the infirmary this instant.

'Happen you're right, boy,' Benedict said weakly. 'But when you've tended the others, I want a full report – at least I can *think* again. I can take that responsibility off you.'

Aidan smiled, gratitude flooding through him. 'It's a burden I gladly hand back.' He picked up the jug. 'I'll return later.'

'Make some more rosehip tea,' Benedict's voice floated after him. 'Not as effective, I grant you, as when the hips are fresh off the bushes, but nevertheless it's . . .'

Aidan went into Simon's cell and put himself out of earshot.

From a misty start, the day soon became sunny and warm. The courtyard, facing south-west, was in shade almost until the middle of the day, by which time Aidan had put a couple of benches out in one corner. It was a veritable sun trap, and he thought his convalescents would benefit from an hour or so in the warm fresh air. Wallflowers were in bloom, fooled by the favourable conditions just there into thinking spring was well advanced. Growing out of the stone walls, their perfume hung on the light breeze.

Aidan took a short rest on one of the benches. He had been working since early morning, taking round water for drinking, water for bathing sweaty hands and flushed faces, refreshing teas and, under Benedict's orders, a thin but nutritious broth of boiled mutton bones and barley which he'd concocted in Mattheus's kitchen. Mattheus was getting better, too: as Aidan had repeatedly hurried back to the dormitory to receive instructions on the next stage in the cooking process, he kept shouting, 'You be careful, now! I don't want to get back to my kitchen and find you've broken something!' and, 'Stir it, Aidan! Don't let it settle on the bottom of the pan or I'll never get it off!'

During a relatively quiet time between the second lot of tea and the broth-making, Aidan told Benedict about the woman. Benedict, he recalled, was Ranald's second-in-command, so it was doubly appropriate that Aidan should reveal the news to him. As infirmarer, he must be told about his patient, and as acting leader, it was to him that Aidan would have to confess, should Ranald remain out of action.

The thought of confession was so forcefully on his mind that before he could stop himself he was on his knees beside Benedict's bed.

Benedict looked at him questioningly as he struggled up again. The thick eyebrows went up further as Aidan said hurriedly, 'I meant to tell you. She woke in the night and asked for water. I gave her a few sips – not too much, just as you said – then she went to sleep again.'

'You meant to tell me,' Benedict repeated. 'Something so important, which you must know I've been waiting for these many days, and you forgot?'

'I'm very sorry.' He didn't want to explain that he'd forgotten on purpose, to keep Benedict in his bed. 'It's just there's so much to do all the time that I – '

Benedict reached out to touch his sleeve. 'Hush, boy, you're forgiven. Believe me, I'm a good one to understand how too much to do can drive even the most crucial thing out of your head. So, tell me, what did she say? And, more important, how does she look this morning?'

'She's sleeping, but it's different now.' Aidan tried to put into words what he'd noticed. 'She moves around more, but like anyone does when they're asleep. She no longer twists her head from side to side, and she's stopped muttering.'

'How does she feel to the touch?'

Aidan felt the hot shameful blood rush into his face. Head down, he thought, he doesn't mean *that!* 'Her forehead is cool,' he said. 'I put my hand on her head and then on my own, and they felt much the same.'

'Good, good.' The infirmarer was nodding. 'I would say, then, that the fever is passed and that, as you suggested, she's now sleeping naturally.'

'Did I suggest that?'

'Indeed. You said she was moving like everyone does when they're asleep.' He laughed. 'We'll make an infirmarer of you yet! Most of what we do depends on observation, and you know how to keep your eyes open, boy.'

'What should I do now?'

'She'll probably wake again by and by. Encourage her to drink, as much as she wants. But only –'

'Only a little at a time,' Aidan supplied.

'Aye. Move on from water to rosehip tea, and stir in some honey. Poor lass, so many days without sustenance, she'll be feeble as a triplet lamb.'

'She didn't really say anything,' Aidan said.

'Hm?'

'You asked what did she say. She just asked for water.'

'Aye.' Benedict looked sad. 'Who is she, Aidan?'

It had to be a rhetorical question, and Aidan didn't respond. 'I must go,' he said.

'Keep me informed,' the infirmarer called as his parting shot.

Aidan thought, would I dare do otherwise?

The broth, or the fresh spring air, or both, did wonders for the convalescents. In the infirmary, making up a tonic from leaves of rosebay willowherb, Aidan smiled to hear Benedict, Simon and Mattheus trying to outdo each other in describing the severity of their symptoms. Elias had sat out with them for a short spell, but soon Benedict had instructed Aidan to see him back to bed.

The worst is over, he thought. Provided none of them has a relapse – please God, they won't – soon we shall be getting back to normal. He glanced over at Ranald. Please God, too, that you recover soon. We need you. *I* need you.

The tonic finished, he set the stone jar in a cool corner. Then he went outside to join the others.

'Why did he not fall ill?' Simon asked the company in general, poking a finger at Aidan.

'He's young,' said Mattheus.

'Not much younger than Elias,' Simon retorted.

'He's healthy,' Benedict said.

'So were the rest of us till we sickened,' Simon said. He grinned at Aidan. 'You must be the Lord's favoured, boy.'

Not I, Aidan thought. No, not I.

'How is the lady?' Mattheus asked, lowering his voice.

Aidan, who didn't want to answer, was saved by Benedict. 'We are not to speak of her. Remember?'

'Oh, yes. Forgive me.'

We may not be speaking of her, Aidan reflected, but sure as death and sunset, we're all thinking about her.

Slowly and carefully, the infirmarer got to his feet. 'Your arm, boy,' he commanded Aidan. Leaning heavily on him, Benedict made his way inside his domain. 'I thought I'd have another look,' he said quietly, putting the door to. 'In case there's been any change while we've been sitting out there.'

He had made straight for his patients the moment Aidan helped him out of bed. Aidan had been impressed by the sight of a man, scarcely well enough to be on his feet, worrying about others.

'He's on the mend,' Benedict pronounced, standing over Ranald. 'Constitution of an ox, our leader. Thank the Lord.'

'Amen,' Aidan said fervently.

The infirmarer moved over to the bed by the hearth. 'Now then, lass,' his tone changed, as if he were speaking to someone very young and delicate,

60

'what about you?' Pulling up a three-legged stool, he sat down beside her, studying her face, his hand to her forehead. 'Are you coming back to us?'

Aidan, watching closely, saw her eyelids twitch at his touch. 'She'll wake,' he said warningly. 'Shouldn't we –'

Benedict glanced at him briefly. 'I'm still infirmarer here, boy. At best, you're my apprentice,' he said gruffly, but he smiled, to show he meant no offence. 'She's slept long enough,' he explained. 'Her skin's dry, there's little water in her – see?' He pinched a fold of skin on the back of her hand, and the fold stayed in place for a moment or two before flattening back. 'Now she needs liquids. Lots of liquids. Mankind and animals, both can die from lack of water, even though the sickness is past.'

The woman stirred, and Benedict spoke to her. 'Come on, my lovely, drink.' He held out his hand to Aidan, who put in it a mug of water. Then, as Aidan had done himself in the night, Benedict held it to her mouth.

As she drank, her eyes opened. At first she squinted, as if the light were too bright. Then her lids shot up and she pushed away Benedict's hand. Alarm evident in the hoarse voice, she said, 'Gawyn?'

'Nay, lass.' Benedict replaced the mug. 'Drink, then talk, if you must.'

Thirst overcame fear, and she finished what was in the mug. 'More,' Benedict said, giving it back to Aidan. 'Warm water this time, and put some honey in it.'

He did as he was told, then watched as Benedict spooned tiny amounts of water-softened honey between the woman's lips.

'That is good,' she said quietly. The croak was going. Honey for dry throats, Aidan thought inconsequentially, hearing in his head the echo of Benedict's lecturing tones.

'You're safe,' Benedict said gently. 'No harm shall come to you here.'

She looked around, eyes going from Benedict to the crowded shelves of the infirmary, to the huddled form of Ranald, in the other bed. To the fire, and to the window with the sunshine beyond. Finally, to Aidan, trying to merge into the darkest corner.

'Who are you?' She was not asking him; she had turned back to Benedict. 'Monks?'

Benedict smiled. 'Of a sort. We wear the black habit, but we do not call ourselves monks. We are hermits, and you are in our retreat.'

'Retreat,' she repeated. 'Where?'

'Above the Wye.'

Slowly she shook her head. 'I don't remember,' she whispered. 'I don't know how I came to be . . . The Wye? The river Wye?'

'Aye.'

'How did I get here?'

'You were in the water. We brought you here thinking you were drowned,' – is it wise to tell her that? Aidan wondered. Will it not distress her, to learn of how narrowly she had escaped? – 'But you were restored to life. Aidan –'

No, he thought. I want no credit for anything I may have done. 'More water?' he asked, stepping forward. 'Anything else? A cloth to refresh her face? Or –'

'Water.' Benedict handed him the cup. 'As I was saying –'

'How long have I been here?'

'Many days, lady.' Aidan noticed the changed form of address: he had to agree, there was something in the tone of voice that made 'lass' somehow inappropriate. Even more so 'my lovely'.

62

'Many days? Have I slept for that long?' She struggled to sit up, but, too weak, fell back. 'Why do I feel so dreadful?' She managed the ghost of a smile.

'You have been sick of a fever,' Benedict said, smiling back.

'For days?'

He nodded.

'I am in your debt. I thank you for my life.' She took Benedict's hand and bowed over it, as if she were a knight swearing fealty kissing the hand of his king.

Visibly moved, he patted her head with his other hand. 'There, now,' he said. 'There, now.'

Before the delicate question of who had fished her out of the Wye could again be raised, Aidan said, 'Come away now, Benedict. He is only out of his own bed this day,' he explained to the woman. 'He too has had a sickness, as have most of our companions.'

'The same sickness as I?' she asked swiftly.

'Nay.' Benedict shot an angry look at Aidan. 'Your fever had one cause, ours another. The symptoms and the course of the two maladies were different – it is not through you that we ailed.'

'Sorry,' Aidan muttered.

Benedict, allowing himself to be helped up, grunted. 'No matter, boy. You meant well.' Turning back, he said to her, 'I shall come to see you tomorrow. In the meantime, drink all you want. Eat, too, if you can find the appetite – Aidan will take care of you.'

Taking first Benedict, then the other two, back to their cells and then commencing on the long list of things he had to do before he was finished for the day, Aidan thought, I will care for her. To the best of my ability. Maybe then I shall start to make amends.

Happiness surged through him at the thought that,

63

conveniently, he'd just been told to undertake the very task he'd have chosen.

* * *

By nightfall he was exhausted. Benedict, watching him closely as he reported for final instructions, said, 'Here's an order you'll obey. Take a pallet into the infirmary, tuck yourself up in a blanket and go to sleep.'

'But –'

'Unless I have your word, not only shall I make sure Ranald knows of your disobedience, I shall send you to your cell and take your place in the infirmary.'

'You're not well enough! You only got back here because I half carried you!'

'Exactly,' Benedict said triumphantly. 'You don't want to think of your poor weak infirmarer suffering a night on a pallet, at the beck and call of a couple of inconsiderate patients, do you?'

'No.'

'So I have your word?'

'Of course.'

'I doubt you'll be disturbed.' He admits now that whoever watches in the infirmary will pass a quiet night, Aidan thought. Now that there's no need to suggest the opposite. The infirmarer turned on his side, settling for sleep. 'Oh, how my bones ache!'

Your bones may still be suffering, Aidan thought affectionately. There's no longer anything wrong with your powers of persuasion.

He dragged a straw-filled pallet into the infirmary, putting it as far away as he could from the woman by the hearth. Lying down, he discovered very soon that this was a mistake: the furthest point from the fire was behind the door, under which the spiteful wind was

64

whistling a south-westerly. A *cold* south-westerly, he thought, giving in and moving further into the room.

All was quiet. Ears tuning in to the small sounds of breathing, he identified the shallow breaths of Ranald. Turning his head slightly, he listened for her. She'd been asleep when he came in, he was sure. Breathing deeply and regularly, her chest rhythmically lifting the covers he had tucked round her.

Yes. There it was.

Satisfied, he relaxed. His guard weakening – Benedict had said you always woke up when a patient called, it was like mothers and babies – he felt himself falling asleep. Of course I'll hear, he thought drowsily. I'm only a couple of paces distant from them. I'll hear if they so much as turn over.

Sliding into the beginnings of a dream, he thought he saw her. She was on a horse, and Benedict held its rein. 'Come along, my lovely,' he was saying, at which she turned into a knight in chain mail, helmet on his head, and swung at Benedict with a broadsword.

'Gawyn.'

Ah, yes. The knight's name's Gawyn. That's right.

'Gawyn.'

Suddenly wide awake, he knew the name hadn't been a part of the dream: someone – she – had said it. And she said it earlier, he remembered. When Benedict roused her.

He got up off the pallet, quietly going across to her.

'My lady?' He didn't know what else to call her.

She didn't hear his quiet voice. 'Not there, with him,' she muttered. 'No-one to help me. Hide.' Suddenly she opened her eyes and said quite lucidly, 'This is a retreat. He said so, the big one. He said it's safe.' Her voice was almost accusing, but he saw her fear in her eyes.

Trying to sound calm and reassuring, he said, 'You're perfectly safe. No-one ever comes here but us. No-one else knows we are here. We have told no-one about you – this is a retreat, yes, and we have no contact with the world.'

Her eyes drooped closed. Briefly she opened them again, and he said, 'Safe. You are safe, as God's my witness.'

She smiled at him. 'Thank you. How could I not believe such earnestness?'

Her eyes closed again, this time staying closed. He watched as the tension gradually went out of her. Soon she seemed to be asleep, although she was frowning, as if, wherever she was, it was not a particularly happy place.

He waited, but she said no more. In time, her breathing deepening, he realized she wasn't going to stir again.

Four

He slept surprisingly well on his pallet, and, as Benedict had predicted, neither of his patients disturbed
him in the night. When the rooster crowed from
the hen hutch, he woke to the early light feeling re-
freshed.

Benedict said they'd all be taking proper nourishment today, and Aidan had orders to make sure there
was milk and eggs in plenty. After washing his face
in the cold water out in the courtyard, Aidan looked
in briefly on his patients in the dormitory – they were
all still sleeping, and he marvelled at how illness had
made them deaf to their usual rooster reveille – then
made his way out on to the hillside to look for Titus.

He'll be in the sheep fold, Aidan thought, striding
off around the contour of the hill that rose up behind
the hermitage. He wished it was a longer walk – the
fresh westerly wind on his face felt wonderful, and
the land just waking up to the sunrise was wild and
inspiring.

Today she will eat, he decided. I shall make her
coddled eggs, and give her hot milk with honey. Oh,
and for the others, too, of course. Perhaps Mattheus
will allow me to make porridge, if I promise to respect
the bottom of his pan.

The soft bleat of a lamb calling for its mother came to him on the wind, and he hurried on. Following the track down into the valley that lay between two sheltering hills, he saw Titus outside his hut, a hurdle under his arm, a length of twine and a mallet in his hands.

'Good morning, Titus!'

Titus turned. 'Aidan! Welcome.' Putting down his load, he hurried over, arms out to embrace his visitor. 'I must just replace a broken hurdle – thank you for these new ones, by the way, I was in dire need – then I will make you a hot drink. There's still the night's chill in the air, isn't there?'

Aidan was glowing from his walk, but he wasn't going to turn down the offer. Titus's hot drinks contained a nip of some wonderful brew that the old man distilled from herbs; on an empty stomach, the mixture shot straight to the head and then descended pleasantly to the legs. 'I'll help,' he said, picking up the hurdle. 'Where do you want this?'

'There.' Titus pointed to a section of the hazel fence where a rivulet ran beneath it. 'My blessed sheep have taken it into their silly heads that the water's better on the far side. I have to persuade them otherwise, or else they'll be out and scattered the length and breadth of Gwent by nightfall.'

They took out the damaged hurdle and replaced it with the new one, Aidan hammering in the posts with the mallet while Titus made the joins secure with twine. The fence enclosed a meadow of rich grazing: fed by the little stream and encouraged by the sheltered south-facing aspect, the grass was thick and lush. The community had used the place for years to bring on the spring lambs.

'A good lambing?' Aidan asked as they went back to the hut.

'Middling.' Titus looked around at his flock, ewes grazing while their offspring suckled, down on their knees, docked tails wagging as if in panic that the food supply was about to be withdrawn. 'I lost a couple of ewes.'

Aidan nodded. 'You told me. How are the lambs you've been raising?'

'They'll do.'

I'll bet, Aidan thought. They'll probably be the biggest of the flock by midsummer.

Inside the hut it was snug. There was an open fire on a patch of bare earth, its smoke drawn out through a hole in the low roof. Titus, a neat worker, had arranged the tools of his trade and his few personal belongings as tidily as Benedict's medicines and potions. On an iron trivet over the fire, a pot of water simmered.

'Drink?' Titus asked.

'Aye.'

Into two pewter mugs – mementos, possibly, of some affluent period in Titus's former life – he poured generous measures of his ochre-coloured herbal drink, topping each mug up with hot water. He handed one to Aidan, and, after touching their mugs together, silently they drank.

After a few moments Titus gave them a refill. For some time there was no sound from either of them except for the occasional long, deep 'Aaaah' from Titus. Eventually, getting to his feet, he remarked, 'That's a strong one.'

Aidan suddenly recalled why he had gone out to the fold. It hadn't been to sit there going 'Aaaah' with Titus.

'I came for the milk, Titus,' he said, standing up on shaky legs.

'Aye. Thought you'd be needing it again round

about now. Two pails for you, behind the hut. They're on the mend, then.'

'Yes, thank the Lord.' He went outside and put the full pails on either ends of the yoke leaning against the hut. 'In a few more days, we'll be sending someone out to give you a hand.'

'I can manage,' Titus replied. 'Not much to watching over a small flock and milking one cow twice a day.'

He walked with Aidan until the path rounded the hillside. As Aidan went on his way, Titus called after him, 'How's the woman?'

'Fever's broken,' he called back.

'Praise God,' Titus said piously.

And how *he* knows about her, Aidan thought, smiling, when he hasn't even been living in the community, I can't imagine.

Ranald and the woman were still sleeping when he got back, so he tended his convalescents first. He'd collected a dozen eggs from the hen house, which he beat up with those stored in the kitchen. The bread was several days old, but sound; it'll do them good to chew on it, he thought, give their jaws something to do other than shout orders at me.

But it was a relief to see the four of them alert. Better they shouted at him than moaned in delirium.

He managed to give Ranald half a cup of water. Ranald held on to his wrist with a hand that shook: Aidan said a prayer for him.

When he went back to the infirmary after eating his own breakfast, she was sitting up, eyes fixed on the doorway.

It was a surprise.

'Hello,' he said lamely. 'How are you feeling?'

She smiled. Even in the drawn face with its spiky

fringe of matted hair, it warmed his heart. 'Hungry,' she replied.

'Wonderful! Wait, I'll bring you eggs, hot milk – there's no fresh bread, I'm afraid, nor will there be till Mattheus is on his feet, but he says that won't be long, he's probably afraid they'll all think I cook better than he does unless he takes over the kitchen again soon – but I could . . .' Unable to recall where he'd begun, he trailed to a stop. Her grey eyes were full of amusement, which further disconcerted him. 'What would you like?' he said quietly.

'I would like eggs and milk,' she said, straightening her face. 'Please, don't take any more trouble than you have to. I imagine you have your hands full.'

It wasn't the moment to begin on a litany of all he'd done over the past few days. There wasn't any moment for that, he reminded himself; just be thankful they all live.

He boiled water and made a fresh infusion for her. 'Drink this,' he said, crossing to her bed – he could smell her as he drew near – 'and I'll fetch food.'

She took the cup, pulling away from him as if she, too, were aware of the smell. He felt a deep pity for her. Hurrying back to the kitchen, he wondered what on earth he could do.

As he prepared the eggs, he discounted the possibilities. Can't ask Benedict to help, he's still weak. Can't ask any of them. Would she want help, anyway? We're men, she's a woman. Women . . . He wasn't certain how women went about the business of washing, but he was sure it was nothing like the bare-chested, down-to-the-waist dip into the communal trough that served him and his companions.

He put a large pan of water on to heat. She shall have hot water, at least. If I make a screen of some sort around the hearth, she can wash in the warmth

71

from the fire. I'll take her soap – it's coarse, but it serves. Then I can find her clean clothes, and when she's dressed, I'll change the bedding.

In the kitchen, it sounded simple. But in the kitchen his mind was occupied with cooking, leaving him no room to think about anything else.

Back in the infirmary, watching her eat like a snow-starved wolf, it was different. It was embarrassing him even to be near her, now that she was conscious. The thought of her washing, taking off the soiled shift and –

Don't think of it.

'I've heated water,' he said in a rush as he took away the empty dish and mug. 'I'll make a screen – I'll hang blankets from the beam, you'll be quite private – and you can wash, if you're strong enough. I mean, only if you want to.'

Too late, he realized his suggestion wasn't very diplomatic.

But she was laughing. It was a weak, hoarse sound, but definitely a laugh.

'You're trying to tell me I stink like a midden, I take it?'

'No! I –'

'Oh, yes, I do. I'm grateful for your consideration – I would love a wash – and a change of garment?' – He nodded – 'more than anything in the world.'

Relieved, happy that he'd done the right thing, he ran back for the hot water.

He was torn between staying in earshot while she washed – in case she needed him – and getting as far away as he could. He compromised by walking round and round the courtyard, humming loudly every time he passed the open infirmary door. Once he thought he heard that laugh again.

After a long time, she called out, 'I've finished.'

He hurried inside. The blanket lay in a heap on the floor, and she was slumped beside it, face ashen. She was dressed in the clean shift he'd given her; it was one of Elias's.

He went to her, kneeling beside her.

'Sorry,' she whispered, 'bit too much.'

He wrapped her in the blanket. 'Can you stay there a little longer?' he asked. 'Just while I put fresh coverings on your bed?'

She nodded.

Working as fast as fire over dry bracken, he stripped the bed and made it up afresh. Then, hands under her elbows, he helped her up and into it. She lay back and closed her eyes.

Bundling up the dirty linen, he was about to leave when she spoke.

'Woman's vanity,' she said. Turning, he saw she still had her eyes closed. 'A man would have had more sense. Hm? A man would lie there and stink till he was well enough to do something about it. Whereas I . . .' The words trailed off. Since he'd been thinking much the same thing himself, and was wondering now whether he'd been wrong to suggest the wash, he made no reply.

But when he came back from the laundry, he picked a few wallflowers and put them in a mug by her bed.

Late in the day, she woke again. He'd been outside with the others, for whom the food had worked miracles; Benedict had spent some time with Ranald, and, Aidan thought, somehow had made him more comfortable.

She called to him as he was tidying up after Benedict's medicine-making.

'You,' came the soft voice. 'Sorry, I don't know what you're called.'

'Aidan.'

'Aidan. Thank you for the flowers. Their scent got into my dreams.'

'I'm glad.'

He kept his back to her. 'Aidan?'

'Yes?'

'Have you the time to come and talk to me?'

'Of course.' He abandoned the pestles and mortars and went over to stand by her bed. 'What can I do for you, my lady?'

She was a lady, there was no doubt. It wasn't only the way she spoke, it was other things. The auburn-gold hair which, although short for a woman, had been properly cut. The hands, blistered as if she'd recently ridden hard, but the skin white and smooth. The clothing she'd worn when he'd found her in the river, well-made and of expensive fabrics.

Her very manner, shouting loud as a fanfare that she wasn't used to being subservient.

For some time she didn't speak. Then she said, 'Aidan, why do you call me "my lady"?'

'I beg your pardon if it's not right,' – he felt flustered – 'only I know no other suitable form of address for you, until you tell me your name.'

She sank back on her pillow, her expression a mixture of anxiety and amusement. Then, the amusement apparently getting the upper hand, she glanced at him. 'Oh, dear. I rather hoped you were going to tell me.'

At first he didn't understand. Then enlightenment dawned. 'You mean you don't know.' It wasn't a question. 'You've forgotten.'

'No, I don't, and yes, I have.' Brave of her, he thought, to make light of it. But suddenly she grabbed at his hand, her nails digging into the flesh. The terror naked in her face, she whispered, 'I don't know who I am!' Then she began to cry.

74

What do I do? he wondered wildly. What does a lady expect from an underling when she's sobbing her heart out?

Then it didn't matter what she was or what he was. For most of the few years of his manhood he'd lived here, where Ranald taught them to look after each other. To comfort, to love, even. It was a better – far better – way than he'd known before.

He sat down on the edge of the bed, put his arms round her and held her till she was quiet.

The tears had exhausted her, and she slept through the evening and on into the night. When darkness fell, Benedict appeared in the infirmary.

'You can go back to your cell, boy,' he said softly – Ranald was restless. 'I'll watch over them tonight.'

Aidan didn't try to object. He knew he should get away. Silently he went to the door, about to open it when Benedict said, 'You have done well, Aidan. We all owe you much.'

'I've done no more than you would have done. Or any of the others.'

Benedict considered for a moment, then said, 'No more than I, perhaps. Than the others, I'm not so sure. You have wits, boy, and you're not afraid to use them to make decisions.'

Aidan wanted to hear no more. Muttering his brief thanks, he went out and shut the door behind him.

In his cell, for the first time in days alone and with no-one to care for or listen out for, his mind turned back to the sin he still carried. It was heavier now, for the days had darkened the stain on his soul, burning it into him like acid. Unconfessed! his conscience shouted. Unconfessed! What if you die in the night and the devil bears you down to the hell he's reserved for fornicators?

He shouted in silent agony, I'm sorry! I'm *sorry!* But there came no balm of comfort, so that he had to ask himself if he regretted what he'd done or merely the pain it was now causing him.

And now I have compounded my sin, he thought. I touched her again, held her body against mine, held her tight so that I felt her –

He tore his thoughts away. It couldn't be right, that they were giving him so much pleasure.

I must not see her again. I cannot trust myself to be with her without setting on her, so I must keep away.

It hurt, to think of keeping away. He took that as an indication that it was the beginning of his penance. I'll do my penance gladly, he thought, and she will fade from my mind. Or else . . .

He didn't let the thought go on.

I shall ask Benedict for leave of absence – I'll suggest that Mattheus has more need of me, cooking for all of us when he's only just up and about again himself. When Mattheus is well, I'll go out and help Titus.

The trouble was that he didn't have a specific job in the community. He helped the others. Sometimes, before it had dawned on him that it was a prideful thought, he would reflect that he was a bit like Ranald, involved in everything but tied to nothing.

No skills, that's me, he decided, harsh with himself. Not wise enough to lead, not clever enough to tend the sick. Not practical enough to cook, nor with the artistry to work as Elias does. No touch with living creatures like Titus, no green thumb to make the crops spurt like a lad with new stockings.

And obviously time on my hands, time for the devil to get into my mind and make me do wrong.

The thought gave him a cold thrill of fear. Quietly getting out of his bed, he slipped his habit over his head, fastened the belt and, barefoot as befitted a sinner, made his way to the chapel. On his knees in front of the altar, he sent prayer after inarticulate prayer up to the God he loved to help him.

* * *

In the morning, eyes scratchy from lack of sleep, he went to the infirmary and tapped on the door. Benedict's voice called, 'Come in!', but he didn't, instead tapping again.

The door was flung open. 'I said come in!' Benedict looked impatient. 'Are you deaf, boy?' He went back into the room, saying over his shoulder, 'See, Ranald's better! Had a good night, he did, and he's taking some nourishment. You come over here and –'

Belatedly he realized Aidan hadn't followed him in. Turning, he stared at him, the cross frown changing to a look of concern.

'Are you ailing, Aidan?' he asked, his voice more kindly. Going back to the doorway, he put his big cool palm across Aidan's forehead. 'You're not fevered, but still . . .' He studied Aidan's face, the frown returning. 'You look awful, boy. Dead white face, and as black under the eyes as if you'd been up all night!'

I have, Aidan thought.

'I'm all right,' he said. 'I came to ask if you could do without me today. I thought perhaps I should help Mattheus instead.' Benedict was still frowning. Aidan reminded himself that the infirmarer had a clever brain and a sharp pair of eyes. 'I mean, I'll stay here if you really want me to, but . . .'

He could almost hear Benedict trying to work out why anyone should want to exchange a day assisting with the light and interesting work in the infirmary for long hours sweating over hot pans, scrubbing vegetables and swilling dirty dishes. Under Mattheus's tyrannical rule, too.

'No, no, you go over to the kitchen,' Benedict said. 'And I hope he rewards you as fulsomely as you're hoping!'

No, that's not it, Aidan thought with relief as he ran across the courtyard. Although if I felt like food, it might well be a factor.

As it was, he hardly ate all day. For one thing, he wasn't hungry, but the main reason was that Mattheus, with several days' routine chores to catch up on as well as food to prepare for people with varying amounts of appetite, kept him hard at it from early morning till dusk. At last, back and shoulders aching, hands swollen and wrinkled from long immersion in cold water, he was allowed to leave the kitchen. Had it not been for the fact that Mattheus looked even more exhausted than Aidan felt, he would have been tempted to feel sorry for himself.

He walked slowly across the courtyard and out through the gate, going a little way down the track and stopping to sit on the steeply-sloping grass beside it. Turning his face to the west, he looked at the near hills and the far Welsh mountains, black now against the setting sun.

Ranald was better. Word had come from the infirmary that, later in the evening, Aidan was to assist Benedict in getting him across to the chapel, where all of them were going to give thanks for the community's recovery from sickness. It looked as if life was getting back to normal.

Only it's not, he thought, circling his shoulders and trying to get rid of the stiffness. It can't be, because she's here, she who has also had a reprieve from death and for whose deliverance we shall, no doubt, be saying our thanks.

Even those of us who are trying not to think about her.

With one last look at the quiet land before him, he stood up and went back to the hermitage.

Five

The day after Ranald had got up from his sickbed to lead them in prayer, he sent for Aidan.

'Ranald wants to see you,' said Simon, acting as messenger. Simon, Aidan noticed, had lost weight during his illness. So had all of them, but it showed more in Simon, whose hitherto jowly face looked quite slim.

'Where is he?' Aidan hoped Simon wouldn't say 'in the infirmary'.

'He's in his cell.'

As he set off, Aidan felt Simon's eyes on him. The close brush with death obviously hadn't made him think better of his gossipy ways: 'Ranald sent for Aidan just now,' he'd tell the next person he spoke to. 'I wonder what that young man's been up to?'

If only he knew, Aidan thought, instantly feeling glad he didn't. Does Ranald know? Is that why he's sent for me? The possibility stopped his hurrying steps, but, since he'd been given a summons and had to obey, he made himself walk on.

Ranald was seated on his bed, back straight, feet on the ground. His pallor alone gave away how ill he'd been. Aidan, moved by a mixture of impulses, fell on his knees before him and, after a moment, felt Ranald's hand on his head.

'Get up, Aidan,' said the quiet voice. 'I have summoned you for two reasons: first, to thank you, on behalf of us all, for what you have done over the past week.'

'I don't . . .' He stopped. You weren't meant to interrupt Ranald.

'Benedict has told me of your devotion. He also tells me you look pale, and he surmises that you have been too long cooped up with the sick. He suggests – and I agree – that the best medicine for you is to go out and work with Titus.'

It was the last thing Aidan had expected. It seemed too much like a reward, and he was not a man who deserved a reward. But Ranald didn't know that.

'I don't think I can go,' he heard himself say.

'Why ever not?'

He couldn't answer. Ranald's voice said, 'Aidan, look at me,' and he raised his eyes, meeting the deep blue ones looking down at him. Now, he thought, now I tell him. Then he'll know how evil I am, and will punish me, not reward me.

Ranald's eyes were full of love. I can't, Aidan realized. I'm not man enough wilfully to destroy the image he has of me. He lowered his head.

'I don't know.'

'I know,' Ranald said. 'You have been overburdened, and you have lost sight of what is important. Some time in God's good air is what you need. Go now, while the sun is out – Benedict says it will rain later.'

Aidan went.

On the hillside later in the morning, he thought back on Ranald's words. I've lost sight of what is important, he repeated to himself. He means, I suppose, that they're all well again, and we must be thankful. So he's sent me out here, where God is close, so I'll truly feel gratitude. And he's right, because I do.

He felt better than he had for a long time.

Titus had seemed pleased to see him, despite his words of the previous day about managing on his own. Perhaps he could manage the work, but, Aidan thought, he must tire of the solitude sometimes. He'd noticed that the old man would alternate between long bouts of silence when he didn't talk at all and brief bursts of garrulity when he didn't stop.

When they had paused for the midday office and a light snack, Titus said, 'If they've sent you to me, it must be for a purpose.'

'Benedict thinks I need some fresh air.'

'Fresh air you could have drawn into your body sitting in the courtyard. No, I think Ranald wants you to learn, so learn you will. We'll begin straight away – I'm going to move the flock to another pasture, and you can help me.'

The rest of the day was pure delight. With Aidan moving hurdles and Titus taking charge of the flock – he controlled them with a combination of stones lobbed to land on the far side of stragglers, which made them turn back towards their sisters, and a variety of violent arm-movements – they herded the nineteen ewes and their twenty-seven offspring two miles further into the hills, to an open pasture bordered on two sides by a copse. From the greater height, a panorama of the bending Wye opened up; for some time Aidan stood speechless with wonder.

'When you've finished admiring the view, lad, we'll go back for the hut,' Titus said.

Aidan hadn't appreciated it was moveable. Between them, they carried walls, roof and contents, and by dusk were settled in the new location. Titus found stones to make a hearth and, using his flint, got a fire going to cook their evening meal. When they'd eaten, he put water on to boil and made them both a herbal drink.

'This'll make you sleep,' Titus said. Curling up on his simple bed, the smell of grass sweet in his head, Aidan didn't think he'd need any help.

Just as he was drifting off, Titus remarked, 'Castrating tomorrow.'

* * *

Aidan spent two weeks out on the hills with Titus. Two weeks weren't enough to make a sheep herd of him, he knew, but they had certainly seen him on his way. Titus taught well: his silent times gave his pupil a chance to digest the torrent of facts and information that had poured out of him when he was talkative.

Aidan wondered if he would have enjoyed it all so much had he not just emerged from incarceration with the sick – even the castrating hadn't been that bad, once he got used to it, and he appreciated that it was the one thing that Titus, now minus three of his incisors, could no longer do. He'd even coped with the dagging, when they sheared away the dung-caked wool from the ewes' backsides to stop blowflies being attracted and leaving their maggots to burrow into the flesh.

From time to time, one of the community would come out to exchange news, and on Sundays the two of them would go into the hermitage for the day's offices.

Ranald's rule that they were not to speak of the woman held firm: all that Aidan knew was that she was still in the infirmary, no longer sick enough to be in bed, but under Benedict's care all the same. They continued to pray for her. Near to her or not, he carried her with him, in his conscience. Sometimes he wondered if it wasn't in his conscience that she lodged but his heart, and he faced the thought – and what admission of it would lead to – without panic. Out on the hillside with Titus and the flock, the thought of living back in the world was easier to contemplate.

He wondered what effect she had on the others. Life in the hermitage seemed to be just as it had always been, as far as he could tell from the brief interludes he spent there. Everyone was busy – spring was flying now, obviously making up for lost time, and Ranald had made working on the community's small acreage a priority – and perhaps doing digging and planting duties as well as all their usual work meant that they didn't have time to dwell on the stranger in their midst. Some of them – Elias, for example, whose grip on the realities of life was slight at the best of times – had probably forgotten she was there.

Setting off to fetch fresh food supplies for himself and Titus one morning, Aidan had reached the perimeter fence when Titus called him back.

'Go and see Benedict,' he shouted. 'Ask him if he's got any waterpepper leaves – I haven't the time to go and look for some myself. That ewe's still bleeding, I'll need to –'

'Yes, I will!' He turned and hurried off. Dagging and castrating he might take in his stride, but a fortnight in the world of recently-delivered female sheep hadn't been enough to harden him to other aspects of the sheep herd's lot; he still felt himself blushing when Titus spoke so forthrightly about wombs and birth passages.

Benedict. Waterpepper leaves. Can I find some? he wondered. That would save me a trip to the infirmary. But I'm not sure what they look like. They grow by the water and the leaves burn the tongue, I know that much, but then that probably applies to all manner of other plants too. No. I can't risk it.

I'll call on Benedict last, tell him I'm in a hurry. Then I won't have to linger.

Unable to think of a better plan, he trudged on to the hermitage.

Mattheus loaded his basket with dried meat, new bread, and a slab of ewes' milk cheese. He put in a few of last year's apples, and told Aidan to help himself to carrots and onions.

'Suiting you, is it, the outdoor life?' He turned from stirring a steaming pan of broth to glance at Aidan, his cheeks scarlet and his forehead beaded with sweat. 'You look well on it, I'll say that. Better not show your face to Simon, he's still smarting about you not falling sick like the rest of us.'

'How's his cough?'

Mattheus shrugged. 'Not too bad. Ranald has put him to light outdoor duties – he's weeding the herb garden – but the sunshine doesn't seem to be doing him as much good as it should.'

'Is Benedict about?' For a hopeful moment Aidan thought the infirmarer might also be working in his precious herb garden.

'Aye, you'll find him in the infirmary, I expect.'

'Oh.'

Postponing the confrontation, Aidan went in search of Ranald, whom he met coming out of the chapel. He made the series of genuflections that constituted the community's formal greeting to its leader; Ranald did not insist on it, but there were times – like now, Aidan thought – when they felt moved to do him the honour.

'Good day, sheep herd,' Ranald said.

'Don't let Titus hear you say that. He told me only

yesterday I was no good with sheep, my hands were about as sensitive as a dray horse's hooves.'

'What had you done?' Ranald smiled.

'Dropped the dagging shears too near his foot.'

'Ah, well, it takes time to learn new skills,' Ranald said calmly. 'Were you looking for me?'

'Yes, but only to pass on to you Titus's report. All's well, he says to tell you.'

Ranald's smile widened. 'Not a man to waste words.'

Aidan wanted to ask how much longer he would be put to work with Titus, but he knew better: Ranald would tell him when he was to come back. He did not encourage them to worry about the morrow, considering that to be his preserve. He believed firmly in his little flock emulating the lilies of the field.

'I'll get back, then,' Aidan said. 'I – er, I just have to see Benedict. Something Titus asked me to fetch.' Why do I feel I have to explain myself? he wondered. Guilty conscience, came the instant reply.

Ranald said, 'Off you go, then.'

And, briefly placing his hand on Aidan's head in blessing, he disappeared in the direction of his cell.

The door to the infirmary stood open. As he approached, Aidan could hear singing, Benedict's deep baritone and a lighter voice above it.

He stood on the threshold. Benedict was busy at his bench with mortar and pestle, and beside him sat the woman, her nimble hands working thin strips of willow into containers for dried herbs. She was dressed in a black robe identical to the ones worn by the community; it would, he realized, be all they had to offer her. Somehow it didn't seem right for her to go on dressing in her own boy's clothes, now that they knew she was a woman.

Neither of them noticed him. He studied her,

noting the new sheen on her short reddish hair, the returning colour in her face. She's better, he thought. And, hard on the heels of that, she'll be going.

'Benedict!' he said. Too loudly – they both jumped.

'Aidan!' Benedict smiled in greeting. 'What can I do for you?'

Fixing his eyes on Benedict's, still he caught the woman's smile. 'Some waterpepper leaves, if you have them, please.'

'I have.' He moved across to his shelves. 'Plenty growing by the river. Where the track bends down, by the willow – you know the place?'

'I do.' He took the leaves, turning to go. 'Thank you, I'll gather them myself in future. I'll wish you both good day.'

'Wait!' Benedict's voice called after him.

He paused. Some other medication that the infirmarer thought might come in useful? A request for Aidan to bring him some plant that grew in the vicinity of the sheep fold?

Neither. Benedict said, 'I was about to take the lady here out into the sunshine. I thought we'd sit a while in the courtyard, let her feel the warmth on her face.' He smiled at her. 'I've still too much to do, so you can take her for me.'

'Can't she –' He broke off. It would sound churlish, to say, 'Can't she go on her own?' 'Of course,' he managed.

'Thank you, Aidan.' There was humour in her voice, as if she knew very well what he'd been about to say and was amused at his awkwardness. Rising from her stool, she came to stand beside him.

'Offer her your arm, boy!' The infirmarer was laughing. 'She won't bite, and she needs the support.'

Awkwardly he held out his arm, and she put her

hand on it. He could see the bones under the flesh and, closer to her, he could hear the breathlessness. No. She wasn't better yet.

He led her to a bench that stood in the corner between the infirmary wall and the side of the chapel, steadying her as she sat down, then settling beside her.

'I hate being weak,' she said vehemently.

He didn't know how to answer, so he just said, 'Oh.'

'Not all women are feeble and dependent, you know!'

He recoiled slightly; she'd sounded quite cross. He had a sudden image of his mother. She was slumped on the flagged floor she'd just finished scrubbing, and the priest whose house it was stood over her, booted feet only inches from her swollen hands. He turned his mind away.

His mother hadn't been feeble. Or dependent – not in the way this woman meant. She'd worked so hard that she'd given up what was left of her strength, and a severe winter – and other factors – had taken her from him.

'I never thought they were.' His anger surprised him.

It seemed to surprise her, too. She said quietly, 'I'm sorry. You get involved in taking me for an airing, a duty you obviously don't relish at all, and I bite your head off. Blame it on frustration.'

He wasn't sure what she meant. He could understand anyone hating being cooped up inside when they were fit, but she didn't seem fit. Then he thought he understood.

There wasn't an easy way to lead up to it, so he just said, 'You still don't know who you are.'

'I don't.'

They sat in silence. He could smell the dog roses that climbed up the wall behind them. An insect buzzed.

Several questions ran through his mind, but they were all equally inane. If she doesn't know, she doesn't know. No use asking if she's tried bringing to mind the last thing she can remember. Or saying all the girls' names she can think of till one rings a bell.

'Ranald's tried to help,' she said eventually. 'So has Benedict. They're both so kind, they keep telling me they only want what's best for me, that I'm not to think what I do think. Which is, as I'm sure you've guessed, that the sooner I remember who I am, the sooner they can send me back to wherever it was I came from.'

'I'm sure they don't . . .' He broke off. He wasn't sure at all.

She smiled. 'Oh, yes,' she said. 'It's for the best of motives, I don't doubt, but they want me to go. Ranald says I must think of someone, somewhere, grieving. Thinking I'm dead. He conjures pictures for me of loving parents, of a husband half out of his mind with worry.'

'And it does no good?'

She shook her head. 'No. Not only that, but – No.'

He wanted her to continue with whatever she'd been going to say. Not knowing how to encourage her, he said nothing. It worked: into the soft peace of the morning she said suddenly, 'I'm afraid. I was running away, I'm sure I was, and I'm very afraid. Sometimes I see something – someone – oh, I don't know who he is, he's richly dressed and powerful. I have to – oh!' She beat her fists against the bench. 'I don't know! It's so vague, just the fear, and the feeling I must get away. And when I remember more, I'll have to go back. Won't I?'

She turned to him, grey eyes candid. He knew he must answer truthfully.

'If what you've got away from is fearsome,' he began slowly, 'perhaps your mind is deliberately hiding it away.'

'No! You must believe me, truly I don't remember!' she said hotly.

'All right, I'm not doubting you. What I'm trying to say is that it could be you have good reason for your fear. If that's so, I don't think Ranald would deliberately send you back to face something bad. I mean . . .'

He knew very well what he was trying to say, but the words wouldn't come. He wanted to say, I know Ranald. He – well, like all of us – has turned away from the world, for his own good reasons. He hasn't much time for the intolerance of mankind, nor for the cruelty. He won't send you anywhere you don't want to go.

'Ranald is a good man,' he said quietly.

'I know,' she agreed quickly. 'Because of that, and because I'm aware what an embarrassment I am in his community, I must find a solution. But what? I've no money, and, apart from this,' – she indicated the black robe, which she'd hitched up to a manageable length by gathering great folds of material above the leather belt – 'the only clothes I have seem to have been made for a squire. I can hardly go back out into the world dressed as a boy, for all that it's how I left it.'

'You'd been riding hard,' he said, remembering. 'You had blisters across your palms.'

'Did I?'

'Yes. And no gloves, or you hadn't when I found you.'

There was a pause. Then she said, 'It was you.'

She hadn't known. And now he'd gone and told her. He hung his head. After a moment he felt her hand on his arm, the merest touch. Now she's going to speak, he thought in panic, tell me how grateful she is, and I'll feel even worse than I do already. Because, unlike her, I know about the wonderful, brave act I performed after I'd found her.

And the legacy of emotions it's left in its wake.

She didn't speak. The sun was strong now, and the scent of the dog roses was heady. He breathed in deeply. Gradually the painful awkwardness abated.

'I ought to go,' he said, standing up. 'Titus will be wondering what's keeping me.'

She had her eyes closed, and was leaning back against the warm golden stone of the chapel wall. 'Yes, you go,' she said. 'I'll sit here a little longer. The sun's making me feel good. And the roses are – '

Suddenly she shot up, eyes wide, face eager.

'Roese!' she shouted.

He took a step towards her, alarmed. 'What's the matter? Do you feel ill?'

She was on her feet, her hands batting against his chest as if unable to contain her excitement. 'Roese! That's my name! *ROESE!*'

She was singing it, 'Roese, Roese, Roese,' bashing him with each repetition. Laughing with her, he gave her a hug.

'Roese,' he said against her hair. 'Like the flower. Oh, it suits you! You -'

He was holding a woman in his arms.

He leapt away from her, and she staggered, almost fell. 'Sit down,' he ordered, his voice coming out harsh. 'You'll trip – you're not strong yet. I'll call Benedict.'

She flopped back on to the bench, the joy draining from her face. She looked frail once more, thin and sick. Frowning, she began to speak, a questioning look in her eyes. A hurt look.

He turned his back on her. His flesh retained a memory of how she'd felt, pressed against him, and it combined with the guilty, haunting picture of her naked breasts he couldn't chase from his mind and the growing feelings for her he couldn't drive out of his heart. It was too much for him: grabbing his basket from outside the infirmary, he leaned inside and shouted out, 'Benedict! See to your charge!'

Then he ran out through the gate and fled away across the hills.

PART TWO

Roese

Summer 1208–Spring 1209

Six

The nauseating vertigo was back. Her head felt as if it were floating away from her body, and the courtyard seemed to be tilting. I can't be sick out here! she thought wildly. I *won't!*

Back pressed to the chapel wall, she closed her eyes. That was worse: without any point of reference – even a tilting one – the swirling sensation increased. Her stomach began to heave, and, sliding off the bench and falling to her knees, she retched into the flower bed.

A cool hand was on her forehead.

'I'm sorry,' she gasped, eyes and nose streaming. I scared him away by singing and dancing, she thought. I wonder how fast he'll run from a woman being sick?

'There, now, lass.' It wasn't him. The voice was deep and kind, and belonged to Benedict. 'When you've recovered yourself, we'll get you back to your bed.'

She wanted to say, I don't want to go to bed!, and stamp her foot. Like I'd do when Ismay told me I must retire and leave the men to their talk. It used to work, because I could make Father do exactly what I wanted.

The wisp of memory had gone before she'd been able to latch on to it.

'Thank you,' she said to Benedict. 'The sickness is going – I'm feeling better.'

'Always the way, just afterwards,' he said. 'You're still going back to your bed, my lady.'

He put his arm round her waist and they crossed the courtyard to the infirmary. He gave her a moistened cloth to wipe her face, and a cup of cold water to freshen her mouth. Then he made her lie down, covering her legs and feet with a blanket.

'Go to sleep,' he ordered. 'You've had enough excitement for one day.'

He turned to go, but she caught hold of his sleeve. 'Benedict?'

'What is it?' His eyes looking down at her were indulgent.

'Out there, with him –'

'Aidan.'

'Aidan, yes. We were talking of –' What had they talked about? She couldn't remember. It didn't matter, it hadn't been anything they'd said that had opened the door in her mind.

'He's a good man,' Benedict said. Slightly defensively, she thought, and was vaguely wondering why when he went on, 'I can't think why he dashed off like that. You must forgive him, lady, he's not used to women. He nursed his companions well enough when they were sick, but perhaps in your case . . .' He left the sentence unfinished.

'I expect he was being considerate,' she said. 'He seems a sensitive man – no doubt he realized how much it'd embarrass me to have a witness to my weakness.'

Benedict patted her hand. 'You don't mind me. Do you?'

She smiled. 'I'm used to you. Anyway –' She debated briefly whether or not to go on, then decided she would, 'You're older than him.'

It was the right decision. Benedict slapped his hands against his thighs and shouted with laughter. 'And a sight less favourable to the eye, eh?' He smoothed a palm across his belly. 'Aye, you're right. Now, let me get back to my work, or I shall never finish.'

She still hadn't told him. 'Benedict!'

'What now?' He frowned in mock anger.

'I was trying to tell you something.'

He came back to stand beside her. She thought, he knows it's something important. No wonder he's so good with the sick, he reads people as if they were letters on a page.

'What is it, lass?'

'I've remembered my name.'

For some moments he said nothing. Then, very calmly, as if he were trying not to alarm her with a display of over-enthusiasm, he asked, 'Your name. And do you recall anything else?'

I'm seeing flashes, she thought. I saw Ismay, and Father. Myself, in a rage because I'd been forbidden . . . What? I don't know, the image has gone. Do those tiny splinters of the picture amount to something worth mentioning?

'No,' she said. 'Just my name.' Since he didn't ask, she told him: 'It's Roese.'

'Roese,' he repeated. Then, his face filling with happiness, he said, 'You will remember, lady. Not immediately, perhaps, but in time.' He put his hand to her temple, and she felt a warm glow where the fingers touched her skin. 'The memory's there, see? It must be, you now know what you're called. The rest will come back to you.'

He looked so pleased about it that she didn't tell him what she was thinking. That, accompanying the flashes, she was experiencing a growing feeling of dread.

'I'll rest now,' she said, summoning a smile. He has work to do, she thought, it's not fair to keep him by me just because I'm afraid. And he'll be close. At least, I hope he will.

She watched him walk back to his bench and pick up the pestle and mortar. Yes. He was going to be close. Somehow the prospect of opening the shutters on her memories wasn't quite so frightening if he was near.

He must have told Ranald what had happened. In the evening, after she'd woken from a long sleep and eaten some bread and broth, Ranald came to see her.

'Good evening, Roese,' he said, pulling up a stool and sitting down beside her bed. They were alone: after removing her empty bowl, Benedict had announced he was going to the chapel. She bowed her head in greeting. 'You have begun to recover your memory.'

She'd noticed before that he spoke with an unfamiliar accent. It was slight, but definitely there. But now wasn't the time to puzzle over it; he was waiting for her response to his remark. 'A little, but nothing that makes much sense, I'm afraid.' She didn't meet his eyes. She thought, he'll know I'm lying. It's ungrateful to lie, when he and the others have been so kind, but I have to.

He said quietly, 'Look at me, Roese.'

She raised her head. His eyes seemed to have the power to move her gaze; staring into the blue irises, she couldn't look away.

'Now. Tell me what's troubling you.'

She shook her head.

He sighed. 'I can feel your fear. You have perhaps remembered that the place you belonged to out in the world was not a good place. You are thinking, I dare say, that the moment you tell me where this unhappy place is, I will send you back there.' A swift emotion ran across his face: she thought it was anger. But when he spoke again, it was not apparent in his voice. 'You imagine, perhaps, that, like Pilate, I shall wash my hands of you. We have restored you to health, I shall say, now go away and leave us alone.'

He was right. He'd used the very words she'd put in his mouth. She understood then why he'd seemed angry; she'd offended him.

'I misjudged you,' she muttered. 'I apologize.'

He looked away from her, frowning. He seemed to be thinking; she'd noticed that all of them had a tendency to pause before speaking, as if they had to consider carefully before they did so to make sure the words that emerged were the right ones. As if they had to watch out and not waste any.

At times, she thought – now, for instance – it really tests the patience.

'We live apart from the world here,' he said eventually. 'For our own reasons, each of us has elected to turn away from society. For us, this *is* the world.'

'You mean –'

He went on as if the interruption hadn't happened. 'You have brought into our community a reminder of what we have left behind. You came to us out of peril; somehow you came to be in the river, alone and with no-one to protect you. More significantly, you were in disguise, which implies that you were concealing your identity. The conclusion I draw is that you were running away.'

'But I can't –'

Again he swept by her protest as if he hadn't heard it. 'Here, as I said, we have *turned* away from the world,' he said, this time emphasizing the word. 'One or two would be more honest and say they had *run* away.' He leaned closer, eyes once more fixed on hers. 'I didn't say to them, go back to the torment of the world, go and suffer it and stop being so cowardly! Why then should I say it to you?'

She said before she could stop herself, 'They're men.'

He recoiled, and for an instant she thought the anger was back. Then he smiled, and the smile grew into laughter. 'I forgot,' he said. 'I've lived without women for so long that I'd forgotten that way they have of bringing you down to earth.' He chuckled again, and she wondered what happy scene he was remembering. 'A man can spend all day pondering on the nature of the cherubim and the seraphim, losing himself in wonder and abstraction, and his woman will fetch him back by reminding him he promised to slaughter the pig.' He shook his head, the humour fading. 'As you rightly point out, we are men. And, of course, you cannot stay here for ever.' He got up, replacing the stool under the bench. 'You should know, Lady Roese, that it's for me to worry about for ever. As for you, let the memories come back. When you are ready, tell me what you have remembered. You have my promise that I shall not send you away from us until you want to go.'

He was leaving. It seemed impolite to let him go without another word, and as he opened the door, she called out to him.

'Yes?'

Feeling stupid, she couldn't think what to say.

She felt the chill night air as he swept out through

the door. Turning back to her, he said, 'I will pray for you.'

It comforted her as if he'd wrapped her in a soft blanket.

Benedict was worried about her, and when he settled her for the night, made her drink a greenish concoction which he said would hold at bay the recurrence of her fever.

'Am I falling sick again?' she asked him.

'I don't know, lady,' he said, fingers on her wrist. 'Your heart beats rapidly, but that may be because you're excited. Quite a day, when a body remembers their name, eh, Roese?' He grinned at her. 'And you're hot, but then you've been out of your bed today.'

'Out in the courtyard,' she added. 'In the sunshine.'

'How do you feel?' he asked. 'Will you sleep? I put some chamomile in your drink, so I shall expect you to.'

'I feel – strange,' she said. 'Sort of light. And sleepy. My head throbs.' She closed her eyes, and against the darkness saw sudden images which went again before they were more than half formed.

'I'll be here,' he said calmly. 'If you wake and need me, just call.'

She heard him move away. The small sounds as he tidied the infirmary and prepared for the night were soothing. She thought she heard a voice – 'I won't do it, Roese. It's no use you calling, I'm not listening,' – but it couldn't have been Benedict, he wouldn't say anything like that. I must have dreamt it, she thought.

Hot, restless, she seemed to be in a state between wakefulness and sleep. Sounds and scenes acted themselves out before her closed eyes, but she found that she could direct them: here was not the random illogic of dreams, where the bizarre held sway like the Lord of Misrule.

I can see Father, she thought. The day he brought me the silk from the merchant at Chepstow. Ismay told him to buy a colour that would not show the dirt – she said she refused to make me any more dresses in pretty colours until I learned to treat them with respect – but I went behind her back and told him to buy pale yellow or bright leaf green. He has brought me both, and she is furious! 'You'll have trouble with that girl,' she tells him – she's shaking her finger at him, as if he were a naughty boy! Oh, *wonderful*, how does she get away with it? – and he's saying, yes, Ismay, you're quite right and I'm very sorry, but he's winking at me behind her back!

The picture faded. She heard the mutter of Benedict's soft voice in prayer. The glow from the fire made patches of moving light on the wall.

Ismay's worried about me. She tells Father I'm old enough to be a wife, that he should think of my future and find me a husband. Be quiet, woman, he says, but kindly. Why should I send my daughter from me when both she and I want her to remain?

It's not what is done, Ismay points out. Just as boys are sent away to learn to be squires, so girls must leave their families and learn to be wives. Make new homes of their own.

Roese is happy here, Father counters.

Ismay sniffs, whispers something. One or two words leap out: *woman*, and *urges*. Father snorts with laughter, says, she is but seventeen! A girl still!, and Ismay sniffs again, but louder.

Seventeen. I'm seventeen, and it's May. All of the summer stretches ahead, and Father has bought me a chestnut mare. William is with me, and we are putting her through her paces in the water meadow.

'You will have to be able to ride hard all day like a boy, Roese, if this wild plan is to become a reality.'

Who said that? Father? William?

No.

Gawyn.

She turned over, and, without meaning to, made a small sound of distress. On the other side of the infirmary Benedict propped himself up on one elbow, staring across at her.

'It's all right,' she said.

She closed her eyes.

They are waiting, Father, Ismay, William. Her defences down, fever weakening the protective forgetfulness that has already been breached, they stand on the edge of her consciousness. She can hold them at bay no more.

Ismay comes to the fore.

* * *

'Roese! *Roese!* You're to come in this instant! I have food to prepare for an army of people and only one pair of hands!'

Roese slid from the mare's back, laughing. 'Would you see to her for me please, William?' There was no need to ask: William was thirteen, but maturing wildly. She was well aware he would do anything for her. The thrill of her new feminine powers tempted her to take advantage of his adoration, but then he'd been like a little brother to her for four years and her affection for him held her in check. Besides, she never knew when he was suddenly going to remind her of some incident in their shared past that showed her in a very different light. Like the time they'd been caught scrumping apples and both got their backsides paddled.

'Will we ride again later?' he asked, taking the mare's reins from her.

'Don't know.' She glanced in the direction of the doorway, where Ismay stood hands on hips waiting for her. 'But somehow I doubt it.'

William groaned in sympathy. 'Food for an army, she said. You'll be too busy to ride ever again, Roese.'

'She didn't mean a real army, idiot.' She punched him playfully. 'Father would like that, wouldn't he? Hordes of rough soldiers pushing into the hall, keeping the fire off him and scratching themselves! He'd make them go and stand outside, just like he makes you when *you* start scratching yourself.' She danced out of range as he swung a fist at her.

'*ROESE!*' Ismay's voice was a bellow. I'll be in for a lecture on behaviour befitting a lady as well now, Roese thought. Just what I need when I'm standing in the kitchen with her cutting up a hundred cabbages.

'Coming,' she said.

By mid-morning Roese felt as if she'd been on her feet for hours. The fresh bright day whose dewy beginning she'd seen with William as they rode seemed to belong to a different lifetime: in the steaming kitchen, where a haunch of Welsh venison turned on a spit over the open fire and thick iron pots of various sizes bubbled on their hooks, all that was needed was someone with a red-hot pitchfork to make the hellish vision complete. And the old drudge whom Ismay had fetched in from the village to scrub the vegetables and draw the pigeons stank so strongly that it made Roese want to heave.

Outside she could see the sunlight dancing on the hills. A kestrel hovered on the wind, and she heard her father's voice calling William. Laughing with him.

A restrained curse called her attention back into the kitchen: Ismay had dropped a pot. Roese went to help her pick up the pieces. '"Make it a memorable meal, Ismay," he says,' she was muttering under her breath, '"Some of your special pastries wouldn't go amiss." As if I had all day and a full staff at my beck and call!'

Roese made soothing noises. It wasn't worth actually saying anything; she knew from long experience that Ismay wouldn't hear. Ismay was her own woman, hers the only voice that penetrated into the efficient, well-regulated mind. Especially when she was trying to do the work of ten with no-one to help her but a stinky old woman and a girl who yearned to be somewhere else. I'll try harder, Roese thought. If I could do more, it'd take some of the burden off her.

But, no matter how she tried, she was no good in the kitchen: unskilled labour was the best she could do. Ismay had stood at her side countless times, going through pie-making step by step until even an idiot would have picked it up. But not me, thought Roese. Poor Ismay. It's her misfortune to be cook, nurse, substitute mother and companion rolled into one in a household where the daughter of the family is as much use to her as a cold in the head.

Ismay had nicked her finger on a sharp shard of pottery, and Roese bound it for her with a strip of linen. Ismay took advantage of the moment of imposed inactivity to rest her buttocks on the table's edge, lifting one foot and then the other to inspect her ankles.

'Swollen up like bladders of lard already,' she said mournfully, 'and not yet midday! If my prince comes today, young Roese, he'll ride straight past.'

'Ah, but you could cover your feet with your skirt,' Roese suggested. 'Give him a smile and a sweetmeat and he'll canter off and win you a kingdom.'

Ismay patted her cheek with the undamaged hand. 'What would I want with a kingdom?' Her red face creased into a smile. 'Just more faddy whims to cater for and more quarrels to untangle, I shouldn't wonder.'

As definitions went, Roese thought, it wasn't bad. She wondered if the king would agree. 'There,' she said, ripping the end of the linen into two and tying it into a knot, 'how's that?'

'It'll do.' Ismay stood up. 'You've a gentle hand, girl, even if the touch doesn't extend to baking.' She cast a quick glance around the kitchen. 'We've almost finished. Go across to the hall and make sure there's space enough at the tables for twelve.' Her eyes came back to Roese. 'Then you'd better go and wash your face. And find yourself something to wear that doesn't reek of boiled onions.'

The morning had been so hectic that Roese hadn't thought to ask for whose benefit they were working so hard. Ismay said a dozen, she thought as she shivered in her room over a bowl of cold water, that's Father, William, Ismay and me, and Roger probably – Father said he'd be back this morning. That leaves seven guests.

Hurriedly she dried her hands and her face and her goose-pimply body, then took a clean smock from the chest at the end of the bed. She fastened the cuffs, then lifted her yellow kirtle from the bed and dropped it down over her head. Ismay had made a short train at the back; she twisted round, trying to see how it looked. There was a girdle in a slightly darker shade of yellow, embroidered with a few precious gold threads. She tied it tightly, then had to slacken it off a little as she found she couldn't draw breath.

I'll find Father, she thought. He'll tell me who's coming to eat with us.

Twitching the unfamiliar train behind her, she closed the door of her chamber and went carefully down the steep steps.

William was in the yard, leading his pony and Roese's father's huge bay off towards their stables. 'William, where's Father?' she asked. 'And you'd better hurry with the horses.' She glanced up at the sky. 'It won't be long till dinner, and you can't come into the hall like that.'

He looked down at his torn and filthy hose. 'Sir Walter got me up on his horse and let me try riding at the quintain,' he said dejectedly.

'Without much success, apparently.'

'That's not fair! I hit the target twice, but the third time I forgot about keeping him running straight,' – he slapped the bay's lofty withers – 'and when he slewed off to one side, I didn't go with him.'

She felt sorry for him – most boys weren't promoted from page to squire till they were older than thirteen, and a page's duties were less hazardous. But he'd grown so fast in the last few months that Sir Walter had made the decision to let him try out his strength. She watched as he turned his back and limped off across the yard, her pity increasing.

But he'd hate it if he knew, she thought – he can't stand anyone offering sympathy, it makes him feel he's a weakling. He has this need to measure himself against Roger all the time, for all that Roger's my brother and not his. And Roger's ten years older, and a big man into the bargain!

She ran to catch up with him, skirt and train

gathered up and draped over one arm.

'Venison for dinner,' she said heartily.

'Umm.'

'And Ismay's pastries.'

'Umm.'

He still didn't look very happy. She prodded him in the ribs and fell back on the old fail-safe.

'Bet I can ride Father's horse round the wood and back across the field faster than you can,' she whispered.

His eyes lit up at the challenge. 'Bet you can't!'

She took the bay's reins from him. 'Give me a leg-up and start counting.'

'Roese, you can't! Not dressed like that!' His eyes were round in disbelief.

'Just watch me!'

As she dug her heels into the flanks of the surprised bay, she heard him muttering, 'One parish priest, two parish priests, three . . .' until she was out of earshot.

The bay had obviously had a hard morning, and wasn't eager to hurry. Used to the weight of Sir Walter, he acted as if Roese wasn't there. Until, as they trotted along the path beside the wood, she snapped off a switch of hazel and brought it down hard across his rump.

It was an action she instantly regretted.

The horse wore a harsh bit, but Roese's hands didn't have the strength of her father's. As they flew off down the track, she realized they weren't going to stop until the horse wanted to.

The track turned in a long right-hand bend, curving round the copse to cross a stream. At that point it branched, one arm going on beside the wood and off towards the hills, the other coming back across the fields to the house. Pulling to the right with all her strength, with relief she felt him begin to turn.

He seemed to take the meadow as a challenge. Eyes streaming, hair tangled across her face, she could hardly see. But she felt the increase of pace, in the wind flying past and in the racing thud of the great hooves on the turf. In a strange way, it was quite exhilarating.

Too soon, the house loomed up ahead, William in the yard still holding his pony and still, she noticed as she approached, counting. He appeared to think nothing was amiss; she wondered briefly what he'd do if she screamed, 'Help, William, I can't stop!'

Pushing her buttocks down into the saddle, she leaned back, sawing on the reins. At last, the horse began to respond, although she thought it was probably more because he'd had enough than because he was answering to any feeble command of hers. Or – she almost laughed – because he could see a yard and a stable wall rapidly coming towards him.

The gallop slowed to a canter, then to a trot.

'. . . fifty-one parish priests, fifty-two parish priests,' William said. 'Fifty-three, Roese!' His voice increased to a shout. 'My turn.'

She thought she'd got away with it. Trotting into the yard, she imagined she and the huge bay must make quite a good picture. Then the two of them noticed simultaneously that they had a visitor: a big grey stood just inside the gate that led out to the road, on its back a dark-haired man wearing the apparel of a knight. The coat of mail caught glints of sunlight as he moved, and the device on the black surcoat echoed the scarlet bear's head on his shield. Under his arm he carried a plumed helm.

She became horribly aware of the blood on her face where branches had whipped back. And of the yellow silk kirtle, whose flowing skirt she'd pushed high up her bare thighs.

She took a hand off the reins to drag down the thin material, but it was caught up in her smock. She heard something tear, making a surprisingly loud sound. The noise startled the bay, who threw back his head. With only one hand on the reins, Roese knew what was going to happen.

Stepping sideways in a sudden rush, the bay dumped her into the pile of sodden, steaming straw that William had earlier raked out of the stables.

Picking his moment, Sir Walter came out of the hall, hand extended to greet his guest. 'Sir Gawyn de Brocéliande,' he called pleasantly. 'Welcome to our –'

Then he saw her. His outraged voice boomed out across the yard, but his words were drowned in the dark-haired knight's laughter.

Seven

If Ismay wasn't such a good-hearted woman, Roese thought, she'd march off and have nothing more to do with me. Which is probably what I deserve.

They were up in Roese's chamber, and Ismay had just seen what Roese's abrupt departure from the bay's saddle had done to the yellow silk kirtle. It was never going to be the same again, no matter how carefully Ismay laundered and mended it.

'I'm truly sorry, Ismay.' It wasn't hard to sound penitent; the shame of what had happened – and, even worse, of having a stranger witness it – was affecting her deeply.

Ismay sniffed.

'Will you help me dress in something else? The green, perhaps?'

Another sniff.

'Oh, please, Ismay! I said I'm sorry, and I am – I didn't mean to wreck the yellow silk, after you'd worked so hard on it. Won't you – '

'It's not the kirtle, you foolish girl!' Ismay spun round from her inspection of the damaged garment, and Roese saw instantly that this was more than anger at a stupid prank. 'It's – it's – oh, dear Lord help me, can't you see?'

Roese stood dumbly shaking her head.

Ismay took a deep breath, then held out her hand. 'Come here, Roese. Come and sit with me a while.'

Roese had got as far as putting on another clean smock. 'But – '

'Oh, never mind that. I'll worry about what you're to wear later. Just you listen for now, because there's something I have to say to you, and it won't wait any longer.'

Apprehensively, Roese went to join her, perching on the chest beside her. 'What is it?'

But the urgency of Ismay's preamble seemed to have deserted her. It was some moments before she said quietly, 'Your dear mother left you too young, Roese. She knew she was dying, God bless her, and she knew also that you would suffer. Roger and your father as well, but it was you she worried about. Only a mite, you were, not yet six years . . . But that's by-the-by.' She shook herself. Roese was relieved that she didn't continue; eleven years was a long time, but sometimes she still grieved for her mother as if the death had happened yesterday. 'Now, your father entrusted you to me – I said he should remarry, but he'd have none of it, wouldn't even *look*, and that merchant's widow from up by Usk way was a fine woman, wealthy, too, but there you are, some men are like that, and who am I to say I'd act any different? When a body's been happily married, I suppose . . .' Roese smiled to herself. Ismay would certainly say her piece, but it might take time. 'Your father is angry with you, my girl, very angry, and that's not like him, now, is it? Apple of his eye, you are, as well you and I both know, and now you've gone and upset him.'

'But –'

'No buts!' Ismay's sharp forefinger prodded into

Roese's ribs. 'I want to see a change in you, young Roese, starting this very moment. Seventeen, you are, *seventeen!*' She said it with as much surprise as if Roese had jumped from babyhood to seventeen in one leap. 'I was married at seventeen, a mother at eighteen and –'

'– And a widow at twenty-one,' Roese finished for her; it was a familiar recital.

'I've tried to tell Sir Walter, oh, how I've tried,' – Ismay's voice soared into the histrionic – 'but he's determined to think of you as a girl still. Now, you take today as a warning – let me tell you, he was all for treating you as a boy this morning, never mind a girl – I only just persuaded him it wasn't fitting for him to give you a good hiding!'

'Thanks,' said Roese, her tone heartfelt.

'It's up to you, my lovie,' Ismay said, arms going round Roese in a sudden intense hug. 'You must show him you're a young lady, then perhaps he'll start accepting the inevitable and treating you like one. Get yourself out of the stable yard, and stop all that horseplay with young William – dear God, you need a man's company, not a boy's!'

'I don't,' Roese muttered, wriggling away.

'Oh, Roese, I'm afraid you do.' Ismay looked at her sorrowfully. 'And I shall tell Sir Walter yet again that he must do what is right. He must start looking for a husband for you.'

The midday dinner was an uncomfortable time for Roese. Apart from the fact that it hurt her bruised hip to sit down, she was aware of her father's eyes on her; the purple in his cheeks indicated that his anger hadn't yet subsided. The guests proved to be a mixed group of clerics – a priest and two monks on their way to Tintern – and merchants, two stout and self-satisfied men up from the south to buy wool, accompanied by their unappealing and over-confident sons. One of the sons was seated next to Roese, and appeared to think she should be grateful for the privilege.

The food was excellent; the roast pigeons fell from the bone, and the venison was strong enough for the most robust palate.

'Your father could be killed for taking the King's venison,' the youth beside her said to Roese.

'No, he couldn't,' she retorted. 'You forget where you are – we're on the border here, and that deer was felled in Wales.'

He pushed the dark, rich meat about with his knife. 'Of course, I prefer beef,' he said disparagingly.

Roese thought of Ismay, working so hard to produce this feast. She looked at the young man's thin-nosed face, screwed up in distaste.

'I'll ask if you may have some beef stew,' she said. 'I'm sure there's some put out for the hounds.'

He shot her a glance. 'I didn't mean –'

Yes, you did, she thought. She said sweetly, 'Perhaps you'd like to go out to the kennels to eat it.'

He hissed something at her – she wasn't familiar with his words, but the meaning was clear – and there was a sudden movement from behind him.

'Not a term a man uses to a lady,' a quiet voice said, 'Especially in her own hall.'

She turned; the dark knight stood there. On his feet, he was much taller than he'd appeared in the saddle. He sounded like a Welshman. The fingers of the hand resting on the young man's shoulder were digging in like a clamp. 'Just you apologize, now. Pretty as you please.'

The youth muttered something.

114

'I didn't hear that,' the knight said conversationally. His hand gripped tighter, and the youth yelped. 'A little louder.'

'I take back my words.' He seemed to be speaking through gritted teeth. 'Please accept my humble apology, lady.'

The knight leaned forward so that he could look into her face. 'All right, Lady Roese? Can you see your way to forgiving him?'

She wanted to laugh. 'Yes,' she said.

The knight let go of the youth's shoulder, pushing him forward as he did so. 'That's good. Now, eat up your venison, boy, it might put some muscle on you.'

She thought he'd gone. But he hadn't: mouth to her ear, he whispered, 'Fine piece of riding earlier, my lovely. Pity about the muck heap, but I expect it cushioned your fall. Bum all right now, is it?'

She felt the hot blood rush into her face. How dare he! To come to her rescue like that, only to turn the tables and insult her, it was . . . it was . . .

Against her will, she heard his melodious voice echo in her head. The urge to laugh was becoming irrepressible; she got up hastily and went to help Ismay.

The clerics and the merchants moved on later in the day, eager to cover the few remaining miles to their night's lodgings before sunset.

Tidying the hall after their departure, Roese reflected that if her father had to spend hours clearing up other people's mess, he might be less keen to throw open his house to all and sundry. But she knew he'd never change: he was renowned for his hospitality, and he thrived on his reputation as a generous host. Little does the world know, Roese reflected, that there's always something in it for him – he wouldn't

do it otherwise. The merchants who stuffed themselves at our expense today, now, they've been
talked into buying Father's wool next spring, and into
calling on us again with the pick of their cloth. And as
for the priest and the monks, well, they've gone away
so grateful for a good square meal that Father will be
remembered in their prayers for weeks.

What, though, of Gawyn de Brocéliande?

A stack of pewter plates heavy in her hands, she
went back to the kitchen.

'Ismay, what did that Welsh knight want with us?'
She tried to make her voice sound casual.

Unsuccessfully: Ismay spun round from the table
and fixed her with a look that would have bored holes
in wood. '*A – HA!*'

'Don't you go a-ha'ing me,' Roese protested, 'I
merely asked a reasonable question.'

'So you did, my girl, so you did.' Ismay's suppressed laugh said much more than her words. 'He's
from the Black Mountains. Has a castle up on a lonely
crag. Wild place, they say.' She rolled her eyes at
Roese, as if suggesting some terrifying country of
mysterious mists and savage beasts.

'He's got a French name,' Roese pointed out.
'What's he doing with a castle in the Black
Mountains?'

'He has a castle in Brittany as well.'

'Oh, well, then. That explains everything,' Roese
said sarcastically.

'Ask your father.' Ismay elbowed her out of the
way and dumped the dirty plates in a deep bowl of
water. 'I'm too busy to stand here gossiping about tall
dark knights,' – she glanced at Roese again – 'no
matter how handsome they are.'

'I – oh!' Roese flung out of the kitchen, banging the
door behind her. But she could still hear Ismay's

laughter. Damn the woman! Insinuating that I. . . that he . . . *OH!*

Ismay brought her an early supper, with the instruction that she was to retire and leave the hall to her father, Roger and Sir Gawyn when they returned.

'Why? And when they return from where?'

'I told you earlier, ask your father. *I* don't know, I'm just the dogsbody.' Ismay thumped the plate of bread down on the table. Roese wondered why she was so disgruntled.

'Very well,' she said meekly.

Ismay paused, hand to her forehead. 'I'm sorry to snap, Roese. I'm tired.'

You're not just tired, Roese thought. Something's worrying you.

She felt a shiver of alarm. Ismay saved her worrying for really important things.

'Here's your father now,' Ismay said. 'Excuse me, I have work to do.'

She swept out of the hall. As she passed Sir Walter, she wouldn't meet his eye. Roese thought her father looked almost sheepish.

'Roese!' he said heartily.

'Hello, Father.'

'Have you heard the good news?' he asked, perching on the table beside her.

'What good news?'

'An excursion!' he said gleefully. 'A chance for Roger and me to see a bit of action, get our fighting arms in working order again! A good opportunity for the boy William, too – he can squire for us!'

She lit on the one word. 'Fighting?'

'Aye!' His eyes were shining. 'Oh, don't you worry your pretty head, Roese,' – he reached out and ruffled her hair – 'it's nothing to be anxious about!

117

Gawyn is having a little trouble with a neighbour – dispute over a piece of land, it is – and has asked for our help. He came to my aid a few years ago – you were just a child, you wouldn't remember – and he's calling in the favour. I can't refuse, Roese. You know that.'

His face had fallen as he spoke. No doubt, she thought, in response to my distinct lack of enthusiasm.

He appeared to be waiting for her to say something. She wondered if it would make any difference what she said. 'I see.' She kept her voice cool. She hesitated over her next words – they would be hurtful, she knew – but then said them anyway. 'The fact that you're an old man doesn't make this Gawyn think twice about asking you? When, as you point out, he's calling in a favour and knows as well as you do you can't refuse?'

She was right; he looked very hurt. 'I don't want to refuse!' he shouted. 'Roese, I'm a better man than Roger – than Gawyn, too – for all my years! It's experience, see! No amount of youth and strength can make up for experience!'

She looked at him. He was running to fat, and his fleshy face had a permanent bluish hue. That Gawyn must see these things too, she consoled herself. Perhaps he's right and it is only a little squabble. Nothing to be anxious about. Surely he wouldn't ask Father if there were any real danger?

'When do you leave?' she asked. 'And how long will you be gone?'

He threw his arms round her in a hug, apparently taking her questions as an indication that she was over her qualms. 'We leave as early as we can tomorrow,' he said happily. 'Gawyn will be back in the morning – he's gone off to rally some more support.

And as for how long –' he frowned, 'two, three days up into the Black Mountains, the same back again, and in between, who can say?' He jumped off the table, almost dancing with pleasure. 'Don't expect to see us back within the fortnight, Roese.'

She was about to ask if Roger and William were as elated as he was about the venture when their loud arrival into the hall answered her. Roger's normally sombre face was creased in a smile, and William was hopping with joy.

They scarcely noticed her leave the room.

The yard was alive with activity from soon after first light. It was impossible to sleep – even had it not been for the noise, she was too keyed-up. She dressed and went down to watch.

Her father's bay stood beside Roger's mount. Both had been groomed till they gleamed – she wondered if William had been to bed at all – and now were being fitted with their caparisons. The cloth draped over their broad backs was green and blue, green for the hills, her father always said, and blue for the Wye. The fact that the Wye was a dull sludgy brown and not bright azure apparently had escaped his notice.

I rode that horse, Roese thought. I rode my father's destrier, and was lucky to escape with a bruise or two.

William's pony looked tiny beside the huge animals. She had a sudden thought, and, walking over to where he stood sharpening the point of Roger's lance, put the idea into action before she could change her mind.

'Do you want to take Arrow?'

His head shot up. 'She's a mare.'

'I know. But she's a hand and a half bigger than him,' she nodded towards his stout, tough pony, 'and she's fast. She's not called Arrow for nothing.' Almost

119

cross that he should make an objection, she felt all the more passionate that he should accept her gift. 'And so what if she's not a gelding? It's only a small boundary dispute, you're not going on crusade! Still, suit yourself, *I* don't care!'

She turned on her heel, but his hand on her arm held her back. 'Roese, why are you cross?'

She spun round. 'Why do you think? Because –' She didn't go on. His young face, thin now as the plumpness of boyhood fell away, was a touching mixture of irrepressible excitement at the coming adventure and hurt puzzlement because she was angry with him and he didn't know why.

'I'm not cross,' she said affectionately. She wanted to hug him, in the warm, happy way her father always hugged her, but she wasn't sure he'd welcome that. Especially standing out in the yard. Instead she punched his shoulder. 'Do as you please. Arrow's yours if you want her – you take care of her, though! I want her back hale and hearty! – and if you'd rather take that old rag-bag of yours, that's all right, too.'

His eyes turned to where Arrow's elegant head poked out over the half-door of the stable. 'What will your father say?' he asked. She felt he was weakening. Hardly surprising, she thought, he's as good a judge of a fine horse as anyone, and Father paid a lot for my Arrow.

'She's mine,' she said firmly. 'Mine to do with as I choose. And I choose to lend her to you.'

He spat in his palm and clasped her hand. 'I accept. I'll look after her, I swear.'

His delight was affecting her, making her ache with tenderness at his youth and his eagerness. She felt again the shiver of alarm she'd felt yesterday, when Ismay had looked so worried. Stop it, she told herself. Stop being a killjoy. 'Go and get her ready, then.' She pushed him away. 'Roger can see to his own lance.'

He ran off. She could hear him singing. He was wearing a new pair of hose and a tunic quartered in her father's colours. Inside her head the words rang out, He's not old enough. Not old enough to be a squire and go to fight.

She found herself a perch on the mounting block and watched as the long preparations wound to a conclusion. Gawyn had returned, with him a band of six knights, helmed and dressed in chain mail; seeing them ride up, Ismay had exclaimed, 'Diew! Have I to feed that lot?' but it was all right, they had elected to ride on ahead.

Sir Walter, Gawyn, Roger and William ate together, and Roese went to help Ismay serve them. Her own three menfolk didn't look like their everyday selves: putting on his hauberk and surcoat had made her father stand up straighter, holding in his belly and squaring his shoulders as if preparing himself for the fray. Roger looked like a stranger; but then he is a stranger nowadays, she thought, more often from home than here with us, so that I scarcely know him any more.

William seemed on the point of bursting with pride. Look after him, she wanted to say to her father. Remember how young he is. And how loyal – don't lead him into needless danger.

Her eyes moved to Gawyn. This is your venture, she said silently to him. My father owes you a favour, I know that, and I think too that if you turned round now and said you'd changed your mind and didn't need him after all, the chances are he'd kill you. All the same . . .

All the same, I have a bad feeling about this.

121

They finished the meal and went back out to the yard. She watched as they mounted, the younger men swinging themselves into the saddle as if wild to be away. Her father used the mounting block. The May sunshine glittered on shields, helms and harness.

'Goodbye, Lady Roese.' Gawyn stood before her, the grey prancing and trying to grasp its bit in the huge square teeth. He was bareheaded, his helm under his arm, and his dark hair shone like the coat of a healthy animal. The black and scarlet surcoat suited him. 'I've enough men now, else I'd have asked you to ride with us.' He grinned, as if, like her father and William, he too could hardly hold in the euphoria. 'Sit a horse well, you do.'

She was about to thank him, make some appropriately ladylike reply to his compliment. Wish him luck, even. But as she opened her mouth to speak, he added, 'For a girl.'

A girl! *A girl!*

Without thinking, she was searching the ground for a stone, a chunk of wood, anything, to fling at him; four years with William and, before that, a childhood with an elder brother had made her deadly with any missile.

Her hand closed on a compacted clod of mud, thrown out of a hoof.

'Come on!' Gawyn shouted. 'If we ride hard, we'll catch the others this side of the foothills!'

Her father led the way out through the gates, head high, voice shouting a farewell. William and Roger rode behind him, and Gawyn brought up the rear.

As his broad back disappeared, the heavy boulder of mud hit him squarely between the shoulders.

Eight

The fortnight extended into three weeks, and not a word came from the Black Mountains.

Roese, reverting to childhood, looked to Ismay for reassurance. But Ismay didn't give any.

Roese took to spending hours in the little chapel attached to the house. A dread was on her, and she tried to find comfort in prayer. The words came readily – she'd been reciting them all her life, since long before the alien language made any sense. She and Ismay had always gone to church together in the village and, unless her father was away, the priest would come up to their own chapel to celebrate private mass for the family. But now, with all of King John's realm under the pope's interdict, nobody went to church any more, not even to be married or buried. Like everyone else, Roese said her prayers alone. The comfort she sought was not forthcoming.

Unable to sleep one night, she became aware of someone walking about in the hall below. Wrapping a shawl over her shift, she went down. She opened the door a crack, to see Ismay pacing to and fro before the dying fire.

Ismay was talking to herself: Roese could see her

lips moving. Perhaps she, too, was praying. She didn't notice Roese.

It was unnerving to see strong, dependable Ismay reduced to pacing and muttering. Without advertising her presence, Roese turned and crept back to bed.

Almost a month after the sunny, optimistic departure, the only one of Roese's household to survive the minor boundary squabble came home.

He led a bay destrier who favoured a wounded off foreleg. His own mount had lost the jaunty step with which she'd danced out of the yard four weeks before.

His face was yellow with fatigue and lined with grief.

She ran out into the yard and caught him as he slid off the mare's back. Tears streaming down his cheeks, William whispered, 'They're dead, Roese. I'm sorry, I'm sorry.'

Then he fell out of her arms on to the cobblestones.

*　*　*

Roese and Ismay, desperate for news, sat at William's side as he slept. He had no wound – Ismay made her leave the room while she checked – but seemed to be utterly exhausted. Late into the night, when Roese sat alone while Ismay took a short break, he woke.

Roese looked down at him, noting how the peaceful expression crumpled as he struggled out of sleep and remembered. 'It's all right, you're home now,' she whispered.

He stared up into her face, his mouth working. 'But your father – Roger – I told you, they're dead! I didn't – I couldn't –'

'Didn't what, William?'

124

'I tried to help, but I couldn't. It's my fault, Roese, but, God help me, I didn't know what to do!'

She watched the horror grow in his eyes as he relived the nightmare. Fleetingly he looked adult as the deep shock lines altered his expression. Then the tears began, and he was a boy again.

She held him as he cried. The hoarse sounds of a child's emotions let out in a youth's breaking voice rent her heart.

Ismay, hearing them talking, had silently come into the room. Standing behind Roese, she put her hand on Roese's arm. The two of them waited until William had cried himself out.

Ismay had brought him something to drink: Roese caught the aroma of mulled wine. Sensing Roese's eyes on her, she smiled briefly. 'I've made it strong,' she said quietly. 'Yes, I know he drinks little as a rule. He's a man now, Roese. Whatever he's been through has seen to that. Now, he needs to rest. Perhaps it'll help him cope with his memories.' She looked down at him tenderly. 'Drink it, William,' she said to him. 'Then sleep. Whatever you have to tell us will keep till morning.'

They sat until his breathing deepened. Lying on his back, he started to snore gently – it was time to leave him.

Roese fell into her own bed, so tired that she'd thought sleep would come instantly. As she closed her eyes, she saw an image of her father, holding in his stomach as he caressed the hilts of his sword. He looked proud and happy.

He's dead, she thought. He was so excited, so pleased to be young again. Now he's dead.

Ismay was there, arms around her, soothing her. She was crying, too – Roese felt the wet cheek against her own. It helped, a little.

In the morning, Ismay took Roese and William into the hall. She made them sit at the big table, William at the head, herself and Roese either side. The formal situation seemed to help William, which was, Roese reflected, precisely why Ismay had arranged it.

Straight-backed, eyes fixed on some distant point on the far wall, he told them.

Gawyn's dispute had been quickly settled; his neighbouring landowner had been daunted by the sight of nine fully-armed knights, mounted expensively and accompanied by a dutiful handful of squires. 'Gawyn said, "There, now, look, he's seen reason,"' William said, the ghost of a smile on his gaunt face. 'Then he thanked us all, and offered us the freedom of his castle. In order to show his gratitude, see.'

Recipe for trouble, Roese thought. Nine knights fired up for a fight, and denied more than a token sortie.

'What a place!' William's face showed how impressed he'd been. 'Right up in the hills – well, they were mountains, I suppose, great crags soaring up with snow on their tops. And the castle was like a fortress – it was up high, with a sheer drop on two sides, the mountain at its back and access up a winding track that went over a drawbridge.' He shuddered. 'It was very narrow, that drawbridge. It wasn't easy getting the horses across – some of them got very nervous. Gawyn said it'd be better if he and his squire rode ahead, their horses being used to it, like. All the same, I didn't try to ride across, I got off and led Arrow.' He shot Roese a smile. 'I'd promised to take care of her, and I remembered that and ignored the other boys who said I was scared.' He shuddered again, more violently. 'I was scared, anyway.'

Ismay put her hand on his arm. 'It sounds to me as

if you were sensible,' she said. 'Often, fear is put into
the heart for a very good reason. Choosing to lead a
horse over a dangerous bridge, instead of taking a
risk and riding, means you took notice of your instincts and acted accordingly.'

William looked at her gratefully. 'That's what I
thought, too. I wish –' He broke off. 'Gawyn was a
very good host. He has people there who look after
him – cooks and things – and there was so much food
and drink!' He stared round-eyed at Roese. 'Honestly, we eat well here, but you should have been there!
They never stopped drinking, all day!'

His face changed; last night's grief began to creep
back across his features. He took a deep breath, as if
steadying himself, then said, 'Two of the knights got
violent, picking fights with the others. Sir Walter and
Roger tried to make them calm down, but they didn't
listen. When Sir Walter reminded them they weren't
behaving like knights should, they laughed at him.
They called him a silly old man who'd forgotten how
to have fun.' He lowered his eyes, as if it shamed him
to have to tell Roese such things.

'What about Gawyn?' she asked. It was hard to
keep the indignation out of her voice. 'What was he
doing while all this carousing was going on in his
hall?'

William shrugged. 'He seemed to be enjoying it.
He wasn't aggressive and wild like the worst of them,
but he didn't really try to control them. Not at first,
anyway. Not till – ' Again he stopped. This time, it
was some moments before he could bring himself to
go on.

Roese sat stiff with anticipation.

'They started challenging each other.' William's
low voice echoed in the hall, the only sound to break
the silence. 'It was the two trouble-makers to start

with. They were making the rest do things like scaling the walls of the courtyard and walking round the top of the balustrade on the tower. They were drunk, and didn't see how stupid they were.

'Then someone said about the drawbridge. I forget who it was. Two of them started it, and another one joined in. Sir Walter and Roger refused, and Gawyn went out to watch.'

'That makes six,' Roese said. 'What about the other three?'

'They'd gone. Their squires packed up and they left. Said they had better things to do than watch a load of hotheads risk their necks.' Again the shudder.

Why didn't you come home, Father? she asked silently. Did you think you ought to stay to make them see sense? Or were you having too much fun?

'One of them missed his footing and fell.' He was hurrying the words out and she had to strain to hear. 'He caught hold of a stanchion of the bridge, and his companion leaned over the edge and grabbed him under the arms. He was slipping down too, the weight of the other man was dragging him – he hooked his legs round a bridge post but then he got stuck. He didn't look as if he was going to be dragged any further, but he wasn't strong enough to pull the other man back up.' His eyes meeting Roese's were wide with indignant horror. 'They were *laughing*, Roese, as if it was just a big joke! The man was hanging there, hundreds of feet over a drop to a rocky cleft below, and they were so drunk they thought it was funny!'

'What happened?'

'Roger said they'd need help. He ran out to help hold the man who'd fallen, and Sir Walter went with him. He was saying something about getting one of the horses, and he told me to put a collar on Roger's destrier and lead him on to the bridge.'

He was sitting with his head bowed. Suddenly he looked up at Roese. 'I don't know how it happened, I swear, Roese! It all seemed to be going all right, with Roger pulling one of them up on to the bridge, a line fixed from the horse to the other one, and me leading the horse slowly forward. Then someone shouted, there was an awful scream, and all at once the horse was walking backwards, faster and faster, and I couldn't stop him, I tried but he was too strong, and he put his hind feet over the edge and someone shouted again – one of the others, I think – then Roger screamed that he was falling and your father got all tangled up with the horse and they disappeared.' He made a strangled sound. 'Then Gawyn came running out, looked over the edge and said, "Oh, God."'

'Wh –' Her mouth was too dry to speak. She wet her lips and tried again. 'Where were they?'

'The horse had fallen on top of Sir Walter. They were on a sloping bit about halfway down. The other man and Roger were right down in the gully.'

'And they were all dead?' Ismay's voice sounded surprisingly calm.

William nodded. 'Yes. You could see they were, but Gawyn took a couple of his people down to check. They brought the bodies up. Not the horse – there was no way they could do that. They had to leave him where he lay. Gawyn said he wouldn't last long out there.'

Roese had a vision of carrion crows round a big felled body. It made her feel sick.

'Gawyn is arranging for Sir Walter and Roger to be brought home,' William said. 'He asked if you'd want that, or if they should be buried there, and I said they should come back here. Was that right?'

'Yes.' She sensed that his need for reassurance

went beyond being told that had been the correct decision. She said, 'William, look at me.' Slowly his eyes met hers. 'I don't see that any of this was your fault,' she began. 'You said last night that you were sorry, that you tried but couldn't help them.'

'I couldn't! I –'

'It's all right. You weren't to blame. It was an accident, William,' – she stressed the word – 'and if anyone was at fault, it was the knights who let the drink get the better of them.'

'And Sir Gawyn de Brocéliande,' Ismay said darkly.

Roese cleared her throat. 'I – do we –?' She cursed herself for the hesitancy and started again. 'Ismay, we must notify the priest. He will arrange the funeral. A requiem mass, possibly.'

She'd forgotten, but Ismay hadn't. 'There won't be any requiem mass. Nor any funeral, not while the interdict lasts.' Her voice was expressionless, as if the misdeeds of royalty and their subsequent punishment were not for her to comment on. 'We'll bury them in the woods.'

'Yes. Very well. But we must tell –' Who did you tell? The overlord of the manor? The king's representative? Someone, surely, should be informed of the death of a knight.

'We will notify the sheriff of the county,' Ismay said. 'He will take what steps are necessary.' She got to her feet. 'Roese, go to the kitchen and see if you can organize the midday meal. A household still has to eat, whatever happens. William, you go with her.' She gave them both a thin smile. 'Look after each other.'

In the weeks between William's return and the arrival of the king's man, Roese finally grew out of girlhood.

Dressed in the sombre black garments she and Ismay hastily made, her reflection looking back at her from the expensive piece of glass in the hall window made her out to be a mature woman. I'm not, she wanted to shout, I'm still me! Nothing's changed!

But it has, she admitted. Everything's changed. I've lost my father and my elder brother. I have no mother, no close relation at all. There is an elderly female cousin of my father's two counties away, but my father fell out with her years ago and she won't acknowledge my existence.

There's Ismay, and there's William. She's house-keeper to a household which no longer exists, he's squire to a dead knight. Far from it being up to them to take care of me, I must do what I can for them. Which seems to be precisely nothing.

The priest had explained that she had no rights. Her father's manor and land did not become hers, as she'd at first supposed: unwed, unbetrothed, she could not inherit because she had no man to take over her inheritance.

Aghast, she'd asked, 'Who does the land go to? And the house, and all our possessions?' The horses, the furniture, the very pots and pans! she thought frantically.

'Everything becomes the property of the king,' the priest answered. He sounded neither pleased nor sorry about it; his neutral tone merely informed.

'What about me? Am I now the king's property too?'

She'd intended it as a joke, wanting to lighten the depressing atmosphere.

But he looked at her and said, as if she ought to have known, 'Yes. Of course.'

I'm mistress here till we're thrown out, she thought on the day a cart arrived from the Black Mountains

131

bearing the bodies of her father and her brother. They were boxed and ready for burial: two days later, one of Sir Walter's friends sent men to help William dig two deep graves in the woods.

Gawyn did not appear. He sent his deepest regrets, and offered her any assistance she might need.

I'm mistress here till someone arrives to tell me otherwise, she thought on the day the sheriff of the county came to report that the king had been informed of Sir Walter's death, and that arrangements would be made.

I'm mistress here, she thought as life slowly began to walk forwards again.

But it didn't last.

The king's representative was Sir Percy Albenham, Earl of Beauhampton. He was a man who knew the law inside out, far better than a rural parish priest. But what he had to tell her amounted to the same thing.

'Your father died while you are still under age,' he explained. As if she didn't know. 'Your brother, being of age, could have assumed the mantle as head of the family and arranged for your dispo– ah, your mar-riage,' he corrected himself slickly – 'but, sadly . . .' He let the sentence hang in the air, hands turned up as if to express his regret at Roger's carelessness.

'I know that.' Don't snap at him, she told herself, it'll only antagonize him. And things are bad enough without that. 'I appreciate my sorry position,' she said more gently. 'Perhaps you would explain just what happens now?'

'Of course, my dear lady.' She had an image of thick oil being poured. 'You are now a ward of the king.'

The king. King John, a distant figure far away in whatever palace it was he lived in. She was his ward. She wondered if he viewed the arrangement with as much dismay as she did.

'What does that mean, exactly?'

Sir Percy leaned back in his chair and pressed his extended palms together as if he were about to say a prayer. Taking his time, he said, 'Your father had not, I understand, entered into negotiations regarding a marriage for you.'

'No.' I didn't want to marry, she thought. He didn't want me to, either. He liked having me here with him. Ismay kept prodding him to do something, but he kept putting it off. Next week, next month, next year.

'That is – ah – regrettable.' He gave her a shallow smile which failed to make any impression on the narrow dark eyes. 'Inasmuch, I hasten to add, that had you been betrothed – officially betrothed, that is, I don't mean some vague agreement with no standing in the law,' – he glared at her as if she'd been trying to deceive him with some such flimsy arrangement – 'had a legal betrothal existed, then naturally the King would have honoured it.'

'Naturally,' Roese echoed faintly.

'As it is . . .' The smile again, and another unfinished sentence. As if she knew the rest.

'Yes?'

'Hm?'

'As it is, you were saying.'

'Ah. As it is, you are, as I say, a ward of the king. It is up to him to arrange your marriage.'

It took a while for the meaning of the words to permeate. When they had done so, she seemed to hear the heavy iron doors of a prison cell clang shut in her face.

'Has he – would he be likely to have anyone in mind?' she heard herself ask. Funny, I seem to be picking up his roundabout way of speaking, she thought. Her mind leapt to concentrate on the interesting phenomenon, shying away from the enormity of what she'd just been told.

'That I cannot say.' Sir Percy awarded her another smile. 'Rest assured, Lady Roese, that the king is accustomed to this sort of thing. He would not disparage a lady by arranging her marriage to someone who was not her social peer.'

Social peer, she repeated to herself. What's that? I know! Of course I do. It means someone who's the same type of person. A knight, like Father. I'm a knight's daughter, so the king won't marry me to a blacksmith or a ploughman. That's something, I suppose.

There was one more thing to ask. She had a feeling she already knew the answer. 'Do I have any say in the matter?'

He looked at her as if she were simple.

'No.'

For some time nothing happened. Engaged in some domestic task, laughing with Ismay as they sorted apples, or riding out with William to inspect the harvest, teasing him as he learned to control the big bay, she would realize she was happy. It was possible to maintain the illusion that it was always going to be like this.

Christmas came. The first Christmas without Father and Roger, and she ached for them. Especially Father. Ismay tried hard, but they all missed the big child who'd loved to dress up and who used to eat so much that he'd been good for nothing in the afternoon but lying back on his couch moaning that his belly ached.

January. Snow and thick ice, making travelling something to be avoided. Safe within the thick walls, the outside world became irrelevant.

It was only a temporary reprieve. In February, the Earl of Beauhampton returned. The king had found her a husband.

They were sitting in the hall in front of a hastily-lit fire that was smoking. For the rest of her life, she would associate the acrid smell of smouldering, damp firewood with a sickening drop of the heart.

'And who is my husband to be?' she asked. She felt hot and cold at the same time, and her knees were shaking.

Sir Percy's manner was hard to read. He was maintaining a pleasant expression – as pleasant as he could manage with limited resources – but he appeared to be on edge.

'A wealthy man, Lady Roese – he is paying a considerable dowry for you! *Very* considerable!'

For an instant she thought the money would be paid to her. Then she understood. No wonder the king bothered with something as mundane as arranging the marriage of an insignificant knight's daughter. She had wondered if, in the midst of the rumoured troubles with Wales and with Brittany, not to mention the ongoing dispute with the pope, the king might have forgotten all about her. No. One thing everyone knew was that the extravagant King John was always short of money.

'How much is the king getting?'

Sir Percy looked shocked. 'That is a matter of the utmost confidentiality,' he said in hushed tones. Roese thought it was unreasonable, when it was herself who was being sold, that she didn't even know how much she was going for.

'. . . a vast estate in Kent, my lady,' Sir Percy was saying. 'And a very pretty part of the county, I'm told.'

Kent. She had no idea where Kent was, except that

it was nowhere near home. A vast estate. A wealthy man.

A thought struck her. Young men weren't usually wealthy, nor the possessors of vast estates.

'How old is my husband?'

Sir Percy appeared to squirm. 'A good man, Lady Roese. A position in the entourage of the king is rumoured. King John thinks highly of him, which of course is why he has decided to bestow on him such a . . .'

She had seen the furtive journey of his eyes over her body before he pulled himself together and returned his gaze to her face.

'How old?'

Sir Percy shrugged as if to say, it's not my problem. 'He is forty-seven.'

Nine

She would have been torn apart with horror, except that even as he told her, she was making up her mind it wasn't going to happen.

Numbly she heard him out, listening with half an ear to the arrangements for a meeting; the bridegroom, it appeared, wanted to inspect the goods before he parted with his money. 'A mere formality, Lady Roese, of that I am certain,' Sir Percy said, smiling at her unctuously as the rogue eyes escaped his vigilance and again roamed over her body.

She was to travel to Gloucester, where Sir Percy would act as intermediary for what he delicately termed 'the negotiations'. He spoke for a long time about how she should behave, what servants should attend her – I only have the one, Roese thought, unless you count William, and both Ismay and I would argue with the description 'servant' – what she should wear, how she should respond to the questions her future husband would certainly ask. You would think it was Sir Percy who was being paid the dowry rather than the king, she reflected. I wonder if he's getting a commission?

She waited until he had finished, then courteously saw him out of the hall and into the courtyard. William was hovering on the steps, and she asked him to fetch Sir Percy's horse. Excusing herself, she wished him a safe journey and then went back inside, closing the door firmly behind her. Let William see him off, she thought – I have to think.

Her prospective husband would be waiting for her in Gloucester in a month's time. Four weeks. Long enough to come up with a plan of action?

It had to be.

Where shall I be in four weeks' time? she wondered. Somewhere. Anywhere but Gloucester, with him.

It was only then that she realized she hadn't taken in the man's name.

* * *

Who to turn to for help?

Once the wilder schemes had run their course and regretfully been abandoned, she came swiftly to the conclusion that she wasn't going to manage this alone. Ismay seemed to have been stunned into silence – Roese imagined it would only be temporary – and would say nothing beyond, 'I kept telling him, but he wouldn't do anything. Wouldn't even listen, curse the man!' at which her eyes would fill with tears she'd hastily turn away to hide.

Belatedly Roese accepted that Ismay had loved Sir Walter.

She's right to put the blame on Father, Roese thought. Yes, he *should* have found me a husband. He'd have taken my wishes into account, of course he would, and together we'd have chosen someone who filled both his requirements and mine. As it is . . .

She didn't finish the thought, but even its beginning caused her heart to race in panic.

Don't worry, she told herself. *It's not going to happen*.

What are my resources? I have Ismay, who is wise and sensible and knows her way around in the world. She'll be my greatest strength, or at least she will be when she's herself again. I have William, who, although I can't rely on him for any bright ideas, will do anything I ask.

She reflected what a shame it was that William wasn't a few years older, then she could have married him. No, I couldn't, she corrected herself, he has no money. No . . . nothing.

Dear God, what's going to become of William?

Of Ismay?

She understood then that running away from a marriage she wasn't going to accept at any cost was only the first of her problems.

Days passed. The household seemed to be frozen, its inhabitants inanimate. They ate, slept, passed a few words with each other, but it seemed to Roese that they existed in a time and a place apart.

They're waiting for me to tell them what to do.

Oh, God, and I don't *know*.

She took Ismay on one side. 'You realize I won't marry him?'

Ismay snorted. 'Of course I do.' She glared at Roese. 'A man of forty-seven, who'll take you away to some Godforsaken corner of the realm so you'll never see your home again?' Roese smiled at Ismay's description of the most civilized part of England as 'Godforsaken'. On the other hand, though, given the reputed sophistication and worldliness of King John's court, possibly the adjective was accurate. And they said now the king would likely be excommunicated, along with his poor Godforsaken people.

'I know you won't do it, Roese. I'm just waiting to hear *how*.'

'I have to get away,' Roese said decisively. 'And well away, leaving no clue to where I've gone, so that when he realizes I'm not going to meet him in Gloucester and comes here looking for me, he'll find . . .'

'Find an empty house?' Ismay finished for her. 'And where, pray, shall William and I be?'

'With me, of course,' Roese snapped.

'Yes?' Ismay looked angry. 'Living on what?'

It was typical of her to have gone straight to the heart of it. Grand plans collapsed under the weight of practicalities such as, what shall we eat?

'You're alone in a wicked world, my girl,' Ismay said. 'You have your looks and your wits, and that's all. Your house and everything in it belongs to the king, and since you're not mistress here, William and I are homeless. You have no relations, and none of your father's fine friends will intervene – they'll say, and who can blame them, that perfectly acceptable arrangements have been made for you, and if you choose to defy the king's authority, on your own head be it!'

For an instant Roese felt her resolve quake. It's hopeless, she thought, there's no way out. I'll go to Gloucester, meet him, see what I think – he may be nice.

He won't be. He's forty-seven, and he'll take me away from my homeland. For ever.

And I mustn't even think of going to meet him, because if I do, I'll never escape.

Ismay was muttering, but Roese cut the sound out of her consciousness. Think. *THINK!* There must be someone, someone Father trusted and liked, who'd come to my aid for his sake.

Once the little pebble of an idea had started to move, it gathered momentum as quickly as a boulder racing down a mountain.

He sent his regrets. His deepest regrets. And offered me any assistance I might need.

Guilty conscience, that's what that was. He was accepting responsibility. As well he might, since if it hadn't been for him and his stupid dispute and his accursed drawbridge, I'd still have a father and a brother and I wouldn't be in this appalling mess.

She stood up, feeling almost that she was flying; after so long in agonized indecision, it felt good to have a purpose.

'Ismay, please prepare my riding clothes. And put out whatever I'll need for a few days away from home.'

Ismay eyed her warily. 'Where are you going?'

'Into the Black Mountains. I'm going to see Gawyn de Brocéliande to point out to him that the boot's on the other foot, and he now owes me a favour.'

Ismay's face registered surprise, then she smiled. 'Now why didn't I think of that,' she said softly. Then, practically, 'You can't go alone. You'd better take William.'

They left at dawn, partly to avoid interested eyes witnessing the departure, partly so as to make the most of the short February daylight. It was cold, but the sun was bright. They travelled light – Roese carried the small pack Ismay had prepared for her, to which she'd added one further small item – and rode hard, stopping only out of absolute necessity, and by nightfall had covered more than half the distance. Roese was thankful for William's powers of observation: he had remembered the way perfectly, never once hesitating when a choice of tracks had to be made. He was invaluable, too, in finding their night's lodging, making her ride on past an inn she would have thought all right, pointing out the soiled and sodden straw in the stable yard as an indication that the human accommodation might not be much better. He took her to a small establishment set back from the road: she wondered, but didn't ask, if he'd stayed here on that other fateful journey, when he was still her father's squire.

Late the next day they were climbing the steep mountain paths that led to Gawyn's castle. She was afraid, for sometimes the paths were narrow and a fall into space awaited the unwary. But William gave her courage: mounted on her father's horse, sound again thanks to his devoted care, he led the way up the hillside as if he did it every day.

As darkness fell, they rounded a rocky shoulder and found themselves on the edge of a precipice. Before them a thin wooden drawbridge spanned the chasm: she heard William give a low moan, and ached for him that she had to make him come here again.

In the silence a loud rattle began, and the end of the drawbridge started to lift out of its bed: Gawyn's men were securing the castle for the night.

William shouted, *'HOI!'*, making the horses start nervously and Roese jump out of her skin.

From across the void a voice called, 'Who goes there?'

'William, Sir Walter Prenville's man.' His voice cracked slightly, making him sound hoarse. And young: he wasn't anyone's man, yet.

She could see a dim figure standing on the other end of the drawbridge, peering out at them. 'You are two,' the man shouted. 'Who is with you?'

William turned to her, eyebrows raised. She

nodded. He called, 'The Lady Roese, Sir Walter's daughter.'

There was a pause – a shocked pause? she wondered – then the figure went back to the great wheel that turned the supporting chains of the drawbridge. As he twisted it, the heavy wooden planks fell back against the packed earth. Before anyone could change their mind, William slid off his horse's back and was leading him out on to the bridge.

Roese dismounted and followed, trying to still the trembling in her hands before her fear could communicate itself to Arrow. Does she remember? she wondered. She's been here before, has smelt death in this awful place.

Don't look down. Don't think about the rocks far below, where my dear father and my brother met their fate.

She gritted her teeth and lifted her chin, summoning anger in place of fear and grief.

Anger would be a far better emotion with which to face Gawyn de Brocéliande.

The man seemed to recognize William: as they stepped off the drawbridge, he stood back to let them pass through the gated archway leading into the courtyard, giving the boy a curt nod. He followed them through the dark passageway – it appeared to have been hewn out of the rocks, and from above drips of chill condensation fell on their heads – and then, moving forwards to take Arrow's rein from Roese, pointed out a doorway.

'The lad and I will see to your horses,' he said. 'The master is in the hall.'

Do I go in? she wondered. Unannounced?

For a second she wanted to laugh. Who's going to announce me?

She said grandly to Gawyn's man, 'I thank you,' then swept up the trailing hem of her riding cloak and walked up the steps leading to the hall.

The studded door opened to her push. She crossed the threshold, and the door swung closed after her. He didn't hear: he was sprawled in a chair in front of the hearth, a mug in his hand, gazing into the flames.

She willed him to notice her, but her thought didn't reach him. Clutching at her courage, calling back the fierce anger that had come to her aid on the drawbridge, she strode forwards into the room.

She was on the point of addressing him when he looked up.

His eyes locked on to hers. In his face she saw surprise, swiftly replaced by a frown. Of irritation? Guilt? She couldn't tell.

Jumping in before he could speak, she said, 'My father and my brother are dead because of you. You sent their bodies home to me, but you did not have the decency to accompany them and see them buried. You sent me word that you would help me if I needed you. And I do.'

She stopped as abruptly as she'd begun, furious with herself for blurting it all out at once when she'd meant to lead up more subtly to her demand. So subtly that with any luck he wouldn't have realized it was a demand at all.

Now she'd leapt in and her bridges were burning merrily behind her.

Her attack had brought out a response in him, and it wasn't the one she'd hoped for. There was no sign of remorse now, no hint in his expression that he would accept his responsibility and come to her aid. She'd attacked him, or so he would see it. I ought to have known better, she thought: attack a fighting man and he hits back.

144

Trying to remedy her error, she began, 'I have responsibilities. To William, whom you know. To Ismay, who kept house for us. And there is no-one I can turn to, for I have no kin. I am under age, and so not my own mistress. I have –'

'You will be made a ward of the king,' he interrupted. His voice sounded hoarse, as if he had been shouting. 'Situations such as yours are not uncommon. The law has an efficient way of dealing with them.'

The fury rose in her. She tried to swallow it, tried to tell herself that getting angry with him – with any man – wasn't how you got your own way. Calm down, she told herself. Be demure, womanly.

His words echoed in her head. Situations such as yours. An efficient way of dealing with them. With me, that means. And he speaks of me as if I were an acreage of pasture. A boundary dispute that's got out of hand.

This has come about because of him. And my father is dead.

Restraining the almost ungovernable urge to throw herself on him and punch him as her brother long ago had taught her, instead she stood where she was. And said, with ice in her voice, 'You asked my father for help in a way that he was honour-bound to accept. I now am doing the same to you. Your – misadventure,' – she invested the word with heavy sarcasm – 'cost my father and my brother their lives. You offered me assistance – I have witnesses, your man gave me your message in front of several of my servants,' – to be accurate it had been Ismay, but he wasn't to know – 'who will swear to the fact. You now have a debt of honour to me.'

He banged his mug down on the table. 'Diew, woman, what the devil do you expect me to do? Plant your crops? Herd your sheep? I'm a soldier, not a farmer!'

She shot forward, leaning her hands on the arms of his chair and imprisoning him before he could stand up. So much taller than she, he would be given an unfair advantage. And he already had so many fair ones.

Face close to his – she could smell the ale on him – she shouted back, 'I'm to marry an old man! And I *won't*! I'd rather die! But I'm not going to die, I'm going to get away!'

He stared at her, mouth open. Then he said coldly, 'And I'm to help you? Put myself in the wrong for the sake of some girl I hardly know? And get you away where? You just said you have no kin – do you expect to earn your living in some distant town? How, pray?'

His golden brown eyes glinted with sudden lust, and she read his thought. The unspoken insult stabbed her like a dagger point, and swiftly she drew back her hand and smacked him hard across the jaw.

As quickly, his own hand grasped her wrist, the strong square palm and the long fingers holding her as fast as an iron band. He said softly, 'Don't do that again.'

His face was livid with the mark of her hand. She watched in shocked fascination as the blood flowed back and the handprint flushed scarlet.

She half expected him to hurl her away from him, then to set about her and beat her senseless. But she didn't read violence in his eyes: they were full of some strong emotion, but it wasn't violence.

Amazingly, he began to smile. 'I don't believe you're a woman at all,' he said. 'You ride a destrier like a boy, you swing a punch like a boy. Maybe your betrothed is being handed a lucky escape.'

She repeated his words to herself, just to make sure. Did he mean it?

'You'll help me?'

'I didn't say that,' he countered swiftly. 'Tell me what you're asking of me, and I'll see.'

She stood up and walked away from him, circling the cold hall as she gathered her thoughts. I'm being given a second chance, she told herself. This time I must argue my case calmly and logically, the way I worked it out beforehand. This time I've got to get it right.

She did one more circuit. The straw under her boots smelt damp, as if nobody had turned it for days, let alone changed it. It suddenly dawned on her that, apart from the man who had lowered the drawbridge and let them in, he appeared to be alone.

She spun round to face him. 'Where is everyone?'

He smiled grimly. 'We're dealing with your problems, not mine. Come on, now. What do you want me to do?'

Slowly she approached him again. A couple of paces from him, she stopped.

'Three things. I want you to find a place for Ismay. She's used to being head of the household – she's been like a mother to me, like a wife –' She'd been about to say, like a wife to my father, but something about his clear amused eyes made her change her mind. 'She's had full charge of everything. She can't go and be someone's drudge, she's too old to change her ways.'

He nodded. 'I understand. Finding a home for Ismay will not be a problem. What else?'

'William. He was my father's squire, although he's only thirteen.'

'He's a good boy,' Gawyn said. 'Strong and sensible, and he has a loyal heart. I can find a new master for William. And what is your third thing?'

'Me. I'm not marrying a man of forty-seven and going away to live in Kent. I need you to –' To what? 'I have to get away, where the king's jurisdiction can't reach me.'

'So you came into Wales, and landed yourself in a castle in the mountains.'

'Not with the intention of staying!' Dear God, he'd be imagining she was offering herself to him! 'There are other places. France, for example. You have a French name, and – '

'I have a Breton name,' he corrected her.

' – and Ismay said – I mean, my father said you also have a castle in Brittany. Obviously you don't live there, but somebody must, and I thought . . .' She trailed off. Yes, perhaps he could get me away to Brittany. But what then? Live in his castle as a scullery maid? Scour the plates and sweep the floors?

It was hopeless. Sagging in defeat, she began to turn away – there was no point in hearing his scornful answer, when she already knew what it was going to be.

'Where are you off to?'

He didn't sound like someone about to ridicule her. He sounded – indulgent.

She turned back, hope flaring. 'I'm not off to anywhere.'

He studied her for some time. Then he said, '*If* I decide to help you – only if, mind – how . . .'

'I can pay you.' She pushed her hand inside her pack, fingers fumbling for the hard linen-wrapped shape. She found it and, dragging it out, hurriedly unwrapped it. 'This was my mother's. It came to me on her death, just as it came to her from her mother, and so on back through the years. It's Celtic, I think.'

She held out her hand to him, the bright object on its fold of linen glistening in the firelight.

He picked it up. The square cross on its heavy chain was so big that it was not dwarfed even by his large hand. Examining it, tracing the spiralling patterns of wrought gold, touching the huge garnets and amethysts, she heard him whistle softly. 'A rich inheritance indeed,' he said. He looked up at her. 'Your mother should not have given it to you without telling you its worth and its provenance. This is not an object to be casually bartered to a stranger.'

'My mother died when I was too young to understand anything but the fact I was losing her,' she said expressionlessly. She glanced once more at the cross. 'And as for bartering it, I thank God I possess something that seems to have the power to move you.'

She hadn't intended the irony in her tone. He noticed – of course he'd notice! she thought, cross with herself – and she saw the comment had found its mark.

'It moves me all right.' He wrapped the linen coverings around the dazzle of jewelled gold. 'For payment of this value, I'd take you to Outremer. *And* back again.'

'You'll do as I ask?' She had to be quite sure.

'I'll get you away, yes. I'll take you to Brittany, and you can hide in my castle until you're of age. Then you can think again, but by that time – how old are you, by the way?'

'Seventeen. Eighteen in a few months' time.'

'In three years, you ought to have come up with something.' He was laughing now, she could hear it in his voice.

She stared at him. He'd just agreed to help her, to do all that she'd hoped for – no, more than she'd hoped for, she hadn't dared imagine he'd offer to take her to Brittany, *and* let her live in his castle for years – and it seemed ungrateful instantly to start wondering what his motives were.

But she couldn't help it. Born nosey, she thought, that's what Ismay says. Never know when to leave well alone, always have to prod and poke till I go too far and get my hand slapped.

She said, 'Why are you helping me?'

He leapt up out of his chair, the explosive movement indicative of his state of mind. *'Why?* You get exactly what you want then ask me *why?* Great God, woman, does it matter?'

She shook her head, ashamed.

But it did matter. Straightening up and facing him, she said, 'Yes.'

'Diew, what am I going to do with her?' he muttered. 'An argumentative woman with too much mouth. All right then,' he said, addressing her, 'I'll tell you why. Because I made a mistake. Because I involved other people in my misjudgement, and three of them lost their lives. One of them was your brother, another your father. The third was – ' He broke off. 'I don't often make mistakes, and this was a bad one. You are suffering because of me, and that sits ill on my conscience.'

She thought he'd finished. But, almost as if it were an afterthought, he added, 'And, besides, no man in his right mind would turn down something as valuable as this,' – he lifted the cross by its chain, swinging it towards her before catching it and tucking it into his belt – 'even if he didn't need money as badly as I do.'

Abruptly he turned away, bending down to pick up his discarded mug and, from under his chair, the flask of whatever it was he'd been drinking. 'You can sleep through there,' he pointed with his mug to a door in the corner beside the hearth. 'It's dry, which is more than can be said for most of this benighted place. Your boy William will be all right out with the horses – Gerald will look after him. I'll see you in the morning.'

She was still standing in the middle of the hall staring after him, some time after he'd slammed the door.

Ten

She slept soundly and long; exhausted from the hard ride and from the emotional scene at the day's end, even her hunger didn't prevent a restorative night. The place he'd sent her to was indeed dry, since the little room backed on to the rear wall of the great hearth in the hall. A bed of sorts stood in the warmest corner, and she'd wrapped up in her cloak and covered herself with a fur rug. It occurred to her to wonder if he'd given up his own accustomed place for her. She didn't lose any sleep over it.

She woke to utter silence. She was cold; the breeze whistling in through the small unglazed window was biting. Getting up, she went to peer out.

And stared out at nothing but sky.

She looked downwards, where the castle walls fell away sheer for several hundred feet, gradually merging with the rocky sides of the mountain. Far, far below she could see the glint of water.

She could have been alone in the world.

She ran across the room and out into the hall. Empty, and just as they'd left it last night – no Ismay here, to come in to clean and tidy, to prepare the table for a wholesome and appetizing breakfast. No cook, either, it seemed, for no food smells lifted into the morning air.

She went outside into the courtyard, wrapping her cloak more closely round her. There was a light dusting of snow on the cobblestones. Across from the hall there was what seemed to be a stable block: she could hear the stamp of hooves. William will be in there somewhere, she thought. And that man – Gerald.

She quietly opened the door and went inside. Several stalls stretched away on either side, partitioned with wooden panels. There was a dusty smell, but otherwise the stables seemed to be cleaner than the castle. She heard movement from the end stall – it didn't sound a big enough noise for a horse. She crept along the passageway and peered over the partition: William lay on his side, raised on one elbow, looking nervously in her direction.

When he saw her he gave an audible sigh of relief, sinking back into the straw. 'Roese! Thank goodness! I thought . . .'

She was about to tease him about being too old to have superstitious fears, but in time she remembered what had happened the last time he'd been here. 'Hello, William. Are you all right?'

He nodded. 'Yes. I'm starving, though. Do you think there'll be anything to eat?'

She shrugged. 'Not unless we go and forage for ourselves. There doesn't seem to be anyone here, apart from Gawyn and Gerald.'

'Gerald's up there.' He pointed to a hay loft at the end of the passage, reached by a ladder.

'He's obviously not making our breakfast, then.'

William said anxiously, 'Roese, where *is* everyone? When we – when I was here before, it was humming with people. He had lots of servants, and we ate and drank like . . .'

Again he trailed off. She said hurriedly, 'Let's go and find some food. I'm starving, too. Gawyn won't mind, I'm sure.'

She wasn't sure at all.

They found their way to the kitchen, William leading, his hunger apparently overcoming his memories. There they found the squalor of neglect, with dirty plates and mugs, empty flagons, odds and ends of leftover food on which mice – or even rats – had clearly been busy. And, in a securely fastened cupboard, bread and a hand of ham. The bread was stale and the ham was too salty, but they didn't care. Washed down with water from an earthenware jug, it was a satisfying meal.

'We should leave some for Gawyn and Gerald,' Roese said.

'Mmm.' William crammed another chunk of bread into his mouth. When he had chewed it down to a manageable size, he said, 'Gawyn doesn't eat. Gerald says he hasn't bothered with proper food for days.'

'What about Gerald? Doesn't he eat either?'

'Yes. He goes out during the day and eats with his relatives down in the valley.'

What an extraordinary set-up, she thought. Nobody here, servants all gone bar one, the castle filthy, no food, and the master keeping himself alive on quantities of drink.

Suddenly she stopped chewing. Stopped breathing, almost, for the thought that had just struck her was breathtakingly awful.

Gawyn had been drunk last night. And this morning would probably say he hadn't meant what he'd said about helping her. Or, even worse, disclaim any memory of having said it at all.

'What is it, Roese?' William asked.

She looked at him. She longed to confide in him, but had told him little about her mission save that she was seeking Gawyn's help in finding new posts for him and Ismay. She supposed he'd heard about her proposed marriage. Things like that never stayed secret for long.

He was my father's trusted squire, she thought, filled with love for him. Why do I keep anything from him, when he has proved himself so worthy of that trust?

So she told him.

He said – predictably, really, since he'd been brought up with the chivalric code since he was small – 'If Gawyn made you a promise, he has to honour it. Even if he was drunk when he made it.'

The five-year gap between them stretched to infinity. She said sadly, 'He *should* do, yes. But if he doesn't, there's nothing I can do.'

I'm a woman in a man's world, she thought. And they want to marry me to an old man I've never seen. She was shot through with fear at her own helplessness.

William said passionately, '*I'll* take you away, Roese! I'll find work, we'll go right away from here, live somewhere – find an abandoned cottage or something, it'll be all right, you'll see!'

She went up to him and hugged him. 'Thank you, William.' Knowing his vision could never become reality, she couldn't bring herself to go along with it. Apart from anything else, she'd won for him, at least, a secure future: Gawyn had promised he'd find him a new master. That was what should happen to William – he deserved better than the uncertain life of a runaway, which could only have one ultimate end.

'You'll just have to ask him,' William said sensibly as she let him go and moved away. 'There's no point in worrying yourself silly over something that may not happen. But I meant what I said, Roese.' She was touched by his earnestness. 'You don't have to marry anyone you don't want to.'

She had a sudden absurd vision of rows of men lining up, vying for her hand. In spite of everything, it made her laugh, and William joined in.

'A long time since I heard laughter in my kitchen,' Gawyn said, appearing noiselessly in the doorway. Instantly Roese wondered if he'd been standing outside listening. What were we saying? she thought anxiously. Anything he shouldn't have heard?

He didn't seem like a man outraged at overhearing ill of himself. He seemed remarkably cheerful and, for someone whom she'd talked herself into believing had gone to bed raging drunk, also remarkably lively.

'We've saved you some food,' she said nervously. 'I hope you didn't mind us helping ourselves, only we were very hungry.'

'And I offered you nothing last night. I apologize for my poor show of hospitality, lady.'

She waited, thinking he was going to tell her the reason, but he didn't. Calmly he tore off a hunk of bread, taking his dagger from his belt and neatly cutting slices of ham. More than anything she wanted to talk to him, to ask for reassurance that everything was all right and he wasn't going to renege on his promise.

'William, go and rouse Gerald, would you?' Gawyn said. 'He'll sleep until noon if we let him, and there is much that I want him to do.'

William caught her eye, mouthed something – she wasn't sure what – and left the room. Gawyn finished his food and then poured water into a ewer and washed his hands. The action surprised her, but she found it strangely comforting, as if he were telling her, yes, I may live like a beast, but I am still a knight. I still know the correct way to behave.

Turning from his ablutions, he said without preamble, 'You need to get to Brittany, and I have undertaken to take you. You have paid me with something of great value, and in exchange I will do what I can to see you safely overseas, to where the king's jurisdiction has no power over you. A fine plan, my lady, but to make it work we now have much to do. You have the threat of an unwanted husband hanging over you if we fail. For me, the punishment would be rather more drastic.'

'You mean . . .'

He made a gesture of cutting his hand across his throat. 'I do. And in no easy way, you may be sure.'

'And yet you'll take the chance?'

'I will. We must restrict the chance element to nil.'

'We can't. There'll always be a risk. Won't there?'

'If not to nil, then we must reduce it as far as we can. We must plan, Lady Roese. Down to the last detail. As tight as if this were a military campaign.'

There was a light of excitement in his eyes. She wondered if this were another reason for his promise to help her – the simple love of adventure.

His expression made him more approachable – he seemed for a moment not much older than William. She said, 'Are you so starved of action, that you'll do something so dangerous?'

His face clouded. 'I have my reasons,' he said curtly. 'Let it be enough for you that I'm doing as you ask. You don't need to know the why of it.'

She felt humiliated, that he'd rebuffed her so thoroughly. Then she was angry with him for putting himself within reach and then withdrawing. She said coldly, 'I have no interest whatsoever in your motives. The important thing is that you accomplish

157

what I am paying you to do. I suggest you concentrate on how best we're going to succeed.'

He looked furious for an instant, then his face cleared and she saw rich amusement. It was like watching the sky when a storm was passing. In a calm, everyday tone, he said pleasantly, 'The first thing is you. You'll have to be able to ride hard all day like a boy, Roese, if this wild plan is to become a reality.'

Not pausing to ask why, she said indignantly, 'I already can! You saw me, you said –'

'I saw you fall off.'

'That's unfair! He only unseated me because –' Because I was pulling my skirt down over my legs with one hand, she'd been about to say. Because *you* were staring at me.

She felt herself grow hot, and couldn't look at him.

'Yes, it was unfair,' he said gently. And gallantly. 'All right, you can ride as well as your William. We'll go out to the stables, saddle your mare, and you can show me.'

She looked down at herself. 'I can't ride like William wearing a gown.'

'No,' he agreed. 'You'll have to become a boy. Like I said last night, I think you may be one already.'

An angry rejoinder sprang to her lips, but he was on his way out of the kitchen. And, laughing as he was, he wouldn't have heard her anyway.

* * *

They spent the larger part of the next week in the saddle. She realized very quickly that the occasional half-hour of hard, fast riding, out for an unobserved gallop with William, was a different matter from riding that way for hours on end. She was used to a

158

slower, more ladylike pace, often with William at her horse's head, and the new muscles she now called into play shouted out at the abuse. But, once over the discomfort, she found her confidence quickly grew, so that she was happy to let the adventurous Arrow have her head and take whatever obstacle she felt equal to, be it ditch, hedge, or perilously steep bank.

The days were happy. With William at her side to give her encouragement, the daunting figure of Gawyn riding ahead soon ceased to alarm her. He unbent as the days went on, often dropping back so that the three of them rode abreast, pointing out to them landmarks and interesting features of his homeland. She sometimes found she had momentarily forgotten the purpose behind the outings.

At the end of the week, Gawyn declared her fit. When she asked, fit for what?, he replied, 'Fit to pass as my squire. At a distance, anyway.'

The grin he gave her robbed his words of their sting: in any case, she was too surprised to notice.

'Your *squire?*'

He made an impatient sound. 'Yes. How else do you think I'm going to get you across England to the south Devon coast? And you a wanted woman?'

South coast? What was he talking about? There were ports on their doorstep! Why ride so far?

'Why can't we take ship from somewhere nearer? If we sail from a Welsh port, I won't even have to go into the king's territory.'

He looked at her for a long moment, as if working out what to say. Then, patronizingly, as if explaining to a child, he said, 'Isn't that just what anyone looking for you would expect you to do?'

'Yes,' she flashed back, 'but English law wouldn't have any power over me in Wales, so what does it matter if they do?'

He frowned, and she felt his growing anger. 'You know nothing,' he said crushingly. 'We follow my plan, or we don't go at all.'

She opened her mouth to protest, but shut it again. What was the point? Without him she would get nowhere – she had no choice but to agree.

He became preoccupied, disappearing for hours at a time and returning either downcast or triumphant. More often downcast: she got the impression something was worrying him badly.

Late one evening – they were just finishing a substantial supper, Gerald having brought in generous supplies – he came in muddy and wet, his face marked with deep lines of fatigue.

'You go at first light,' he announced, pouncing on a leg of roast chicken and cramming it into his mouth.

She could hardly take it in. 'Go where?'

'Home,' he mumbled through the chicken.

'*Home?* What do you mean, you –'

He swallowed. 'Only temporarily. When you get there, go in after dark, so nobody sees you. Pack whatever you can't do without in your new life – some boy's clothes wouldn't go amiss, and good ones at that – tell your Ismay to do the same, and leave again before dawn. It'll be the last you, or William, or Ismay, will ever see of your home. It's not yours now, it's the king's.'

Shocked by the brutal words, she felt as if he had hit her.

My new life. Never see my home again. Not my home now.

The full realization of what she was doing at last dawned. Until then, the need to escape had been paramount: getting away from a union with an old man had driven her on to the exclusion of all else.

160

She hadn't stopped to think what she would be giving up along with an unwanted marriage.

Then she thought, but he's right. It's no longer mine to give up.

She had nothing to say to him. Rising from the table, she said to William, 'Go and do whatever you have to for an early start. Then get some rest – we have two long days' riding ahead of us.'

He did as she ordered, pausing only to collect another piece of chicken and some bread from the rapidly emptying dishes before Gawyn beat him to it.

When he had gone, she wished Gawyn a quiet good night and went through into her small bed-chamber. Lying long into the night, waiting for the sleep that refused to come, she tried to gather her courage for what lay ahead.

As they neared home at nightfall on the second day, she wondered what Ismay would say to her riding dressed in a patched tunic and a pair of Gerald's old hose. Anything of Gawyn's would have been far too big, and William had no spare clothes, so she had been reduced to wearing the cast-offs of a serving man.

It had been no time for pride. She'd beaten out as much of the dirt as she could and suffered.

It was quite a relief to have something so mundane to worry about; for most of the journey she'd been trying to convince William that there was absolutely no way he could go with her to Brittany. In the end she'd had to fall back on Gawyn: 'You heard him!' she shouted. 'He's said to me more than once that we do it his way or not at all! He has found you a good home, William. Please, *please* don't upset all the plans – if you do, he might back out of helping me at all!'

The thought was so alarming that she didn't have to force the fear into her voice – it was already there.

He'd acquiesced. Or she thought he had – he hadn't actually said, very well, I'll do as you say, but at least he'd stopped arguing.

They waited in the copse behind the house until it was fully dark, then William went ahead on foot, hurrying back to say it was all right, Ismay was alone and there was nobody else about. Then, for the last time, she rode into her courtyard.

Ismay took less persuasion than William. A fortnight on her own, facing a horribly uncertain future, seemed to have put her in the sort of panicky mood where, Roese thought, she'd have agreed to anything.

'He'll have found you a good place, I know it,' Roese said fervently.

Ismay gave her a look, and, putting her finger right on the weak spot in the argument, remarked, 'He's found me a roof over my head, yes, and I'm grateful. But I don't see how you can be so sure it'll be a good place, when you hardly know the man.'

Roese sighed. 'All right, then, I *don't* know. But isn't it better than the alternatives would have been? Moving with me to Kent, so far away from your home that you'd never come back, or, if this husband had been of a ruthless nature, thrown out into the cold?'

Ismay nodded. 'Don't think I haven't thought of that, my girl.' She, too, sighed, far more dramatically and noisily than Roese. 'All your poor dear father's fault, God bless him. If he'd done as I said and chosen you a husband, my wishes and my future would have been taken into account. As it is, I'm being uprooted, sent away, after all I've done for this family, too.'

Roese swallowed her irritation. 'I know, Ismay, and I'm truly sorry. I'm doing my best, but – '

Ismay's mood abruptly changed and she hurried across to Roese, enveloping her in a warm hug. 'I know you are, my lovely, I know.'

Roese felt the emotional tears prick at her eyes, and gently disengaged herself. 'We must get on, Ismay,' she said. 'A small pack, remember. We'll have to ride back to the Black Mountains with only two horses between the three of us, so we must keep our baggage to the minimum.'

She left the hall and went into the chamber that had been her father's – and her brother's, when he was at home – to search for suitable garments. Perhaps, she thought, something positive to do will take my mind off the regrets.

Her brother had been short and broad in the shoulder. He – or more probably, it had been Ismay – had also been pernickety about his clothes: in the chest in the corner of the room, she found shirts, drawers, tunics and hose, neatly folded and layered with pieces of old linen and sprigs of lavender. Stripping down to her skin, she tried on for size a shirt and a pair of drawers; their fabric, fine wool, felt little different from her own accustomed shift. But the shirt didn't hang straight; she took it off again and, tearing the old linen into strips, bandaged her breasts so they were flattened against her ribs.

Into her mind came a memory of Gawyn, eyes unreadable as he stared at her.

She selected a pair of padded hose, which would save her thighs from the chafing of the stirrup leathers that long days in the saddle otherwise gave – Gerald's smelly old hose had been thin, and the soft skin on the insides of her legs was almost raw. Cut on the cross, it didn't matter that Roger's hose were a little too big for her. Finally she took out a felt hat, a tunic and a cloak; they'd been Roger's second best, she remembered. He'd dressed up in his best to ride off to his death.

He felt very close as she held his garments to her breast. Her father, too, seemed to hover round her as she stood in the dim light in his chamber. It seemed an appropriate moment to say her farewells.

She was so afraid of sleeping past the dawn that she only dozed intermittently through the short night. When there was the faintest glimmer of light in the east, she called Ismay and William, then took some hot water from the pot over the kitchen fire and went to wash. It was a private ceremony: she recalled Roger's ritual bathing and his night of vigil before he was given his spurs, and she felt she was doing something similar. I've had the night of vigil, she thought, even if I was in the house and not kneeling before the altar. Now I'm purifying myself. Putting on a new garb.

When she had finished, she went to find Ismay.

'Ismay, cut off my hair.' She handed her a pair of shears. They were sharp – she'd tested the blades on the hairs of her forearm.

Ismay blanched and said, 'Roese! No!'

'Yes.' Roese wasn't in the mood for argument. 'If you won't, I'll do it myself, which will look awful as I've never cut hair before. You, on the other hand, are renowned for your skill.'

'But –'

Roese sat down on a stool, draped a piece of linen round her shoulders and handed Ismay the shears.

A short time later an acrid smell of burning filled the air: most of Roese's waist-length reddish-gold hair was melting in the flames of the kitchen fire. She

164

shook her head, feeling the short bob swing against her neck.

'How do I look?' She grinned at Ismay.

Ismay sniffed. 'Not like my lady Roese, more's the pity.'

Roese hugged her. 'Good. That's the whole idea. Now let's go, before the sun comes up.'

William was waiting in the yard, in the saddle of the big bay. He held out his hand to Roese, who swung up behind him; Arrow was to bear Ismay.

William and Roese led the way out through the gate. She fixed her eyes forwards, staring resolutely ahead over William's shoulder.

It was still too dark for any final, longing look back at her home.

* * *

They met few people on the road. On the second day, a few miles short of where the track began to climb up to Gawyn's castle, they saw a mounted figure standing under trees to the side of the road. He seemed to be watching them as they approached. Her heart filled with fear, until she realized with huge relief that it was Gawyn. Wearing a nondescript brown robe to cover his mail, he looked different; not like a knight, but like any ordinary traveller.

Her relief was short-lived. 'We're not going to the castle,' he said tersely, not pausing to greet them. 'Roese, get down,' – she obeyed him – 'you wait here in the wood. I'll take Ismay and William on to where someone's waiting to escort them to their new homes.'

'But why –' she began.

'Don't ask!' he snapped back. 'There's no time. Take Arrow and water her down there at the stream.' He pointed under the trees. 'Ismay'll have to ride behind William – it's not far.'

Ismay, stunned into silence, emerged from it to say rebelliously, 'How far's "not far"? My old bones won't allow me to –'

Gawyn grinned. 'A few miles, Ismay. And at the end of it, a warm welcome, I promise you.'

Roese almost said, there! I told you so.

Gawyn was urging them to haste, almost pulling Ismay off Arrow's back and trying to bundle her up behind William. Roese wanted to ask if she could embrace them – this was goodbye, and it was so sudden that if she didn't watch out, they'd be riding off before she could wish them God's speed. God bless.

William must have had the same thought. He said in a surprisingly dictatorial tone, 'Wait.' Then, leaving Gawyn to hold the bay, he ran over to Roese.

She couldn't think what to say. Nor, apparently, could he: putting his arms clumsily round her, he leaned his face against hers, then kissed her cheek.

She whispered, 'Goodbye, William.'

His only answer was a sort of croak. Running back, he leapt into the saddle, and, with Gawyn pushing and him pulling, got Ismay up behind him. Roese went to take Ismay's hand. 'Good luck,' she said, the tears spilling down her cheeks.

She saw a corresponding glimmer in Ismay's eyes. 'And to you, Lady Roese,' she whispered. 'And to you.'

Then Gawyn was trotting out on to the track, and, almost violently, William yanked the bay's head round and set off after him.

*

Gawyn was not gone long. She was ready for him, Arrow rested and watered. He said grimly, 'We must hurry. We have much ground to cover before we rest for the night, and the weather's closing in. Come on.'

She fell into line behind him. He was right about the weather: the orange of the sunset was being swiftly covered by grey clouds billowing up from the west. There was rain on the air, and she pulled the hood of her cloak up over the round felt hat.

Even when they did at last stop – far too late for Roese, who was past exhaustion and only staying in the saddle because she seemed to have frozen into it – it was not at any cosy inn. They unsaddled the horses, removing their bridles and hobbling them, then, under cover of trees that kept off most of the fine misty rain, ate a hasty meal of dried meat and bread then lay down on the ground. She'd never slept on the bare earth before. Never slept in the open.

As she tried to get comfortable, she felt him nudge her. Silently he handed her his flask and, after a moment's hesitation, she drank from it. Whatever it was, first it burned her throat, then it began to warm the rest of her. The bumps underneath her felt a little less sharp.

Gratefully she handed it back.

The next day was much the same, except that it rained harder.

In the early evening of the following day, he said they must cross the Wye. She had no idea where they were, had given up trying to work it out and hadn't even contemplated asking him – he seemed lost in his own thoughts, and, judging by his expression, they weren't cheerful or reassuring ones. But they'd have had to bear north, she knew that – the Wye couldn't be forded in its lower reaches, and they'd have to make for the ferry up above the Yat.

On the summit of a hill above the river, he halted.

'We'll stop here and eat. Rest a while,' he announced. She wondered why they didn't press on for the ferry in what was left of the daylight, but the time was gone when she was prepared to badger him with her questions.

He unsaddled the horses and tethered them, then the two of them sat down, backs to the broad trunk of a sheltering tree, and he shared out the food.

'Drink?'

She glanced at him. The flask was in his hand, and he was offering it to her.

'No thank you.'

He smiled. 'Go on, it'll put heart in you.'

'But I —' I don't drink such fierce liquor, she'd almost said. It isn't suitable for a lady.

He was laughing, aware of the reason for her refusal. 'What do ladies drink, then, Roese? A little sweet wine? Small beer? Or was that for boys like you?'

His laughter was directed at her, and it stung.

'Yes!' she shouted. 'We had both of those at our table, and more besides. My father —'

My father. She couldn't go on.

After a while she felt his hand on hers. 'I'm sorry,' he said. 'I didn't mean to make you think about what you're trying to forget — and don't think I haven't noticed and been grateful for the fact that you don't keep reminding me of my obligation to you.' He paused, then went on, 'And I'm sorry for teasing you.' He glanced at her, and his face wore a wry smile. 'You make a fine boy.'

She found herself smiling back. 'Thank you.'

The moment was past. Or so she thought, beginning to pack the uneaten food back in the leather bag.

168

She felt that he was still looking at her. Lifting her head, she met his gaze.

He said, staring right into her eyes, 'But I miss the woman you used to be.'

She opened her mouth, but could think of nothing to say. Shutting it again, she went back to her packing.

The ferry was a simple wooden platform, attached to ropes with which the passengers pulled themselves across. In the daytime there was a ferryman, but Roese and Gawyn were late, and he'd gone off to his home. The sheeting, relentless rain could, she reflected, have influenced his decision.

The river was running high. The past months had been wet, even more so than usual for the time of year, and the swift-flowing, black water ran silently, awesome in its power. She shivered.

'Come on,' Gawyn said. 'They've tied up for the night, or maybe they think the river's too high for safety.' He was busy cutting the ferry's mooring ropes.

'Should we cross?' she asked nervously. She shivered again.

He glanced at her, not pausing in his cutting. One rope lay severed, the other was on the point of parting. 'We'll be all right. Better to go over now, when no-one's here to see us and remember.'

She couldn't argue with that. England was on the other side of the river. From now on, they must be even more careful.

He led his horse on to the ferry. Well-schooled and, she thought, probably used to such strange manoeuvres, the tall grey stood unconcerned, calmly chewing on his bit.

She went next, pulling at Arrow's bridle, expecting her to follow the grey's lead. But Arrow wasn't happy: arching her neck, she blew at the water rushing by so close to her feet, alarm in her eyes.

Gawyn pushed them off from the bank, hauling hand-over-hand at the rope. He seemed to be finding it hard work; she could see the strain in his face, in the bulging muscles of his arms and shoulders. The fast current was trying to sweep them downstream, and he was having to use all his strength to pull them towards the opposite bank.

When they had almost made it – a mere ten yards of black water separated them from safety – some large object being dashed along by the river banged hard against the platform. Gawyn paused momentarily in his hauling, then, as Arrow threw her head back and started to dance in terror, urgently resumed.

'Hold her, Roese! For God's sake, hold her!'

His own horse was affected by the mare's panic, and began shifting his great feet; Roese hung on to both his bridle and Arrow's, but her weight wasn't sufficient to make much impression. She tried talking to them, trying to soothe, to calm them, but, weak with fear herself, couldn't make her tone convincing.

With a jerk, Arrow pulled the rein out of Roese's hand. Roese lunged towards her, trying to grab a handful of mane, but Arrow sidestepped out of the way. Grasping at thin air, Roese felt herself topple. Her foot slipped on the wet planking, and suddenly there was nothing between her and the sinister force of the water.

In total, icy darkness she tried to gasp in air, and took a mouthful of water. Turned over and over by the vicious current, she had no idea which way was up. Throwing her arms out, for a split second she felt his strong hand close around her wrist.

She was soaking wet, and her hand pulled through his grasp.

The river was punching her, bruising her, its secret power pushing on her so that she went down, down into the black below. Eyes wide, she could see nothing.

But she could hear: he was calling her name, again and again.

Her head broke the surface, and she saw him. He had reached the bank, and was dragging the horses on to dry land, throwing their reins over a hitching-post, racing along the path after her.

His speed was no match for the river.

She was swept under again. She thought desperately, must get to the edge. Must get my mouth up, got to breathe.

Once more her face was exposed to the air. Long enough for one quick gulp, then the water closed over her head.

She heard him again. 'Roese! *Roese!*' She thought she saw him plunge into the water, a long severed branch in his hand, but if he was trying to reach her with it, she knew it was no use.

She went under again. His voice, still calling, hoarse now, sounded a long way away.

As she gave up and stopped struggling, she thought what a pity it was to have ruined Roger's second-best cloak and tunic.

Eleven

She lay in the faint light of very early morning, wondering if the agony of not knowing who she was had been better or worse than the despair of remembering.

No home, no-one to take me in, she thought. My one hope gone, ridden off into the night without a backward glance.

Then she saw Gawyn again, plunging after her into the water, shouting her name until his voice cracked and he couldn't shout any more.

Shivering, for the memory of being in the river had been all too real, she huddled into the blankets.

I know now, she thought. I can lie here and retrace every step of my last journey, from when I left my home until I slipped out of Gawyn's grasp and was swept away down the river for that young monk – Aidan – to find me. I can also dwell on all the details of what led to that journey. Whether or not I want to do either is a different matter.

But she couldn't stop herself thinking. In a combination of dreams and awakened memories – perhaps, she thought, also visions induced by the drink Benedict had given her – she now had the full story of her life up to that moment.

The future, conversely, was an unguessable blank.

Eyes wide, she stared out through the little window at the waxing daylight until the rest of the hermitage began to stir.

She knew without even asking that this was a matter for Ranald. When Benedict greeted her with his usual solicitous enquiries as to how she felt and how she'd slept, it was enough to say to him, 'I have to speak to Ranald.'

His eyes widened as he considered this. Then he nodded. 'Aye. I'll tell him. He'll come, as soon as he is able.'

He gave her food and drink, then went off to join his brothers in chapel. In the still morning she heard the echo of their chanting voices. Then they went to the refectory.

At last Ranald came.

Closing the door behind him, he crossed the room and sat on a bench at the foot of her bed. His eyes on her face, he said, 'I believe you have something to tell me.'

A long time later, when she had finished, he stood up, stretching his long frame.

Lying back, for the talking and the tension had exhausted her, she watched him. She wanted to ask him what he would do, but the effort was too great. She felt her eyelids drooping.

His hand was on her head. He said, 'Sleep now. We will talk again later, when you are ready.'

'You won't make me –' she began.

Eyes closed now, she heard the smile in his reply. 'I won't make you do anything. I told you before, I shall not send you away until you are ready to go.'

Hearing him close the door, already she was

drifting into sleep. There's nothing I can do now, she thought drowsily. It's in his hands.

She dreamt of Gawyn, holding her at arm's length while he looked at her and saying, 'You're not really a boy, so you can live with me in Brittany.'

It was evening before Ranald returned. She'd wondered if Benedict would refer to her memory having miraculously returned, and what it had revealed to her about her past, but his conversation remained firmly in the realms of the mundane. She concluded that either Ranald hadn't told him, or else – and this seemed more likely – he had, but had kept back all but the generalities and told Benedict not to question her.

She went to sit outside in the sunshine for a while in the late morning. One or two of the other brothers crossed the courtyard – Mattheus from the refectory, and a thin, rather unhealthy-looking monk with an absent expression who looked at her in great surprise as if he wasn't aware of her existence – but that was all. She didn't see Ranald, and there was no sign of Aidan. No wonder, she thought. I discomfited him so much yesterday that he's probably keeping well away.

Ranald came to her after supper.

Without thinking, she greeted him as she'd seen the others do, making the genuflections and muttering, 'Pray God to make me a good Christian and lead me to a good end.'

The surprise in his face was almost instantly wiped out and he made his usual reply: 'May God be prayed that He make you a good Christian.'

After a moment, he said, 'Why did you do that?'

Embarrassed, she said, 'I'm sorry if it was wrong. It's just that I've seen the rest of them do it, and I thought –'

She broke off. She hadn't thought, she'd just acted. Obviously, it hadn't been the thing to do – perhaps the little ceremony was reserved for members of the hermitage.

'I'm sorry,' she repeated.

But he was smiling. 'Why? You've done nothing to be sorry for.' Then, his smile deepening, he added, 'That, I fear, is a sweeping statement. You may have done many things you are sorry for.'

She returned the smile. 'I have, but I know what you meant.'

He was pulling up the bench to its position at the foot of her bed, and she prepared herself for what she was well aware was coming; he'd said earlier that they would talk again, and she knew it wouldn't just be about how she was feeling or what she'd been doing all day.

Anticipating some proposed plan of action for her, she was taken aback by his opening remark.

He said, 'Roese, what, do you think, was Gawyn running away from?'

'Running away?' It took a moment for the idea to sink in. 'It was I who was running away, he was merely helping me. I paid him, remember? I paid him with my mother's gold cross. I told you.'

'Yes, I remember.' Ranald's expression revealed nothing. 'But I have thought long over what else you told me.' He paused, as if gathering his thoughts and summarizing them. 'You asked him to take you to Brittany, and, in exchange for a valuable item of jewellery and because, on his own admission, the deaths of your father and brother lay ill on his conscience, he agreed, promising that you should be allowed to take up residence in his castle in Brittany until you were of age. Did you never wonder why he should suddenly be willing to leave his Welsh

175

stronghold and take to the road? Did you not think that it surely should require longer for a man with his responsibilities to abandon them and set off?'

'He had several days,' she said. 'More than a week. He was away for much of that time, no doubt making what arrangements had to be made.'

'A week,' Ranald repeated. 'Only a little over a week. When, as far as you knew, he was leaving his Welsh domain for the foreseeable future?'

She had to admit, it didn't seem a very long time to make his preparations. 'I don't know what his plans were, but I suppose he –'

'And, although you noticed the squalor and the absence of any retainers save one, did you not think it strange?'

'Of course! So did William!'

'And what did you conclude was the reason for that state of affairs?'

'We thought – we thought –' Yes, we thought, she admitted silently. But not very hard or for very long. And we didn't come up with any answers.

'You observed that Gawyn seemed preoccupied. And "downcast", I think was what you said. You didn't work out what was worrying him so much?'

Dumbly she shook her head. I had my own worries, she thought. I had no time for his. She said, 'No, I didn't. I was so thankful he was going to help me that I didn't stop to wonder why. It didn't occur to me to question his motives.'

As if responding to her despondency, he said, 'Very understandable. Please do not think I am castigating you. I am merely trying to ascertain if perhaps you noticed anything that you haven't mentioned.'

'Such as?'

He shrugged. 'A chance remark? Mention of someone who could have been threatening him?'

She searched her mind. 'No. There was nothing like that. Only his reference to the third knight who died. You know, in the accident. He implied that being responsible for his death was a bad mistake.'

He nodded. 'I know. And you're not aware of the knight's identity?'

'No.'

He was silent for some time. Then he said, 'Consider these facts. One, and perhaps most importantly, Gawyn was taking an enormous risk in getting you away. The king himself had arranged your betrothal, and in aiding your flight Gawyn was indeed risking his life, just as he said. If you'd been caught, he would have been executed for treason, and that, as I dare say you know, is neither a pretty nor an easy death. Would he do that, even for a gold cross and to salve a guilty conscience?

'Two, think back to your amazement when you learned you were to take ship from the south coast of England. Quite rightly, you asked why you had to go so far, why indeed you needed to go into England at all when it would be far safer for you to stay in Wales, where the king had no power over you.'

'Yes!' She was pleased to have him remember a moment when she'd been perceptive. 'That's right, and he said we couldn't sail from a Welsh port because that's just what they'd expect us to do and where they'd be looking for me . . .'

Glancing up to meet his eyes, she knew he had in mind exactly the same objection. 'But they wouldn't have been, would they? Because the king has no jurisdiction in Wales, so nobody would have been looking for me at all.'

'No. The obvious plan would have been for you to sail from some port on the south coast of Wales. When you argued the point, I believe you said that he told you somewhat forcefully that either you did what he ordered or he wouldn't take you at all.'

'Yes.'

'Roese, it was he who dared not use a Welsh port. Someone – maybe a group of people – was on the lookout for *him*.'

'That was why we had to be so furtive,' she said, suddenly seeing the whole misadventure through new eyes. 'Why we had to ride through such difficult country, why we couldn't use proper roads or inns. Why, even, we had to cross the Wye when darkness and flood made it so dangerous. Because *he* was on the run!'

Indignation poured through her that her life had almost been lost because of his need for secrecy.

Ranald said calmly, as if aware of her turmoil and wanting to soothe it, 'You could have ridden the roads openly and crossed the river in the daylight, at a time when the ferryman judged it to be safe.' He paused, perhaps wanting to make quite sure she was paying attention, then said, 'Nobody was looking for *you*, Roese. Your arranged meeting with your betrothed husband was not for many days yet, so you were free to go wherever you wanted. You were not yet officially a runaway.'

'But he was,' she finished.

'Yes. He took advantage of the fact that you had to escape to finance his own flight.'

Neither of them spoke. She suffered the barrage of her emotions – mostly anger and resentment, but underneath a small sense of hurt, that he could have used her so.

The hurt gradually increased. Reliving the awful moment when she had grasped at Arrow's rein and missed, she felt again the terror of having the cold black water close over her head. Felt her arms flail,

178

and his hand momentarily encircle her wrist as he tried to save her.

Heard his anguished voice calling her name.

Saw his light brown eyes looking at her as he'd said, 'I miss the woman you used to be.'

Hating the weakness that made her utter the words, she said, 'If that was all – if he was just using me – why did he sound so desperate when he thought I was lost? He already had his payment, my mother's cross wasn't shooting off down the river with me.'

Ranald looked at her with compassion. 'Perhaps he had more humanity than we give him credit for. Perhaps, given the choice, he would have stayed and searched until he found you, alive or dead.'

Keeping back the self-pitying tears, she whispered, 'Why didn't he, then?'

Ranald shrugged. 'I can't say, other than to suggest there was a good reason why he had to hasten away.'

'Being on the run, you mean.'

'Yes. That is certainly one reason. Another is that, throughout, he seems to have been in a hurry. We may conclude that he had to be in a certain place by a certain date. Possibly, even, he was racing to make a rendezvous with a specific boat to get him over to Brittany. Who can say?'

She waited until she felt in control of herself. Then she said, 'We can't say anything for certain. Can we?'

'No. However, we may surmise.'

She didn't know what he meant. 'Surmise?'

'We may look at the situation in broader terms, trying to fit Gawyn's actions into a wider picture.'

She smiled suddenly. 'You might be able to, but I can't. I know hardly anything about the wider picture.'

The compassion was back. He said, 'No, that I

appreciate. Boys are educated, girls learn how to keep house. Yes?'

'Yes.'

'Well, Roese, the king faces threats on many fronts, in particular from the disputed duchy of Brittany and from the quarrelsome chieftains to the west, where –'

'The Welsh lords. Yes, I know about that, and about the war with Brittany. And about the interdict – that was why we couldn't bury my father and Roger in the churchyard, with a proper funeral.'

He bowed his head. 'Yes. Of course you know of these things. Now we need to think how they may be relevant to what has happened to you.'

'You mean because Gawyn is a Breton?'

'It appears from what you say that, like many, he holds lands in what are now two different countries. Indeed, that he holds allegiance to two different over-lords.'

She didn't understand. 'Why?'

He hesitated, then said, 'In the reigns of King John's brother and his father, the English crown ruled over lands across the sea – Brittany, Normandy, Aquitaine and Anjou, for example, were allied to England through marriage and inheritance. A man who held estates in Normandy and in the Wye valley, let us say, faced no conflict of loyalties, since both lands were ruled by the English crown. But now that these overseas lands are lost to England, such a man must choose – he can only swear allegiance to one king, and must, in effect, decide if he wishes to be an Englishman or a Frenchman.'

'A Welshman or a Breton,' she added.

'Yes, although in that case the conflict is less clear-cut since the knight of a Welsh castle would not own to owing allegiance to anyone but himself. And even if Normandy now belongs to the French crown,

Brittany does not, though since every Breton holds King John responsible for the death of their young Duke Arthur, the duchy will never again submit to English domination.'

She shook her head, trying to clear it. 'Then why is this situation you're describing relevant to Gawyn's flight?'

He looked at her, the blue eyes candid. 'I don't know. I'm merely trying to look at the possibilities.' He sighed. 'The more I look, the less I see clearly. And, rather than running from the king's realm and seeking refuge over the border in Wales, your knight seems to have done the opposite. Although it seems strange to think of any man seeking refuge under King John.'

She didn't know enough about it either to agree or disagree, so she kept silent. And she felt anyway that comment would have been superfluous: Ranald appeared merely to be thinking out loud.

After some time, he got to his feet. 'There is nothing further we can say at the moment,' he said decisively. 'We may conjecture, but that will not advance us.' He glanced down at her. 'For now, you must rest and continue to build your strength. In the time that it takes for you to be restored, perhaps we shall arrive at a plan of action. Even, indeed, at some accurate answers.'

She wanted to be absolutely sure she had interpreted his remarks rightly. 'You mean I can stay till you've worked out what's happened and what I should do next?'

To her surprise, he laughed. 'That is what I mean, yes. And I apologize for using twice as many words as I needed.'

He came to stand over her, and she heard him mutter something. She thought it might have been a blessing. Then he bade her goodnight, and left.

* * *

She lay waiting for sleep, but it was slow in coming. She heard Benedict enter the infirmary to check on her, and then heard him leave again; presumably he was to sleep in the dormitory with the others now that she was no longer likely to need his care during the night.

It felt strange to be on her own. Until very recently, she had always shared her bedroom with someone else, at first her mother and father, later Ismay. During the time she had spent in Gawyn's castle she had slept alone, but for the last two nights out in the wild before she'd fallen in the Wye, she'd had a man lying beside her.

And since being recovered from the dead, there had been the brothers' devoted care.

Now I'm quite alone, she thought. In every respect.

It wasn't something to dwell on; it was too frightening. Even if Ranald had said he wouldn't make her leave till she had somewhere to go, it was still frightening because she couldn't even begin to think where that somewhere might be.

Gawyn flashed back into her head, but she pushed that thought out too. He's gone, she told herself. Ranald has convinced me he was on the run, and, since no doubt he's long ago given me up for dead, there's no point at all in hoping he's going to turn up and provide the answer to all my prayers.

No. No point at all.

Wakeful still, it occurred to her that there was very little she could think about with equanimity.

She found herself thinking of Ranald. In one short session, he had shown her how very important it was to look beyond the obvious. Now, as she remembered all that he had said, it seemed that his instruction was working against him: how, she wondered, can a man who lives in an isolated community know so much about what goes on in the world he claims to have left?

Stray phrases came back to her. Aidan, assuring her she was safe with the monks, telling her they had no contact with the outside world. Ranald himself, assuring her they lived apart, that for them the lonely hermitage *was* the world.

Who, then, had told this self-sequestered community's leader about the quarrelling Welsh lords? About King John's dubious reputation? About the rumoured slaying of the Duke of Brittany?

A shiver went through her. Apart from the fact that he sounded foreign – she'd almost got used to his slight accent, only now, when it suddenly seemed to have become significant, remembering its existence – there was more to Ranald than the humble leader of an unsophisticated community of monks. Not even monks, she remembered – Benedict's voice said in memory, 'We wear the black habit, but we do not call ourselves monks.'

What, then? What were these strange men, living a life apart?

I trusted them, she reminded herself, before I thought to question. To do as Ranald encouraged, and try to see below the surface. Why may I not go on trusting them? Whatever they are, they've saved my life.

But she discovered that trust once lost was not so readily regained. Father let me down, she thought, bless his kindly, irresponsible soul. And so did Gawyn. But Ranald? And the others, Benedict, Aidan?

She saw Aidan in her mind's eye, looking at her with shining honesty as he tried earnestly to convince her she need not be afraid. She realized she missed seeing him about the hermitage, and wondered when he'd be back. There was something about him that was oddly endearing.

Her thoughts of him had allayed her fears; no-one so sincere, she decided, could be anything but trustworthy.

She was feeling sleepy. Closing her eyes, she murmured, 'Goodnight, Aidan. Wherever you are, thank you.'

Spring 1994, April

I don't care what Peter says, Nina thought as the party made its way back down to the car park, it's not right to disinter those whom someone else has buried. Over whom someone's said words, for whom they've carried out ritual. No matter *how* long ago.

Or – thinking painfully of that tiny skeleton – how young and insignificant they might have been.

As the track led under the shade of some stunted shrubbery, an image of the small round skull hovered in front of her. Then, as if her mind couldn't bear to see it so, the baby's head was abruptly clad in flesh, in pale skin with a delicate pink flush, in downy reddish hair. Slate-blue, sleepy eyes opened, and their gaze for an instant met hers.

The long-ago dream came back to her, the dream she'd had when her own child should have been born. And, just as on that night, she thought she held a living, breathing child in her arms.

The path moved out from the shadows and into the sunlight, and the image faded.

She thought dully, I thought I'd put all that behind me.

Ahead, Peter called to them to hurry up, it looked

as if it was going to rain. Telling herself it was stupid to feel like crying, and she certainly wasn't going to be so feeble as to do so, she did as he said and hurried up.

Once they'd got over the shock of what they'd found up on the monastery site, the talk, predictably, had been of little else. Peter had become dictatorial, the small drama prompting him to adopt the role of wise, capable leader telling the subordinates what to do next. You have to admit he seems to know what he's talking about, Nina had thought grudgingly, helping Gus and Bryn erect a barrier round the trench while Peter covered the contents with blue plastic. But does he have to be such an arrogant little shit?

It had been lovely having Mark there. Watching his back as he walked down the track ahead of her, she remembered how he'd hugged her. Gone on hugging her, in fact, till they were interrupted by Peter calling out a greeting from the graveyard and telling him to come and have a look.

Something that had felt so natural had changed, once an outsider was looking, into an action that clearly embarrassed Mark. So much so that he'd hastily let go of her and hurried in to see what it was Peter wanted to show him. Once he'd seen, though, to Nina's triumphant joy he turned back to her, his expression anguished. He didn't need to tell her what he was thinking – the moment of rapport had shouted out as loud as trumpets.

She half wished that Peter were not so insensitive, then he might have noticed. Might have realized that being emotional wasn't entirely a female prerogative.

Now, as if he perhaps were thinking of that moment, Mark paused to wait for her.

'The track's wider here, we can walk two abreast,' he said.

'Oh. Yes.'

She couldn't think what to say. After a moment, though, it didn't matter; clearly he could.

'I feel – sort of dirty,' he said quietly. 'You know?'

'Yes!' She bit back the exclamation, *you* feel dirty! I was there all day! 'We're involved, aren't we? Even just by standing there looking at it – I wish we didn't have to call it "it" – we've contaminated ourselves. Like –'

'Like people who stop to stare at road accidents,' he supplied.

'Exactly. Or people who follow racing ambulances.'

'They're usually reporters, so I suppose they have the excuse that they're only doing their job.'

'Are they? I –' She caught his eye and belatedly realized he'd been making a joke. Rather a small one, she thought, but smiled nevertheless. Talking to him about it was making her feel better, and she didn't want the conversation to end through her own lack of response.

'Perhaps he'd say he had the same excuse for all this.' She nodded down the track towards where Peter was leading the rest of the group. His voice came faintly back to them: still in knowledgeable expert mode, Nina thought.

'He has.' Mark sounded angry. 'In a day or two that little skeleton will be down in the university lab with the others, and a few days after that they'll be telling us what sex it was, how old it was when it died, and what it died of. Then they'll put it –'

'I don't want to know,' she interrupted, in a tone far more harsh than she'd intended. '*Any* of it.'

She felt his hand grasp hers. 'Sorry.'

They walked in silence for some moments. He had let go of her hand. Then, unable to help herself, she said, 'What do they do with them?'

He smiled. She thought it was nice of him not to say, I thought you didn't want to know. 'They re-bury them. With a proper religious ceremony, I think.'

'In a churchyard?'

He shrugged. 'Suppose so. Before they start digging they have to get a special licence from the Home Office, and one of the conditions is that they re-bury the remains, unless there's some overwhelming reason not to.'

She imagined it. Would that be the right thing, to take the baby away and put it in a churchyard? Don't think about it! Forcing her mind off on another tack, she asked, 'What if they weren't Christians?'

'That's not very likely. Everyone in England was Christian in the Middle Ages. Everyone was Catholic, come to that.'

'What about heretics? Bryn said something about Wycliffe.'

'He was later. Thirteen something.'

'Weren't there any heresies at all in the twelfth century?'

He frowned, then said, 'There was a group called the Cathars. They must have been twelfth century, because they were wiped out in the thirteenth. But before you say what you're about to say,' – she shut her mouth, smiling – 'I don't think there were any in England. It was a religion that came from the East, possibly brought into Western Europe via Byzantium. Some people think it may have been spread by returning crusaders. There were followers in the Low Countries and northern France, but persecution drove the Cathars south into the Languedoc.'

'Oh.' She was aware she wasn't really taking in what he was saying. Her mind was still on the baby.

'It would be nice if it – they could be re-buried up here.'

'Mention it to Peter. Maybe he'll say, yes, that's just what we're going to do.'

'Do you think so?'

'No. Not really.'

They were almost back at the mini-bus. She wondered what would happen now – would he say he had to return to his falcons and leave her to go home with the others, or would he suggest meeting up somewhere back in town?

He said hesitantly, 'Would you like a lift?'

At the same time Peter grabbed her arm and said, not hesitantly at all, 'Hurry up, Nina! Get in, I'm taking you all for a drink. We've earned it!'

'Mark's giving me a lift,' she said.

'It's okay.' He looked slightly awkward. 'You go, Nina,' he muttered. 'I wasn't one of the working party, I don't expect Peter to treat me, too.'

'But –'

'I'll see you on Monday.'

Before she could stop him – find out from Peter where they were going and tell him to join them later, when Peter's benevolence had run out and they were all buying their own drinks – he'd turned away and was striding off towards his camper van.

She said under her breath, '*Sod* it!'

Bryn was holding out his hand to her, and he helped her up into the back of the van. She didn't meet his eye – sympathy was the last thing she wanted.

In the middle of the week Peter sent them a copy of the report. Since hers came top of their three names on the envelope – quaintly conventional of Peter, she thought, to put ladies first – Nina felt entitled to read it before either of the others.

It was headed

THREE SKELETONS FROM WYE MONASTERY SITE:
PRELIMINARY FINDINGS

She skimmed through the summarized findings on
the two monks: one was estimated to have been in his
early sixties, which was, the report pointed out, a
good age for the 1200s. 'His bones show evidence of
extensive and advanced arthritis,' the report continued, 'particularly in the shoulders, wrists and
hands, supporting the suggestion inherent in the
presence of the tools discovered in his grave that this
man was an agricultural or horticultural worker. No
evidence from the bones suggests that death was
other than from natural causes.'

Died from old age, Nina thought. In his early sixties.

The second monk had been younger, probably
no more than his mid-twenties. 'The condition of
the remains suggests he died from malnutrition,' the
report said baldly. 'Certain malformations in the
knees and feet seem to imply much time spent in an
attitude of prayer, on his knees with his feet turned
backwards and pressed against the ground.'

He was a monk! she wanted to write in the margin.
Monks do pray.

The small skeleton from the Wye monastery is
thought probably to have been a full-term baby.
Slight compacting of the skull confirms that the child
was in fact born normally (had the mother died and
the child been delivered by Caesarean section, no
such 'moulding' would be present) although it is
impossible to say whether it was a live or a still birth.
If born alive, the child can have survived no more

than a few days, after which time the 'moulding' would have disappeared.

The skeleton is exceptionally well-preserved; this would appear to have been deliberately engineered, the body having been carefully buried between large rocks placed around and above it to protect it. The radius from the left forearm had become detached and was found three centimetres above the skeleton. Possibly this displacement was brought about by early wild animal interference.

The sex of the skeleton cannot be determined until the results of DNA testing have been obtained. However, the grave goods found (see below) suggest it may have been male.

Underneath the skeleton was found a broad-bladed cutting sword and a pair of rotating rowel spurs. The iron sword is late twelfth/early thirteenth-century British, engraved with an inscription (yet to be deciphered). The spurs are thought to be of late twelfth-century French manufacture (confirmation awaited).

Slowly she put the pages of the report back in order and sat back in her chair. Closing her eyes, she saw again the graveyard in its protecting hillside, the scars of the open trenches cutting into the soft grass like swordswipes. Imagination supplying details that never would have been included in a scientific report, she watched as the graveyard became peopled.

Monks in dark habits carried first an old man, then a young man to their graves, each accompanied by mementos from life, reverently placed beside them down in the earth. There was low chanting, male voices lifted to the mountains and the wide sky.

A smaller procession came; two habited men bearing cloth-wrapped bundles, one small, soft and round, one long and pointed. The sharp sound of a woman weeping, the deep hum of a man's inarticulate comfort.

Her visions were too real: Nina opened her eyes.

She could no longer see them, but they were still with her; something of their raw emotion seemed to linger in her mind so that, absurdly, she felt like crying. It's inevitable, she thought, trying to rationalize, the past fascinates me and I've always gone out of my way to investigate old places, in the hope that one day I might pick up some vibration of long ago. Now that it's happening, I can't possibly complain!

But is that why? Or is it because I'm all too ready to identify with a woman who has lost her baby?

Whichever way she looked at it, it was unsettling.

She put the report back in the envelope. Bryn's name came next, so she got up and took it across to his desk. He was typing out an editorial on hunt sabotage for the next newsletter, and she waited till he came to the end of a paragraph.

'That's good,' she said, reading as he typed to a full stop.

'Mark would do it better,' he acknowledged. 'More poetically, so as to move the masses to protest.'

'Yes, I expect you're right, but you've covered the salient points like where they're to meet and what they should bring with them. And you've included a reference to closing gates and not irritating farmers by trampling across their crops.'

'Who needs poetry?' he grinned. Eyes on the envelope, he asked, 'What's that?'

'Peter's preliminary report on the monastery.' She put it down on his desk.

'Have you read it?'

'Yes.'

'And?'

She didn't want to talk about it. 'It's interesting. Why not read it yourself?'

He watched her for a moment, then said, 'Okay. I'll give it to Mark when I've finished.'

She was turning back to her own desk when he said, 'Nina?'

'What?'

'Don't – Look, I know we said the other night that we'd go and help Peter again next Saturday, but you don't have to. I mean, if it upsets you, I'm sure he'd understand.'

'Are you? It's more than I am!' she said heatedly, then added immediately, 'Sorry, Bryn, I didn't mean to bark at you. And it's nice of you to have noticed how I feel.' And not to come over all patronizing, she could have added. 'To be honest, part of me wants to go away, stop thinking about those bodies and have no more to do with it.'

'But the other part has had its curiosity thoroughly aroused and can't wait to get digging again?'

She was about to protest – it wasn't exactly what she meant – then, seeing his face, made herself laugh. 'Got it in one. Besides, I wouldn't give Peter the satisfaction of saying I couldn't cope.'

'Well, you are a woman,' Bryn said. 'Overflowing with emotions and irrationality.' He winked at her, to make quite sure, she imagined, that she knew he was joking.

'I really ought to be left at home sewing my sampler,' she remarked.

'Quite right. As should every other woman who ever dared put her nose out of doors into this man's world.'

'Does he have a girlfriend? Wife?'

'Who, Peter? I shouldn't think so. Would you?'

'She'd have to be remarkably tolerant.'

'Or bigger than him and able to shut him up.'

He was pulling the report out of the envelope and, she guessed, eager to start reading. 'You'll come on Saturday, then?' he asked.

She hesitated, then: 'Yes. I will.'

When she got back from a short lunchtime sortie into the town to take back a library book and get some shopping, the report was no longer on Bryn's desk. She wondered if Mark had read it yet, and how he'd reacted – he'd have had time to, he never went out for lunch. Sometimes he brought in sandwiches, or cold and rather unappetizing chunks of pie which were clearly leftovers. He lived in a small and attractive house on the outskirts of the town, on his own, apart from a cat, and she gathered that his former fiancée had left him and married someone else. It would be hard, Nina reflected – although surely not impossible – to live with a man whose mind was so totally taken up in his work. She wondered disloyally how long it had been after the fiancée's departure before Mark had noticed she'd gone.

Wonder if he kissed her like he kissed me, she thought before she could stop herself. Wonder how she could have left, if so.

Then, angry at her inability to put the episode out of her mind, she hissed bitterly, '*Stop* it! Stop mooning after someone who doesn't want you!'

Dumping her shopping, she went through to his room.

He was sitting at his desk staring out of the window; the report was in front of him. It was so unusual to see him doing nothing that she felt sure his reaction must be similar to hers.

He looked up at her. 'Hello, Nina. You've read this?'

'Yes.'

'What did you think?'

She drew a breath. 'I think Peter and his colleagues should stop buggering about with those poor bodies and put them back where they found them.'

He didn't respond at first. She thought, I've blown it! I've got it all wrong, he's found the report fascinating, been talked into approval by Peter's eloquence and now he'll think I'm –

'So do I,' Mark said.

She sank down into the chair by his desk. 'Oh, good,' she said lamely.

He pointed to his word processor screen, and she read, 'Dear Peter . . . Thank you for the copy of the Wye monastery report . . . very interesting . . . much food for speculation . . .'

The second paragraph was where he began to talk business:

EARTHWORKS includes in its remit the responsibility of spokesman for those who cannot speak for themselves. To date, we have found ourselves called upon to take up arms on behalf of such threatened species as the whale, the dolphin, the fox and the badger, but we are perpetually vigilant, ever willing to put our shoulder to the cause of any who suffer through the insensitivity, albeit unwitting, of other, stronger forces.

We wish to request the immediate return of the Wye monastery skeletons, plus burial goods, to the graves in which they were found. Whoever buried them intended them to stay where they were; no-one, be they thirteenth-century monk or present-day parent, buries their dead with the expectation that, one day, they will be dug up for examination under the bright lights of a laboratory. Neither do they perform their funerary rites, whatever they may be,

with the thought in mind that in the future, a different ceremony and different prayers will accompany a
re-interment.

The advancement of knowledge has been sufficiently served by your actions so far. We await your
earliest notification of the date on which the bodies
will be returned to their graves.

She said, 'Phew!' Then, turning from the screen to
look at him, 'Are you sure about this? You're not
just –' No, she couldn't say, you're not just doing this
because I was upset? Anyway, of course he wasn't!

She didn't think he'd heard. 'I still feel dirty,' he
said quietly. 'I'm acting on the promptings of a guilty
conscience.'

'What have you got to be guilty about?' She knew
she'd never spoken so frankly to him before – never
said anything that appeared to question his judgement – but she couldn't stop. 'You weren't with us,
you didn't do any digging-up of bodies! It's not your
fault!'

'"Any man's death diminishes me, because I am
involved in Mankind",' he quoted. Then, angry suddenly, 'That's what this is all about, Nina! Earthworks, all that we're trying to do! Modern man is a
selfish sod, taking what he wants, raping the poor
silent earth and she has no voice to protest! They call
it progress, or advancement of science, but they're
just excuses for people to do what they want – no
doubt Peter feels he's doing us all a favour by digging
up skeletons and, as you so graphically put it,
buggering about with them!'

He had leapt to his feet and, voice still raised, was
pacing the room. Out of the corner of her eye she saw
Bryn in the corridor, listening.

Mark spun round to face her, grabbing hold of her

196

shoulders. 'I can't reverse the greenhouse effect or slow down global warming. I'm powerless, and I know as well as you do how little of what we're saying actually gets *read*, never mind getting through. But I can prick Peter's conscience and make him do what's right. And I'm bloody well going to.'

Face to face with him, she could see the passion in him. She was about to reply, assure him that she agreed and was with him every step of the way, when suddenly he whispered, 'Oh, Nina,' put his arms round her and kissed her.

She was so amazed that initially she froze. Then, the eager verbal response she'd been about to give translating easily into a physical one, she was kissing him back. Feeling as if, wound together, they were beginning to spin, she heard Bryn discreetly clear his throat.

Abruptly Mark let her go. He muttered an apology, then, visibly turning in on himself, went back to his desk.

Feeling herself dismissed, she left the room.

Bryn was already seated at his desk, and for some time neither of them spoke. But she knew he'd heard everything, probably seen everything, too, and she couldn't bear not talking about it.

Hearing Mark's voice speaking on the phone, she whispered, 'Do you think he's doing the right thing?'

Bryn looked up. '*You* do. Does it matter what I think?'

'I just asked you, didn't I?'

'Okay, then. I don't entirely agree with him, but I'm behind him. To quote Voltaire, "I disapprove of what you say, but I will defend to the death your right to say it."'

'But you don't agree about the bodies?'

He sighed. 'I would have said yes. Certainly, seeing that baby's skeleton gave me a jolt – I felt for a second as if someone were threatening me, telling me to keep away. But now I've seen the report, and read about the sword and how they buried the child so as to protect it, I'm hooked. I want to know more, and I'll be going on Peter's dig on Saturday. So it's hypocritical if I say I thoroughly disapprove.'

'Oh.' She hadn't considered what she was going to do about Saturday. 'But what if Mark asks us to sign the letter?'

'Stand up and be counted, you mean?' He smiled. 'If he does, I'll sign. Mark's a fighter, a champion of the underdog. He's got a lot of courage, and I admire that. All right? Can I get back to work now?'

She laughed with him. 'Yes. Oh, just one more thing.'

'What's that?'

'Well . . .' Now she came to put it into words, it sounded less than loyal. As if she didn't believe in Mark. But it was important for her peace of mind to have his opinion. 'Do you think Peter will take any notice?'

Bryn studied her for an instant, then said, 'You didn't read right to the end of the letter, did you?'

She thought back. 'Not right down to the signature, no. Why?'

He indicated the local telephone directory and an edition of *Who's Who*, both lying open on the end of his desk. 'If you had, you might have noticed that Mark's copying the letter to several fairly influential people who are more than likely to see his point of view. Such as our MP, who happens to be pushing a Private Member's Bill on the abolition of fox-hunting and with whom Mark's having dinner next week. Such as that naturalist chap on TV, who lives not a million miles from the monastery and loves nothing better than a punch-up with academia. Such as that bishop who recently had wide coverage in the national press on this very topic. And he hasn't finished with *Who's Who*, yet. So, in answer to your question, I have to say yes, I do think Peter will take notice. I don't think he'll be given any choice.'

Nina's feelings about Earthworks underwent a sea change that afternoon. From being vaguely embarrassed about what she did for a living – 'only just a living,' her mother was wont to point out when Nina paid one of her rare visits dressed in more than usually threadbare jeans – and from hoping people wouldn't think her hopelessly naive to be working to save the planet, she began to feel proud. It was, she decided, partly Mark's fervour rubbing off on her (nothing at all to do with the kiss), partly that she was impressed by his having influential contacts. Going to dinner with an MP! Writing to bishops and people on TV!

And I'm part of it, she thought. I work for Mark's organization, a brave David about to take on the Goliath of an established discipline. A giant of academia, as Bryn would say.

'We're going to win, too,' she muttered.

'What's that?' Bryn asked.

'Nothing.'

Bryn went promptly at knocking-off time – it was his night for playing squash, and he missed his slot on the court if he was late – but Nina wasn't in any hurry to leave. She wanted to see Mark, but she wanted him to come in to her room rather than going to find him in his. So she sat catching up with the filing, hoping he wasn't so absorbed in whatever it was he was doing that he'd be there till all hours.

At half past six, she heard him get up and open a drawer in the cabinet. Then she heard his steps come out into the corridor.

'Nina? Still here?'

Feeling slightly nervous, she wanted to say no, I went hours ago. 'I'm doing the filing,' she said instead. 'You know how it is – there always seems to be something else to do during the day.'

'That's good of you.' He came to perch on her desk. 'I can't pay you overtime, you know. Wish I could!'

'It's all right.' She wondered if he'd done any more about trying to get sponsorship, but decided it wasn't the moment to ask. On the other hand, was it worth suggesting he dropped a hint to the local MP over dinner? Or to the TV celebrity, if and when he responded to the letter copied to him?

What would he do if I said, I don't want money, I'll do it for love?

It definitely wasn't the moment for that.

'I posted off the letter,' he said.

'Did you?' She hadn't noticed him leave the office.

'Yes. I went out while you were making tea.'

'Oh.'

He was looking down at his foot, idly kicking against the wall. 'Nina, I'm sorry about earlier.'

'Which bit of earlier?' *Damn!* It was out before she could stop it. 'I mean –'

He put his hand under her chin, lifting her face so that she was looking into his eyes. 'Not that bit.' He smiled slightly, letting her go. 'I wouldn't –' He broke off. 'I meant about shouting at you. It wasn't you, and I hope you know it – I was angry about the bad things, and you had the misfortune to be there.'

'It's all right.' She felt moved by him. The bad things. Yes, she knew how they angered him, made him feel impotent, a lone voice that nobody heard. 'I'm glad about the letter,' she said fiercely. 'It needs to be said.'

'Thanks.'

He didn't go on, and she thought he'd get up and return to work. But, standing up and looking out of the window so that his back was to her, he said, 'I can't get that skeleton out of my mind.'

She said, 'Neither can I.'

'Yes, I thought you'd say that.' There was a pause, then he said, 'Nina, what did you feel? When you saw it?'

It was important to him, she was well aware. Concentrating, she tried to remember. To get it right.

'They gave me the arm bone first,' she said. 'The one that was mentioned in the report – the left radius. They didn't know it was a baby's bone then, or if they did, they didn't tell me. I thought it was from an animal. And I felt . . .' She paused, thinking back. 'I felt it sort of *shook* me. Sent a shudder through me, as if it – or someone – was saying, "you must take note of this!"'

Eyes fixed on his back, watching for reaction, she saw him nod.

'What else?'

'When they uncovered the remains, they all went quiet. Moved away. I asked what was wrong, but they wouldn't say. I went to look for myself, and I felt –'

I cried, she thought. I ran out and you were there, and I cried in your arms.

'You were upset, weren't you?' His tone was soft. 'I was, too. I felt a stab of pure grief, as if it were my child lying there. Well, perhaps not mine, but the child of someone I loved very much, and I was having to bear her pain. It's weird, but – ' he turned round, eyes on her, 'I got confused. I'd just been hugging you, and when I looked up from the grave back at you standing on the path, for a second you changed, and I thought it was this other you that I'd been comforting.'

She felt her skin creep.

'Another me?'

'Yes. You were wearing a long black dress, and a white headdress. I could see your hair, though – deep gold, just like it really is. In that moment I knew what you – the other you – felt like. I could still feel the rough material of your robe under my fingertips. And the tears – of both of you, of one of you, I don't know – on my shirt.'

She didn't want to hear any more. 'Mark, it's scary. Please, I –'

He came over to her, hands reaching for hers.

'Sorry. It's not scary, but I can see how you might find it so.' He smiled, and went on in a voice obviously intended to cheer her up, 'You're very real, Nina. You're not likely to fade into a ghost, you're too alive. I –'

His eyes were fixed to hers. Whatever else he'd been going to say about her liveliness faded away; perhaps, she thought wildly, he's already convinced himself.

Nothing happened. She said shakily, 'Don't look at me like that.'

Still he stared at her. Then, moving slowly as if tearing himself away, he got up and went out.

She heard a gentle but firm click as he closed his office door behind him.

PART THREE

Gawyn

Spring 1209–Early Spring 1210

Twelve

He stood staring at the wild black water which had torn her out of his grasp. He knew it was hopeless, but he couldn't move away.

He'd raced along the path, the branch in his hand, but even running harder than he'd have thought possible, he wasn't as swift as the current. He'd lost sight of her, long before the path gave out and the steep banks prevented him from going any further.

I could plunge into the water, he thought. Except that I don't know which side of the river she's been carried down and I can't swim. We'd end up with two corpses, not just one.

The realization that indeed she probably was a corpse by now at last penetrated. He turned away and went back the way he had come.

Collecting the horses – I'm going to have to lead the mare, he thought, I can't turn her loose for someone to find and wonder about – it crossed his mind that he might try to find a road that ran parallel to the river's course. He might hear tell of a body washed up and would know then, for certain.

He abandoned the idea. Riding down along the river would take him out of his way, and he couldn't afford to lose any more time.

Anyway, he concluded, what would it tell me that I don't already know?

She's dead.

Hunched against the everlasting rain, he turned the grey's head away from the water and struck out for the Severn crossing below Gloucester.

He'd seen shock in other men, seen it and known how to deal with it. In himself, it was a different matter; for some days he lived in fear that he was falling ill of some sickness, for what else could account for the strange lightness in his head that prevented him from concentrating and made him all but lose sight of his urgent purpose? One morning when at last the rain had stopped and the sun came out, he found himself on the southern shore of the Severn estuary contemplating a day's rest, thinking, even, to find some inn where he might put up for a while.

For a frightening moment he had forgotten where he was going.

Head swimming, he kicked the grey to a canter, the mare falling in step behind. When did I last eat? he wondered. Is lack of food the reason why I feel so strange?

He rode hard until noon, turning south away from the sea and into the red lands of Devon. Coming across an isolated farm, he tethered the horses and went into the yard, where a surly, silent woman was willing to sell him bacon, bread, milk and apples in exchange for coin. She also provided him with a flagon of cider.

He stopped a few miles further on and ate the lot, finishing with a long draught of the cider. Good, he thought, savouring it, but not as good as they brew in Normandy.

For the first time since the Wye, he turned his thoughts to what was ahead. His mind moving on to

Brittany and arriving in Brocéliande, he suddenly thought, I don't have to go home now – there's no need to make the detour. She is no longer with me, to be delivered and settled into her new life in my castle.

Until he finally faced that reality, he hadn't understood how much the idea had appealed to him. A woman like that, waiting in my castle for my return. What could it have led to, being together, living so close to each other? Someone with her independence, her refusal to give up even when that would have been the easier option. What couldn't I have done with her? What couldn't she have made of me?

Sitting there alone on the edge of the Devon moors, his grief for his loss rose up and poured out of him.

Some time later, when he was restored and the fed and watered horses were thoroughly rested, he set off once more. The mechanical part of him was now in control: the ruthless instincts of survival which had kept him alive and, usually, thriving for twenty-five years were once more in the ascendant. The next steps in his journey were firm in his head, the ultimate goal a fixed purpose. It was now merely a matter of events going sufficiently well to get him there on time.

Face turned towards the south coast, resolutely he closed his mind to the past.

Or so he told himself.

*   *   *

He had crossed between Devon and Brittany on many occasions, and now was not the first time he had needed to make the journey furtively. The busy ports he avoided, instead skirting town and village and making for a little-known cove to the west of the

Yarty river mouth. There, as he'd expected, he found riding at anchor the ships of a small group of independent seamen, as they called themselves: everyone else referred to them as pirates.

He recognized one vessel, the *Kermaria*, a light ship with a disproportionately large area of sail which meant a swift and efficient crossing in calm weather and, as he knew to his cost, a nightmare voyage on something more akin to a twig in a mill-race when any kind of sea was running. He stood looking out across the Channel, which was as flat as a field. What there was of a wind was gentle and moist, blowing in from the west.

Making up his mind, he rode on down into the cove.

The master of the *Kermaria* he also recognized; he reached into his pouch to count his money, for Eustace drove a tough bargain. On the other hand, Gawyn had never known him fail to carry out what he promised, unless a total deterioration of the weather or some other act of God got in the way.

Tying up the horses at the end of the short jetty, he walked out to where Eustace stood with three other men, apparently doing nothing except watch the flowing tide and turn the occasional eye to their ships and the men at work aboard. He greeted them, and they turned, slowly looking him up and down. He felt the reaction as they took in the sword at his side.

Hands held out, palms towards the sailors, he said, 'Eustace. A word, if you please,' and, after a brief glance at his colleagues, Eustace gave a curt nod and followed him back along the jetty.

'A fair day for a meeting of old friends, Gawyn,' Eustace said when they were out of earshot of the others. The Cornish accent was marked; for all that Eustace named his boat for the Breton Virgin and spent more time sailing French than English waters, his allegiance was to the land of his birth.

Gawyn smiled thinly; 'friends' was, he considered, an exaggeration. But he responded amiably, 'Aye. How goes business, Master?'

Eustace spat into the water. 'Not bad, not good. Traffic's still down – John Softsword ruined the livelihood of many a corsair, when he let slip Brittany and Normandy from the English crown. Did he stop to think of us who live off the sea, eh? Tell me that!' He spat again, this time with more force.

'I doubt it,' Gawyn said. The king, he thought, had probably had weightier considerations on his mind than worrying about how the pirates would manage with a fraction of the former number of ships to rob.

'Still, I survive. I have my letters of marque,' – Eustace patted his tunic – 'and I thank King John for that. Whoever plunders the *Kermaria* brings down undreamed-of revenge on the fellow vessels of his nation!'

'Come on, Eustace,' Gawyn dug him in the ribs, 'to plunder a ship, first you have to catch her.'

Responding to the flattery with a huge laugh – as Gawyn had hoped he would – Eustace thumped him back. 'Aye, well, perhaps sometimes I'm mistaken and I just imagine I've been plundered.'

'It could happen to anyone,' Gawyn agreed. Then, sliding it in while Eustace was still laughing, 'How much to take me and my horses to Brittany? Into Paimpol, with the best possible speed?'

The amusement fell from Eustace's face as fast as if he'd just been told Devon was riddled with plague. Casting a rapid eye at the grey and the mare – Gawyn cursed himself for leaving them where Eustace could see them, for the grey and the gear he bore were obviously worth a small fortune and Arrow looked like almost pure Arab – in the next breath Eustace named a figure so high it was Gawyn's turn to laugh.

'Absurd,' he said flatly, and offered half.

They haggled for some time – Eustace was obviously enjoying himself, and Gawyn hoped his desperation didn't show – and finally agreed a sum that was only a little more than Gawyn had anticipated.

'When do we sail?' he asked.

'Now.' Eustace waved an arm towards the sea. 'Tide's all but full, wind's in the west. We'll go before it shifts to the south.'

'I'll lead the horses on board, then.' I'll have to cover the mare's eyes, he thought, she'll play up otherwise. He turned to go, but Eustace shot out a hand and grabbed his sleeve.

'Not yet.' He rubbed fingers and thumb together. 'Money first.'

Gawyn grinned. 'I ought to have known you better.' He counted out the coins.

'Aye, you should.' Eustace put the money away in a leather purse, then shook Gawyn's hand. 'Here's to a kindly sea.'

'Amen,' Gawyn echoed fervently.

Overnight a strengthening wind blew steadily from the west, and the *Kermaria*'s sails, sharply angled, billowed out as she ran almost due south for the Brittany coast. Responding to the increasing westerly, the flat sea grew restless, and Gawyn, awakened by the different movement, left his berth below and went up on deck.

The seaman at the tiller nodded a greeting, which he returned. A trio of sailors were sitting in the lee of the ship's gunwales and, from the clicking sounds and the clink of coins, he guessed they were passing the time playing dice.

He went up into the ship's bows, leaning his arms on the rail and looking down into the water creaming up around her forefoot. The figurehead was in the form of a Venus-like figure, generous-breasted and with flowing hair, but high above her on deck, set into the fore mast, Gawyn had noticed a medal of the Virgin; Eustace, prudently, was a man to hedge his bets.

The night sky was rich with stars, and a thin moon lay on her side high above. Cloud was mushrooming in the west – there will be rain, he thought, before dawn. He listened to the spiteful slap of waves against the *Kermaria*'s starboard midship. Rain would be no bad thing, if it kept the sea calm.

His mind ran ahead. Tomorrow, some time in the afternoon, we shall arrive in Brittany. God willing.

He sighed. This crossing, where for the time being he put himself in another's hands and need be nothing but an idle passenger, was hard to endure: it was easier to keep his thoughts under control when he had to be active rather than passive.

Trying not to be depressed by the many hours still ahead, he went back to his bed.

The rain came, flattened the sea and took away most of the wind. It was late evening of the next day when at last the coast of Brittany came into view, the red rocks of the island of Bréhat glowing like garnets in the last light of the sunset.

'It'll be dark by the time we sail into Paimpol,' Eustace remarked, standing at Gawyn's side in the bows. 'No bad thing, for you.'

Gawyn made no answer.

'Ask me no questions and I'll tell you no lies, eh?' He heard Eustace chuckle. 'Don't worry, I'm deaf and blind when it comes to my passengers.'

'I know,' Gawyn said quietly. 'That's why I pay your exorbitant rates.'

'Discretion has its price,' Eustace commented dryly. Then after a short silence, 'Will you be making the return trip? I'll be around, for the next week or so.'

'No.' He wouldn't be going back within the week. He wasn't sure he'd be going back at all.

Eustace looked at him, shrugged almost imperceptibly, then went aft to talk to his men.

The *Kermaria* slipped silently into Paimpol, and Gawyn concluded that, unless anyone had been specifically looking out for her, her arrival would have gone entirely unnoticed. They berthed at an apparently little-used end of the quay, tying up with a swift efficiency that came from years of performing the same drill. A ramp was let down, and Eustace came below to help Gawyn lead out his horses. The grey was restless, eager to be on the move; Arrow was showing the whites of her eyes, her coat moist with nervous sweat. Against his will, he wondered if this re-acquaintance with water was making her recall her terror on that other night.

'Thank you, Master,' Gawyn said formally, shaking Eustace by the hand.

Eustace studied him. Then, unusually for him, said, 'God go with you. Wherever you're bound.'

As Gawyn led the horses off the quay, he was already running back up the ramp and signalling for it to be raised.

He rode some way out of the sleeping town, once out beyond the last habitation letting the grey have his head, running the stiffness out of his legs. Gawyn, prepared to check his pace in case the mare couldn't keep up, found there was no need; although a good two hands shorter than the grey, she was lighter, less heavily laden and more flexible, and her turn of speed was surprising. Screwing round in the saddle to watch her, the beauty of her movement gave him a keen pleasure.

'What shall we do with you, lass?' he asked her as they eventually pulled up. 'Sell you? You'll fetch a handsome price. But Lamri and I would miss you – shall we keep you, and find you a squire who'll thank God for his good fortune in such a mount?' He leaned over and patted her neck as she nudged close to him; although the idea of selling her had its appeal – it was awkward, at times, leading her, and he was attracted by the thought of a purse full of gold – he had an idea he wasn't going to part with her.

'Too good to waste on some Breton who doesn't know an Arab from a mule, aren't you?' He patted her again. 'And, besides –'

No. Don't think of that. Don't let the picture form of her on the mare's back, face set against the exhaustion and the rain, skin marked with blue dye where the colour had run out of that absurd felt hat that mercifully concealed the shorn hair.

'Come on.' His changed tone made the mare start, and she tried to pull away. Spurring the grey, he set off at the trot to look for somewhere to spend what was left of the night.

In the morning it was raining again as he rode back towards Paimpol. It was still early, and he was banking on the town being as yet quiet. The house where he was bound was set apart, but, later in the day, there would be people about.

He approached under cover of trees, only emerging to enter through the archway that broke the high walls. A man stood on watch but, seeing who it was, waved him in. The man called out, and a boy came running from the stable block to take the horses.

'Get them out of sight,' Gawyn said. 'Feed them and water them, then, later, take them out in turn for exercise.'

The boy nodded. Removing his packs, Gawyn went up to the stout door of the house, which opened as he thumped on it.

'Welcome,' said his cousin. 'Fourteen days late, but I'm sure you have good reason for the delay.'

'Diew, I have.' Gawyn followed him inside and the door banged shut. Yves would, he had already decided, only receive an edited version of the tale – some of it there was no need for him to know. Switching to his cousin's Breton, he said, 'Will we still be in time? Do we yet know the day and the place?'

'Yes to all those things.' Yves turned to smile at him. 'I have much to tell you, but first let me see to your comfort. Water and soap, yes? A change of linen?'

Gawyn was already unbuckling his sword belt and taking off the plain, concealing robe he had worn for the long journey. The two days on the *Kermaria* had given him a chance to take off his mail, but donning the hauberk again on arrival in Paimpol had reopened sores not yet healed. Removing the front and rear parts of the leather cuirass, he reached up under his arms to unfasten the mail. Yves took the items from him, treating them with reverence, and the small ceremony was strangely heartening; he wondered if Yves, too, was prompted by the handling of the garments into an instinctive reminder of all that was inherent in knighthood.

The quilted tunic underneath the mail was wet with both sweat and rain; standing at last in his linen shirt and breeches, Gawyn followed Yves out to the small inner courtyard where the water trough stood.

'I'll leave you to it,' Yves said as Gawyn stripped naked and plunged his head down into the water. 'Call for more hot water if you need it. When you've finished, come and eat, and while we do so, we will talk.'

Amid the sensuous pleasure of washing the dirt of too many days from his body, Gawyn hardly heard him leave.

Thirteen

Dressed in clean linen and a borrowed tunic of Yves's – his cousin was considerably shorter, and the tunic finished at his shins – he went through to where food and drink had been set out. Yves looked up from the papers he was studying and smiled.

'You look human again,' he remarked.

'I feel it.' His mouth watering, he stood back from the table, waiting for Yves's invitation. At first, still preoccupied with the documents, Yves didn't notice, then, raising his eyes again, said hastily, 'Please! You must be starving – help yourself!'

He managed to stop himself falling on the food, but only with difficulty; his cousin's board was always generous, the fare of the best. Tactfully, Yves took a small plateful to keep him company, but Gawyn could tell by the way he was merely picking at it that he wasn't very enthusiastic. He seemed much more interested in his papers.

'Have you had sufficient?' he asked Gawyn after some time.

'Aye. Thank you – it was excellent.'

Yves inclined his head. 'We'll take a fresh jug of wine and sit in the courtyard, and I'll tell you the news.'

Settled in chairs in the sunshine, Gawyn waited while his cousin put his papers – and, presumably, his thoughts – in order.

'I told you of the happenings last spring,' he began. 'Pope Innocent obviously isn't a man for whom the impact of an injury diminishes with time – quite the reverse.'

'The man who was killed was his papal legate,' Gawyn commented. 'No man would forgive the slaughter of a representative sent on a peaceful mission of enquiry.'

Yves snorted. 'Many of the people of the Languedoc – some of the bishops, possibly, Raymond of Toulouse certainly – might argue that Peter of Castelnau didn't know the meaning of the term "peaceful mission".'

'He was the pope's man. For nearly five years he'd been trying to find a way to root heresy out of the south. God knows, no-one could envy him the task – the Languedoc nobility's riddled with it, and every peasant from the Rhône to the Pyrenees will follow suit and turn Cathar if we don't take a firm stand.'

'"We"?' Yves echoed, his tone amused. 'The crusade's being preached to the knights of France. The pope would be surprised if the lord of a castle in the Welsh mountains responded to his appeal.'

Gawyn closed the thought of his Welsh castle into a fastness at the back of his mind. 'Also the lord of a domain in Brittany,' he said mildly. 'Which, if I'm going to have to make the choice, I shall remind myself is by far the more lucrative possession.'

'Forgive me,' Yves said, smiling, 'I don't seriously consider you an outsider. It's just envy – all my mother left to me was a draper's debt.'

'So, what's the present position?' Gawyn steered him back to the matter in hand. 'Has King Philip put his full weight behind the crusade?'

217

'He's agreed to let it happen – since he's Raymond of Toulouse's overlord, no-one can act to re-take the Languedoc without his permission. He's certainly hostile to the Cathars, but he's still too worried about more immediate threats to do much more than lend verbal support. The pope has repeatedly asked for either the king or the Dauphin as leader of the crusade, but Philip refuses – apparently he told the pope he has two fierce lions at his flanks, and cannot turn his back on either of them.'

'John of England and the emperor Otto? I can't speak for the emperor, but King John is still paying for the Aquitaine expedition of three years ago. I can't believe he's busy planning a renewed attempt to win back the French territories.'

'Yes, but King Philip can. Still, even though he won't involve himself or his son, he's promised Pope Innocent a contingent of knights.'

'Ah. To include us?'

Yves caught his eye, his excitement obvious. 'Guy of Brittany swore fealty to the crown this last Pentecost. There's nothing to stop any of his knights from responding to a papal appeal that's been sanctioned by the king.'

'What terms?' He tried to keep an answering eagerness out of his voice.

'The usual. Forty days' service, and a plenary indulgence equal to what we'd earn crusading in the Holy Land.' He hesitated, then: 'I don't like to mention material rewards in the same breath as spiritual ones, but it's rumoured there'll be good lands in the Languedoc for distribution. They're going to confiscate the heretics' estates and offer them to any of us who can take them.'

'Lands in the Languedoc,' Gawyn repeated. A country of sunshine and lazy days, of spreading vineyards and ancient cities which retained a breath of the Romans.

'And there,' Yves had lowered his voice, 'is the heart of the matter, from the king's point of view.'

Gawyn, still dreaming of heat, said, 'What?'

'The Languedoc is virtually an independent fiefdom,' Yves said quietly. 'If an army acting with the king's authority takes it over, whether or not it's in the cause of eradicating heresy, the end result is the same: the land comes into the King of France's realm.'

'And France increases her territory yet again.' The protest forming as he uttered the words, he said, 'But I don't accept that's the heart of it. These Cathars, these Albigensians, they're wrong. Aren't they? They've fled to the Languedoc because it's the only place that will tolerate them – they've been hounded out of Flanders and the North, burned and branded for the evil influence they are.' He leaned towards Yves, his manner intense. 'Do you know what they say? That God didn't make the world. He is perfect, they say, and since nothing in the world is, then the world wasn't made by God. They reject the Old Testament God, our God, Yves, and tell us God's world was made by Satan. They tell us Jesus Christ is an illusion, hell and purgatory don't exist, and the priests of Holy Mother Church have no more power to intercede with God and the saints than has any other man.'

'Yes, I know,' Yves said gently. 'I've heard nothing else since first this crusade was preached,' he muttered. 'But –'

'There are no "buts,"' Gawyn said forcefully. 'The Cathars are wrong, and they're dangerous. They have to be stopped.'

'Not just stopped. Annihilated. Have no doubt, Gawyn, that's what this will lead to. I've been with the knights, they're spoiling for a fight. The pope and the king have given them a legitimate target, which they'll be allowed to attack as ferociously as they like. Whatever they do, they'll be rewarded with remission of sins and exoneration of guilt. Not to mention the likelihood of a nice piece of fertile southern land.'

'The Cathars deserve annihilation,' Gawyn said coldly. Yves's mention of guilt had unnerved him; fight, he thought. Fight, and I'll forget. Fight a holy war, and God will forgive me. He said suddenly, to his cousin's evident surprise, 'I want to hear Mass. Today.'

'Very well.' Yves recovered himself quickly. 'We'll go together, although we can't take communion as we've just eaten. But it'll have to be this morning.'

'Why?'

Yves looked apologetic. 'I know you've had a long journey – and a hard one, judging from the look of you – but, as I said when you arrived, you're a fortnight late. There's no time to waste.'

Understanding, he said, 'Where? And when?'

Yves's face broke into a wide smile. 'Lyons. The twenty-fourth day of June.'

'Only just over two months.' And my horses – especially Lamri – and I have had insufficient rest. *And* I have yet to recruit a squire. 'Will we make it?'

'Yes.' Yves's emphatic answer brooked no argument. 'We'll make it.'

They set off for the great muster that was to launch the Albigensian Crusade early in the afternoon. Yves's own squire, a sturdy boy named Barr, had worked so hard on both Gawyn's horses and his gear that he rode out of Yves's yard looking fresh-minted. The boy's younger brother Cadoc had been recruited to squire for Gawyn; 'I trained him,' Yves had assured him, 'and were it not for an older loyalty to his brother, I'd have chosen him for myself – he rides like a centaur, and he's full of pluck. He was born for the job.'

Gawyn studied the youth as they rode. He was of a slighter build than Barr, taller, and less self-assured. When he had been given to understand that Arrow was to be his mount, he'd looked like a child given a honeycomb.

'The mare?' he'd said incredulously.

I'll have to work on this Breton accent of his, Gawyn thought. 'Aye,' he replied. 'Her name's Arrow.'

'Arrow,' he whispered. 'She's – she's –'

'What?' he asked kindly.

The boy turned brown eyes to him. 'Beautiful,' he whispered. Then, as if afraid Gawyn might say he'd only been joking and he wasn't giving this paragon of a horse to his new squire after all, had leapt lightly into the saddle.

Gawyn thought, Roese, your Arrow has gone to a worthy successor.

* * *

The days fell into a pattern. From riding alone – and under the stress of flight – Gawyn found the journey a pure delight. He'd always got on well with Yves; the same age, they'd been flung together as children on the many occasions when their fathers had visited each other. As the elder brother, Yves's father had inherited the patrimony, which had gone in turn to Yves; Gawyn's lesser inheritance of the estate in Brocéliande had been compensated by the addition of the stark castle which came to him from his Welsh mother.

It was a good feeling, Gawyn reflected, to ride off to war beside someone you knew almost as well as you knew yourself. As well, he amended, when it comes to fighting. We were each other's natural opponents from the time we could first pick up and brandish a stick – I know exactly how he reacts to any threat from a broadsword swipe to a charging warhorse, and he could say the same of me.

Prompted by the thought, he caught up with Yves and punched him. 'Hoi! Remember that time I unseated you three times running when we were tilting?'

'Remember that time you fell off your father's old destrier?' Yves replied equably. 'The half-blind one that moved a little slower than a snail?'

Gawyn had a flash of memory: Roese landing in the midden. The joke turned sour on him, and he dropped back.

When they stopped that night – it was the fifth on the road – Yves waited until the boys had settled and then said, 'You never told me why you were delayed.'

'Didn't I?' I'm not sure I'm going to.

'No. Anything you want to talk about?'

'No.'

There was a short pause, then Yves said, 'I may be speaking out of turn, but I wouldn't like to go into battle with something on my mind.' He glanced at Gawyn, then added piously, 'I might perform less than my best, and be a liability to my fellow knights. And I wouldn't want that, particularly if one of them happened to be my cousin.'

Gawyn had to laugh. 'Very well. Not that it's anything that bad,' he added hastily. Another lie, he thought. 'I had a dispute with a neighbour over some land – it was mine, always had been, but he moved his sheep on to it and told me I was in the wrong and anyway I didn't seem to be using it for any very important purpose. When I told him that wasn't the point, he turned nasty and rounded up a group of armed men to defend the new and highly imaginative boundary he'd drawn.'

'Silly man.'

'That's what I thought. What he thought, too, when I arrived with eight mounted knights in full war gear.'

'What did he do?' Yves was grinning.

'Herded up his damned sheep and put the fence back where it had always been. He'd have swept up the droppings, if we hadn't started edging towards him to hurry him along.'

'That doesn't sound like trouble. What happened next?'

Gawyn leaned back against his pack, sighing. 'I did something I shouldn't have done. Something my better judgement told me was a mistake, but – you know how it is.'

Yves waited patiently for him to go on.

'They'd been robbed of a legitimate excuse for action, my band of knights, and I wanted to compensate them. So I took them home and opened my hall to them.'

Yves whistled softly. 'Your better judgement was right. Got a bit out of hand, did it?'

'Yes. Three dead.'

'*Dead?*'

'Aye. Drunk, clowning around, they fell off the drawbridge.'

'Great God.'

Gawyn glanced at him. 'That's not the worst of it.' Nor is this that I'm about to tell you, he added silently. I intend to keep to myself the worst of it. It's between me and God. 'One of the dead was related to Llewelyn ap Iorworth.'

'Llewelyn ap Iorworth! Sweet Jesus, Gawyn, whatever made you involve *him?*'

'I didn't, not directly,' Gawyn objected. 'The man was only a distant relative. And Llewelyn and his followers don't normally concern themselves with matters outside their own territory – the thing is, it's becoming difficult to judge where that territory ends.'

'No longer only Anglesey and the north?'

'No. Apparently he now has powerful allies in the Marches. New allies, I would guess, keen to show just how loyal and reliable they're going to be.'

'By offering to act on Llewelyn's behalf and knock out an upstart knight who's been stupid enough to send one of Llewelyn's kin to his death?'

He was about to protest, say, no, it wasn't like that. Only it was like that. He'd made a mistake, a costly one that had brought down on his head a wrath so furious that he'd had to flee for his life. Had to let go a whole castle full of staff, for he knew the nature of the enemies he'd attracted to himself: they were the sort of men who, robbed of their victim, would take it out on his retainers. The sort of men who would impale a man on a stake or lop off his limbs one by one, then mock him in his agony.

The one piece of good fortune had been to have land in his lap someone also on the run, someone who was prepared to pay him to make an undercover journey he'd been going to make in any case. Pay him handsomely – he thought of the jewelled cross, hidden in his pack – for the privilege of his protection.

His thoughts running on out of his control, he was grateful when Yves said, 'Would you have come to join me anyway? Had you not had to leave Wales, I mean?'

I've no idea, Gawyn thought. But he didn't say it. 'Yes, I would.'

'For the honour of fighting in God's war against the heretics?'

'Aye.' Forgive me, Lord, Gawyn prayed, if that's not the whole truth.

'And not,' Yves went on relentlessly, 'because a crusading army is a convenient place to hide? *And* earn glory at the same time?'

Gawyn didn't answer.

They sat for some time deep in their own thoughts. Gawyn didn't try to guess what Yves was thinking about; for himself, he was praying silently, the superstitious dread on him that God would know he was not joining the crusade for the pure motive of destroying His enemies, and that, knowing this, He would punish him for his deceit. I'm sorry, he repeated, sorry for the original misjudgement that led to the deaths of three men. Sorry that I robbed Roese of her brother and her father, so that she was forced to escape from an arranged marriage that would have been intolerable for her. Sorry I took her into danger, so eager to get out of Wales and away from my enemies that I crossed the river when I knew full well it wasn't safe.

Sorry, much more than sorry, that because of me she lost her life.

As, eventually, they settled for the night, Yves's voice came to him out of the darkness.

'I don't know what else it is you've endured that you're choosing not to tell me about,' he said softly, 'but it sits ill on you. If I can't help, I pray God can.'

* * *

Out of Brittany and through Anjou and Blois, on towards the junction with the main route south at Bourges. At first, when they numbered only four, they maintained the fastest speed, riding as long and as hard each day as the horses could tolerate, making

225

only the briefest stops for food and drink, reluctant to search any longer than they need for supplies so that their diet became monotonous. When anything slowed the pace – one day the rain fell with such force that for safety's sake they were forced to seek shelter, once Yves's horse seemed in danger of showing up lame – Gawyn and Yves would stare at each other in anxiety, sharing the same thought: will we be in time?

As they neared Bourges, their fears were calmed; along the way they began to meet with other knights, in pairs, in bands, a vast contingent from Burgundy wearing silk crosses on their chests, all bound south for the Languedoc. The group was further swelled by wives, craftsmen of all trades from sapper to pastry cook, camp followers and hangers-on. And by armies of priests, who never missed an opportunity to hop up on to a cart and encourage the travellers, telling them they were part of a great cause, God's own holy cause, and that they must not let fatigue, or hunger, or any other of the privations of the road, deter them from their magnificent purpose.

Sometimes it seemed that the whole world must be on the move, taking up arms against the Cathars.

The two months had been long enough; Gawyn and Yves thought they'd probably travelled further than most of the train, but they took the cross and were among the first at the muster on 24th June. Lyons, Gawyn reflected, must have wondered what had hit it; he didn't know how many they numbered in all, but judged that the wild rumours of hundreds of thousands of souls were probably an exaggeration. The senior knight in their company said authoritatively that there were forty thousand of them, and, in the absence of any better estimate, Gawyn accepted his.

The papal legates were jubilant. In the midst of a shifting, restless crowd, Gawyn and Cadoc stood together listening to the fierce, fanatical haranguing of Arnald-Amaury, who called down God's wrath on the Cathars, prayed for His aid in this the most vital of crusades, and, spreading his arms as if to embrace them all, told them they were the greatest Christian army ever mustered.

Other speakers took to the platform, bishops who listed yet again the numerous sins of the Cathars – surely even they can't be guilty of all of them, Gawyn thought incredulously as a bishop from the Midi (who, he supposed, ought to know) told in graphic detail of the sexual perversions practised by the senior Cathars – Perfects, they were called – on the younger of their adherents. Another bishop reminded the company that any group who rejected marriage and refused to swear on oath couldn't possibly be normal and decent.

The military men, too, had their turn; lacking the practised rhetoric of the clergy, they were briefer in their remarks. For the first time Gawyn set eyes on Simon de Montfort, who, they said, was tipped to be commander in chief. He was, Gawyn judged, in his middle to late forties, old to be a commander of men. Yet he gave the impression of carrying his years lightly; tall, built like an ox, he had a great shock of greying hair. He brought with him a reputation as an ambitious man and a courageous soldier. Watching the determination in the craggy face as de Montfort spoke of seeing himself as the instrument of God's anger, Gawyn saw no trace of fear or doubt.

De Montfort stepped down, and yet another priest took his place. Gawyn found he was no longer listening. He'd gone along merely to hear what they all had to say; in an army this size communications were going to be difficult, and he'd made up his mind not to miss any chance of news. But what he'd heard wasn't news, and he began to feel he was wasting time that he and Cadoc could have better spent on their equipment. On resting, even.

But, against his will, he felt himself drawn into the mass fervour. When Arnald-Amaury returned to the platform to lead them in prayer and give a last address, urging them on in their battle on God's behalf, Gawyn went along with his every word.

At his side, bringing him down from the heights, he felt Cadoc tug at his sleeve. He hadn't understood more than one word in five, and Gawyn found himself whispering a repeat of the ringing address, translated into colloquial Breton.

Fourteen

The great army rolled south out of Lyons towards Montpellier, the authority of its leaders – both spiritual and temporal – and the sheer weight of its numbers making its reputation even more alarming than its actuality. Many nobles didn't wait for the feared attack, instead surrendering their castles and making their peace with the Church, adding themselves and their followers to the already vast train.

Some time after they had set out Yves, riding for a morning with the knights of the Duke of Burgundy, came back to report that Raymond VI, Count of Toulouse, had met the crusade leaders at Valence and taken the cross.

'I understood he was a heretic himself,' Gawyn said. 'From what I've heard of his court, I can well believe it. Decadent, they say, men wasting their time on making songs and writing poetry.'

'The jongleurs and troubadours aren't just a feature of the court of Toulouse,' Yves replied. 'They existed in the south long before Raymond decided he preferred singing to fighting.'

'I was told his wife was a Cathar. How can such a man join the crusade?'

'He may sympathize to the extent that he's never

actually prohibited them, but he's not a heretic himself, so it's all right to allow him in.' Yves spoke lightly. 'And with any luck he won't be called on to attack the very Cathar convent that houses his wife. If he is, he can tell her to duck.'

'It's not a joking matter.' Gawyn's annoyance overflowed. 'This cursed Raymond's typical of what's wrong with this place. It's – they're –' He struggled to find words for what he was feeling. How to say, it's unhealthy, this anarchic society where women have as much power as men, where they all sit up there in their fortified hilltop castles, doing just as they please with no thought to the good of the land as a whole? Great God, no wonder they can't form any opposition to our advance – they're decadent and demoralised. 'It's not what I expected,' he said eventually, aware that it went almost nowhere towards expressing his thoughts. Then, 'We're going to run through them like fire across a cornfield. It won't be a fair fight, under anyone's definition – they won't stand a chance.'

Yves studied him gravely. 'Remember?' he said quietly. 'All those weeks ago, back in Paimpol, I told you we were going to annihilate them.'

Gawyn didn't reply. The finger of unease that had been regularly running up and down his spine was growing into a fist.

Raymond VI's turncoat action meant that the main thrust of the crusade would now be directed against his nephew, Raymond-Roger Trencavel, Count of Béziers and Carcassonne. As the army reached Montpellier, word went round that he had sought audience with the papal legate, begging for forgiveness and offering to join the crusaders – have none of them any guts? Gawyn wondered – but his appeal was dismissed. Rumour had it that he'd most probably flee to the walled city of Carcassonne, leaving Béziers to look after herself; 'He'll be hoping the inhabitants will hold us up long enough for him to get his Carcassonne defences in order,' Gawyn said disgustedly to Yves, 'and God help them in Béziers, because *he's* not going to.'

Montpellier was unlike any city Gawyn had seen before. It had an almost tangible air of prosperity, and its people looked well-fed and satisfied with themselves. The port won for itself a good proportion of Mediterranean trade, both goods – particularly the locally-produced salt – and human; Montpellier lay on the pilgrimage routes to Santiago de Compostela. There was a huge market and, ensuring that the cerebral side of life was given due importance, a school of medicine. The city had a cosmopolitan feel; the Spanish influence was strong, and in the crowded streets Arabs and Saracens rubbed shoulders with Christians with all the assurance in the world.

Gawyn's unease increased.

On the twenty-first of July the crusade crossed the Hérault river and entered the territory of Raymond-Roger of Carcasonne. The weather was stifling – Gawyn had never known such heat, and the very high humidity made it hell to ride in a mail coat, plus the linen and padding layers that went under it. He appreciated the sense of those knights – no doubt veterans of crusades in Outremer – who had chosen light colours for their surcoats; we of the cold north, he realized, forget that the original purpose of the surcoat was to deflect sun from the metal of the hauberk so that you felt less like a lobster being boiled alive.

A black surcoat was about as effective as no surcoat at all.

He sweated, drank voraciously from the water in his flask, and sweated some more. Cadoc, who as his squire should also have worn the black marked with the scarlet bear's head, had escaped; unable to equip him properly because of the haste of their departure, Yves had found him a garment of plain white. From time to time he would glance sympathetically at Gawyn, frequently offering to dismount and fill his flask. But the water from the ponds by the road tended to be brackish, and it looked stagnant and unappealing; towards the end of each march, Gawyn preferred to go thirsty.

The taking of Béziers was effected without the mounted knights even having to swing a sword. On a slight rise beyond the outer defensive ditch hastily dug by the townspeople – blessedly, in the shade of a stumpy group of some prickly sorts of tree quite unknown to him – Gawyn stood with Yves watching the whole thing.

Before the army had arrived, a respected elder of the clergy had been sent ahead carrying terms: the town would be spared the inevitable sack provided that it handed over two hundred heretics known to be living there. Alternatively, the faithful were invited to come out, leaving the heretics to whatever fate the crusaders chose to administer.

Both offers were rejected. Do they underestimate us so badly? Gawyn wondered. Can't they see what they're taking on?

The town grabbed the initiative and sent out a sortie under the protection of a white flag, a ploy that proved deceptive since the men suddenly opened fire on the crusaders, shooting several flights of arrows into their front ranks before they had time to react.

In the shocked silence that ensued, someone screamed. It was a woman's voice, and Gawyn guessed it was some camp follower who'd just seen her man cut down. The solo voice was joined by others, shouting, uttering fierce, piercing cries, and the woman's companions began moving in a body towards the city walls, waving sticks and clubs and racing for the gates.

They're as surprised as we are, Gawyn thought, staring fixedly at the walls, where there were signs of hasty panic action. Sweet Jesus, they're not ready for this!

Alarm bells rang out as the dirtiest, lowest element of the crusader train proceeded to press the advantage. The vanguard who had carried only makeshift weapons were joined by the better-prepared; the harsh sun glittered on the metal of swords, axes and daggers. They'll finish the job, Gawyn thought desolately, before we've even had a chance to –

'MOUNT!' came the repeated shout of a rapidly relayed order from somewhere to his left.

'Mount!' Yves echoed. 'Come on! Mount and we'll take the town!'

In a great surging, pounding throng, they galloped down the slope towards the bleeding city, pausing at the bottleneck of the gates, then riding on into the streets. All around him Gawyn saw knights break off from the rush to kick down doors and plunder, often not bothering to seek booty for themselves, merely grabbing it from the hands of furious camp followers, who instantly made good the loss by turning on the inhabitants and helping themselves anew.

He smelt smoke. Some savage impulse – thwarted avarice, he guessed – had prompted the foot followers to fire a building, and in the heat the flames caught ferocious hold.

233

Through the rest of the day the fire spread. Back on the mound beyond the defences, Gawyn watched as the very city took on the look of a glowing coal; even from a distance, the heat radiating out in regular waves was all but intolerable. Word came that the cathedral had burned to the ground, incinerating the bodies of the massacred within. From time to time a slight breath of wind would bring across a billow of smoke.

And the stench of burning flesh.

He wondered if the jubilant reaction of the crusaders was totally sincere; did we mean to do this? Is this really how men of God pursue a war, even if it is a holy war against His enemies?

What does God say to the sight of women and children – defenceless men, too – cut down by a mob, their bodies slung into His holy house to be burned like the carcasses of plagued cattle?

What, in God's name, have they done to deserve it? Were they all Cathars, every last one?

He'd asked Yves that question. Yves had replied, his voice expressionless, that when the pope's representative had been asked how faithful Catholics could be distinguished from Cathars and so left unharmed, Arnald-Amaury apparently replied, 'Kill them all. God will know his own.'

The general attitude seemed to be that they'd brought it on themselves by rejecting the crusaders' generous offer of terms. Gawyn detected a sort of pride in the fact that neither age, nor sex, nor status had been spared, as if it were a matter for self-congratulation for soldiers to have overcome the defenceless.

The only common cause for regret was that the fast-spreading fire had destroyed far too many rich homes, whose contents could otherwise have left Béziers stuffed into the crusaders' packs.

* * *

The army moved on, leaving the deserted ruins of Béziers smouldering under the scorching sun.

Along the road, town after town was taken with no resistance; how could they resist, Gawyn thought, when they're empty? The people have heard how we take towns on this crusade. They've heard, and they prefer to run and leave us to it; with their homes undefended, they may lose all their worldly possessions, but they'll keep their lives.

Increasingly, he was riddled with a deep sense of shame.

The brief action at Béziers had given Raymond-Roger Trencavel little additional time to fortify Carcassonne, but as the crusaders rode up late in the day on the first of August, it was clear that there hadn't been much more he could do in any case: the walls of Carcassonne made it the most heavily-defended city Gawyn had ever seen.

It was clear from the outset that Carcassonne wasn't going to be the pathetically easy victim that Béziers had been. One thing Raymond-Roger had managed to do was to arrange for the collection or destruction of anything edible or drinkable within a wide radius of the city; unless the crusaders could live off their own supplies, they were going to have to forage far afield for the enormous amounts required to sustain their vast numbers.

The attack was organized in stages, one area at a time. The crusaders' onslaughts against a section would be met by short savage forays from within; casualties on both sides were high. The scaling ladders employed were rebuffed by a deluge of boulders and accurately-fired arrows; Yves's Barr was wounded in the shoulder, although he was lucky in that the stone had only bruised him. 'If it had hit your tough Breton skull,' Yves told him, trying to cheer him up, 'you wouldn't have felt a thing!'

It was a stalemate. Inside the walls, conditions must have been deteriorating; they had little water, and the heat was intense. The smell of rotting flesh grew increasingly strong, for there was nowhere in the city to bury so many dead. Great clouds of fat black flies were everywhere, and from time to time sounds of hysteria reached the besiegers from within.

Outside, life was slightly better. They had water, and enough manpower for parties to be spared for food collection. The heat had brought on the harvest; Raymond-Roger hadn't been able to destroy what hadn't yet appeared above the ground. The crusaders had commandeered the salt pans of the coast and had set up a barter system, exchanging salt for the bread made in the homes of the outlying population.

Time went on, and the decision was made to bring up the siege engines; for half a day the hot air vibrated to the sound of rock hitting masonry. The same part of the walls was hit repeatedly, and, undermined by the sappers' digging into its foundations, eventually it began to crack. Under cover of darkness, the sappers completed their tunnels; when they were fired in the morning, a substantial section of the walls collapsed.

A party of knights, Yves and Gawyn included, was detailed to go in through the breach. Barr and Cadoc, Barr still in pain from his wounded shoulder, were eager to go too, and Yves told them to mount up.

But Gawyn countermanded him.

'Why?' Yves, keen to be moving off, seemed more surprised than irritated. 'They're as wild for action as the rest of us!'

Gawyn was responding to an instinct so strong that there was no way he could ignore it. However, it didn't come accompanied by an explanation: shrugging, he said feebly, 'We're leaving a lot of our gear here. Given the plundering tendencies of this lot,' – he indicated the army camped all around them – 'how much do you think'll still be here when we get back?'

It was an acceptable reason. Yves wasn't to know that Gawyn had already removed from his pack the only thing he was concerned about: Roese's cross lay against his hauberk, under his cuirass.

Yves frowned, then nodded. 'Very well. Boys, stand guard. Now, *come on!*'

Together they joined the heavily-armed, mounted knights pressing in wedge formation towards the ragged gap in the walls. High above, on hastily-constructed wooden platforms, the defenders fired arrows down on them, but as soon as the knights got in close to the walls, the angle became too acute for any possibility of accuracy. Gawyn was about to take off his helm, preferring to take the chance than slowly suffocate, when beside him, just the other side of Yves, another knight who had done the same thing had his head nearly torn from his shoulders by the force of an arrow right between the eyes.

They were in a suburb of the city whose sloping streets were lined with well-maintained houses, clearly the dwellings of the wealthy. As usual a few knights were seduced into breaking down doors and helping themselves to the choice of what was within, although the majority seemed keener on riding on, encouraged by the prospect of action.

They weren't disappointed. At the turn of a particularly narrow street – dear God, we should have been on our guard! Gawyn thought desperately, it's a perfect place for an ambush – an armed force of men awaited them. They had used to the full the advantage of having time to prepare: they had formed themselves into ranks, so that if those at the front fell, immediately their places were filled by those behind. From the windows and balconies of houses above came a steady stream of arrow fire, and those inhabitants who had no other weapons resorted to throwing, with great accuracy, a variety of missiles from sticks and stones to broken crockery and, from one window, heavy glass ornaments.

With drawn swords, Yves and Gawyn fought side by side. As they pressed on up the street, the defenders gradually falling back, they got into the formation they'd practised for such situations. Gawyn turned his horse and proceeded backwards so that, both of them right-handed, he and Yves had a sword to defend both sides, each free to move with no danger of impeding the other's sword-arm.

Sensing that they'd gained the upper hand, the knights began to howl their victory. Breaking out into a little square, they dismounted to race after the fleeing defenders, and from all around echoed the cries of dying men. Some on foot, some still mounted, they forced a way on, further into the heart of the town, and, as the fighting men were decimated and the attackers found it harder to find targets, they began to storm into the houses, dragging out women, children, the sick and the elderly.

It was infectious, the brute urge to kill, and Gawyn

found himself revelling in the great surge of collective power, responding in a manner that was almost sexual. In the middle of a band of shouting, jubilant knights, their horses abandoned as they systematically hacked their way through a group of screaming women trying to run before them, he reached out with his left hand and caught by her long black hair a young girl, pale gown already splattered with either her own or someone else's blood.

He pulled her head back so that her wide, frenzied eyes stared right into his. They could have been alone, the only people left in the world: as he sheathed his sword and pulled out his dagger to cut her white, exposed throat, it seemed to him that everything went quiet.

Suddenly the smell of urine rose up. He heard the splatter of liquid hitting stone, saw a small cloud of steam.

In her terror, she had lost control of her bladder.

He loosened his fierce grip on her hair, horrified at how he must have been hurting her. Guilt ravaging him, leaving him shaking, slowly he removed his helm; he tried to control his panting breath and formed the words, 'I'm sorry.'

She shook her head, pulling away from him, looking over her shoulder to where the other women and their pursuers had run off round the corner. She doesn't understand, he thought, and she must.

He threw his dagger away from him, turning open, empty palms towards her. 'I'm sorry,' he repeated, knowing even as he did so that it was hopeless, that they spoke quite different languages. 'I will not harm you. See?' He reached out to take her by the shoulders, some vague idea forming that, if words failed, he might show what he meant by embracing her. Giving her, Christ-like, the kiss of peace.

Then, swift as lightning and catching him totally off-guard, she raised her knee and caught him accurately and violently in the crotch.

For good measure, she spat in his face as he went down.

He crumpled, elbows and knees bending in towards the middle of his body where the agony from his bruised testicles seemed to explode again and again. Whooping for breath, he felt hard stone against his back as he slumped against a wall. His head cracked against the paving slabs of the street, and he felt the vibrations of running feet.

No need to run away, he said silently to her. I won't be coming after you.

Then everything went black.

He knew he couldn't have been out for more than a few seconds; when he came to the running feet were louder, and they didn't belong to the girl but to a fresh wave of knights, pounding up from the square below.

'Where did the women go?' the man in the lead demanded. He was thickset, with bright red hair and a boil on his chin.

Gawyn struggled to his knees, a hand against the wall for support.

'I – there, I think.' He pointed down a side alley. Wherever she'd gone, it hadn't been down there.

'Are you wounded?'

He shook his head. 'It's nothing. It'll pass.'

'Fall in, then,' the knight said. Then, looking around, 'Put on your helm, man! And here,' – bending down, he picked up Gawyn's dagger, tossing it to him – 'you'll need this.'

Standing up, Gawyn caught it and transferred it to his left hand. He drew his sword.

'Down there, you say?' another of the knights asked.

'Aye.'

'Are you sure? I hear screams from that way.' The lead knight pointed on up the slope. Turning round to his companions, he said, 'Follow me. This fellow's talking no sense – must have had his brains knocked sideways.'

There was some laughter, and, intent on hurrying off towards where the faint sounds of fear floated down from above, the man spun round again.

To find Gawyn standing in his path.

'Get out of the way, idiot!' he shouted. 'There's action up there, action of the sort we haven't seen since we left our homes, most of us! Know what I mean?'

Gawyn could hear the leer in his voice.

'Yes,' he said calmly. 'You're not going to see it now, either.'

He had in his favour the element of surprise; out-numbered, it was all he had. He caught the leading knight a blow with his sword that, sliding off the man's helm, bit through the mail and deep into his shoulder, nearly severing the arm. He crowned an unhelmed knight with the flat of his sword, simultaneously stabbing him in the belly with his dagger, but the blade turned on the hauberk and twisted out of his hand.

His sword was too long to be an efficient weapon at such close quarters, and he managed only another few swings before it, too, was taken from him by the combination of one man holding his forearm and another bending his hand backwards; he heard – felt – a bone snap in his wrist.

Then a numbing blow caught the base of his skull, a blow with some weapon that thrust up underneath his helm. He felt blood running down his neck.

He couldn't see properly. They were going, the knights, the one, two, three of them still on their feet jumping over their fallen colleagues and hurrying away.

His body shaking with pain, he fell back against the wall.

He could still hear the screaming. As he lay there, it grew louder.

'I'm sorry,' he whispered. 'I hope you can get away. You and the others.' He paused, fighting for breath. 'Not right, to make war on women. Not women, not anyone who doesn't fight back. Not what God wants.'

He closed his eyes, and the sounds from up the street faded.

Struggling for one more gasp, he said again, 'Sorry.'

Later – much later, it was quite dark – he thought he heard footsteps. There was the sound of slowly-turning wheels, and someone cried out.

Trying to see through the gloom, he watched as two men lifted the knights he'd injured up on to a cart. One of the men came to look at him, peering through the eye-slits of his helm, roughly pulling him away from the wall to inspect him.

He tried to move a hand, tried to speak with a parched mouth and a tongue that had stuck to his palate.

'No point taking this one,' a voice called out. 'He's sitting here in a river of his own blood. If he's alive now, he won't be for much longer.'

Gawyn felt a thump as the man let him go and his head hit the stonework.

The cart trundled away.

It was very quiet.

After a time, he felt his feet grow numb.

Spring 1994, April

On Friday morning Peter phoned to say Saturday's dig was cancelled.

Bryn, who had taken the call and relayed the news to Nina, was smiling, as if the news pleased him. She recalled his remarks about admiring Mark's courage, his willingness to champion the underdog.

'Aren't you disappointed?' she said. 'You were looking forward to finding out more about our mysterious monks.'

He wasn't to be drawn. He just said, 'A bit.'

'Did Peter tell you why he's cancelled it?'

'He said he was having problems with Admin, whatever that means.'

It means, Nina thought, that Mark's campaign is beginning to bite. That someone – the MP, or maybe the bishop – has received their copy of Mark's letter protesting about what's happening at the dig, and has taken action. Got in touch with Peter's Admin, perhaps, and told them to bring their archaeology department in line. Or else.

Or else what? An exposé in the gutter press? Someone earnest on the telly saying how awful it is?

She didn't know.

'He must have made some follow-up phone calls,'

Bryn said suddenly. 'Mark, I mean. Those letters only went out the day before yesterday. I wouldn't imagine that any of the recipients would have registered their protest so soon unless Mark prompted them.'

She had to agree, it did seem incredibly fast work.

'I'll go and tell him about Peter's call.' She got up from her desk. 'He'll be pleased.' She tried to quash the peeved little voice inside that was saying, wish he'd told me. Wish I didn't feel so left out.

Mark's door was open. He was sitting hunched over his desk, absorbed in a thick book which looked like an encyclopaedia. A cup of coffee stood untouched in front of him; she'd made it an hour and a half ago.

She went to stand at his side. Picking up her presence he said, without looking up, 'I'm trying to find out what sort of monks they could have been.' Reading over his shoulder, she saw the book was open at a page dealing with early medieval religious orders.

Both the Carthusian and the Cistercian orders were founded in direct reaction to the decadence which had become endemic in older orders and in the Church in general. A religion in which supposedly celibate clergy lived openly with "housekeepers," and in which men vowed to poverty lived in as much luxury as the nobility, was not to be tolerated by those who yearned for an austere lifestyle modelled more closely on the teachings of Christ.

Skipping the details about founding saints and location of original abbeys, a paragraph further down caught her eye.

The orthodox church's descent into worldliness was also one of the fundamental causes of the growth of heresy. Deeply dissatisfied with the "establishment," men hungry for reform challenged the Church's declarations with their own perceived understanding. When the Gregorian movement failed to live up to its promise of reform, disappointed expectations made men search for their own solutions.

Heresy. I was talking with someone about heresy just the other day. Mark, it was. What were we saying? He told me about some group with a strange name. Cathars.

As if it had been lying in wait, the word jumped out at her from the page.

Such movements as the so-called Albigensian Heresy (from the Languedoc town of Albi, an important centre for the breakaway faith) capitalized on people's need of an alternative. One of the strongest weapons of evangelist Cathars (from the Greek, "pure ones," the name given to senior avowed aesthetes) was to alienate their listeners from the orthodox church by pointing out, quite justifiably, how far the clergy had fallen from the ideal life outlined for them in the gospels.

She nudged Mark. 'Cathars again. You were talking about Cathars last Saturday, on the way down from the dig.'

Slowly pulling himself out of his concentration, he nodded. 'And here it is in black and white. Which goes to prove you can believe every word I say.' He looked up at her, grinning.

'I do, I do,' she assured him. Then, because she was feeling guilty about having disturbed him, she said quickly, 'We've just had a call from Peter. The dig's off – well done!'

She saw a swift joy in his face, but then he frowned. 'What do you mean, well done?'

'The letters! And whatever else you've done. Bryn

says you must have been chivvying them – the people you copied the letter to – and it's worked.'

'I haven't.' He reached out to the stacked trays at the back of his desk. 'I haven't even sent the copies yet,' – he extracted them, waving them at her – 'I've been trying to compose a hard-hitting covering letter.'

'But you said they'd gone off! You told me on Wednesday you'd sent them!'

'I sent the one to Peter. That was all.'

'Then that's what's done it! He's read what you said and either seen reason or else been so afraid at the thought of those other people taking action that he's abandoned the whole thing.'

Mark looked almost angry. 'Nina, don't be idiotic. Stop and think, and you'll see that's highly unlikely.'

'But –'

He was on his feet, pacing between his desk and the window. 'Peter has the authority of his university behind him. Digging up and examining dead bodies is an accepted part of archaeology, and if you think he's going to be shaking in his shoes because of a mild rebuke from a tin-pot organization like us, you're even more naive than –' He stopped. After a moment, he muttered, 'Sorry.'

More naive than I look, she finished silently for him.

She thought, it's only because he feels bad that he can't put the world to rights single-handedly. He didn't mean it, it's just that he gets frustrated. I was being silly, anyway. Naive.

The horrible word seemed to ricochet around in her head, more scathing and hurtful with each repetition.

'Well, the dig's off, for whatever reason.' She turned to go. Then, the pain of having him shout at her suddenly demanding more than a passive retreat,

'You won't have to champion that dead baby any more, so you can go back to your sodding falcons.'

She banged his door so hard that the walls shook. Storming through the outer office, not looking at Bryn, she said, 'I'm taking an early lunch.' And, she added to herself, I may well not come back.

But she did. The faint hopes she'd held that Mark might apologize, however, were to remain mere hopes; his office door stayed closed and she didn't see or hear him for the rest of the day.

As Bryn's watch bleeped the hour at six o'clock, he pushed his chair away from his desk and stood up.

'Knocking-off time,' he said. 'Come on, Nina, I'll buy you a drink.' He glanced at her. 'Two drinks.'

She smiled back. 'Thanks.' There was no point in trying to cover up, Bryn would have heard every word; in such a small building, you didn't have to go to the trouble of creeping about listening at keyholes. Especially when someone had his door open and was shouting.

Bryn trotted down the hill and she free-wheeled beside him. They entered the pub at eight minutes past six, but still had to wait behind several other prompt people who'd beaten them to it: the Friday evening syndrome, she thought.

They put away the first round in silence, and Nina bought another. On the third – true to his word, Bryn had bought her two drinks – she started to feel less miserable. And more truculent.

'I'm *not* naive,' she said abruptly, interrupting Bryn's musings about what he was going to do over the weekend. 'Am I?'

'No more than any other girl in her mid-twenties,' he replied loyally. 'Don't take it to heart. He wasn't really angry with you.'

'I just happened to be there,' she finished. 'I know. I seem to be making a habit of it.'

Only last time, she thought, he *did* apologize. And he didn't call me naive, that time.

'You could always leave,' Bryn said. 'Tell him to stuff his job and his sodding falcons' – he grinned at her – 'and find yourself something that pays you a wage commensurate with your efforts.'

'You mean – oh! Thanks.' Belatedly she realized he was complimenting her. 'Perhaps I should do just that.'

Bryn went on looking at her. She heard him mutter something about pigs flying, then he nudged her and told her it was her round.

Ten minutes later Peter walked in.

Oh, shit, she thought, just what I need! She caught Bryn's eye.

'Shall we slip out the back before he sees us?' she whispered.

'Why?'

'Oh, because –' She couldn't think how to put it briefly. Anyway, it was too late, because he'd seen them and was coming over.

'Hi. I'll get you both a drink,' he said, 'since I came to find you to apologize. What'll you have? Oh, you've got full glasses – I'll put one in the pipeline for you.'

'Still want to leave?' Bryn asked softly as Peter made his way to the bar.

'I'm prepared to reserve my decision.'

'Till we've heard him out?'

'Quite.'

'This is a bit embarrassing,' Peter said as he returned to their table and sat down. 'But since it's only fair that I tell you, I'll make myself look foolish and you can jeer at me if you like.'

248

'Curiouser and curiouser,' Bryn remarked. Nina caught his eye, mutely agreeing; it was hard to credit this new apologetic Peter.

'This is about the dig and why you've cancelled us for tomorrow, I take it?' she asked. Peter nodded. 'You told Bryn you had problems with Admin. Was it – ' She stopped. If she said, was it anything to do with Mark's letter? and it wasn't, it might give Peter the opening to say, no, of course not! We didn't take any notice of that.

'That was only part of the truth,' Peter said. 'The fact is –' He broke off, and she watched as an expression of incredulity spread across his face, as if he found it hard to believe his own words. 'Bloody hell, I never thought I'd hear myself say this – I'm a scientist, damn it, I've been trained to test and test again, not to believe anything till I've proved it, and definitely not to get carried away hypothesizing!'

'The fact is?' Bryn prompted him.

Peter sighed. 'The fact is, half the archaeology department believe those skeletons carry a curse. Like the Tutankhamun business – disturb these bones at your peril.'

Nina's instant reaction – so powerful that she almost spoke it aloud – was, no! You're wrong. Not a curse. They have power, yes, but not an evil power.

She kept quiet. Because if, as he probably would, Peter asked her how she could be so sure, she wouldn't have had an answer.

Bryn said calmly, 'What makes half the archaeology department believe anything so fanciful?'

'I knew you'd poke fun at me,' Peter grumbled. He glared at Bryn, anger in his face. 'Well, just listen to this. We've had the two adult skeletons for a couple of weeks, right? No problem. Not, that is, till we brought the baby in to join them. They're all there in the constant temperature room, low lights, quiet atmosphere,' – Nina could see them, all too clearly – 'and there's – it's –' He frowned furiously. 'I don't know, it's as if there's a presence watching over them.'

Nina felt a long shudder go up her spine.

'And that's not all,' Peter went on defiantly. 'There have been accidents – Gus dropped a Petri dish and cut his hand open picking up the pieces – had to have four stitches. One of the girls slipped going out of the lab – she was hurrying, you might like to know, because she was bloody scared – and she's now at home nursing a broken shoulder.'

'Accidents happen,' Bryn said neutrally.

'Oh, yes, they do. But explain this.' Peter leaned towards them, lowering his voice. 'A cleaner was in the lab late last night. She knew nothing about the skeletons – couldn't have done, she only came back that day from her holiday in Rhyl – and she was so bothered she went and got the night porter out.'

'Why?' Bryn and Nina spoke together.

'Because,' – Peter looked from one to the other – 'she heard a baby crying.'

Baby, tiny, little fists waving. Knees drawn up in pain. Crying. Crying. Cuddle him, croon to him, he won't stop. Crying.

Nina shook her head violently, and the images went away.

After some time, Bryn said, 'What are you going to do?'

Peter shrugged. 'It's not been decided yet. Admin don't believe us – they're muttering about hysteria and imaginations working overtime – and all they're prepared to do at present is to halt further excavations and leave the skeletons where they are till we all see sense and get back to work.'

'And will you?'

'God, *I* don't know!' Peter seemed to be at a loss. 'I've never experienced anything like this before. Maybe it is mass hysteria. Jackie – the girl with the broken shoulder – is the fanciful type, but that cleaner isn't.'

'What about the men?' Nina asked. 'Or is it only the women who are sufficiently sensitive to pick up anything more than a vague feeling of unease?'

Peter looked at her. She had an idea he remembered as well as she did his remarks about women being emotional and irrational. 'Perhaps it is,' he said. Then, surprisingly, 'If so, it's men's loss.'

He smiled at her, and she smiled back. Truce, she thought.

'Surely you must consider whether or not there is really any danger to your staff and act accordingly,' Bryn said practically. 'By which I mean that if they start believing in this curse,' – his tone suggested he didn't – 'then they may subconsciously make things go wrong. They'll be expecting them to.'

'Accidents waiting to happen,' Peter said. 'Not a reassuring thought, in a laboratory.'

'Or anywhere else.' Bryn added.

'Why don't you just put them back?' Nina said quietly.

Peter put his face in his hands. 'Because there are so many unanswered questions. So much the skeletons and the grave goods can tell us, if we examine them fully.'

'And we *have* to have this information?'

He removed his hands and stared at her.

'No. Of course not. The world won't grind to a halt without it. It's just that it's so fascinating. So challenging.'

'You should replace them,' she heard herself say.

'The skeletons and the grave goods belong up there on the hillside. It is their special place.'

She had no idea where the words were coming from.

'They react together,' she went on, 'the power of the place, the bodies and what is with them. They should be left undisturbed.'

Again she heard the baby crying. And the woman sobbing. And, encroaching on those sounds till it blotted them out, a man's voice, loud and deep, hoarse with grief and pain. Saying, Leave them here.

In split-second snatches, she saw shadowy figures. Here one moment, gone the next.

Then Bryn said, 'Nina? Are you all right?' and she was back in the pub.

She took a sip of her beer, and then another. Peter said to Bryn, 'How many of those has she had?' and Bryn said, 'Too many, apparently.'

I'm not drunk, she thought. Or am I? Joan of Arc heard voices, and they burned her. I'd better shut up.

She got to her feet. Standing, she wasn't so sure about not being drunk. 'Sorry,' she said. 'I think I may have had a couple too many. Time I went, anyway.'

'Do you want me to come with you?' Bryn asked.

'No, I'm fine.' She smiled at them both. 'You can't be done for drinking and driving on a bike, can you?'

'Take care,' Peter said.

'Right. You too.' She added, not knowing quite why, 'Watch out for vengeful knights.'

Out in the cool night air she felt better. And not in the least drunk – whatever had been influencing her in the pub, it hadn't been the alcohol. She cycled slowly home, trying to remember exactly what she'd heard. And seen, if the flashes of vision could be called seeing.

The graveyard, carefully tended with clipped grass and a well-maintained wall. Men in black. A woman in a dark robe. A tall man in whose face were the marks of suffering.

A sense of awe in all those unknown people as a wrapped object was placed in the ground.

Leave them here, he said. Someone said. Leave the bodies? The objects? Perhaps both?

And we haven't. The objects are being studied and examined. The skeletons are lying exposed on tables in Peter's lab.

Again, the shudder went through her. For the first time, she began to feel afraid.

* * *

She spent much of Saturday in a despondent mood, attempting to get a few useful chores done but going about them in such a desultory way that in the end it seemed best just to give up.

What shall I do? she wondered. I don't want to do anything.

Yes, I do. I want to go to the graveyard.

What?

The realization shocked her. But as the shock faded, she knew it was right. It was what she wanted, and the only thing that she wanted.

I can't. There's no point – they'll have roped it off. Stopped anyone from going in. There'll be a notice – 'Keep Out, by order of Peter's Admin.' Even if I get up there, I won't be able to do any more than look in over the ropes. No, not ropes, they'll have used that holey orange plastic stuff that workmen put round trenches in the road.

Against the objections scuttling round her head came the impulse again. I want to go to the graveyard.

But –

Barriers can be climbed. Notices can be ignored.

Suppose they've put someone on guard?

They wouldn't. They couldn't afford to pay a night watchman for however many nights it'll be before a decision is made. They'd have to have a *day* watchman, too. Wouldn't they?

Night, day. Which would be better?

Night. Go at night.

Go tonight.

What would be the purpose of going? she asked herself as she sorted out warm clothing. There's nothing to see that I haven't seen already, unless I take a spade and start digging. And surely that's exactly what these voices, whatever they are, have been urging against?

Just go. Be there.

All right. I will.

Coming to a decision brought relief. The rational part of her brain back in control, she was able to convince herself that she was drawn to the graveyard simply because it was, indeed, a special place. And one that might not be available for private visiting for much longer, whatever happened. If the investigations go on and something awful happens – what? she asked herself, annoyed at the drama of the thought – then the whole place will be fenced off as thoroughly as a minefield. If the bodies are reburied, there's bound to be publicity, and it'll no longer be secret and peaceful.

Whatever happens, it won't be the same.

She waited till late afternoon. Then, feeling distant, almost as though she were watching herself perform the actions, she went into her bedroom and put on the jeans, thick socks, and sweater she'd laid out earlier. Stuffing a woolly hat, gloves and a torch in the pocket of her waxed jacket, she picked up her hiking boots from the bottom of her cupboard and went out into the living room.

It'll be cold, she thought, I wonder if this'll be enough? Yes, I'll get warm climbing the hill. *And* cycling out there. How long will it take? Ages, a couple of hours at least.

Then I'd better start out right now.

She couldn't cycle in boots, so she fixed them to the bike's carrier and put on a pair of trainers. She rode quickly through the town, confidently weaving in and out of the homegoing traffic; the shops had just shut, and all the cars seemed to have bulging plastic bags loaded on the back seats. Someone tooted at her, and she was just about to make a rude gesture when, turning to look, she saw Mark's camper two cars behind. He was signalling to go left, down the street that led to her flat. He waved and mouthed something, but she couldn't make it out. She waved back.

She wondered if he'd been going to see her. Well, I'm not there, she thought rebelliously. She hadn't forgiven him for shouting at her, and quite liked the idea of him fighting his way through all the traffic only to find he'd had a wasted journey. Turning her back on him, she cycled off.

Two hours had been a good estimate. She reached the car park by the river a little before eight o'clock. The spring daylight had faded – she'd had her lights on for some time. She realized that she needn't walk all the way up this time – the track was quite adequate for a bike, and, in lowest gear, she might make it almost to the top.

There was nobody to be seen, although she could hear voices and laughter from the pub along the river bank. There were a couple of cars parked, and a trailer loaded with canoes. That was all.

She set off along the riverside path.

Very soon the track began to get steep, much steeper than she'd remembered. She got off her bike and, after changing into her boots, hid it in some bushes, using her torch to put on the D-lock just in case. She remembered Bryn remarking that you couldn't leave anything around nowadays unless it was bolted down. She smiled – it was nice to recall friendly words right at that moment, when the darkness was becoming slightly oppressive.

'Not *that* oppressive,' she said aloud. She could see well enough to walk without the torch, so she put it back in her pocket. Then she continued the ascent.

Soon she was panting, and for some time all her energy was taken up with the effort of climbing, in the dark, a path whose contours seemed to be different from the last time she'd gone up it. It was daylight then, she reasoned. And I was in a group.

Now I'm alone, and it's dark.

She stopped. I'm going back, I don't want to . . .

She heard a baby crying.

Oh, *God!*

She took three great leaping paces back down the hillside, then pulled up. The baby cried again, and she felt a sob rising in her breast.

Go back? Run into that lovely warm pub full of jolly canoers and demand a large brandy?

Or go on, pick up that poor child and comfort it?

The dream image was back. Once more, she seemed to feel the soft-solid shape of a baby in her arms, smell the warm milky smell.

She could hear reason shouting in her head, *GO BACK!*

But reason didn't seem to be capable of holding its own against instinct. Turning her face up towards the summit, up towards the graveyard waiting for her in the dark, steadily she resumed her climb.

Perhaps all this is meant to be, she thought hazily. Perhaps I'm being given a chance to make amends. I conceived a child, and I lost it. Part of me still mourns, part of me still feels guilty, even though I manage to put it out of my mind most of the time.

Perhaps I'm here because it's up to me to get that child buried.

She wondered fleetingly why, if that were so, she should be tramping up here, when she'd do far more good petitioning Mark's list of influential people or chaining herself to the university's railings.

After all, there wasn't really a child crying up there!

But, before that sensible thought could take hold and make her go back, it seemed to be blown away.

She reached the summit, and sat down on the low wall around the courtyard to recover her breath. A damp breeze blew from the west, carrying some quite heavy drops of rain, but she was too hot to put on her hat. It'll stop, she thought. The clouds are going to break up and we shall see the moon soon.

She wondered how she knew. She also wondered, with a shiver of fear, why she'd thought *we* and not *I*.

She leapt up. Sitting still wasn't a good idea if it allowed time to think things like that.

She went along the path to the graveyard. As she'd thought, it was surrounded by a barrier of posts supporting a temporary fence.

She stood for some time, looking into the sheltered enclosure. Just as she was reaching into her pocket for the torch – for there under the hillside the light was too poor for her to see – the last cloud cleared from in front of the moon and the graveyard was suddenly flooded with light.

The beauty of the scene reached deep into her. She thought suddenly, I'm not afraid!, and the realization surprised her. She felt as if people were near, but they were good, and she knew they meant her no harm. She thought she saw a man sitting by the smallest grave, a tall man, hunched over with long legs bent up in front of him.

She looked around to see if there were any other figures, and when she looked back, the tall man had turned into a notice fixed to a stake.

She searched for a way to get over the barrier, which had been constructed with some thoroughness. Climbing a little way up the slope of the hillside made the task less formidable; she managed it with no more damage than a rent in her jeans and a long scratch on the inside of her leg. Smiling briefly, she saw that she'd got over right next to another of the notices; shining her torch on it, she read, DANGER: EXCAVATION SITE, KEEP OUT, and, in smaller letters underneath, the university's address and a warning that trespassers would be prosecuted.

So prosecute me, she thought.

She didn't know what to do next. She wandered across to look down into the first two graves, but they were covered with polythene sheeting which had been stapled into the surrounding earth. Turning to look out towards the path, she had an impression of a small group of dark figures walking towards her. One was carrying a tall cross, and male voices were chanting.

I've seen you before, she said silently to their dark shapes. When I read Peter's report, I saw you burying your dead companions.

I don't fear you, although I don't know why I don't.

She went over to the small trench where they'd

found the baby. It, too, was sealed with sheeting. She clasped her hands on top of the stake that held the notice, and rested her chin on her hands. DANGER. KEEP OUT.

It's not dangerous, not for me.

I want to help.

A deep voice said, *We know. We welcome you.*

He spoke with a strange accent. Welsh?

Then, right beside her, she heard the woman sobbing. Spinning round – for the sound was so close that Nina was sure they must be shoulder to shoulder – she saw a slim figure, clad in black, crouched in grief and leaning against a man.

For a moment he looked right at her. His face was boyish, and his mouth, although now showing the signs of strain and grief, looked as if he smiled readily. His arms supporting the woman held her in a way that seemed to express the utmost devotion.

They were burying the child. Tears on her own face, sobbing even as the woman sobbed beside her, she watched as others put a long cloth-wrapped shape down into the ground, then, grunting with effort, placed four squares of rock in a rectangle.

Then they took up the child, wound in its shroud, and tenderly placed it down in the earth.

She covered her face with her hands, slowly sinking to the damp grass.

My baby's dead. I'm burying it, grieving for it.

No, not *IT*. The words seemed to be put into her head from somewhere else.

Him. The child was a boy.

My baby? A boy?

Yes.

Conception, pregnancy, and a child that was not to be.

This isn't my child, she protested, finding some

vestige of herself. This was a full-term baby, whereas mine . . .

She couldn't go on. The tears overcoming her, she lay down and gave herself up to the grief she'd kept locked away.

After a time, she thought she felt a hand on her shoulder. The touch was light, so light that she wasn't even sure it was there. She felt comforted, all the same. Opening her eyes, she looked back towards the path. The man was helping the woman away. Behind them, almost like a shadow, the tall man watched them go.

She went on staring at the place where they'd walked out of sight. And watching the figure standing there.

He had less difficulty than she'd had in getting over the barrier. But then, she thought, smiling, resentment forgotten, he's got longer legs than me.

She got up and went towards him, and Mark held out his arms to her.

'How did you know I was coming here?'

'I didn't.' He still had his arms round her. 'When I saw you earlier, I was on my way round to ask you if you wanted to come up with me. I thought you must have other plans, so I came on my own.'

'It must have given you a start, seeing someone lying on the grass!' She gave a laugh, stepping away from him slightly – it was embarrassing, to think he'd seen her lying there. Possibly heard her sobbing, too.

He started to say something, then stopped. She said, 'What did you say?'

'I was about to say, what are you doing here? Then I thought you could ask the same thing of me, so I didn't.'

She shrugged. 'I don't know why I came. I just felt I had to.'

He turned to look at her, but despite the moonlight she couldn't read his expression. He said quietly, 'Funny you should say that.'

'Did you hear the – did you hear anything?'

After a moment he said, 'Oh, yes.'

'And see anything?'

'Mm.'

She didn't want to ask him to describe what he'd seen and heard, and he, apparently, didn't want to tell her. Perhaps, she thought, he too realizes there's no need.

'We have to make them put him back,' she said urgently. 'The baby, I mean.'

'I know who you mean. The monks, too.'

'Yes. But . . .'

He said, 'Yes. Still, we shouldn't ignore them.'

There was a pause. Then she said, 'Why were we summoned here?' No, that was impossibly melo-dramatic. 'Why do we –'

'It's okay, you don't have to rephrase it. I think you were right the first time – "summoned" is certainly how I'd describe it. But as to why, I don't know.'

The atmosphere was peaceful. Without tension or trauma, now. She could still sense the presence of the dark figures, but they were remote. She walked slowly round the grave. Once, twice.

Mark sank to his knees and lifted a corner of the polythene sheet.

'What are you doing?'

'Don't know. Just having a look.'

She knelt down beside him and handed him her torch.

'It's okay, I've got one.' He had, and its beam was bigger and brighter than hers. He shone it down into the earth, and side by side they leaned forwards.

The rocks that had sheltered the little corpse had been removed – she recalled that Peter's report had mentioned a sword and spurs extracted from underneath the skeleton, so they'd have had to take the rocks out or the grave goods would have remained hidden. There were depressions in the ground, presumably where the items had lain.

She reached right down and ran her hand along the long line that must have marked where the sword had been.

'Careful,' Mark warned. 'They'll be coming back to do more digging, they'll notice if anything's been disturbed.'

Quite calmly she said, 'Let them.'

She heard him laugh quietly.

She felt, quite distinctly, a hand on hers. A strong square palm and long fingers held her wrist as fast as an iron band. Guided her, moved her hand in a direction against the way she'd been going.

It wasn't Mark's hand: one of his held the torch and he was leaning on the other.

Unafraid – numb, almost – she let her fingers trail along the soft damp soil. Then, feeling a downward pressure, the tips were pushed down, disappearing into the earth. For a strange instant it looked as if they'd been chopped off. Then she felt something. Something hard, and fairly small.

Reaching down with her whole hand, no longer needing any guidance, her fingers closed round the object.

'Gently!' Mark whispered.

Very slowly, she inched it out, letting the earth fall back into place in the little hollow it left behind. It felt cold to the touch.

She knelt back on her heels, and Mark shone the torch on to her hand.

It was an oval medallion, about two inches long. On it was a figure. Black – it was made of some heavy metal – it looked like someone in a hood and crown.

Looking closer, she saw the hood was a veil. And the figure held a baby in its arms.

Her arms. Quite obviously, despite the corrosion and the residue of soil, it was a medallion of the Virgin and Child.

BOOK TWO

June 1994

For some time they heard nothing from Peter. Whenever she thought about it, Nina found herself wondering if the deafening silence meant the archaeology department was quietly forgetting about the whole thing. It didn't seem very likely, she had to admit – much more likely was that they were up there in the laboratory, working away on the skeletons and the grave goods, stoically ignoring psychic manifestations in the interests of the advancement of science.

She carried in her mind an image of that tall, dark figure, crouched over the baby's grave.

I wouldn't like to anger him, she thought. Then, the words forming before she realized what they implied, I'm glad he's on my side.

The Virgin and Child medallion hung above her bed, sharing a hook with a picture called 'Fairy Patchwork' which she'd had since she was a child. She'd asked Mark if he wanted it – it seemed fair, since they'd been together when she found it. No, she amended, I didn't find it – it allowed itself to be found.

She didn't like to think of that firm, invisible hand guiding hers.

As if thinking along the same lines, Mark said, 'No, you keep it,' adding after a moment, 'It was meant for you.'

They'd gone back to her flat and Mark had taken a careful impression of the medal's front and rear faces, covering it with paper and gently brushing a soft-leaded pencil over the raised design. 'Like a brass rubbing,' she said, watching over his shoulder.

'Mm.' When he'd finished, he gave her the medallion. 'Look after it,' he said, his face earnest. Then he smiled. 'As if you wouldn't.'

She hoped he'd stay, offered him a coffee, a beer, a sandwich (was there anything in the fridge?). But he said he ought to go. Standing in the doorway seeing him out, he looked down at her, and the light in the hallway was too dim for her to read his expression. It seemed he was about to make some momentous utterance, but he must have changed his mind: all he said was, 'Night, Nina. See you on Monday.'

Sometimes, lying in bed, she would reach up and touch the medallion, lifting it on its chain so that its weight rested in her hand. Around the figures was a border of letters: M – A – something – I – O, two dots, then, in smaller letters, D something. Then upper case R – O – C and something that looked like a benchmark sign, without the central stroke. A letter like a W, another bench mark, a chip where a letter was missing, then O – U – R. There were more letters round the other side of the border, but she couldn't make them out.

Why have I got it? she wondered. I can't believe I was made to go up there and find it purely to hang it over my bed. She relaxed and emptied her mind, trying to pick up the faintest prompting as to what she should do next. There was nothing.

Except the feeling that someone was saying, not yet.

* * *

Some weeks after she and Mark had made their night visit to the monastery site, two things happened at once. It was towards the end of the university term, and Nina had begun to think there would be no further developments till the autumn – wouldn't they all be preparing to take off for the summer? Making plans to go and dig up dead bodies in some other corner of the world?

Apparently not, she concluded as she answered the phone to Peter, because, almost before she'd said hello, he said, 'I have to talk to you lot. It's about the skeletons.'

She felt as if she'd just seen a nasty accident. Heart racing, she said, 'What about them?'

'Not over the phone!' he hissed. 'I'll come and see you this evening.'

'In the pub?'

'No. Wait for me in your office. About six.'

'Yes, Peter, that'll be fine,' she said to the dead line.

'Who was that?' Bryn asked.

'Peter. He's coming up to see us after work.'

'Can't wait.'

She smiled, getting up to go and tell Mark. His word processor was on and he appeared to be in the middle of a piece about clean beaches. Topical, she thought, with the summer holidays about to start.

'Sorry to disturb you, but Peter just rang.' She relayed the message.

'Something about skeletons,' Mark repeated. He looked at her speculatively. 'That's funny.'

'Why?'

He opened a drawer, extracting a paperback in which he'd placed a folded sheet of paper. Opening the book and unfolding the paper, he said, 'Remember this?' It was the rubbing he'd taken of the medallion.

'Yes, of course.'

'Well, look.' He pointed to an illustration in the book: apart from the places where the medallion's border was chipped, the two drawings matched.

She leaned forward to read the caption. SPORT-ELLE FROM ROCAMADOUR: THE VIRGIN AND CHILD MEDAL WAS THE BADGE OR INSIGNIA OF PILGRIMS WHO VISITED THE SHRINE.

She whispered, 'Where's Rocamadour?'

'France. In the south, to the north of Toulouse.'

'Where did you get the book?' She looked at the cover – *The Medieval Pilgrims*.

'That's what's funny – I was going through some tea chests in my loft last night, looking for something quite different, and I found this. I'd forgotten I had it.' He stared at it as if its presence in his loft was a matter for concern.

She picked it up, inspecting it. 'It says G. Hawthorne on the inside cover. Who's G. Hawthorne?'

'I've no idea.'

'You probably bought it second-hand. I've got hundreds of books that say G. Hawthorne. Well, not exactly, but the equivalent.'

'I know what you mean. Yes, I expect I did.' He met her eyes. 'It is funny, though, isn't it? That it should turn up just now?'

And she had to agree that it was.

'What do the words say? Round the border?' It seemed a good idea to concern themselves with the tangible.

'*Siellum Beate* Mario de Rocamadour, I think.'

'Something of the Blessed Mary of Rocamadour?'

'Yes, that's as far as I got. I gave up Latin before 'O' level.'

She looked at him. 'I bet Peter would know.'

'I bet he would, too. But we're not going to ask him. Are we?'

'No,' she said firmly. 'Not yet, anyway.'

He held her eyes for a long moment, then, turning away, returned to his beaches report. She thought as she went back to her own office, we share a secret. Even if we don't share much else.

Peter arrived at five past six, and Bryn made them all a cup of tea. Peter hardly noticed his; closing the outer door of the office with, Nina thought, an unnecessary amount of drama, he took up occupation at Nina's desk and loosed his opening salvo.

'I can take it that you all swear what I'm going to say will go no further?'

They all nodded dutifully.

'You've probably wondered what's been happening,' he said. Clearly not deeming it necessary to wait for their confirmation, he went on, 'Well, listen to this. We were good boys and girls, we left those damned remains alone while our powers that be thought the matter through to a decision. And they didn't hurry, I can assure you! Do you know what they came up with at the end of their weeks of deliberation? I'll tell you! They said we should replace the two adult skeletons and their grave goods, since we'd already investigated those pretty thoroughly, taken the samples and photographs we need. So we did that, they're back where we found them and they – '

'What about the baby?'

Peter turned to her, face surprised as if he wasn't used to being interrupted. 'I'm coming to that.' He hesitated.

'Go on, then!' Bryn flashed her a smile, and she felt he understood her impatience. Thanks, Bryn, she thought.

'They told us we could proceed with caution,' Peter said, his voice heavy with sarcasm. 'Whatever that meant! We interpreted it as working very carefully, not doing anything without a good reason, and touching the bones as little as possible. We –' He stopped, laughing uneasily. 'God, you're going to think this is stupid! Grown men – and women,' – he glanced at Nina – 'behaving like kids playing murder in the dark!'

'How do you mean?' Mark asked.

'We put the skeleton in a little room off the main lab. It's quiet, whoever was working on the remains wouldn't be disturbed.' He looked down at his hands. 'Nobody wanted to be alone in there. All of us, me included, felt we were being watched. Even with someone else with you, you got the feeling something was trying to stop you getting on. Imagine that!' He glanced at them in turn, his distress clear. 'You're about to do some test you've done hundreds of times before, you're chatting to a colleague about Bristol City's performance last Saturday, and you're trying to convince yourself the scraper in your hand hasn't really just become as heavy as lead, it's all in your imagination!'

'Perhaps it was imagination,' Bryn said. 'You all must have been in a state of heightened suscep- tibility, after all.'

'You're telling me!' Peter cried. 'But all of us? Every single one on a team of five, plus a caretaker who, since he saw what he says was a tall man with a sword, refuses to go near the lab and a cleaner who still hears a baby crying?'

'Mass hysteria?' Bryn suggested.

'Hah! I've never been hysterical in my life, and d'you know what happened to me?' Peter leaned towards Bryn, face working. 'I thought I'd beat this thing – I'd go and work on my own one afternoon, and let them all see that everything was perfectly normal. Maybe then, I thought, they'd stop bleating on about shivers up the spine and feeling unseen eyes on them. Know what happened?'

Nina watched him. He was pale, and there was a tick in his left eyelid. She touched his hand. 'What happened?' she asked gently.

His eyes locked on to hers; for a fleeting moment she thought she saw gratitude in his face. Perhaps people didn't often act gentle with Peter.

'It was all right, to begin with. I wanted a bone sample for the DNA test which, amongst other things, would determine the sex. I only needed a fragment, and I was careful not to take more than necessary, believe me.' He swallowed. 'I – I was cutting a piece from the exposed end of the left arm – if you recall, the radius had broken off – and I was just putting it into the container when someone spoke.' He closed his eyes. 'But it wasn't one of us. Couldn't have been – we haven't any Welshmen on the team.'

Nina whispered, 'What did he say?'

'He said, "Leave him alone."'

Him, Nina thought. *Not it, him. The child was a boy.*

She reached for Peter's hand again, this time grasping it and not letting go. 'What did you do?'

'I laughed, thought it was one of the others geeing me up. "Huge joke," I said, "now let me get back to work." But he didn't, he did this.'

Taking his hand back from Nina – she was touched to see he smiled at her briefly as he did so – he drew back his opposite cuff. Across the wrist of his right hand was a thick red weal; the flesh was swollen and darkly discoloured.

'Jesus,' Bryn muttered.

Nina touched it with delicate fingertips. 'Have you had it X-rayed?'

'Yes, it's not broken, though it feels like it. When it happened, it hurt so much I thought my hand was being cut off – I suppose it was the pain, but I had an image of a heavy sword crashing down on my wrist, and I thought I saw blood spurting.'

'The effect of the pain trauma,' Bryn said authoritatively. 'Does funny things to the –'

'I wish you wouldn't keep being so fucking rational!' Peter exploded.

Bryn looked at him coolly. 'It seems to me someone has to be,' he remarked. 'As I said just now, mass hysteria. As fine a case as I ever heard of.'

'How do you explain this?' Peter waved his injured arm towards Bryn.

'Either something fell on you, which in the ensuing panic you blotted out of your memory,' – Peter reacted so violently to the word 'panic' that Nina grabbed his good hand again, restraining him – 'or you're the victim of auto-suggestion.'

'I'm not! I –'

'You feel guilty about what you're doing,' Bryn went on inexorably, his own voice raised to drown Peter's, 'you said yourself you were at pains to take the smallest possible bone sample. Your mind provided the punishment you thought fitting.'

'Bollocks! *You* try it!' Peter was on his feet, the challenge apparent in every line of his body. 'Come with me now, all of you, and see for yourselves! I *dare* you!'

In the startled silence that followed his words, Nina suddenly wanted to laugh: I dare you, she thought. Like kids in the playground.

But it wasn't funny.

Mark – trust Mark, she thought lovingly, to step into the breach and make the right suggestion – said quietly, 'I think we should do as Peter asks. But I

274

think, too, we must recognize that we're dealing with something beyond our present experience. Something has happened, we can't dismiss it,' – he glanced at Bryn – 'or, at least, we're foolish if we try to. Maybe we should remember the old truth: there are phenomena in the universe we can't hope to understand until we've discovered the rules they operate by.'

'"There are more things in heaven and earth, Horatio, than are dreamt of in your philosophy."' Bryn smiled at Mark, apparently taking the admonition in good part. 'And until we understand, we'll continue to be scared shitless?'

Mark grinned. 'Something like that. Well, do we go?'

Bryn and Nina looked at each other. Both together they said, 'Yes.'

Mark took Nina and Bryn in the camper, and they followed Peter's Ford through the evening traffic up to the university. There were plenty of people still milling around the campus although – significantly? Nina wondered – the archaeology department appeared to have been locked up for the night.

As if in confirmation, Peter said as he let them in, 'There's nobody here. I can assure you, if you hear anything going bump in the night, it's no longer human.'

'He means it as a joke,' Mark whispered in her ear; she flashed him a grateful smile.

The building had a long hallway, along which were display cases containing rocks and artefacts whose significance she could only guess at. Peter led the way up the stairs to the second floor, through big double doors labelled LABORATORIES. Through a couple of long rooms furnished with benches and cabinets, then off through a door into a smaller room.

As Peter reached to put on the overhead strip lights, she said, 'Is it here?'

He glanced at her. 'In there.' He pointed at a metal door with a Yale lock. Crossing to a stoutly-constructed wall cupboard, he was reaching in his pocket for keys. 'I want to show you something first.'

I knew it – he – wasn't close, she thought.

Peter reached in the cupboard – it was more like a big wall-safe – and took out a long object wrapped in thick plastic. Looking up to see they were watching – it's okay, Nina thought, you have our full attention – he removed the plastic and held up a huge sword.

'The blade's almost three feet long,' he said softly as they stared, 'it's top quality, strong yet flexible. The handpiece is decorated in spirals, but the pattern's worn away where it was held – this wasn't some decoration worn for show, this was a soldier's weapon.'

Nina stepped forward, holding out her hand. Peter looked as if he would refuse, then slowly he laid the flat of the blade across his forearm, offering her the hilt.

The handpiece was far too big for her grip: her fingers and thumb nowhere near met round it. Into her mind flew a memory of a powerful hand enclosing her wrist, pushing her fingers with easy strength down into the ground.

'He was a big man,' she said. I see you, she thought, you're standing in the graveyard. She stared down at the brutal blade, her eyes following the inscription. 'Have you deciphered the words yet?'

Glancing up at Peter, she saw he was gaping at her with his mouth open.

'Why do you say that? About him being big?' he asked.

I've met him, she wanted to say. Instead, she muttered, 'It's obvious. The blade's too long for anyone much under six foot, and the handle's too thick unless you've got large hands.'

Peter seemed to shake himself. 'Right. You were asking about the inscription. Yes, we know what it says.' Moving to stand next to her, he ran his finger along under the swirling writing. 'It's in medieval Welsh, and it says, "Carry me always beside you and I'll keep you from all dangers." Or perhaps "hurts", we're not sure.'

'What about this bit, where the writing looks different?' Mark pointed.

'We've made no progress with that. It could be some sort of magic spell, in a secret alphabet. The Anglo-Saxons used to do that, not that they were the first; a sword was found at Lincoln with an inscription in the Futhark alphabet, which consisted of twenty-four runes. It said something like *Antananantanantan*, and it's thought it was a chant which warriors shouted when they went into battle. They believed its secret meaning gave protection.'

'Is this in the Futhark alphabet?' Bryn asked. 'No, it wouldn't be,' – he answered his own question – 'your preliminary report said it was twelfth or early thirteenth century.'

'Right. No, the best guess we've had so far is that it's an ancient Celtic script.'

'You mentioned spurs in the report,' Mark said. 'Can we see them?'

Peter took the sword out of Nina's hands – she let it go gratefully; it was very heavy, and holding it even for a few minutes had made her arms ache – and wrapped it up again, replacing it in the cupboard. 'Here,' he said, 'twelfth-century French spurs, made in the last few years of the 1100s.'

'How do you know?' Mark held one up.

'They have a rowel – this toothed wheel, see? – instead of a prick. And rowels didn't come in till then.'

'A sword with Welsh and Celtic inscriptions and French spurs,' Bryn said. 'Did they belong to the same man?'

Peter shrugged. 'How can we know? But they were buried together, so it's possible. Don't forget that England ruled a vast portion of France under the Plantagenets – that's why we fought the Hundred Years War, in a vain attempt to regain our French possessions after John lost them for us.'

'So you're saying it's quite likely a knight might buy his sword in one part of the kingdom and his spurs in another?' Mark asked.

'Yes. Highly likely. Until Philip II of France won back the Angevin empire, many English knights held lands in both England and France.'

'But the sword is inscribed in Welsh,' Nina said quietly. 'He wasn't English, was he?'

There was silence in the small room. Are we all thinking the same thing? she wondered. We are. We're all remembering Peter saying that someone spoke, but it wasn't one of them. Couldn't have been. They haven't any Welshmen on the team.

Peter put the spurs back beside the sword. 'Now, if you still want to, we'll look at the skeleton.'

Nobody said they didn't want to. We don't, though, Nina thought. Oh, we don't.

Peter unlocked the metal door, put on a low light and, once they were all in, closed the door again. 'We keep it at a constant temperature,' he said.

They stood in a circle round the central bench. Peter folded back the green covering material to reveal a tiny skeleton, the bones brown with age and slightly glossy, as if they'd been polished.

'We've cleaned off the soil,' he said, voice hushed. 'You can see the left arm's incomplete – the radius bone's over there.' He nodded towards a workbench by the wall. 'We need another tiny bone sample because we –'

She didn't hear why they needed another bone sample. He was standing right beside her, towering over her, face dark with anger and light brown eyes narrowed with hate. The long hair, streaked with grey, hung to the shoulders, which bulged with muscle under the mail coat. He emanated such overwhelming power that she stepped back.

He seemed to step with her, as if somehow he was bound to her. Into her head that remembered voice said, *Put him back.*

She said, her voice emerging dreamily, 'Put him back.'

The three of them spun round to her.

'What have I just been saying?' Peter sounded on edge. 'We have to stop this, we're taking too much of a risk by going on. You feel it, don't you? I knew you would, and you do, all of you. Don't you? There's a sort of singing in the air, as if some great generator were humming. And it's – I –' His voice trailed off.

'You must put it back.' Mark didn't sound like himself.

The child belongs in the graveyard, she thought. But there's something else – what is it? She frowned, trying to concentrate, trying to focus on the thought forming in her mind. Him? Is it him? *He* has to be up there?

Aye.

She was smiling, glad to have got it right. 'Why?' she whispered.

She could see the graveyard, but then she was no

longer looking at the defiled site. She was in the courtyard of the monastery, looking at the chapel. 'I don't understand,' she said, and once again she was visualizing the baby's grave.

She said again, 'He must be re-buried, the sword and the spurs with him.'

They were all staring at her. Bryn said, 'Nina, you're – *Nina!* Mark, *look* at her!'

She was aware of them. Could see them, Peter by the skeleton, Bryn next to him, Mark in the very action of stepping towards her. They were dim, though, as if she viewed them through a dark fog. Peter whispered, 'Oh, dear Christ, it's –'

Moving between them, she gathered up the green cloth, folding it around the little skeleton, tucking it in as tenderly as if this were a living baby and she was anxious not to disturb its peaceful sleep. 'Rest,' she said, 'rest, my lovely one.'

With the skeleton covered up, the humming in the air faded. As if its power had been all that was supporting her, abruptly Nina's legs gave way and she crumpled on to the hard floor of the lab.

* * *

Somewhere on the way back from unconsciousness to awareness, she heard him say, *I'm sorry, lass.*

She opened her eyes. Mark's face came into focus above her – he looked unspeakably relieved when she smiled up at him.

They'd carried her out of the controlled temperature room and into the main lab; she seemed to be lying on a bench – she could see a pair of gas taps to her right – and it was uncomfortably like waiting to be dissected.

She said to Mark, 'I'm not dead.'

280

'I know.' He was holding her hand. 'You're quite the opposite, as I've told you before.'

She was glad he remembered too.

She sat up, and saw that Peter and Bryn were hovering behind Mark. Peter said, 'I shouldn't have brought you here,' frowning and sounding cross as if it had all been her fault, as if she'd pleaded and pleaded and at last he'd said, oh, very well then!

'You suggested it,' Mark said coolly. 'Don't get angry with Nina for succeeding too well in picking up exactly what you wanted us to pick up.'

Peter ran his hand over his high forehead – Nina suppressed a giggle, recalling that Bryn had taken to referring to him as 'slap-head'; it wasn't really a moment for laughter, and she wondered if she'd picked up the lab team hysteria. 'Yes, you're right,' he said. 'Are you okay, Nina?'

'Yes.' She squeezed Mark's hand to say thank you for sticking up for me, and he squeezed back.

Peter grinned. 'Sufficiently okay to tell us what happened?'

Not really, she thought. But she said, 'I just felt a presence. He's insisting that we put the skeleton back – he said so.'

'You did, too,' Bryn said.

'Did I?' Suddenly she remembered something else. 'He wants to be back at the monastery, but he can't because the baby's here,' she said in a rush. 'Perhaps he has to watch the baby and the monastery, and he can't do both while the baby's down here.'

'Yes, you could be right,' Peter said. 'And if he – God! Listen to us! What the hell are we saying? We're talking about this as if it were real!' He stared at each of them, his expression amused and irritated at the same time. Then, shaking his head, he said, 'I don't know about you lot, but I can't cope with this. I'm

281

going down the pub, where I intend to have far too much to drink.'

There was nothing else to do but follow him out.

Bryn said he'd go and have a beer with Peter, but Nina didn't want to. Mark drove her home – he said he didn't feel like a drink either, for which she sent up a brief prayer of thanks.

'I'll come up with you,' he said as he parked outside the house. 'You still look a bit shaky.'

Glad I tidied up this morning, she thought as they went in. It would have been awful if I'd suddenly noticed Mark was sitting face to face with my underwear drying on the rack.

He'd only been to her flat once before, but he'd picked up enough to move confidently round the kitchen making tea. He made her lie down on the sofa, and he brought her tea over to her.

'What next?' he asked, sitting down beside her.

'They must put it back.'

'I imagine they will. Don't you? That wasn't really what I meant – I was thinking that there's something very strange going on, and wondering how we might shed a little more light on it.'

'What's strange about it?' As soon as she'd said the words, she realized how inappropriate they were. 'Yes, okay! What's strange apart from having a powerful presence protecting the remains of a baby who died almost eight hundred years ago?'

'What about the medallion? Why was it important that you should find it?'

'I don't know. Perhaps it belonged to the baby. A christening gift, or something.'

'A gift all the way from southern France?'

'Well, whoever put it in the grave must have been on a pilgrimage to Rocamadour! *That's* not strange, is it?'

'A Virgin and Child medallion, a sword inscribed in Welsh and a pair of French spurs,' Mark mused. 'Don't you find that the least challenging?'

'Of course. I just feel that, since it's totally impossible to discover what the link is – if any – then there's not a lot of point in us worrying ourselves over it.'

Mark was shaking his head. 'Oh, dear,' he muttered.

'What's the matter?'

'I was just thinking about Einstein. Picturing him remarking to his wife, I'm sure there's some connection between mass and energy but it's totally impossible to find out what it is so I shan't worry myself over it.'

'He was a scientist,' Nina mumbled. Mark looked at her reproachfully. 'All right then, smart arse, what do *you* suggest?'

He watched her for a moment without speaking. Then he said quietly, 'You believe in this ghost of yours, don't you?' She nodded. 'Yes, well I do, too. I haven't seen him, but I did see something. Remember? When they unearthed the baby's skeleton and I found you there in tears, for a few seconds I got you confused with someone else. Maybe I was someone else, too, because I felt -' He stopped abruptly. 'It's not important. What *is* important is that I've seen enough to accept you've really experienced some sort of contact.' He paused. 'I can hardly credit I'm saying this, but I think your ghost guided you to that medallion for a reason.'

'What reason?' she whispered.

'Perhaps it's like a treasure hunt. You get led to one place, and there you find the clue that sends you on to the next.'

'But that'd mean we'd have to –' She broke off abruptly. Have to set off – together, since he's just said he's as involved as I am and I can't see him letting me follow the trail on my own – and make our way to Rocamadour.

He didn't answer. He just looked at her as if he understood as well as she did the implications of what he'd just said.

Does he? she wondered wildly. *Really?* Or has he stopped far, far short of thinking of the two of us, away on our own, and what that might lead to? Is he just thinking of how impossible it is right now to put this mystery aside and get on with boring everyday life?

He seemed to be waiting for her to go on. Abruptly she made up her mind – there was a major obstacle which seemed to make all discussion of whether they went or not totally superfluous.

'We can't,' she said flatly, 'we haven't got any money.' He raised his eyebrows, and she realized her statement was rather tactless. 'I mean, *I* haven't.'

He smiled. 'No you didn't. You were assuming from my down-at-heel lifestyle and the parsimony with which I run the office that I haven't two farthings to rub together. You're quite right, I haven't, but I do manage to take a holiday each summer. I take my camper over the Channel, which is the major expense – once there, I camp and feed myself. And, since the camper starts to complain if I drive much over sixty, I don't use too much petrol.'

'I didn't mean to pry.' She felt awkward.

'You didn't, I volunteered the information. Can you afford to go halves on the ferry ticket?'

'Yes, but –' Suddenly it was all happening too quickly, and she might in any case have got it all wrong. 'Mark,' she said, with a boldness she didn't feel, 'are you really suggesting we go on holiday together down to Rocamadour?'

'I am.' His eyes on hers, she saw some fleeting expression that was gone before she could identify it. 'Purely in the interests of research,' he added lightly. 'We won't be going with the intention of having fun!'

She managed a smile. 'Perish the thought.'

'What do you think, then? Shall we go?' He'd got up, was standing at the window twitching back the curtain as if he had no greater thought on his mind than whether or not it had started to rain.

In the same offhand vein, she said, 'I suppose we might as well.'

He told Bryn the next day. They spent most of the morning going over what Mark wanted him to do with the various projects that couldn't be put on ice till Mark got back.

When Bryn was back in the outer office with her, she waited for some pointed remark. But he didn't make one – he just said wistfully, 'Wish I was going,' and, with obvious warmth, 'You'll have a great time.'

She wondered if Mark had told him why they were going to Rocamadour. Somehow she doubted it; the medallion, she was quite sure, was still their secret.

PART FOUR

Aidan

Spring 1209–Midsummer 1210

Fifteen

There was one particular part of the pasture land which, since the wild roses had come into bloom in the spring, always made him think of her. He never could make up his mind whether he was glad or sorry when the day's round took him there.

The roses grew in a stretch of ancient hedgerow, climbing exuberantly all over the bramble and the sapling trees. They lifted their soft pink faces to the sun, as if basking in the warmth. Sometimes he would lie on his back, eyes closed, breathing in the scent. Remembering.

Gwenhwyfar didn't venture far from the farmhouse; certainly, never as far as the pasture with the wild roses. Aidan was glad she didn't. With her there, he'd somehow have felt disloyal both to her and to Roese.

As long as he didn't go there too often – and only when he had to, never from choice – he felt free to enjoy his memories. And to keep them to himself.

Looking back, he knew it had been inevitable he'd leave the hermitage. The business with Roese had merely been the flint that set off the fire – because of it, he'd had to face up to the facts of his own nature.

A man who could be so stirred by a woman, whose one touch of her naked breast could create such restlessness in him, wasn't going to be happy in a life of celibacy.

From a distance, he could almost laugh at himself. Almost.

But I was a fool, he thought as he sat under the hedge and unwrapped the food Gwenhwyfar had packed up for his noon break. I talked myself into thinking I'd as good as raped her, and I allowed the whole thing to grow right out of proportion. If I'd told Ranald straight away, done a bit of penance and got it off my conscience, how different things might have been. I probably wouldn't be sitting here now.

Finishing the bread and the slice of cold mutton spread with pickle, he took a long drink of ale from the flask. There was something else wrapped up in the cloth – investigating, he found a honey cake. He smiled. She's pleased with me today, he thought. Bless her.

I'll sit here a while longer, see that the flock settle in all right. I can watch for any gaps in the fence – they'll find them out fast enough, with that stream tinkling away invitingly over the other side.

He had decided months ago that the life of a sheep herd suited him. He discovered that he'd learned more from Titus than he'd have thought possible – enough, anyway, to look after Gwenhwyfar's flock as well, if not better, than her late husband had done. But then, from what Gwenhwyfar said and from his own observations, her late husband didn't seem to have done anything very well.

He'd left the hermitage very soon after the morning when Roese had remembered who she was. His wild flight off into the hills that day had taken him miles away, and, sitting alone in a strange valley when at long last he'd exhausted himself, he'd suddenly re-alized that there he was, out in the world again, and that his main emotion wasn't fear but a tentative excitement.

He had eventually got back to Titus late in the evening. He was still carrying the basket full of Mattheus's supplies and Benedict's waterpepper leaves, although, since Titus was already settling down for the night, neither were of any use until the morning.

Titus had accepted his explanation – 'I had to get away. I had things to think about,' with no more than a grunt. The next day, however, he had suggested – in the sort of tone that made it clear it was an order rather than a suggestion – that Aidan should go and see Ranald.

It had been a bad half-hour. Ranald, who didn't seem nearly as shocked as Aidan had expected, listened patiently while Aidan stammered and stut-tered through an extended version of what he'd said to Titus. I have things to think about. I want to get away.

When it became clear to both of them that nothing more was forthcoming, Ranald said calmly, 'You say you want to get away. Have you anywhere in mind?'

Aidan shook his head.

'Periods of doubt can often crop up in the early years of a life of devotion,' Ranald said carefully. 'Is this, do you think, such a time?'

'No.' Aidan's response was unhesitating. He didn't doubt his love for God, or for His gentle Son whom Aidan had long looked on as a sort of helpful, sup-portive elder brother. It hurt him, that he now felt himself to be in a state that wouldn't be pleasing to either Father or Son. 'I don't doubt my faith. I –'

The words stuck in his throat as if he were choking.

The silence went on. 'If you can't be a little more articulate about what is troubling you, Aidan,' Ranald said, after what seemed like hours, 'then I don't know how I can help you.' Aidan looked up at him, and his superior's troubled frown cut right into his heart. I'm hurting him, he thought wildly, I'm nothing but a bother, to her, to Ranald, to everyone.

'I want –' I want to go, he'd almost said. Run away and never come back. But no, Ranald would *make* him say what the matter was if he announced that.

Ranald watched him, waiting. Then he said, 'Perhaps you don't know what you want.' Aidan muttered something inarticulate. Ranald put a cool hand on his brow. 'Go and pray,' he ordered. 'Sit in the chapel, and let its peace wash over you. You needn't actually say any prayers – just allow God's goodness to enter your heart.'

He rose, and Aidan, thinking himself dismissed, got up too.

Ranald said softly to his back as he set off towards the chapel, 'God will let you know what you must do.'

He left in the middle of the night, climbing over the wall because he knew he mustn't unbolt the gate when he wouldn't be able to secure it again to keep his brothers – and her – safe against the darkness.

He'd have left word for Ranald, if he'd been able to write.

He walked throughout the remaining hours till dawn, then lay down in a hollow in the hillside and slept. Waking some time in the mid-morning, he walked again. He didn't know where he was going – he was heading westwards into Wales, but he had no idea of geography and couldn't have said what towns and villages he skirted as he hurried on.

He had brought a little food with him – half a loaf and some scraps from Mattheus's larder – and there was water to be found in the streams.

Two days later, so hungry that he kept feeling dizzy, it began to rain. It rained all afternoon, the original drizzle turning to a downpour so heavy that the drops hurt his bare head. Then thunder clouds gathered, and as night fell the storm broke as if the floor of heaven were cracking up and crashing down on to the earth.

Some time during the night he woke from his light doze to find that the hedgerow under which he'd been sheltering was no longer a shelter at all – a large section of it had been blown away, he was soaked through and so cold that his teeth were chattering. Swirling water was around his feet. If I stay out in the open, he thought, I'll die. It crossed his mind to think that might be what God wanted for him, but then he thought, no. Whatever it is, it's not that.

He struggled down off the exposed hillside and into a valley. In the distance he could see a group of buildings, and he thought he saw a faint light.

Someone's awake, he thought. Let it be some good Christian soul who won't turn me away.

He ran, faster and faster, afraid that the light might go out and he'd be left in the darkness all alone.

As he got nearer, it appeared that the buildings comprised a small farm: stout farmhouse, barn, byre. The light was in the uncurtained window of the house.

Nervously, he raised a numb hand and tapped on the door.

Almost immediately, it was wrested open and a voice said, 'Thank God! Oh, thank *God!*'

It was a woman. Dark-haired, her face white with anxiety, she grabbed at his arm and pulled him inside, banging the door behind him.

'She's over there, I made up the fire because she was shivering so,' she panted, pointing to a shakedown bed in front of the hearth on which a small shape lay covered with a blanket. 'Help her, oh, please help her!'

Abruptly the woman sat down on a bench, as if she didn't know what to do next.

Aidan went towards the hearth. Kneeling down, he drew back the blanket. A child of about five lay huddled on her side, face pale and sweaty. He put his hand on her forehead: it was burning.

'How long has she been in this state?' he asked.

'She was poorly yesterday, and the fever rose last night. She's been like this all day.' A sob escaped her, and, obviously embarrassed, she put her hand over her mouth. 'I'm sorry,' she mumbled.

He looked at her over his shoulder, smiling briefly. 'It's all right. I understand.' Turning back to the child, he said, 'Did she complain of a sore throat, or say that her head hurt?'

'Yes!' the woman cried. 'Both of those. Crying with the pain in her head, she was, my poor lassie.'

'I need some cold water to bathe her with,' he said, 'and a piece of cloth. Also, some water for her to drink.'

'She won't drink! She's unconscious, see?' The woman's voice was near panic. 'I tried to give her some bread, she hasn't eaten for days, must be so weak, poor love, but – '

'Her mouth is too dry to eat,' he said patiently. 'She needs liquids more than food – that can wait till she's better.'

There was a pause. Into the tense silence the woman said, 'She'll get better?'

He turned round again. His eyes on her terrified face, he saw the depths of her mother-love. Father, what do I say? he asked. If I tell her the child will be all right and it – and I'm wrong, that would hurt her worse than if I hadn't given her any hope in the first place. But I'm sure, I'm quite sure, that this is the same sickness they had in the hermitage. And they all got better, even poor weak Elias. So . . .

A quiet voice said inside his head, she will be well.

Aidan said to the woman, 'Yes. She'll get better.'

He removed most of the sweltering blankets, and sponged the child's body with the cloth wrung out in cool water. Benedict said, he recalled, that fever patients often got worse instead of better when they were kept too hot. The woman fetched a clean shift to replace the sweat-soaked one, and they settled the child down again further away from the fire. Supporting her head with one arm, Aidan held a cup of water to her mouth. At first she made no response but, as he let a tiny drop run out on to her lower lip, she opened her mouth, put out the tip of her tongue and licked the water off. He tipped the cup a little more, and she licked again. Then, eagerly, she began to drink.

When she'd finished the cup, he laid her down and she relaxed into deep sleep.

He raised his eyes to the woman. 'In the morning I'll go out and gather some things,' he said softly. He thought for a few moments. 'I'll need selfheal and lime flowers, and I don't suppose you have any rose-hips?'

'No, but I know where I can get them.' She sat on the edge of the bench, tension apparent throughout her body. 'They'll help?'

'Yes. In a few days, she'll be up and about again.'

'You're sure?'

He smiled. 'I'm sure.' He knew what to do, knew it would help the child recover. He'd done it for others, now he was doing it for her. *God* is doing it, he corrected himself, I'm just giving Him a hand.

It suddenly occurred to him that this might be exactly what God had had in mind for him.

He sat with the child for the rest of the night, giving her sips of water whenever she stirred. The mother, clearly exhausted, lay slumped in a chair, fast asleep.

At daybreak a cock crowed out in the yard. The woman leapt up, face shocked, and as consciousness came, rushed over to him.

'How is she?'

'She's better.' Taking the woman's hand, he placed it on the child's forehead. 'The fever's down.'

The woman turned delighted eyes to him. 'She's much cooler!'

'Yes, but fevers always run hotter at night. All the same, it's an encouraging sign.' He got up, flexing his stiff legs. 'Put some water on to boil – I won't be long.'

Letting himself out of the door, he trotted across the yard and up a little way into the hills. He found selfheal growing under the first hedge he looked into, and he'd noticed a row of lime trees the previous day. It was too early in the year for their flowers to be out, but he thought the buds might serve nearly as well.

Back at the house, a pan of water was bubbling on the fire. There was also a smell of bacon frying; his mouth filled with water.

She greeted him with a smile. 'Are you hungry?'

He nodded.

'By the time you've finished with those flowers, breakfast will be ready.'

He didn't allow himself to hurry, instead preparing the leaves and the flowers as Benedict had taught him, hunting round the well-stocked kitchen for the various implements he needed. At last, with the infusions set to cool on the windowsill, he sat down to eat.

He realized, as he mopped his plate with a thick hunk of bread, that she'd been watching him. And that the laughter bubbling up in her had knocked several years off her – with the strain and the fear wiped away from her face, she was very comely.

'When did you last eat?' she asked, putting another slice of bacon on to his plate.

He grinned. 'About a month ago, at least.'

She sat down opposite him, her face suddenly serious. 'I don't know who you are, or what you are, but you came in answer to my prayers, and I thank you with all my heart.'

Her eyes held his. Swallowing the mouthful of bread, he said, 'I'm glad I came by.' He wanted to say more – to tell her he believed he'd been sent – but he was embarrassed, and didn't.

She'd understand, though, he thought as she got up to fetch him a drink. *She said she was praying, last night, and when I knocked at the door she seemed quite prepared to accept I'd come in answer to those prayers.*

I think I agree with her.

By afternoon, the child was well enough to drink her linden tea and gargle with the selfheal infusion. Looking up at Aidan in one of her first moments of real awareness, she'd said accusingly, 'You're dressed in black! I don't like black,' then gone back to sleep.

The mother, overhearing, said, 'Your robe probably reminds her of mine, when my husband died.

Only a mite, she was, but it's funny how they re-member.'

The equanimity with which she referred to her husband's demise made Aidan think it mightn't have been a great tragedy. 'Was that long ago, when he died?' he asked.

She seemed to have to think about it. 'Ooh, let's see – Nesta would have been three, so it's two years ago or more.'

'Oh.' There didn't seem a lot he could say.

'I'm Gwenhwyfar,' she volunteered. 'Might as well know each other's names, mightn't we? What's yours?'

'Aidan.'

'Aidan,' she repeated. 'My husband's name was Arthur. Arthur and Gwenhwyfar, we were. My old mother used to say what I could do with was a Launcelot. Never got one, though.'

And the grieving widow went off into a peal of laughter.

Later in the day Gwenhwyfar went off to fetch some rose-hips – an elderly neighbour, apparently, kept them and would let her have some. When she re-turned, she seemed to have made up her mind about something; sitting down across the table from Aidan as he set to work to make rose-hip tea, she said, 'I've been thinking.'

'Oh, yes?' He kept his eyes on his work.

'I don't know who you are or where you've come from,' – he began to speak, but she wouldn't let him – 'and I don't want to know.' She'd raised her voice slightly for emphasis. 'I was desperate last night – if I'd lost my Nesta, I don't know what I'd have done.' She glanced over at the child, and again he saw the profound love in her face. 'My life, she is, for all that she's a baggage of mischief at times and much too clever for a girl of her age. Still,' she sighed indulgently, 'my fault, as much as anyone's, for spoiling her. Anyhow, you answered my prayers, or maybe God did by sending you,' – he was impressed by the way she spoke of God as if He were a benevolent neighbour; it was heartening, somehow, to know he'd fallen in with someone who enjoyed such a trusting and loving relationship with the Lord – 'and I'm truly grateful. Now I've been thinking while I was out, and I'm going to make a suggestion. If you've nowhere better to go,' – she sounded as if she were quite sure he hadn't – 'you could sleep out in my barn there and work for me. In exchange, I'll feed you. Might even find you some old clothes of Arthur's, so you look more like an ordinary man and less like a runaway monk.'

His head shot up and he stared at her. Blushing, he was about to protest, to explain.

But there was no need. Her dark eyes were full of compassion, and there was a softness around her mouth. 'I said, didn't I, that I don't want to know,' she reminded him gently.

For a few moments he couldn't speak. After a while, returning to his rose-hips, he said, 'All right.'

Sixteen

Gwenhwyfar's barn was dry and wind-proof, and she gave him a simple wooden-framed bed from the house and some blankets. He set up his little domain in the far corner, behind the rusting plough and the broken hurdles. There were quantities of old hay, which he baled and stacked up to make a partition. He found a lamp, which only needed a new wick to get it working again, and he built a rough table out of pieces of wood.

True to her word, Gwenhwyfar looked out some clothes for him, breeches and woollen stockings, darned but still with plenty of wear in them, and strips of linen to bind them to the leg. There was a thin shirt and a heavier knee-length tunic, and a large weatherproof cloak to go over the top. Arthur had obviously been shorter and stouter than Aidan, but the clothes fitted well enough. More importantly, however, he'd had the same-sized feet; the short boots were made of good quality, supple cowhide, and Aidan considered them a great improvement on sandals.

She proved to be a woman with good organizational skills – she must have been frustrated, he thought soon after he began working for her, that there were so many jobs she knew needed doing that time or lack of strength prevented her from carrying out. She took him over her acres one morning, Nesta hopping along behind picking flowers, and she told him how the farm was meant to be run and what she wanted him to do. She kept sheep, which he thought he could cope with quite well, three cows and some pigs, and there was a hen-run in the yard.

'I'll see to the hens and the pigs,' she said. 'I always did, even when Arthur was alive. The sheep and cows were his concern – not that he ever did it properly, lazy . . .' She called her late husband a name Aidan hadn't heard before. But he had a pretty good idea what it meant.

'I can look after your livestock,' he said. He would have time on his hands, he knew. 'Maybe you'd like me to make you a garden?' he offered. 'To grow herbs and things. I could teach you about medicines, too. Not that I know a lot,' he added, afraid she'd think he was boasting.

'You'd do that?' She studied him, dark eyes interested. 'Diew, I never knew a man volunteer before,' she muttered. 'I'd be grateful. Especially if you teach me how to make people well.' She glanced behind, to where Nesta had sat down in the grass to make a daisy chain. Her eyes coming back to meet his, she said, 'You knew enough. Didn't you?'

The gentle look was back. It seemed only to soften her face when she was thinking about her daughter.

He looked away. 'Right, then. Show me where you'd like your herb garden, and I'll work on it when I'm not doing anything else.'

The amount of work varied – at that time of year there wasn't much to do for the sheep except move them from pasture to pasture, but milking the three cows

301

took him some time, until he was used to it – and he had the herb garden dug out by the end of the summer. He would bring on seeds and cuttings in the winter and the following spring, and he promised her a crop by next year.

'You've a green thumb,' she said.

'We don't know that yet,' he replied cautiously. 'Wait till next year!'

She smiled, but he saw some other fleeting expression cross her face.

There was work to do on the house and the outbuildings; some of the problems had no doubt arisen in the two years since Arthur's death, but everywhere Aidan saw signs of sloppy workmanship and botched-up repairs. When he asked Gwenhwyfar for supplies of materials, she obtained them for him without demur – he guessed she had enough money to get by. Every week she set off in the pony-cart to take her produce to market – eggs, butter, and cheese, the special honey cakes whose recipe, she said, was a closely-guarded secret handed down from mother to daughter for hundreds of years – and more often than not, she returned with empty baskets and a purse full of coins.

He found he enjoyed mending things. At first he tackled only small jobs – a hole in the roof that let in the rain, a broken gutter – but as his skill grew, so did his confidence; before winter set in, he put a new roof on the byre.

Arthur's tunic and breeches became too tight – Aidan's muscles had thickened in response to the challenge of his new life. Gwenhywfar, noticing the stretched and tearing garments, bought cloth home from the market and sewed new ones for him.

The wool of the tunic was fine and soft. She said, as she held it up to him before starting to cut out, that the colour made his eyes as green as the mountain streams.

He wondered if she'd ever remarked on Arthur's eyes.

Christmas was coming, and the house was full of secrets: Nesta had asked him to help her string together a holly garland for her mother, Gwenhwyfar had got him to make a cradle for Nesta's doll. After the child had gone to bed, Gwenhwyfar would sit on one side of the hearth sewing doll-sized blankets while Aidan sat opposite carving the cradle's headboard.

She said suddenly one evening, 'Will you be thinking of your loved ones when Christmas Day dawns and we're all celebrating?'

He paused in his carving, and Ranald's face came into his mind. Ranald was praying, and the others – Benedict, Mattheus, Titus, poor Elias – were kneeling before him. Were they his loved ones? He supposed they were.

'Yes,' he said shortly.

They fell silent. But soon she asked, 'Do you have any family, Aidan?'

He closed his eyes. For some reason, the picture he now saw was of Gwenhwyfar herself, face full of love as she looked at Nesta.

Why? She's not my family.

Then he knew. It wasn't Gwenhwyfar that was important, it was the look. The look of a mother, protective and adoring. His mother had looked at him that way, too.

His mind had raced back, and against his will he was seeing things he'd thought locked away for ever.

He fought the images, but they had already broken through. Before he was fully aware of it, he found he was speaking.

'There was my mother,' he said. 'Just her. My

father died the year after I was born, so I never knew him. He was a carpenter, but my mother couldn't take up the trade when he was dead. She couldn't go back to her family, either, so she used to do work for other people. Cleaning, washing. You know.'

'Why couldn't she go back to her family?' Gwenhwyfar's voice came softly out of the shadows on the far side of the dying fire.

'Her father had disowned her. For marrying a carpenter, see. He reckoned a carpenter was beneath her, her being a wealthy merchant's daughter. My father went to do some work for her father, and he and my mother fell in love.' His mother had often told him the story. 'When her father said she was too good for a carpenter, she told him that Jesus was a carpenter, and then she ran away with my father and they got married.'

He heard Gwenhwyfar sigh, and he thought she muttered, 'Lovely!'

It wasn't, he thought. Not lovely at all. Better for my mother if she'd done as her father ordered and waited to marry a man of her own class. 'She worked so hard!' he burst out passionately. 'And people – he –' The picture was there again, that awful picture of the priest in his boots standing over his mother as she lay on the wet flagstones. The boots were muddy, and he'd just told her she had to get up and scrub the floor all over again.

'Who?' Gwenhwyfar asked gently.

So he told her. About having been hungry all the time, and his mother worrying constantly because she couldn't give him enough to eat, so that when the priest had said he wanted a housekeeper, she'd accepted the position with humility and gratitude. 'We've found safety at last, Aidan,' she'd whispered to him. 'And security, here in a holy man's house.'

But the security had been an illusion. As had the safety – Aidan's mother hadn't understood about the extra duties some priests expected their housekeepers to perform. He'd woken with a bellyache one night – hungry again – and cried out for her. She hadn't come. He cried louder, frightened now, and still she didn't come.

Someone came, in the end. The priest, in a dirty shift smelling of something Aidan didn't recognize. He'd kicked him and told him to shut his bawling mouth.

Terrified, desperate for his mother, Aidan had crept after him when he went. And, through the open door of the room where the priest slept, seen his mother lying weeping.

She'd stayed, he now knew, because life in a priest's house, even with those extra duties, was better than life without any house at all. She'd stayed for his sake.

'What happened to her?' Gwenhwyfar's voice seemed closer. Looking up from the fire, he saw she'd left her chair and come to crouch by his.

He swallowed. 'She died,' he said briefly. Died from the work, the distress, the hunger.

'And what of you?'

'I was ten then. I left.' To be accurate, he thought, he threw me out.

'Where did you go?'

He remembered, much too vividly. Trying to find food, trying to find shelter. Given scraps here and there, enough to keep him alive when often it would have been easier to lie down and fall into the cold sleep that ended in death. Something, though, had kept him trudging on, some faint spark of resistance that said, she endured misery and humiliation to keep you alive! You're not allowed to die now, or her sacrifice will have been for nothing.

He thought of the places he'd found in which to survive one more night, of the nauseating, rotten food he'd grubbed out and, in his despair, gulped down. Of the rare acts of kindness he'd received which stood out like beacons in the general unconcern – not to say cruelty – of those more fortunate than himself.

I'm not going to tell you any of that, he thought.

Then, when he was thirteen, thin as a reed and sick with some summer fever, he'd met Ranald. He'd been sleeping – trying to sleep – under a bridge that forded one of the streams that flowed into the Wye, below the hermitage. Ranald, returning from some mission, had heard him coughing.

He'd seen the black robe and, when Ranald put out his arms to help him up, had kicked out for all he was worth and tried to run away.

Only later – much later – had he accepted that some holy men really were holy. Kind and loving, caring for their fellow humans as God intended they should.

'I found a refuge, eventually,' he said after a long pause. 'I stayed there for six years. Now, I know that it wasn't truly the place for me, because – ' No. She'd said she didn't want to know. 'Never mind. At the time, I just knew I'd found security at last, and people I could care about who cared about me. I was safe, I was no longer hungry. That was enough.'

He felt her hand reach up and take his. He heard her sniff, and then she wiped her eyes.

Her hand slipped away as she got up to kneel in front of him. Wordlessly she put her arms around him, hugging his face against her soft breasts. For some time she held him like that, then, pulling away slightly, she put one hand to his chin, cupping his face and staring into his eyes. Hers, still showing the signs of her tears, were full of the tenderness they held when she looked at Nesta.

Then she kissed him.

They went to her bed, and on the way she looked in to the little curtained recess where Nesta slept. Nesta was sound asleep, and Gwenhwyfar quietly closed the curtain.

She made him sit on the bed, and, as he watched, slowly she took off her gown and her shift. The sight of her naked body, pale in the soft light, fuller than Roese's and with white marks on her stomach, filled him with wonder. Kneeling again before him, she lifted his tunic over his head and unfastened his shirt. He stood up to take off his breeches and stockings, and they stood face to face. Then she smiled at him, and once more put her arms round him.

Now he could feel her bare skin against his, feel the little hard bumps of her nipples, feel the round belly pushing against his groin. She was warmth, she was softness, and the touch of her hands as they danced lightly down his back made him stiffen all the harder.

'Gwenhwyfar, you don't –'

But she shushed him, the gentle finger she put to his lips replaced by her mouth, opening to his.

She pushed him back on to the bed, and they lay down side by side. She took hold of his hand and guided it to her breast, and for the second time in his life he felt soft, intimate female flesh. For a split second he saw Roese, lying in the infirmary, the picture swiftly replaced by Roese dancing, hugging him close the day she remembered his name.

But Gwenhwyfar was moving his hand down over her stomach and in between her thighs, and her own hand was stroking his hard penis.

Roese's image faded as his mind and body filled with delight.

When the rooster crowed in the yard at daybreak, he got out of bed. Feeling him move, Gwenhwyfar opened her eyes.

'Are you going?'

'Yes. Back to my barn.' He smiled, leaning forward to kiss her. 'Better for you to be here on your own, when morning comes.'

She nodded. 'Aye.' She pulled him down to her, kissing him more thoroughly. 'You're a considerate man.'

'Gwenhwyfar –' So much he wanted to say, but he didn't know how to start.

'Yes?'

He stared at her, taking in the thick dark hair swirling on the clean white pillow, the face still blurred with sleep, the mouth that now he saw was clearly made for passion. The outline of her breasts, under the blankets. Desire swamped him again, and he slid his hand down into the bed, caressing her breasts then moving down across her stomach to find the warm, wet centre of her.

Laughing softly, she turned back the blankets and he lay down beside her. She whispered, 'Nesta never wakes as early as this.'

* * *

He had never had a Christmas like that one. Gwenhwyfar had invited friends to share the feast-day, and they brought food and drink with them, as well as a band of children of all ages and a few elderly folk who did little more than sit in corners waiting to be fed, occasionally burping surreptitiously and complaining about their teeth and their indigestion.

Nobody seemed to be curious about him – he heard her say to one robust-looking farmer from up the valley that he was a distant relative of Arthur's helping her out with the livestock. He wondered if she'd have told the small lie before he'd gone with her to her bed.

But he didn't waste any time worrying about it.

There was so much food that he thought they'd make scarcely a dent in it. As well as the vast amounts that the guests had brought, Gwenhwyfar herself had laid a whole table full of meats – ham, a side of beef – with small round mutton and onion pasties, steamed puddings and sweetmeats, and a large plateful of her honey cakes. In one of the few moments when nobody was actually eating, presents were given; he had already exchanged gifts with Gwenhwyfar and Nesta, and been touched to find Gwenhwyfar had had a pair of boots made for him, knee-length.

'I only have this to give you,' he'd said apologetically, giving her the little collection of baskets he'd woven and filled with dried medicinal herbs. She'd whispered, 'You've given me far more than that.'

He imagined she was referring to how he'd tended Nesta.

In the evening there had been singing and dancing, the table pushed back against the wall and the rag rugs rolled up out of the way. The robust farmer had danced with Gwenhwyfar several times, and Aidan saw him slap her bottom playfully. She didn't seem to mind.

When finally they'd all gone home, the last of the sleepy children, the chatty old women and the querulous old men, Gwenhwyfar went to put Nesta to bed. Aidan began straightening the kitchen, picking up mugs and dirty plates, but she came back and stopped him.

She stood in front of him, winding her arms round his neck.

'I do believe you've grown since you came here,' she said, kissing the tip of his chin. Her hand stroked along his shoulder. 'You've certainly grown outwards.'

'I've grown outwards today,' he said, uncomfortably aware of a bloated stomach. He kissed her forehead, lips against the thick hair.

She pulled back slightly, looking at him thoughtfully. 'You were a boy when you came to me,' she said. She was slightly flushed, and he thought she was probably a little drunk. I am, he admitted to himself. More than a little.

She was still looking at him. 'You're not a boy any more,' she whispered huskily. 'Are you?'

He took her face in his hands, holding her firmly while he kissed her, long and deep. Her body pressed against his, eager, demanding. He gathered her up, easily lifting her in arms that now had the strength to do anything he asked of them. He carried her to her bed, where he took off her clothes and his own and, with the single-mindedness he knew she liked, began to make love to her.

In a brief pause when he was neither kissing her mouth nor her breasts, at last he answered her question.

'No,' he said. 'I'm not.'

Seventeen

He knew from the sun that he'd been sitting under the wild rose hedge for too long. He'd eaten his food and finished off the ale – that, he admitted, had probably been what had made him fall asleep – and there was no longer any excuse to be there.

He stood up and stretched, breathing in the scent of the roses. Before any more thoughts from the past could come to the surface, he set off at a trot around the boundaries of the pasture, pausing at frequent intervals to check that the sheep would be securely fenced.

Then he started on the long walk back to the farmhouse.

The midsummer daylight not only lasted long enough to see him home, but, after he'd stoked up his energy with a bun and a drink of milk with Gwenhwyfar in her kitchen, allowed him to complete the day's tasks before sunset. When at last he had finished and was dousing his head in the trough in the yard, the first stars were just appearing.

She came out to meet him as he walked across to the kitchen door.

'Supper's on the table,' she said. 'I've put Nesta to bed.'

'I'll go and say goodnight to her.' He paused by Gwenhwyfar, about to kiss her cheek, but she had already turned back inside.

'Don't be long,' she said. He thought she sounded tense, and, going down the short passage to the recess where Nesta slept, he wondered if the child was ailing. It was early for her to be in bed – Gwenhwyfar usually let her stay up longer, when the evening light lasted so late.

The child was almost asleep. He knelt on the hard stone beside her bed and bent over her, kissing her forehead. Quite cool.

Nesta opened her eyes for a moment, saw it was him and smiled.

'Sleep well,' he whispered. And, even more softly, 'God bless you and keep you safe.'

He wasn't sure he had any right to ask God to bless anyone, but it had become habit. When he stopped to think about it, he couldn't see why God should resent being asked to bless a small child, even if the person who asked it of Him was, as Gwenhwyfar had said almost a year ago, a runaway monk.

Nesta put her arms round his neck, hugging him for an intense second before abruptly letting go and settling down again. Smiling, he crept out of the room, pulling the door to. Living all these months so close to her had made him realize he loved children. Loved this child, anyway.

Another reason, he reflected, why I should not have made a contented celibate hermit.

Gwenhwyfar was sitting at the table, cutting bread for their meal. He went to the larder and fetched a jug of ale, pouring some in their two mugs.

312

He was just reflecting how homely it all was when she said, 'Ivor bach was here today.'

He looked up, the mug to his lips. Lowering it, he said, 'Who?'

'Ivor Gwynllyw. You know, from up Caerleon way.'

The robust farmer who'd danced with her at Christmas. He'd been before. Several times, since Christmas.

'Oh, yes?' he said non-committally.

'Yes.' Glancing up, he noticed she seemed to be having some difficulty slicing the rind from the cheese; it certainly appeared to be taking all her attention.

After a moment he said, 'Keeping well, is he, Ivor bach?'

Her face flushed slightly. Then she smiled. 'Ivor Gwynllyw will do, for you. You don't –'

I don't have to call him bach, he finished silently for her.

There was silence in the kitchen. He thought, this is daft! He said, 'Nice for you, Gwenhwyfar, to have company. Especially when I'm away all day, as I've been today.'

'Oh, yes.' She looked up, frowning, as if recalling with difficulty that he'd had a long day. 'How were the sheep?' She seemed to find the question as ludicrous as he did. 'I mean, the pasture. The fence was –?'

'It was fine, and so are the sheep.' He thought guiltily back to his sleep under the hedge. And to the memory-jerking scent of the roses. Then, leaning across the table to take her hand, he said, 'Gwenhwyfar, what's the matter?'

Her hand clasped his. 'Nothing. Eat your supper.'

He got up, going to kneel behind her and wrapping his arms round her. It was some time since they had made love – somehow, since the roses had come into bloom, he'd had other preoccupations.

313

She turned to him, dark eyes full of pain. Staring into her face, he noticed again the lines that ran across the smooth skin. Raising his hand, gently he outlined them with his forefinger. Then, because her nearness was affecting him, he leaned forwards and kissed her.

She responded at first. Then, pulling away, said in a tumble of words, 'He wants to marry me. Says he's willing to take on my Nesta, says he'll take care of us. He says we're neighbours, near enough, and that we could run our lands together, if he buys out Wilfred Thomas's lower acreage. He says he –'

Aidan didn't want to hear any more; if she tells me anything else he says, he thought, I shall walk out.

I knew, though. Knew she was leading up to something, soon as she mentioned his name.

I wondered, even at Christmas.

He saw again Gwenhwyfar and Ivor, relaxing after dancing, his square hand with the reddish hairs on the back resting familiarly on her bottom.

Gwenhwyfar not brushing him away.

He interrupted her recital of Ivor's intentions. 'What did you tell him?'

'Said I'd give my answer at Michaelmas.'

'That's more than three months away! He's patient, this Ivor bach!'

She smiled briefly, the anxiety banished by a flash of humour. 'Wanted me to tell him on Midsummer's Day, but I told him he'd waited three years and I wasn't going to be rushed into making such a decision in a week.'

He was smiling with her until he was hit by the implications of what she'd just said.

Ivor's waited for three years. She's telling me he's been sweet on her since her husband died. He glanced at her, at the shining dark hair, the healthy glowing skin, the habitually solemn expression which, as he well knew, could soften into tenderness so that she was suddenly beautiful.

Did Ivor bach know that, too?

He pushed away the thought – it wasn't fair to her. I have neither reason nor right to be jealous, he thought. No reason because hasn't she just been honourable enough to tell me the very evening after he's asked her to marry him? And no right because, whatever she may be about to promise to him, she's promised nothing to me.

His rationalizations failed abruptly as he pictured her in his arms. Pictured them together in her bed in the secret night, in the quiet dawn.

He got up, muttering a quick 'Goodnight' as he left the kitchen for the privacy of his barn.

Lying back on his hay-stuffed mattress, sleep was far away. The soft night sounds gradually faded, leaving the darkness to the silent predators, and he felt more alone than ever.

I *do* feel jealous, he thought, whether or not I have any right or reason. I keep seeing him dancing with her, smiling at her, his cheerful round face full of happiness. She's smiling back. They dance well together. They *look* well together. He's older than her, but only by a few years. He has a prosperous air. Good boots, fine wool cloth for his tunic.

Now they're walking away from the other revellers, and he's patting her. She turns her head to look at him, and her eyes don't say go away.

His mind racing on to invent what he hadn't seen, he pictured them embracing. Kissing. Touching.

He lay tormenting himself in an agony of sexual jealousy until, at last, he fell asleep.

* * *

He kept away from her over the next few days and, as if she knew full well what he was doing and understood, she took to leaving his food in the barn for him. He might have wondered if she was displeased with him, except that the wrapped bundles always contained some of his favourite delicacies; honey cakes one day, a jar of mead the next.

It was easy enough to keep occupied for most of the time, and on the rare occasions when the hours loomed ahead with nothing to do, he would take himself off walking in the hills. One afternoon he found he had gone several miles in the direction of the hermitage; as he took a short rest sitting on a rock, he wondered idly what would have happened if he'd gone on walking and turned up at the gate.

It began as an idle thought. But in no time it had taken over his mind.

He imagined them all going about the day's work. Mattheus, sweating and quietly cursing in the hot kitchen. Elias, head in the heavens, poring over his illuminated letters. Did he still suffer from piles? Simon, laughing until he coughed.

Benedict, mixing potions, grinding seeds with his pestle and mortar. Ranald.

Roese. No! He hastily arrested the thought. Not her, she won't still be there. Not after a year.

Do they miss me? Ever wonder where I am, if I'm all right?

In a flash of understanding, he suddenly saw the past year in a different light. Instead of being the start of a new life, he realized, it was the transition from the old one. Gwenhwyfar, bless her, has been a crucial part of that transition, showing me once and for all what I am. What I want from life, what I have to offer.

If she's been using me – it was a thought that had

occurred to him with unpleasant frequency – then I have been using her, too. And if she doesn't begrudge it – which clearly she doesn't – then why should I?

He stood up, clear-headed, happier than he had been for a long time.

As he turned and set off down the path that led back to the farm, the last suppressed thought emerged from the depths of his mind: she has been more honest than I, for she has made no secret of the other claim on her heart.

He had walked further than he'd realized, and the farm was in darkness when he got back. In the barn, Gwenhwyfar had left him a plate of mutton stew – congealed and cold now, but still palatable for a man as hungry as he – a big hunk of bread, an apple, two honey cakes and a jug of ale. He ate everything, wishing there was more – it seemed days since he'd had such an appetite – then went outside to relieve himself and wash his hands and face before settling down for the night.

He was drifting into sleep when she came. One moment he was alone, some vague dream beginning in which Benedict was singing to Nesta, then a movement close beside him brought him back to wakefulness.

'It's me,' she whispered.

'What are –'

'Ssh.' She put her lips to his. 'Don't say anything. Sometimes words won't do.'

He wasn't sure he agreed, at first: there were many things he wanted to say. Wanted to ask, too. But very soon, as her hands slid down his naked body and her mouth closed on his in a kiss that seemed to be unending, his own eager response doused the words he would have spoken. We are talking, he thought abstractedly, our bodies are communicating our tenderness for each other, our concern. Our gratitude.

She whispered something – he wasn't sure what it was – and after that, the only sounds for a long time were sighs of pleasure.

'I must go back,' she said later. 'In case Nesta wakes.'

'Yes.' He hugged her, kissing the top of her head as she lay against him.

'But –'

'But what?'

'There's something I must say.'

He laughed quietly. 'I thought you said words wouldn't do?'

'Ah, that was *then*. Now, I –'

'Now you're going to talk till morning,' he supplied.

'Aidan, this is important.'

He picked up the change in her voice. 'Yes. I know. Go on, then.'

She drew a deep breath, held it for an instant and said, 'I've made up my mind and I'm going to tell Ivor I'll marry him.'

He felt her body tense against him, as if she were expecting some violent reaction. To reassure her, he pulled her closer and kissed her again.

'Did you hear?' she said.

'I heard. I thought that's what you would decide.'

There was a pause. Then she said, 'And you don't *mind*?'

'Of course I mind.' His hand lingered on her breast, fingers stroking the soft skin. He knew, suddenly, that this would be the last time they would lie together, flesh on flesh. It seemed a moment for total honesty.

'You have given me more than I can say, Gwen-hwyfar. You have –' He wanted to say, you have shown me which path I must take or, more importantly, which I mustn't take. But he didn't know how to tell her that without it sounding as if she'd merely been an instrument in his decision-making. He couldn't have her thinking that. 'You were almost right when you called me a runaway monk,' he began. 'Yes, I know you don't want to know,' – he felt the protest in her and stopped her before she could voice it – 'and I'm not going to tell you. Only what you have to know, which is that I had taken no vows and so was free to –' He didn't know what word to use. To love you? To bed you? Neither was right – 'to lie with you. If ever your conscience should trouble you, let it only be troubled with the lesser sin of sexual union outside wedlock, not seduction of one sworn to the Lord.' He kissed her again, in apology – 'seduction' suggested that it had all been her idea which, even if it was true, wasn't gallant. But she didn't seem to mind – he thought he heard her laugh softly.

'Shall you return to your monastery?' she asked.

'No. You've – I've learned, from my time with you, that I was right to leave, and I shan't go back. Well, I shall go to see them, because there are – Because I left without saying the things I wanted to say.' I couldn't have said them, then. I was too confused. 'I shall not become a monk.'

She said – this time there was no doubt that she was laughing – 'I think that's the right decision.'

'Now, that's –'

'Aidan,' she interrupted, 'you have an appetite for the things a monk cannot have – Yes, I'm saying that. But those aren't exclusively the things we've just been doing, now, are they? What of children? You think I haven't noticed how you feel about Nesta? How she feels about you? If any monk shut away from the world has dealings with children, I've yet to hear of it!' After a moment she added, 'She'll miss you, Nesta will.'

I'll miss her, he thought. Perhaps I can come to visit, see how she's getting on? See both of them, make sure –

Make sure Ivor Bach's taking care of them? Yes, he'd appreciate that.

It wasn't a good idea at all. He kept quiet.

She said suddenly, 'Do you think it would have lasted, you and me?'

He hesitated, then said carefully, 'I don't know.'

'I know. Aidan, we've had a year of happiness, and that's a gift not many are given. You came in answer to my prayers, and you saved my Nesta.'

'I didn't, she –'

'Be quiet!' She put her finger to his lips, and the gesture turned into a caress. 'You, a holy man, to question someone's faith in the power of prayer!'

'I didn't, I only meant that –'

'I know what you meant. What I'm trying to say is that I felt such gratitude to you that when you told me about yourself – remember that night?' He nodded. He thought, how could I forget? 'When you were sad, because you'd been thinking of things that hurt, I wanted to comfort you, and I did it the only way I knew how.'

He closed his eyes, remembering.

'But, Aidan, I'm older than you, and in time this,' – she pushed back the covers, indicating the generous curves of her body – 'this would no longer appeal to you. Maybe I'll have more children, acquire a few more of these marks, a few more handfuls of flesh, and – ' She paused, looking into his

320

face. 'Not a child of yours,' she said gently. 'At least, I doubt it.'

He wasn't sure he understood. 'How do you know?'

'I was not pregnant when I came to your bed tonight. It's not likely that I shall have conceived – when I wanted to start with Nesta, the midwife told me the best time was halfway between your courses.'

Now there wasn't any doubt: he knew he didn't understand. So, in the concealing darkness that made it easier to ask, he said, 'What do you mean?'

She told him. In more detail than he'd expected – than I need, he thought at one point – she told him exactly what she meant.

He couldn't help but wonder, as at last she finished, whether Benedict knew as much about women as he now did.

He made love to her again before she left him. It was touching, the way she'd spoken so dismissively about her lovely body which gave him so much pleasure; although the thought never fully formed (he couldn't think and make love at the same time), he realized afterwards that he'd had in mind to reassure her. To say mutely, I don't think the time would ever come that I'd not find you comely. He guessed she understood; afterwards, her tears wet on his chest, she'd said, 'Thank you.'

When he was alone, he thought about her with Ivor Gwynllyw. Even about her bedding Ivor Gwynllyw. It didn't hurt quite so much, now.

She's right, he reflected. Right to imply that our year together is enough. Not because I would tire of her – even in her absence, he still couldn't imagine tiring of her – but because I would not make her as good a husband as Ivor. He has wealth, position, land. He can offer the security of a man who has made his mark in the world, whereas I have nothing but my youthful body – he smiled at himself – and a willingness to work. She's right to choose Ivor, both for herself and for Nesta. He'll do what he's undertaken to do – he'll look after them.

A direct woman, Gwenhwyfar had decided to tell Ivor Gwynllyw straight away rather than make him wait until Michaelmas. Nothing coy about her, he thought, she's not the sort to keep a man waiting in suspense just to make him all the more grateful when she finally accepts him.

'I think it would be best if I leave,' he said to her the evening before she was to go into market; she usually seemed to meet up with Ivor on market days. 'He might want to come back here with you to celebrate.'

She looked at him, arching her eyebrow, and he burst out laughing. 'None of that!' he said affectionately.

'No, indeed,' she agreed, 'not until the wedding band is on my finger!'

'Gwenhwyfar, shall I go? Today?'

She appeared to hesitate. 'Perhaps that would be for the best. I was going to leave Nesta with you, but I could take her with me. She enjoys market day.' Her eyes met his. 'I told him you were one of Arthur's relatives. Helping out, like.'

He didn't look away. He watched as the humour spread across her face once more. 'I did that, didn't I?'

The laughter faded, and she sighed. 'Oh, yes.'

Then she turned away.

Eighteen

He returned to the hermitage late in the afternoon, a day or so after Midsummer Day. Even had he not been thinking of her, she would have sprung into his mind as he walked in through the gate: in the still, sun-drenched courtyard, the scent of the roses seemed to hover like a tangible presence.

He stood for a moment, breathing in the atmosphere.

In the infirmary, Benedict was singing. Aidan remembered a day, more than a year ago, when the rich baritone voice had been joined by a light soprano which soared above it.

He crossed the courtyard and stood on the threshold. Benedict, his back to the door, was bending over his workbench.

'Come in or go out,' he said, breaking off the song, 'you're blocking the light!'

Aidan smiled, about to step aside. Then, changing his mind, he stayed put.

A twelvemonth, it appeared, hadn't been long enough to improve Benedict's patience by any significant amount: spinning round, a thunderous frown on his face, he shouted, 'Didn't you hear? How can a man be expected to –'

Then he saw who it was.

'Let me look at you,' he said as the shock faded. Hands on Aidan's shoulders, he studied him closely. 'Hm. You've grown, boy, I swear it.' He punched Aidan's arm. 'Put on muscle, too. What've you been doing?'

'This and that,' Aidan replied. Force of habit – for surely he was no longer answerable to Ranald – made him feel he should give the first detailed account of himself to the leader of the community.

'Labouring?'

'Yes.'

'Out in the good fresh air?'

'Oh, yes.'

Benedict frowned – it was perfectly obvious his curiosity was far from satisfied – but then his face cleared. 'Aye, well, no doubt we'll be hearing all about it, as the days pass. You are coming back to us, aren't you?'

'I –' Aidan hesitated. Then, looking into Benedict's eyes, full of affection and happiness, he found he couldn't lie to him. 'No, Benedict. I'm not.'

'But –'

Aidan put a hand on his arm. He said gently, 'I think I should speak to Ranald first, don't you?'

Benedict, head on one side, gave him a considering look. 'Only a year, it's been,' he said, half to himself. 'Yet you've grown out of boyhood, Aidan.' Then he smiled. 'Aye. You're right. Go and find Ranald.'

'Where is he?'

Benedict's expression grew grave. 'You'll find him in the near pasture.'

'He's out with Titus?' Aidan was eager to see Titus again – apart from anything else, he wanted to tell him all about Gwenhwyfar's sheep and how he'd acquitted himself as her sheep herd. He also had a couple of questions to ask about liver fluke.

'Aidan, Titus is dead,' Benedict said quietly.

'Dead? But he was strong! He didn't catch the fever when you others did, he was –'

He'd almost said, he was invincible. But no man was invincible.

Instead he asked, 'How did he die?'

'He fell. February, it was, in the snows. He went out looking for a lost ewe, and as he was bringing her in to shelter, he slipped. Broke his hip.' Benedict frowned ferociously, turning away. 'Bad break,' he muttered, 'couldn't do much for him. Lying there, having to keep still because it pained him so to move, his lungs filled up. Couldn't breathe, in the end. The fever saw him off.'

Aidan remembered Titus kneeling on the chapel floor, in vigil beside the trestle on which they'd put Roese. He never complained, he thought, not about painful knees, not about anything. He imagined the old man lying in the infirmary, suffering in silence as his breath grew shorter and shorter.

'Poor Titus,' he said.

'Aye,' Benedict sighed. 'May God keep him safe in His care.'

'Amen.' Aidan paused respectfully, then, reflecting that the practical Benedict would be the first to remark that life must go on, said, 'So Ranald is minding the flock?'

'Aye. He says he's the obvious choice – the rest of us, according to him, can be less easily spared from our usual tasks than he can.'

'How are the others? Well?'

'Well enough. Mattheus is the same as always, possibly a little more irascible,' – Hark who's talking! Aidan thought – 'Simon is all right as long as he does nothing very arduous, since anything energetic brings on his cough, and Elias is – Elias is still Elias, only more so.'

Aidan smiled, understanding perfectly.

Another name hung in the air between them. But she, too, Aidan thought, is a matter for Ranald.

'I'll go and find him, then,' he said.

Benedict nodded; Aidan knew quite well the infirmarer didn't think he was about to search out Elias.

Before he turned westwards out into the hills, he went along the path a short way in the other direction and found the new grave in the graveyard. For a few quiet moments he stood over the plot where Titus lay, then he set off to find Ranald.

From some distance off he could make out the tall black-robed figure; Ranald was standing on a rocky outcrop, hand shading his eyes, staring into the west. The sheep were dotted across the pasture, grazing unconcernedly; Ranald, Aidan thought, didn't seem to be over-burdened by the sheep herd's lot.

What wind there was came from the south-west, obscuring any sounds Aidan made as he approached. Ranald was still gazing into the distance when Aidan, standing just below him, said, 'Hello, Ranald.'

He turned. As he dropped his arm, Aidan saw his face, and watched as the expression flew from amazement to a brief flash of joy. Then, looking down so that he didn't miss his footing, Ranald stepped off his rock.

'Aidan,' he said. 'Welcome.'

Aidan was just thinking, with a disappointment that surprised him, that it was a somewhat muted reaction for the Prodigal Son when suddenly Ranald put his arms around him and held him in a brief hard hug.

326

Releasing him, he said in his usual calm tone, 'You knew where to find me, so you have obviously been to the hermitage. You will have been informed of how we fare, and of the death of Titus?' – Aidan nodded – 'So now, if you will, it is time for you to return the favour. Tell me what you have been doing.'

It was as close to an order as Ranald ever gave. They sat down side by side on Ranald's rock, and obediently Aidan began his account of the last year.

He thought perhaps Ranald would let him get into his stride before he asked any questions – particularly any awkward ones – but he was wrong. When he'd got only as far as climbing over the hermitage wall and setting out in the darkness, Ranald said, 'You did not think to come and tell me you were going?'

'I thought about it, yes.' I wanted to, he added silently, only I was afraid you would press me to tell you why. And I couldn't.

Ranald watched him. Then, nodding slowly, he said, 'Go on.'

Aidan described coming across the farm, Gwen-hwyfar crying that he had been sent in answer to her prayers, tending Nesta. Staying on.

When he came to what had happened at Christmas, he dried up.

Ranald sat patiently for some time, waiting for him to continue. When he didn't, Ranald remarked, 'Sometimes a storyteller has to pause in his narrative in order to fill in some information he should have given at the start. Perhaps, Aidan, it is this that is holding you up.'

Aidan shot him a glance – could there have been a clearer hint that Ranald knew exactly what was coming next? – but Ranald's face was impassive.

Now is the time, Aidan thought. I'm still carrying

something on my conscience that I should have shed a long time ago.

Briefly he thought back to the terrified boy he'd been, who had touched – with innocent curiosity, he now knew, not with lust – the breast of an unconscious woman. Who had suffered torments of shame, who had been unable to rid his memory of that lovely sight.

Who, unable to come to terms with his guilt, his nature or his feelings for the living woman, had run away.

'There's something I should have told you a long time ago,' he said. 'It was the day we brought Roese in, when we realized she wasn't dead after all and took her to the infirmary to put the warmth back in her. I was standing by her when Benedict took off the last of her garments,' – he remembered the long strips of linen that she had worn, and briefly wondered again why she'd been disguised as a boy – 'and I saw her when she was revealed as a woman.' He drew in his breath. 'I touched her breast.'

He'd said it. The world hadn't been riven in two, the heavens hadn't fallen. But, although he was now rational about the whole thing, perfectly able to see it for what it was, still he felt a tremendous sense of relief.

Which quickly turned to shock as Ranald said quietly, 'I know.'

He knew! He must have seen, must have watched me through my agonies of guilt as I did everything I could to keep away from her. Waiting all the time for me to go to him and confess.

Instead I ran away.

'You must think I'm very weak,' he muttered.

'Why should I think that?'

'I couldn't face you. I ran away.'

Ranald paused, as if considering carefully what to say. 'I did not think you weak then. I certainly do not now.' Aidan detected a slight lightening in his tone. 'You were presented with something you could not cope with, and, quite naturally, you were afraid. No doubt you thought that if you told me, I would send you away.'

Aidan thought, no. I never thought that. 'I thought it meant I wasn't suitable for a celibate life,' he said, 'and that scared me, because I didn't think I could live out in the world again.'

'Understandably. Your youthful experiences made a deep scar, and you believed the world to be a fearful place.' Ranald leaned towards him, his face earnest. 'But, Aidan, I admitted you to the hermitage because you needed a refuge. Not because I expected you to become a celibate hermit.'

Aidan let the words sink in. When he was quite sure he'd understood correctly, he said, 'You didn't expect that?'

And Ranald said, 'No.'

Aidan's astonishment slowly faded. Eventually he said, 'What would you have done if I'd said I wanted to take my vows?'

Ranald smiled. 'You didn't.' Aidan thought he'd finished, but after a moment he said, 'And, besides, what vows?'

'The ones monks take!' Aidan said, surprised he should ask. 'Celibacy, poverty and obedience.'

'Monks take them, yes,' Ranald agreed. 'But we are not monks. Are we?'

'But –'

'Have you ever known anyone take vows in the hermitage?'

'No, but I suppose I thought you'd already taken them, you and the older ones.'

'And what of Elias? He joined us after you, didn't he?'

'Yes. I never thought about him taking his vows – maybe I assumed he'd come from somewhere else, some other community, and he took them there.'

Ranald shifted his position slightly, as if getting more comfortable, then said, 'How much did you know about monastic orders when you came to us?'

Aidan laughed. 'Precious little!' The laughter froze as he remembered. 'I knew about priests, though.'

Ranald bowed his head. 'Yes, I know. Do not think about him, now. What I am saying is that, in your inexperience, you assumed we were monks; not a particularly devout boy, you –'

'I'm sorry.'

Ranald touched his sleeve. 'There is no need to apologize, I am merely making an observation. You were not devout in the way, let us say, of Elias, or of Paul.'

'Paul heard voices,' Aidan interrupted, remembering the pale, thin young man who had died two years ago.

'Quite. Since you were not devout, like them, you were happy to jog along in your life at the hermitage, not concerning yourself with questions of vocation or of faith, assuming that, one day, you would be required to make some sort of commitment and, without thinking about it overmuch, would do so. Until something happened to shake up that neat and tidy plan, such as it was, and turn it upside down.'

Aidan had been on the point of asking, if we're not monks, what are we? But Ranald had just offered him the opening he'd been waiting for, and he leapt into it.

'It was my feelings for Roese that turned everything upside down,' he said quietly. 'I couldn't stop thinking about her. That's why I went away, because she'd been brought to our door for help, not for me to – Not for me. But I realized I was a –' A normal man, he was going to say. But that would sound as if he were implying that Ranald wasn't a normal man. 'That I liked women,' he said instead. Then it was easy. 'I lay with Gwenhwyfar. Many times. And it was – I was –' He trailed to a stop.

'You cannot imagine going through the rest of your life without lying with a woman again,' Ranald finished for him. Then the dark blue eyes fixed on Aidan, and once again Ranald was back in the role of leader, taking upon himself the spiritual well-being of his little community. 'You have been in sexual union with a woman to whom you are not wed,' he said neutrally. Aidan wondered if he was going to impose a penance. But he continued on an unexpected tack. 'And now you have come back to us. Unless we are to assume that this is only a brief visit, it means you have abandoned the lady.'

'No!' Aidan said emphatically. And he told Ranald about Ivor Gwynllyw.

He was almost certain that, at one point, Ranald suppressed a laugh.

'There's something else,' he said when the whole tale of Gwenhwyfar was out in the open.

'Yes?'

'Just now you said I'd come back to you. I haven't. I mean, I want to be here – for the time being, anyway – but I don't – I can't –'

'You don't want to live in a celibate community. You don't want to take any of these non-existent vows.'

'No. That's right.' He knew Ranald was amused, but resisted the temptation to respond in kind.

Ranald had another long thinking pause. Then he said, 'Aidan, do you think I make a good sheep herd?'

Aidan ran an eye over the flock and around the perimeters of the pasture. 'Yes,' he replied.

'Thank you. And do you think I make a contented sheep herd?'

Aidan glanced at him, and saw vexation struggling with amusement in the lean face. He saw in a flash what Ranald was trying to say.

'No, I don't imagine you do.' He wondered if what he had in mind to say next might be construed as disrespectful, but decided to say it anyway. 'I imagine you wish you were back at the hermitage, meditating in your cell, or sitting in the chapel, or doing whatever it is community leaders do all day.'

'Ha!' The laugh was brief. 'Indeed I do. But were I to indulge that wish, who would look after the sheep in my stead?'

Aidan paused, deliberately and unnecessarily. Then he said, 'Me?'

And Ranald replied, 'I was beginning to think you were never going to offer.'

They walked back to the hermitage together. Ranald remarked casually that, even though Aidan would not be one of the community, he might care to attend the occasional office. It was, Aidan reflected, another of those suggestions that carried the force of a command.

He would live in Titus's hut, collecting his supplies from Mattheus, cared for, should he ever need it, by Benedict. 'You will be of us, but not bound to us,' Ranald said. 'And, of course, free to go whenever and wherever you please without leave from me.'

Where would I go? Aidan wondered as the conversation lapsed while they fell into single file to negotiate an outcrop of rock. There's only one place I want to be, other than here with Ranald and the others. And I have no idea where that place is. Neither Benedict nor Ranald has given me the slightest clue – nobody's even mentioned her name, except me.

For the last couple of miles back to the hermitage, they spoke of lambing, the cultivation of herbs, the treatment of fevers and the best way to put a new roof on a barn.

Only when the walls and the gate finally came into view did Aidan take his courage in both hands and say, 'Ranald, do you know where Roese is?'

Ranald didn't seem surprised – he's probably been expecting the question ever since I turned up in the pasture, Aidan thought. Not breaking his stride, not even turning to look at Aidan, he said calmly, 'Yes.'

Their crossing was in the middle of the night, when the fare tariff was cheapest. On the ferry he showed her the road they'd be taking, the autoroute which curved out eastwards to Reims and avoided having anything to do with Paris and the boulevard Périferique: even in the middle of the night, Mark said, it'd be too busy for comfort.

Late in the evening they stopped in a rest area between Dijon and Lyons. After they'd had supper – provisions they'd brought from home – he showed her how the camper's daytime sofas converted to a big bed; a second one was revealed when the roof was raised. He offered her the choice, and she took the upper one. There were loos, basins and showers in a sort of blockhouse next to the car park; the water was tepid, but she didn't mind. She took her nightshirt with her and changed in the lavatory: she'd bought the garment specially, an elongated T-shirt with elbow-length sleeves and a picture of Woody Woodpecker on the front. It was the most unseductive piece of nightwear she'd ever come across – I'm not, she'd thought, having him think I'm after anything he doesn't want. Even if I am.

But, no matter how businesslike and platonic they

were being – he is, anyway, she thought, and I'm taking my cue from him – still there was a sense of strain as he slid the camper door closed and got into bed; like her, he'd got changed in the washroom. She didn't like to look too closely, but he seemed to be wearing navy pyjamas, as sexless as Woody Woodpecker. It felt most peculiar to be lying up in her comfortable bunk, only feet away from him; she didn't want to investigate in what way it felt peculiar. As he turned out the dim light, he said calmly, as if he did this sort of thing all the time (perhaps he did), 'Goodnight, Nina. Sleep well.'

She lay awake for some time, listening to his even breathing; it sounded as if he'd gone straight to sleep. He must be tired, she thought, he's been driving all day and we were up all night. She wondered why she should feel so wide awake, when she was equally worn out.

It's because this is all so weird, she thought, trying to turn over quietly. Here I am with a man whom I've liked – she found herself hurrying over the word 'liked', not wanting to give her subconscious time to substitute anything stronger – for simply ages. Who sometimes seems to like me too, but then draws back into himself and seems as distant as Pluto. Who can kiss me with apparent pleasure one day, then the next shout at me as if I were a total imbecile.

And who suggested we come on this holiday which, although we're being so careful to refer to it as some sort of task we're compelled to do, still involves the two of us being thrown into intimate proximity for a fortnight.

Even in the warm air, she felt herself shiver.

A fortnight, she thought, beginning to feel drowsy at last. If I can't encourage the liking – damn it, the *kissing* – side of him in the course of a fortnight in a camper, I'd better give up and take a permanent vow of celibacy.

Smiling, she let herself drift into sleep.

The next day was even hotter than the first. She noticed regular displays on gantries over the road showing the time and the temperature: twenty-nine degrees, thirty, thirty-one.

It gave her pleasure to read the names on the boards. Valence. Avignon. Nîmes. Montpellier. Leaning forwards to let a current of air dry the sweat on her back, she thought vaguely, how uncomfortable you'd be on horseback in this heat, sun beating down on your armour.

Mark pushed the camper beyond the sixty he'd said was its maximum; she noticed the speedometer was closer to eighty. It seems slow, she thought, compared to the speed they're going in the fast lane. Then – for he was demonstrating a remarkable ability to pick up such thoughts – she added, but all those BMW and Merc passengers won't be seeing nearly as much of the scenery.

At Lyons they turned west for Clermont Ferrand, circumnavigating the town as quickly as traffic allowed: down in a valley with the extinct volcanoes of the Auvergne all around, it seemed to be gasping for breath in the humid airlessness. South-west to Brive, ignoring the many signs pointing left towards the holiday delights of the Dordogne, then due south to Rocamadour.

'I thought,' he said when they were only a few miles away, 'we'd find a camp site and settle in this evening, then tackle the town tomorrow.'

'Fine.'

'It's not high season yet – the French don't take their *vacances* till August, and the English schools haven't broken up yet – but all the same, it'll be crowded. It always is.'

'It always was,' she said automatically. Then, 'I mean, it's a pilgrimage site, isn't it? There would always have been heaps of people.'

'Right.' She thought he looked at her strangely. 'Anyway, I suggest we make an early start in the morning, then we might have an hour or so with it relatively quiet.'

'Fine,' she said again.

There was a village called L'Hospitalet above the town, and outside it several camp sites. They found space in a field under olive trees, and Mark opened out an awning from the side of the camper, securing it with tent pegs.

'We may as well be comfortable,' he said. 'We'll be here a day or two.'

She hadn't thought beyond Rocamadour. She wondered what he had in mind to do next. I could make some suggestions, I suppose, she thought as she filled the kettle for a cup of tea, only I've never been to southern France before. Perhaps – the thought had leapt into her mind before she could stop it – I'll suggest we head for the sea and lie on the beach all day rubbing sun-tan oil on to each other's near-naked bodies.

She watched him banging in the last tent peg. His shirt had ridden up, revealing his lower back. As he moved, the muscles moved over his ribs. He's far too thin, she thought, he ought to . . .

It's nothing to do with me.

But, against her will, she imagined how it would feel, rubbing oil into that lean body. As if he'd felt the thought – liked it? – suddenly he straightened up and smiled at her.

'All right?'

'Yes.' No, I'm not. I want to hug you, you idiot.

He came across to her, dusting his hands on his jeans. For a long moment he looked down into her eyes, then, turning away, said, 'Let's go and buy our supper.'

In the village there was a delicatessen, where they bought a baguette, large chunks of both bleu d'Auvergne and a promisingly runny Camembert, pâté and tomatoes for supper. Mark selected a bottle of Minervois, and one of pastis to whet the appetite. She picked out two slices of some extravagant gâteau from the shop next door: the nice woman behind the counter threw in the one remaining slice free of charge. Nina's 'A' level French stood up to translating her remark: I won't sell the last bit now, so you can have it.

When they'd eaten and cleared away – Mark said two people in a camper had to keep clearing up, and after only a couple of days she could see his point – they went for a walk along the top of the gorge; standing on the rough path, they gazed ahead to where Rocamadour clung in apparent defiance of gravity to its cliff-face.

'The pilgrims used to go right down to the bottom of the gorge and approach the Holy City from below,' Mark said, binoculars to his eyes.

'They climbed the Great Stairway on their knees,' she added.

'Oh, have you been reading it up too?' He seemed pleased.

'No, I just –' She stopped. 'I must be thinking of somewhere else.'

He patted the top of her head. 'Too much sun,' he said kindly. 'You're all the same, you fair-skinned people. Half an hour in the heat and you've gone irredeemably *troppo*.'

She moved towards him and briefly he put his arm round her waist. It was a moment of sweetness; too soon, he disengaged himself and lifted the binoculars again.

She felt a brief flash of anger. What's wrong with me, she wanted to shout, no longer kissable? No longer the Nina who lights up your days?

No, she thought wearily. I've no right to be so demanding. No right to be demanding at all. And if I was, if I came right out with it and said what I want, he might well tell me, kindly but oh so firmly, that I'd got the wrong idea entirely, that he didn't feel that way about me at all. Then I'd lose him, and I'd be unhappy.

But you're not happy now, reasoned a voice in her head. So what have you got to lose?

Standing so close to him, the impossible beauty of Rocamadour in the last of the sun right before them, she was overwhelmed.

'Mark?' she whispered. She thought he hadn't heard, and was about to speak again when he said gently, 'What is it, Nina?'

He was still staring through the binoculars. She didn't know if it made it easier or harder, not looking into his eyes. 'Mark, how do you – I mean, what . . .' She couldn't find the words. Then they came out in a rush. 'Sometimes you're so lovely to me, kind, and you hug me, kiss me,' – she felt the furious blush rise across her face – 'then you act as if I'm nothing to you.'

'Never that,' he said quietly. She hardly heard.

'Now we're here, together,' she rushed on, 'miles from home, and I keep thinking, I mean I wonder if –' He began to say something, but she went on regardless. 'I know you said we're not here to have fun, because we have a purpose, something we both feel we have to do, but –'

339

There was nothing else for it. 'But is that all? Don't you feel anything, being here together?'

The silence ached between them. I've blown it, she thought, he'll tell me now, once and for all, that I'm barking up the wrong tree.

He said, after some time, 'You mean a great deal to me. You always have done, since you came to Earthworks. And not just because you work hard and carry out all my unreasonable demands without complaint.' She heard the smile in his voice. 'You brighten up the place with your cheerfulness, and sometimes your optimism keeps me going when I'm tempted to jack the whole thing in.'

'You said I was naive,' she muttered.

'I know. I've been kicking myself ever since.'

'I probably am,' she said hurriedly – if he was going to be penitent, she could at least meet him halfway.

'It isn't a fault, even if you are.' He reached out for her, putting his arm round her waist and pulling her close. 'And as for whether I feel anything, being here alone with you, of course I do.'

She waited for him to go on.

'Yes?' she prompted eventually.

He turned her round to face him, cuddling her head into his chest. The binoculars slung over his shoulder pressed into her hip. 'Can't we just leave it at that, for now?' he said.

She pulled away from him, searching his face. 'But –'

His expression was unreadable.

She stepped back, and his arms fell from around her.

'Let's turn in,' she said dejectedly. 'I'm whacked,' she went on, almost angrily, 'and the earlier we go to sleep, the earlier we can start tomorrow.'

Walking ahead of him, she could hear the steady thump of his footsteps as he followed her back to the camper.

Lying in the hot darkness, far too aware of him to relax and fall asleep, the prospect of the long night ahead was not attractive.

She thought she heard him sigh. Then he cleared his throat.

'Are you asleep?' His soft voice startled her.

'No.'

'Can I talk to you?'

'Yes.'

She held her breath.

'Nina, this isn't easy for me to say. No easier than your brave outburst just now was for you.'

He'd noticed that much, then.

'I don't know if anyone told you, but I was engaged.' His voice sounded strangely neutral, as if he were talking about anything but a past love. 'Her name was Lynn, and we'd been living together for a year or so when she decided I was impossible and she didn't want to marry me after all.'

I can't ask him why, she thought as the pause extended. Can I?

'I'm far too involved with my work,' he said. 'That was Lynn's opinion, and she was probably right. I was marginally worse then, the poor woman scarcely saw me other than sitting hunched over my desk.'

'Couldn't she have got involved too?'

He laughed briefly. 'She could, only I was very bad at deputizing. I used to think that unless I did a job myself, it wouldn't get done properly.'

You're still a bit like that, Nina thought. But she didn't say so.

341

'Do you miss her?' It wasn't a question she could have asked face to face in the daytime.

'Yes. At first I missed her like hell. I went after her and begged her to give us another try, but she wouldn't.'

It was hard to imagine him begging anyone for anything.

'Do you still love her?'

There was a long pause, and she heard him sigh again. 'No. I don't know.'

She imagined he'd finished. He's explained why he's not interested in another relationship, she thought, I suppose I should be grateful to him for that. Even if I do –

'Nina?'

'Still here.' She hoped he hadn't heard her sniff.

'This may be incredibly big-headed, but earlier you seemed to be asking, in a roundabout way, if I fancied you.'

'I didn't –'

'I do. Of course I do. But you're quite a lot younger than me, and, as I've just told you, I have a poor record with women. Those two things, plus the fact that you're an extremely able assistant and I don't want to cock up our working relationship, have made me hold off.'

There was the rustle of bedclothes, and suddenly his face was on a level with hers. 'Or used to, until now.'

The light was poor, but she could see his features. He looked sad and excited at the same time: it touched her deeply.

'What are you doing?' she whispered.

He smiled. 'Nothing. I'm just going to kiss you.' He did so, a light touch of his lips to her mouth. 'All right?'

'Yes.'

She heard him settle down again. 'Mark?'

'What is it?'

She wanted to say, what next?, or, where do we go from here? But she guessed it had cost him quite a lot to say as much as he had done; maybe she should be satisfied with that. For now.

'Nothing.'

He laughed quietly. 'We've got work to do, Nina,' he said. 'We've got a ghost to lay. For now, let's concentrate on him.'

Her mind raced back to the reason why they were there. To that tall, powerful presence who at times seemed to have come from the Wye valley with them.

When he muttered, 'But just you wait till I get you home,' she almost missed it.

She was already awake when the alarm on Mark's watch went off at seven. The rest of the camp site was clearly still fast asleep, so they tiptoed to the wash-rooms and talked in whispers as they had breakfast. There was a new sense of closeness between them, as if whatever it was that had been agreed last night – and she still wasn't quite sure what it was – had made them conspirators. By eight, they were walking along the road to Rocamadour.

Above the town were the ramparts of some ancient fortification: Mark said a fort had been built there in the fourteenth century, but now the ramparts protec-ted nothing more threatening than the chaplains' castle.

'Fourteenth century,' she muttered.

A steep, winding path under trees took them down into the Holy City where, after tunnelling under a huge basilica, they emerged into the Parvis des Eglises, from which the pilgrimage chapels radiated.

343

Mark was stopping frequently, checking each building and place of note against his book. I'm not interested, she thought, possessed by a strange impatience: there's no point in looking at all that stuff. It wasn't there, then.

When? she wondered, panicky suddenly.

'What's the rush?' he asked, catching up with her.

She stared at him. 'Which is the original bit?'

'None of it is truly original.' He glanced at the book. 'The first oratory was plundered, rebuilt, enlarged after a fall of rock, burned, ransacked, and generally abused throughout its history. What we see now is largely nineteenth-century restoration.'

I don't recognize any of it, she thought. Then, chilled, why on earth should I?

'I'm going to find the Lady Chapel.' Driven by something she didn't understand, she left him absorbed in his book and followed the sign that said Notre Dame Chapel.

The worn steps wound round in front of the chapel wall, emerging into a small courtyard. There was a huge bulging overhang of raw rock; someone had stuck a sword into a crevice.

There were few people about – it was still early – and, peering inside the chapel, she saw that it was almost empty.

She went in.

It was lit only by candlelight. She was just taking in how small it was when the thought flashed through her head: it used to be even smaller. A third this size.

She moved forwards between the two rows of pews. Beyond a stone rail was the altar, tall, ornate and gilded – even without Mark's guidebook, she knew it couldn't be any earlier than nineteenth century.

It's not what I expected, she thought, it's all too new, too –

Then she saw the Virgin and Child.

She stared up at the serene face of the Holy Mother, who was smiling slightly, her expression calm and benevolent. The Child, its face older than its years, had once held something in its hand, but whatever it was had broken off. Mother and child had their eyes closed: they seemed to be listening to some inner blissful sounds audible only to them.

Nina, moved by an emotion so strong that it made her knees weak, fumbled behind her and found the edge of a pew. Collapsing on to it, eyes still fixed on the statue, she found herself full of joy. *This* was here, this is a part of what this place was. Is still, she realized as she sat there, for slowly the everlasting peace, the core of the place that transcended the ravages of man, reached out and claimed her.

Some time later Mark found her.

'You've been sitting in here for half an hour,' he whispered.

'Have I?'

He seemed to pick up her mood – he would, she thought, smiling, sometimes we're as close as if we really were lovers – and he said no more, making himself comfortable beside her. He wasn't even reading his book, she noticed; he too seemed overwhelmed by the powerful atmosphere of the chapel, content to do nothing more than sit and absorb it.

In time others began drifting in, in twos, in threes. Then a group came in, and someone started lecturing in a carrying voice which she thought was German. As one, she and Mark got up and left.

As they crossed the courtyard and went down the steps, she tripped and he caught hold of her hand. He didn't let go, even when they reached the bottom.

Below the Holy City were shops and food stalls. Glancing into one, she stopped.

'Look.'

'At what?'

She pointed. Hanging on a board were medallions of the Virgin and Child.

He turned to her, and she could see from his face that he was affected in the same way she was. 'Nothing changes, does it?' he said softly. And went in to buy one for her.

They had a cup of coffee sitting under a fig tree, then strolled back towards the Holy City to look in the Treasure Museum. On the way Mark spotted a display of guidebooks, and she waited while he looked through them. Coming out of the shop, he held one up for her to see: it was called *The Cathars*.

'We keep coming across the Cathars,' she said. 'Is this where they were?'

'No, further south, in the Languedoc. But many heretics were sent here for repentance. If they chose to renounce their faith rather than to burn, the priests sent them to Rocamadour under constraint as punishment. They had to take back one of those medallions – a "sportelle" – to prove they'd been here.'

She shivered. 'Come on, let's get on.'

There was a queue for the Treasure Museum, so they went into the Pilgrims' Hall instead. Mark stood staring up at a huge fresco of St Christopher, and Nina moved away to look at the collection of votive offerings. There were many china and stone plaques, most with the single word *merci*, and other, older gifts bearing witness to miraculous healings of the sick, freeing of prisoners, saving of sailors from the sea. There were crutches, chains, manacles, swords.

346

She had been staring at a dagger for some moments before she realized why.

'Mark,' she said. He didn't hear, so she went over to him. 'Mark, come and look at something.'

Standing back on the same spot, she pointed. 'Does that look familiar?'

He stared. Then said quietly, 'Good God.'

'It's as if they were a pair, isn't it?' she said, excitement making her voice tremble. 'Sword and dagger, with the same patterns, the same inscriptions.' Hardly daring to say it, she whispered, 'Do you think they belonged to the same man?'

Eyes still on the dagger, he said, 'They must have done. Even the other inscription's there, the one Peter said was a magic spell.'

You *were* here, weren't you? she thought. Were you healed, and left your dagger as an ex-voto? Were you wounded, and the Blessed Virgin made you well? Is that why I keep sensing your presence? Why I feel that I've been here before when I know I haven't?

Mark was leaning forward, staring at a card under the dagger. She looked, too; the writing was in French. She recognized *chevalier* and *blessé*, but she couldn't concentrate well enough to put the whole thing together. She asked, 'What does it say?'

Mark was flipping rapidly through the pages of his Rocamadour book. 'I've read about this before. Where is it?' She tried to see over his shoulder. Finding the right page, he held the book so that they could both read it.

The section was headed THE BOOK OF MIRA-CLES. Underneath, after an introduction describing how it was the duty of one of the monks to record all the merciful wonders brought about by the intervention of the Blessed Virgin Mary, was written, THE MIRACLE OF THE BRETON KNIGHT.

She read on.

In the early years of the thirteenth century arose the cult of the Miracle of the Breton Knight. The legend, which has passed into the folklore of Rocamadour, tells how a wounded knight returning from the war made his way to Rocamadour, where a priest tended his wounds. But the knight was possessed by the devil, and all the priest's devoted care couldn't make him well. So the priest took him to the Lady Chapel and, in front of the statue of the Black Virgin of Rocamadour, knelt beside him, wrestling with all his might for the lost soul of the poor knight. The devil, unable to tolerate the power of the Blessed Virgin, burst out of the knight's mouth and fled from the chapel, leaving a scorch mark on the stone which can still be seen today.

For many years the shrine was a centre for the healing of the possessed, those whom we would now refer to as the mentally ill.

The Breton Knight is reputed to have left his dagger in gratitude. Among the collection of ex-votos in the Pilgrims' Hall is a dagger which is traditionally associated with the Breton Knight, although it should be pointed out that the inscription is not in the Breton tongue, although it is in some similar language.

'It's in medieval Welsh,' Nina whispered. 'Peter says so.'

'The two languages *are* similar,' Mark said. 'There were strong links between Wales, Cornwall and Brittany in Celtic times, and lots of place-names in Brittany sound Cornish or Welsh.'

'The person who wrote your book didn't work out that the inscription was Welsh.'

'Well, he'd hardly have expected it to be, would he?'

'No. I suppose not.' She added, 'It's quite something, isn't it, to know something nobody else knows?'

He turned from his book and his eyes met hers. He said quietly, 'Yes. And how.'

The town was far more crowded when they emerged once more out into the courtyard. She didn't feel like queuing to look at any of the other attractions, and Mark said he didn't either.

'Shall we go and find some lunch, then?' she suggested. It seemed ages since breakfast.

'Yes, if you like.'

'Here?'

'No, let's go. It's too crowded.'

They climbed up out of the town by the Way of the Cross; she was quite surprised that he gave the Stations of the Cross hardly a glance. They're a bit lurid, she thought, but that hasn't stopped him so far. She concluded that a surfeit of wonders was responsible for his lack of interest.

She was wrong.

When they were back in L'Hospitalet, he opened the camper and went straight for the pastis bottle, pouring them both a more-than-decent shot. Adding water and turning the liquid cloudy yellow he said, 'Which war?'

She didn't follow. 'Huh?'

'In that bit about the Breton Knight, it said he was returning from the war. Which war?'

He had got another book out of a locker and was flipping through it. She wasn't sure if his question was rhetorical. 'A crusade?' she guessed.

'Early thirteenth century. . . Yes! Here we are. There was the Fourth Crusade, which was in 1204, but that ended in the sack of Constantinople – there's no way a knight on his way back from Turkey to

Brittany would go via Rocamadour, unless he was terrible at navigation. They went there and back through Venice.' He turned another couple of pages. 'There was a crusader port in the Languedoc – Aigues-Mortes – but it was built by Louis IX.' He looked up. 'It wasn't even started till 1270. Children's Crusade,' he muttered, returning to the book, 'no, I don't think so.' After a moment he said, 'There's a far more likely war for him to be returning from. One that took place in the early thirteenth century, in which the action was exclusively in a region not a hundred miles south of Rocamadour. One in which the fighting force was comprised totally – almost totally – of French knights.'

'Go on.' She already knew what he was going to say.

'The Albigensian Crusade.' He stared at her triumphantly. 'I bet you anything you like our knight with the French spurs and the Welsh sword fought against the Cathars. That he was wounded, or possessed, whatever, and came to Rocamadour to be healed. He left his dagger in thanks, bought himself a souvenir, then buggered off back to Wales.'

'Stopping off in the Wye valley to plant his sword, spurs and sportelle in some stray baby's grave?' she said. His face fell, and she instantly regretted that she'd crushed his enthusiasm by throwing up something that didn't fit. 'Sorry,' she said, 'one thing at a time. Go on, you're doing well!' She smiled encouragingly.

'I can't stand it when you're patronizing,' he said, grinning. 'There isn't any more.' There was a reflective silence. Then he said, pouring them another drink, 'But I know where I'd like to go next.'

Again, she knew what was coming. This time, she thought she'd demonstrate the fact. 'Cathar country?' she said.

And he said, 'Yes.' Then, his smile becoming a laugh, 'However did you guess?'

* * *

Mark's book said the Albigensian Crusade had been launched from Lyons in July 1209, and that the first objective, Béziers, had been flattened, the town left a smouldering heap of ruins and all the inhabitants slaughtered.

Mark said, with what she felt was remarkable detachment, 'No point in us going there if everything pre-crusade no longer exists.' He glanced at her, smiling as if amused at his own whimsy, and added, 'There won't be any vibes for you to pick up. We'll make straight for Carcassonne.'

'That wasn't flattened?'

'No, the heretics made terms with the crusaders, I think. But check it in the book.'

They were driving south out of Rocamadour, the Quercy countryside too hilly for straight roads, and reading made her car-sick. In a series of brief looks at the text, she confirmed what Mark had said. 'They took it by siege,' she reported. 'The Cathars were allowed to go, but they had to leave all their worldly goods behind.' Looking on, she said, 'Someone called Raymond-Roger Trencavel was Count of Carcassonne, and Simon de Montfort cheated him – he promised him safe conduct if he came out to parlay, and de Montfort seized him, took him away in chains and flung him into prison. The official story was that he died of dysentery, but apparently everyone reckoned de Montfort poisoned him.'

Mark said, 'No holds barred, when you'd convinced yourself you were fighting on God's side. Reneging on an oath and poisoning someone was nothing compared with what came next.'

I'm not sure I want to know, she thought. Deliberately changing the subject, she said, 'Wasn't Simon de Montfort something to do with the English crown?'

'The de Montfort you're thinking of was this one's son. He led a revolt against Henry III, whom he defeated and captured at the battle of Lewes, but he was in turn defeated by Henry's son Edward – who became Edward I, the Hammer of the Scots – at Evesham, some time around the mid 1200s.'

'They were one of these families you referred to with interests in both England and France?'

'Yes. There was some claim on the Leicester earldom, and the family had lands somewhere near Paris.'

'You know a lot.'

'I read,' he said.

So do I, she thought, but I don't necessarily remember.

North of Toulouse they got on to a stretch of autoroute, and she went back to Mark's book. It seemed a good idea to start trying to catch up with him.

Carcassonne was a spreading modern town, and she was preparing to be disappointed when he said, 'Watch out for signs to the cité – it's separate from this bit.'

She was busy watching out when suddenly he said, 'Look.'

They were climbing a hill, the wide summit of which was filled, as far as the eye could see, by the towering ramparts of a walled city.

He said, 'Is that all you can say?'

She'd been too stunned to say anything at all. She heard him laugh quietly; he reached out and gently touched her cheek. For a long moment he stared straight into her eyes, then he turned away.

They left the camper in a big car park, taking a path which led up the grass embankments to a bridge across the wide ditch on the outer side of the walls. Inside the outer walls was a second set of fortifications, which the book said had been built after the crusade.

They went in through a narrow gateway, up a winding street hemmed in by houses and shops. It was busy and bustling, and there were sounds of people chatting and laughing.

They turned a corner, and an image flashed through her mind: this same corner, but now the houses were closed and shuttered, the streets deserted. She thought she heard someone scream, and a heavy pot crashed to the stones in front of her, making her leap backwards.

Mark caught her arm. 'Mind, the cobbles are uneven.'

She felt very strange.

They climbed up to the St Nazaire basilica in its square in the middle of the old town. On a wall was Simon de Montfort's tombstone, depicting a knight in armour with a lion beside him.

'Did he die here?' she asked.

'No such luck, from the heretics' point of view. He was elected leader of the crusade after the defeat of Carcassonne, and lived another nine years. He was finally killed at Toulouse.'

'In battle?'

'Sort of. The crusaders were besieging the city, and the inhabitants were throwing the usual assortment of large objects at them. They say he was killed by a siege stone thrown by a woman – she must have had a remarkably good aim, as she scored a direct hit on his head.'

'That stone's carved with a siege scene.' She

353

pointed at a glass-covered stone. 'Do you think it was the very one?'

'There wouldn't have been much of him to bury if it was.'

They emerged from the church and went to have a beer, sitting in a square under trees. Mark was occupied in reading and making notes, and she let her mind wander.

It was peaceful in the square. The other café customers were clearly also visitors, enjoying a rest and talking in low voices. She thought about the narrow street and the bend where she'd fleetingly seen into another time.

She heard the scream again, this time accompanied by coarse laughter. Before her in the square a group of men in chain mail and brightly-coloured surcoats had surrounded some women – girls, most of them – and as she watched, the first man – a stocky redhead with a boil on his chin – pounced on one of them, putting his gloved hand in the neckline of her dark gown and tearing it, exposing a thin white garment under which her breasts could be clearly seen. The man didn't even pause to remove his gloves before grabbing at them.

His assault seemed to be the signal for the rest to follow suit. Not knowing how to shut off the vision, she saw the knight with the boil throw the girl to the ground, tearing off what was left of her clothing, then lifting his mail coat and tugging at whatever he wore beneath it. Then he was on her, pushing her legs wide apart and thrusting himself between them, armour on pale white flesh, brutal marked face rough against the soft cheek. Either the girl had fainted or he'd knocked her unconscious when he threw her down, for she made no move.

354

When he'd finished – it seemed to be over in no time – he rearranged his clothing, then, bending down as if to a hare caught by his hounds, drew his dagger and casually slit her throat.

Nina covered her face with her hands, fingers pressed against her closed eyes. But she couldn't press out the image of the still white body bleeding on to the stones.

Mark said, 'Are you all right?'

'No,' she whispered. 'I'm going to be sick.'

Quickly he helped her up, and she was aware of curious stares as he hurried her into the café. 'Go on,' – he pushed her through a door marked with a male silhouette – 'Yes, I know it's the gents, but this is no time to be fussy. I'll stand guard.'

He banged the door after her and she bent over the lavatory. For a second or two nothing happened, then, as that awful picture shimmered into her mind, she felt her stomach heave and she threw up.

Eyes streaming, she straightened up and flushed the toilet, turning on the tap in the tiny basin and splashing her face. She heard Mark say something – 'Mon amie est malade,' which the man had probably worked out for himself – then she opened the door.

Mark put his arm round her. A dark man standing beside him flashed her a kind smile.

She said as they went out into the sunshine, 'Do you think we could go?'

'Of course. Soon as we've paid the bill.' He hesitated. 'What was it? Something you ate?'

'No. Something I saw.'

It wasn't sufficient explanation, and she hadn't thought it would be. On the road out of Carcassonne, he stopped on the side of the road, holding her in his arms while she told him the rest.

He didn't speak for some time after she'd finished. At last he said, 'Had you read about a scene like that?'

'No. Your book doesn't go into that sort of detail.'

'What *did* it say about the siege of Carcassonne?'

'Oh, I can't remember. There was lots about military tactics and siege engines. Why?'

'I thought your imagination might be fitting what you'd read to the place it actually happened.' He paused, then said, 'I hoped you were, because I find the alternative – that somehow you're actually picking up events from eight hundred years ago – a bit disturbing.'

'*You* find it disturbing!'

He kissed the top of her head. 'Yes, sorry. It must have been terrible for you.'

She saw it again, but it was mercifully brief this time. The ginger knight leered at her, then was gone.

She suddenly had a frightful thought. 'Mark, what if –' She stopped. Mark might agree, which would be even worse.

But, 'What if what?' he prompted.

She said in a small voice, 'What if that knight – the one who raped the girl – what if he's the Breton Knight?'

'What if he is? Probably lots of them raped girls, it wouldn't make him any worse than the rest of them.'

Yes, it would, she thought. Because I'd expected better of him.

Then Mark said, 'You said this redhead was short and fat.'

'Yes.'

'There you are, then. Your knight's tall, isn't he?'

The relief was overwhelming. She had a brief sharp picture of the golden brown eyes under the greying hair looking at her, half amused, half affronted. Then he was gone.

* * *

They travelled through Cathar lands for a week, following a meandering trail that took in the most significant of the places mentioned in the book. Sometimes she picked up a whisper of reaction – in a wide river valley north of Carcassonne, and in a tiny, lonely village called Minerve, where all that was left of the Cathar fortress was a single tower pointing heavenwards like a saint's finger in a medieval painting – but in the main her inner eye stayed blind.

She didn't know whether to be relieved or disappointed. On balance, relief won. Especially as the days went by and they learned more about what the crusaders had done – she didn't think she'd have been able to cope with actually seeing mass burnings or decapitated bodies thrown down wells, especially if the visions had the sort of vividness she'd experienced in the square in Carcassonne.

Without the intrusion of the past, she was free to think about what was happening between herself and Mark. The evening after she'd been so disturbed in Carcassonne, he'd treated her with such kindness that she'd almost begun to think he'd got over his misgivings at last and was about to make some further move towards her, even though their ghost remained resolutely unlaid. But the following morning, after asking solicitously if she was okay, he reminded her it was her turn to go out for their breakfast bread; she wondered if he'd still have insisted it was her turn if she'd said no, she wasn't okay, and decided charitably that he wouldn't. By the time she got back, he was immersed once more in his books.

Any thoughts she'd had that he might be about to take her in his arms and declared his undying passion, if not his love, quickly fled.

But, when they'd finished packing up and were about to leave, he leaned over and kissed her cheek. He said, 'We don't have to go on with this, you know. We could turn for home this morning, if you wanted to.' He gazed at her, his expression soft. 'In some ways, it wouldn't be a bad idea.'

'But we haven't finished yet! We –'

'All right, it was just a suggestion.' He reached down and turned the key in the ignition.

'Don't you want to go on?' She could hardly believe it.

'Yes, I do,' he said briefly. Glancing across at her, he added, 'I was thinking of you. It made you ill yesterday, this bloody ghost hunt.'

She was overwhelmed at the thought that he'd been prepared to give up just because she'd been unwell. It must mean – She stopped herself. There was no point in speculation, even if she was quite sure she was right.

'I really don't want to give up,' she said. He grunted. 'It's okay, Mark,' she went on, the temptation proving too strong, 'I promise not to embarrass you ever again by being sick in a gents' toilet while you wait outside.'

He didn't deign to reply.

By the end of the week, they were in the foothills of the Pyrenees. The Cathars had fallen back southwestwards towards the mountains, securing themselves in strongholds against the relentless advance of the crusade. She and Mark had read that it took almost forty years for the heretics to be wiped out: the last place to fall, a fortress called Montségur high in the mountains, was finally taken in March 1244.

'Shall we go and see the site of the last battle?' Mark asked her.

She felt she'd been waiting for this: she said unhesitatingly, 'Yes.'

They camped for the night on a shingly patch of beach beside the river Aude, going in to the small town of Couiza for their supper. In the morning they drove on into the mountains; rounding a bend in the road, she spotted, on top of a distant peak shaped like an upturned cup, the outlines of a building.

She pointed it out to Mark. 'Do you think it could be Montségur?'

He looked where she was pointing. 'God, I hope not.'

She knew what he meant – it seemed to be an impossibly formidable climb. 'And us without our ropes and pitons,' she muttered.

But it wasn't as bad as it looked – the road wound steadily upwards, so that by the time they were pulling into the car park beyond the village of Montségur, they were already halfway up the mountain.

It was bad enough. They put on trainers and Mark filled a water bottle – ominously, she thought – then followed the sign to the start of the climb. They passed a modern memorial stone to '250 PARFAITS MORTS PAR LES FLAMMES.'

'What's a *parfait*?' she asked.

'A perfect. It was what they called the avowed Cathars, who'd taken an oath giving up all the things of the flesh, like eating meat and having sex.'

She said before she could stop herself, 'Doesn't sound much fun.'

He smiled. 'They didn't have to take the oath till they were ready. Before they did they were known as adherents or sympathizers – people who supported the Cathars but lacked the commitment for the final step. Lots of them left it till they were on their death beds.'

'The best of both worlds.'

'Exactly. They enjoyed a normal life till they were past enjoying it any more, then swore to give up all the naughties, assuring immediate passage to paradise at death.'

She laughed. 'I'm surprised the whole world didn't turn Cathar.'

His tone suddenly serious, he said, 'The whole world looked as if it was going to. Which is why the established Church stamped them out so ferociously.'

Mort par les flammes, she thought. Died in the flames. Ferociously is right.

They fell silent as the climb grew more difficult – trying to keep her footing on rocks made treacherously slippery by the passage of feet, looking out for handholds that weren't covered in prickles, gasping for breath as the ascent became almost vertical, she didn't have any reserve capacity for conversation. Judging by the way Mark was panting, he didn't either.

But the strenuous exertion didn't stop her thinking. Give up your faith or be burned to death. Tied to a stake, or herded into some building, the doors sealed as the flames took hold. I couldn't, not for anything and certainly not for my faith.

Do I have a faith?

She didn't know.

Out of the blue she thought of her lost child. The image became confused with the baby's skeleton, so that her instinctive pang of protective sympathy was for both children, the one that was never to be born and the one that left the world almost as soon as it had arrived. Symbols of mother love flashed through her mind: a robed figure cradling a tiny baby; a mother giving the breast; the Rocamadour virgin with Christ on her knee. Herself, standing in her sordid little bathroom staring down at the white wand of a pregnancy testing kit which showed a fateful double blue line. *Pregnant*.

The frustrated, suppressed maternal instinct burst out of the corner where she'd confined it. I'd die to save my child's life, she thought. But that's different – that's programmed into us, so that the species goes on.

Faith is another matter.

The path crawled on up the hillside, out above the tree-line and on to bare rock. The sun beating down made her skin burn, and she could feel sweat pouring down her back. Risking a glance upwards, she was dismayed at how far there was still to go: the girl in the ticket booth had said thirty minutes' more climb, and that had been ages ago.

She fixed her eyes on the rocks in front of her – they seemed to be climbing straight up a dry water course – and kept them there. If I don't see how slowly I'm progressing, she thought, perhaps it won't be so depressing.

Some time later, the track flattened out on to a sort of platform, from which steps led up to the great walls: they were there.

Together they dragged themselves up the stairs and into the ruined fortress. In the shade of the walls, they lay down flat and waited for their breathing to return to normal.

'Drink?' Mark said after a while, offering her the water bottle.

'Yes please.' Lukewarm, it was still wonderfully welcome.

They sat looking around them. The interior of the stronghold was quite small, and she wondered how two hundred and fifty people had lived there. She mentioned it to Mark.

'They constructed huts out on the north side,' he said, 'through there. We'll have a look in a minute. The people only came inside when they were threatened.'

'All the same, what an incredibly restricted – constricted – life.'

'Better than the alternative.'

He was right.

They got up and went through the gateway on the north side. The view was stupendous, comparable, she thought, with what you'd get in a low-flying aircraft. The mountain seemed to fall away sheer, the fortress filling in every inch of space right to the very edge, so that one too many step in any direction would have sent you plummeting down thousands of feet to the valley below.

She felt slightly vertiginous.

They stepped cautiously along a ledge towards the western end of the fortress, where another ladder led them back inside. It was a relief to have something to grab on to again: at the top of the ladder, she turned to look out into the mountains.

Mark had gone on ahead, so that she stepped down into the remains of the small room alone.

Abruptly the walls changed from bright golden stone to dimly-lit, cool brown: it was as if the ruined roof were complete again, blocking out the light. The room was almost bare, although there was a strange five-sided ornament hanging on a wall. She felt a stab of pain run down her neck, from her hairline to between her shoulders; she put up her right hand to rub it and the hand fell limp, sending out an agonizing protest.

She shrieked, *'MARK!'*

Then she was back in the sunshine, Mark hurrying towards her.

'What? What is it?'

She shook her head. 'It's all right. But he was here, Mark, and he was wounded. I felt it, just for a second I was in such pain . . .'

He helped her to sit on the edge of a deep window embrasure. 'Has it gone?'

She nodded. 'Quite gone.' Again she heard that voice. *I'm sorry.*

He settled down on the rough stones at her feet, leaning against her legs. After a moment he said, 'This is unbelievable, I hope you realize.'

She laughed shortly. 'You're telling me.'

'I meant this particular aspect.' He put a hand back over his shoulder, and she took it. 'Don't you see?'

She thought. Then she saw. 'You mean, because of where we are?'

'Yes. Unless the narrow beam of what you're able to pick up has suddenly got much wider – which I suppose is possible, as possible, anyway, as the rest of all this – then it means something very strange has happened.'

'It has. I've just picked up the scent of my crusader knight in a Cathar castle.'

They drank some more water, then returned to the main courtyard of the fortress. There were a few more people there now, and the powerful atmosphere felt less intense.

'Let's think this through,' Mark said as they sat down again in their patch of shade. 'First, are you sure it was your knight you felt?'

'Quite sure. I felt his pain, then when it had gone he said sorry. I think he meant, sorry I'd suffered what he suffered.' She shivered. 'Poor man, I don't know how he could stand it for long.' Absently her hand went up to her neck, soothing the flesh.

'Knights were made of stern stuff,' Mark said. 'So, perhaps he was wounded in the fighting, and lay in that room waiting to be tended.'

'Yes, that's possible. When did they fight here?'

'Not till the end.' He frowned. 'No, that won't do – they didn't take Montségur by force, they starved them out, so there wouldn't have been any chance for a knight to be wounded.'

'Do you remember the details?'

He looked at her, amused. 'I should have brought the book, shouldn't I?'

'Yes, I can't think why you didn't. You could have carried it in one hand and the water bottle in the other.'

'The details,' he said slowly. 'Let me think . . . It was March, and they'd run out of food. The crusaders offered to spare their lives if they re-nounced their faith and did penance – you remem-ber in Rocamadour we read about repentant her-etics being sent there forcibly and made to do pen-ance? – and the Cathars requested two weeks to think about it. The two weeks were up at the end of March, just after the spring equinox, and when they were asked for their decision, the Cathars all opted to die.'

'I wonder why they wanted the two weeks, when surely they all knew straight away what they'd decide?'

He shrugged. 'Who can say? Perhaps when death is waiting for you, every extra day is precious.'

'Perhaps they needed the time to prepare,' she said suddenly. 'So that anyone who hadn't already done so could take that oath you mentioned.'

'The Consolamentum.'

364

'Yes. Wouldn't you want to do that, if you knew you were about to die? And if you believed that taking it meant you'd go straight to heaven, you wouldn't mind dying so much.'

'You wouldn't mind dying at all, if you were a Cathar,' he said. 'They believed that the earth was intrinsically bad, and that all of us were here on sufferance, dragged out of paradise by an evil spirit and thrust against our will into these vile human bodies. Cathars looked on earth as a sort of giant waiting room where they had to be till their spirits could return to their souls in heaven.'

'Well, then,' she said vaguely. She was thinking about something else. 'Mark, the timing's wrong. The Rocamadour book said the legend of the Breton Knight began in the early years of the thirteenth century. If he was wounded then and seeking healing, already on his way home from the crusade, then he can't possibly have been here when it fell. It was forty years too late.'

Mark didn't say anything.

'Well? Can he?'

Slowly he shook his head. 'No. And if he was in his prime in 1209, assuming he was there at the start of the crusade, he'd hardly have still been fighting in 1244.'

'So what was he doing here?'

He stared at her, some expression in his eyes that she couldn't read. It was as if he was regretting that he couldn't solve the mystery for her, couldn't put her mind at rest. He said, 'I have absolutely no idea.'

PART FIVE

Gawyn

Late Summer 1209–Early Autumn 1210

Nineteen

Awareness came intermittently. Sometimes he was conscious for long enough for anxiety to start – where am I? Is it safe? – but sometimes it only lasted for brief flashes; once he was being moved and cried out, only to be hastily shushed; once he thought he was flying, the dark night sky all around dotted with stars, the earth far below a faint pattern in shades of grey. Once he opened his eyes to a moonlit room and saw a frowning face bending over him, felt a cup put to his lips from which he swallowed sips of some bitter drink.

Always, no matter how long or short the waking, the pain was so bad he was relieved to go under again.

In his wild dreams he was running, on fire from a burning arrow in the back of his neck. Then he'd be trying to catch up with Yves, yelling for him to wait – 'I can't find Cadoc!' he heard himself shout. 'I must, he's my squire and he's too young to be thrown off the walls!'

In a blessed moment of lucidity, he remembered he'd left Cadoc behind, guarding the gear.

He dreamt of her. Saw her white naked body swept along in fast black water, saw her face, mouth open and gasping for air, heard her cry out to him.

'I've sold your cross and I can't help you,' his dream self said.

I haven't! he protested silently. I've kept your mare, too. I could have done with the money, but I've managed, so far. Don't want to part with anything that's yours.

'I'll give it back,' he muttered.

'Hush,' said a calm voice.

And he remembered he couldn't give anything back to her.

* * *

There came a morning when he woke up and stayed awake.

It's not a dream, he thought, looking around. I'm here, wherever 'here' is.

He was lying on a narrow bed with white sheets. He was dressed in a clean white shift. The walls of the room were whitewashed. The early sun coming in at the small window was bouncing off all the white with a force that hurt his eyes, so he closed them again.

In his mind he reviewed and assessed what he'd just seen. Walls made of large stones, and, judging by the window embrasure, several feet thick. Outside the window, I got a glimpse of some rocky summit but otherwise just the brilliant blue sky, with birds freewheeling as they ride the thermals.

And I can hear absolutely nothing.

Wherever I am, it's not Carcassonne.

It seemed to take him some time to frame the next questions: how did I get from there to here? And *who brought me?*

Whoever it was, they might be hostile. He opened his eyes again, searching the room for his sword, his dagger. But there was nothing of his to be seen. Nothing of anyone else's, either: apart from the bed, above which hung an ornament in the shape of a pentangle, the room was bare.

Relaxing again – he realized he was too weak to maintain any strong emotion for longer than a few seconds – he had the reassuring thought that if they'd been hostile, they'd have killed him where he lay. They certainly wouldn't have gone to the trouble of transporting him here and caring for him.

After a while he risked opening his eyes again and looked down at himself. His right hand lay outside the sheet encased in strips of bandage – white again – and appeared to have been splinted. He remembered the two knights wresting his sword out of his hand – *of course* my sword and dagger aren't here, they were taken from me in Carcassonne – and snapping the bone.

Very cautiously, he tried to move his fingers. A sharp pain shot through his wrist, so he stopped.

My right arm. My sword arm.

His groin hurt with a dull ache that never varied in its intensity.

Very slowly, he raised his left hand, feeling with the fingers round the back of his head. At the base of his skull, the hair had been shaved away; feeling down his neck and between his shoulders, he found that the long, bumpy cut continued. He could detect very many stitches, holding the two sides together. Extending his fingers and thumb, still he couldn't touch both ends at the same time. And, he thought, I've got big hands.

The prodding of his fingers made the cut throb and burn. The flesh around it felt hot.

371

Gradually the pain in all his hurts increased. He gritted his teeth. It'll do no good to call out, there's nobody here. I've been tended, cared for, but whoever did it has gone. Been killed, perhaps.

Anyway, there's no point at all in yelling.

Just when he'd realized that if there really wasn't anyone there it didn't matter if he screamed as hard as he wanted to, the door opened and a man in black came in.

His pleasant opening remark – something on the lines of, 'Oh, I see you're awake, then,' – was entirely drowned by Gawyn's violent and wordless cry of agony.

'I'm sorry I didn't come earlier,' the man said – he'd given Gawyn a long draught of the bitter drink, and slowly the pain was receding – 'but I was delayed. Also, when I looked in on you at dawn, you were still deeply asleep.' He leaned forward, staring intently at Gawyn. 'A healing sleep, it has been. For all that you still hurt, you are better.'

'Aye,' Gawyn said. He wondered how the man knew to address him in a language he understood; it wasn't pure *langue d'oil*, but then it certainly wasn't *langue d'oc*. Then he thought, no, he wouldn't use the local tongue, I'm crusading against the Languedoc.

Or I was.

The man's hands were either side of Gawyn's head, turning him so that he could inspect the wound. 'It is good,' he said, gently laying him back on the pillows. 'The cut was very badly infected – I cannot imagine what that knight had been doing with his sword – but now the infection is losing.'

'Losing?'

'Your own strong body is defending itself successfully. With,' he smiled modestly, 'a little help from our nostrums.'

Gawyn had no idea what he was talking about. But the general drift seemed to be that the man had healed him, so he said, 'I must thank you. For my life.'

The man bowed his head. 'God has saved your life. We have merely helped.'

'Well, thanks all the same.'

There was a calm silence in the room. Gawyn felt he should be asking a hundred questions, but he felt too drowsy. Watching him, the man quietly began to back away.

'I shall close the shutters,' he said, doing so, 'and leave you to sleep. Later, we will bring you food.'

He crossed to the door, opening it and gliding out. Gawyn heard the murmur of prayer; although the words were in an alien tongue, he recognized the Paternoster.

He woke to some savoury smell that made his mouth water. The man was standing by his bed, and he'd brought a small table on which was a mug.

'Drink this first,' he said, 'for if you are in pain it will remove your appetite.'

Gawyn did as he was told.

'Now, when you are ready, we will help you to sit up a little.'

We? He looked beyond the man, and saw a woman, also dressed in black. She gave him an encouraging smile. In her hands she held a tray, on which there was bread and a bowl of something that steamed fragrantly.

'We have brought you soup,' the man said.

'Thank you.'

The woman put the tray down on the table, and

she and the man moved to opposite sides of the bed. Arms holding his elbows, they lifted him into a semi-sitting position, adjusting the pillows to support him. Instantly his head began to swim.

'Yes, you will feel faint, I fear,' the man said. 'Try to eat – nourishment is what you need.'

He wasn't sure he could eat. It seemed more likely he was about to be sick. But they put a piece of bread in his mouth, dipped in the soup, and, after a bad moment or two, suddenly he was eating it. After that, the two of them could hardly keep pace with him.

The woman, laughing, said something in her own language. The man said, 'She says to slow down, and please not to bite off her fingers.'

'I won't,' Gawyn said, smiling up at her. 'If she made the soup, please tell her it's the finest thing I ever tasted in my life.'

The compliment was passed to her, and she responded with a spate of words, patting his arm, looking earnestly into his face. He turned to the man for elucidation, but the man shook his head. He said something to the woman, then, to Gawyn, 'Not yet. You must rest still – time for everything else when you are strong again.'

After the soup they gave him water to drink, then the woman peeled an orange for him, feeding him the segments one by one. Then they gave him more water to rinse his mouth.

'Now, sleep,' the man said. 'Tomorrow, if you are well, we will talk.' He went out, beckoning to the woman to follow.

She moved to the table to collect the tray. But before she picked it up, she glanced over her shoulder and, seeing the man had departed, suddenly bent down and kissed Gawyn's forehead.

She said haltingly, 'God to – bless.'

Then she hurried out after the man.

The man came alone in the morning, and proceeded to tend to Gawyn in ways that wouldn't have been seemly for a woman's eyes, even if she was old enough to be his mother. When he'd finished, he went away again and came back with food – a bowl of some cereal with nuts and fruits in it, moistened with juice.

He inspected the wound on Gawyn's neck, and lifted his right hand to move the fingers.

'It hurts?'

Gawyn nodded. 'Not so much, though.'

'Good. The bones are knitting, and soon we will remove the splints. You must exercise the limb and re-build the muscles.'

'Will it –' He'd been going to ask, will it be strong enough for me to wield a sword?, but stopped. Such a question wasn't very diplomatic, all the time he didn't know who his rescuers were.

He was beginning to have a good idea. Black robes, no meat in the soup nor milk in the breakfast bowl. And the man recited Paternosters whenever he wasn't engaged in conversation.

'Your wrist will heal straight,' the man said. 'You will be able to go back to crusading, if that is your choice.'

Gawyn couldn't read the expression in the dark eyes. It wasn't hostile – this wasn't a victim staring into the face of the man who'd been trying to kill him. But neither was it encouraging – this man wasn't going to send him back out to the slaughter with a prayer of encouragement.

He said, 'Who are you? Cathars?'

And the man nodded.

After some time, Gawyn asked, 'Why did you save me?' Then: 'You know what I am, don't you?'

The thought had suddenly struck him that he might be here under false colours, that the Cathars might have found him, stripped and bleeding, and taken him in out of common decency.

'You are a knight, I think from Brittany.' He glanced down, and answered the question Gawyn was about to ask. 'You talked much, in your sickness, in Breton and in a language we didn't understand. We have Bretons in our number, and one of them sat by you for a time. You came south with the crusaders, and you were of the party who penetrated the walls of Carcassonne on the eighth day of August.'

'I am your enemy,' Gawyn said baldly.

'Yes. But your own knights attacked you and left you for dead. Do you not remember?'

'Aye.' It wasn't something he wanted to dwell on.

'And you remember why?'

'Why they attacked me? Aye, I do.'

The man leaned forward. 'The girl you saved is my niece. The daughter of the woman who was here yesterday, who is my sister.' He paused, straightening. 'We are both very attached to our little Estella.'

'I didn't save her,' Gawyn said. 'I almost –' He stopped, unable to relive that moment when his blade was at her smooth throat.

'She told us what you almost did. And how she then misunderstood what you tried to do next.' He looked down, as if unable to meet Gawyn's eyes. 'She thought, you see, that you were going to rape her before you killed her.' Steel entering his voice, he went on, 'That, unlike many of your fellow crusaders, you preferred live, struggling flesh to dead meat for the satisfaction of your carnal appetite.'

There was a pause. Then he said, 'I apologize. You were not going to rape her, alive or dead. But she was not to know that. She is very sorry that she hurt you so badly. And that, injured already by her, you were further wounded in trying to save her – yes, she observed how you stopped them and tried to send them off in another direction, for she was hiding in a house just above you.'

He said, 'Tell her I forgive her. She was only trying to defend herself, I understand that.' He shifted in the bed, trying to ease the pain in his crotch. Quite a fighter, your niece, he thought. Lashes out like an unbroken stallion.

'She will be happy to have your forgiveness,' the man said. 'She has been praying for you.'

A tremor of superstition went through him. Prayed for, by heretics? The strange God they worship petitioned to care for me?

No! I don't want her to . . .

His thought came to a halt. He pictured the girl, wetting herself in her terror. Saw the concerned face of the man, whose skill had saved his life. Saw the woman, understanding now that what she'd been trying to express to him the previous evening had been gratitude.

They're good people, he realized in surprise. Kind, caring, good.

With the realization came another: he'd been taught to despise these people as the agents of Satan, ordered to hunt them down and kill them without mercy, for they were despicable in the sight of God. But if they weren't despicable, where did that leave him?

Trying to concentrate on the dilemma, his mind wouldn't fix but kept sliding off. There were, he decided as he gave up the attempt, more immediate things to worry about.

He said to the man, 'What is this place?'

'A refuge. For the time being, anyway, although we do not know how long we shall be safe here.' He paused, as if working out how much to reveal to a former enemy, and eventually went on, 'The crusaders have a new military leader: Simon de Montfort now commands the army, although, we understand, he accepted the post with much reluctance.'

'Aye.' Gawyn could well believe it. If the army now held Carcassonne, many might consider that the job was done. Besides, most of the crusaders had taken the cross some time in June; their forty days would soon be up, and their thoughts would be turning towards going home and getting the harvest in. Simon de Montfort might well find himself a commander without an army.

Did they hold Carcassonne?

'The city fell, did it?' He felt a rush of shame as he asked the question. Remembering how they'd left Béziers, he wondered if Carcassonne, too, was now a smouldering ruin haunted by the tormented spirits of the newly dead.

The man stared at him again with that assessing look. 'It did, although there was no further loss of life. Negotiations took place – neither defenders nor besiegers were able to gain the upper hand – and the army allowed the inhabitants to leave unharmed. They were, however, permitted to take nothing with them, not even their clothes; they left the city in their underlinen.'

Gawyn frowned. 'You speak of "they". Were you – we – not among them?'

The man walked slowly across to the window. Looking out through the gap between the shutters, he said, 'We had advance information of what the terms of surrender might be. Whilst material things are not of great importance to us, still we did not wish to leave everything we owned in the city, for the crusaders to purloin and desecrate. In addition, we had sick and wounded in our number – we had no idea what would become of those who could not walk out of Carcassonne unaided.'

The explanation seemed to have come to a halt. 'So you found a way to get out before the end?' Gawyn prompted. 'Some of you left secretly, taking with you whatever you didn't want to leave behind. In God's name, how?' He pictured the besieged city, a vast enemy army camped all around. How had it been done?

The man turned, regarding him with humour in his face. 'Some things it is better you do not know.'

Translating, Gawyn changed his remark to, there are some things I'm not going to tell you. I don't blame you, he thought.

He said quietly, 'Why did you take me with you?' Why encumber yourselves on a perilous journey with a wounded, unconscious man who wasn't even one of you? Suddenly he remembered the sensation of movement, of crying out as he was jolted, to hear someone urgently say, 'Hush!'

'Had we not, they would have killed you.' The man spoke with total authority. 'Your actions were witnessed, and they would have concluded that you had changed sides. The crusaders work on the rule that those who are not with them are against them.'

'But surely they –'

'You have not heard what happens to knights who change sides? No? Well, let me tell you of the son of a Cathar family who initially pledged himself to the crusade. When he saw the treatment that was being meted out to the defenceless, he discovered that his strongest loyalty was to his own. He went to his sister's aid, but he was not able to be much use to her. De Montfort has just had him hanged.'

He crossed back to the bed. 'We did not want you to be hanged. Not that they would have needed to bother, for you were on the point of death when we took you in. We did not want you to die, for obviously you cannot have been prepared. A man who defended some of our number, who put his life in jeopardy on our behalf, did not deserve to depart this life unconsoled.' He glanced at Gawyn to see if he understood. 'Unconfessed, I suppose you would call it,' he said. 'In the orthodox church, you call a priest and confess your sins, hoping you will have time for repentance before death claims you and takes your soul to hell. Time enough, anyway, to earn some remission of your time in purgatory. We who believe in neither hell nor purgatory prepare for death in our own way. If we have not been given the Consolamentum already, it is administered as we die.'

'What is it? What does it do?'

The man smiled. 'It is too great a subject to be discussed briefly. I will tell you, if and when the time is right. For now, merely know that for those who die consoled – the perfect, we call them – the soul is at last permitted to leave its earthly body and be reunited with the spirit it left in heaven.'

'I see.' He wasn't at all sure that he did. But the message was clear: you helped us, and we couldn't leave you to your fate. 'And it was you who tended me?'

'Not I alone. I am not skilled with my hands. Another stitched your head.'

'He did a neat job.'

'She. Yes, she is deft. She learned the craft by practising on the carcasses of pigs. We do not touch meat, so being prepared to handle a dead animal was proof of her devotion to her art.'

Gawyn raised his hand to feel the long row of stitches, trying not to think about dead pigs. 'She also set my arm?'

'She did.'

'Will she come soon? I should like to thank her.'

'She will. There will be no need for thanks – she, too, had reason to help you, for she was among the women fleeing before you that day. She also is my niece, the elder sister of Estella.'

'You speak of family relationships, of children. I was told you didn't believe in marriage. Are all your children –' He'd been going to say, are they bastards?, but stopped.

'We believe that all matters of the flesh are evil. Marriage and procreation involve the sexual union of man and woman, and as such represent evil. However, many of our number were married and had produced children prior to joining us. My sister was one such.'

'But –'

'Enough. I could talk to you all day and still you would have questions, and you need to rest.'

If he's about to go, Gawyn thought, there's something I must ask him. And since it's not about this weird mystery of Cathar belief, he might just answer.

'When you took me out of Carcassonne,' he said, 'was I clad only in my underlinen?'

If he was surprised at the sudden change of subject, the man didn't show it. 'You were. But have no fear – such personal belongings as you had about you were also brought out.'

'My weapons? My hauberk and cuirass? My helm?'

'Yes, all those things. They are below, waiting for

you.' He looked at Gawyn wryly. 'You might care to know that the man who bore the burden remarked that he'd let you reward him for his trouble, when you were able – not an easy task, to flee under cover bearing a knight's armour and weapons.'

'I don't suppose it was.' He smiled dutifully, wondering how to frame the next, most important question. 'There was something else. I was carrying it under my breastplate. Did you find it?'

Even as he asked, he thought of how long he'd lain there in the street. Of all the knights who must have passed, intent on theft and not above robbing one of their own, even if they didn't know he'd just turned against them. It's hopeless, he thought.

'We found a cross,' the man said. 'On a heavy gold chain. A beautiful piece.'

He felt weak with relief. 'Would you bring it to me, please?'

The man bowed his head and did as he was asked. Returning, he put the cross into Gawyn's hands.

'I admire your devotion,' he said quietly after some minutes.

Gawyn, who had closed his eyes the better to enjoy the pictures of Roese that were flooding his mind, opened them again. He was tempted to let it be thought he'd been praying – thanking God for his delivery from death? – but in the end honesty won.

'It's not devotion,' he said.

The man looked at him questioningly but, when Gawyn didn't go on, after a moment turned away and left the room.

Closing his eyes once more, Gawyn held the cross to his chest and retreated into his thoughts.

*

He slept for most of the next few days, knowing that they were passing only by the regular arrival of small, light meals – one in the morning, one at noon, one at dusk – and by the fact that quite often he woke to find it was night and not day. Sometimes he was disturbed by the sound of hammering, and once he thought he heard footsteps running along an echoing wooden platform. He guessed his deep sleep was promoted by some drug they were putting in the bitter drink, for he doubted that he was still sufficiently sick to slumber away quite so many hours of the day. Sometimes, when he could get his mind to concentrate, he wondered at himself that he didn't protest, at least by asking what they were giving him.

He made the discovery that he trusted them. Totally.

Awake as day broke one morning, he went through the familiar tally of his injuries, and found that the hurts were almost gone. Moreover, when he tentatively hitched himself up to a sitting position, his head didn't swim. Slowly swinging his legs out of bed and putting his feet to the floor, he sat wondering what to do next.

More than anything, he thought, I want to look out of that window.

The embrasure was some five paces away. Until he reached it and could cling on to the shutters, there were no handholds to help him along.

'I can do it,' he said aloud.

Using his sound left hand to lever himself, he stood up.

He waited until the sickness passed, then tried a step. Another. Then three more all together, and a fourth that took him right to the window, where he banged into the shutters and forced them apart.

It's as well, he reflected, that they built the sill high, or I'd have flown straight out of the window.

Holding on to the shutters with his left hand – whose knuckles, he noted with amusement, were white – he stared out into the early daylight.

Looking straight ahead, there was nothing to see but sky. For a moment, his mind playing tricks, he thought he was back in his castle in the Black Mountains. But no, Welsh skies weren't like this. Even when the sun shone and the clouds went away, the blue of home skies was light.

Not like this.

Looking down, he saw walls that fell away sheer, merging at their base into the living rock from which they sprang. The rock was sheer, too, or as near as made no difference. Leaning out over the sill – his brain gave out warning signals, hitting him with the dizziness not only of vertigo but of recent fever – he caught a glimpse of trees and greenery far below. Pulling himself back, he let his eyes lift to the distant blue hills and to the long valley they encircled.

How, he thought, how in God's name did I get here? Did they carry me? No! Diew, I'm no easy load even for two men on a straight track.

How, then?

For a moment, he began to believe that the rumours might be true. That Satan, looking after his own, had given the Cathars the gift of flight.

The nausea was getting out of control. Turning away from the frightening view, and the even more frightening question of how they'd got him up there, he staggered back to bed.

Some time later the man – his name, he'd told Gawyn, was Olivier – came in with the usual bowl of cereal and fruits. Glancing at Gawyn, he said, 'You have been out of bed.'

Gawyn smiled. 'Aye. How did you know?'

Olivier's face remained serious for a moment, then he too smiled. 'I could pretend that some special sense permitted me the information. But that would be untrue. No – it's the shutters. I left them almost closed last night, and now they are open.' His eyes met Gawyn's. 'However, I was aware that, as soon as you were able, you would crawl across to the window to try to discover where you are.'

'I didn't crawl,' Gawyn said mildly. 'I just about managed to walk.'

'You did well. And what did you discover?' He looks almost smug, Gawyn thought. As if he knows full well I'm none the wiser.

He took a mouthful of cereal, preparing his reply.

'To begin with the obvious,' he said eventually, 'we're in a mountainous region, I would guess the foothills of the Pyrenees. Possibly this is a strong-hold, and I imagine, from the sounds I hear of wood being sawn and of nails being hammered in, that you are in the process of further fortifying it. Maybe you're building firing platforms on top of the walls.' He paused, but Olivier made no confirmatory sign. 'This fort, or whatever it is, is oriented with its long sides running east-west; this room faces south.' He paused again, glancing quickly at Olivier. This next discovery hardly rated the description, since it was almost entirely speculation. But he thought it was worth mentioning, if only to observe Olivier's reac-tion. 'We're now in August, and today the sun rose over there.' He waved his good hand in the appropri-ate direction. 'By late September, when the autumn equinox occurs, the rising sun will be directly in line with your building.'

Predictably, Olivier neither agreed nor disagreed. For an instant, Gawyn thought he caught a glint of surprised approval in the dark eyes, then it was gone.

'If I'm right about the new fortifications,' Gawyn found himself saying, 'perhaps I can help. You may say that's the last thing you need,' – he was hurrying the words out now, finding the impassive face of Olivier somewhat disconcerting – 'but I think you'd be wrong. Who better than a former enemy to tell you how to spot the weak points? And to tell you how the minds of your attackers work?'

Olivier took his time over his response. I'm not surprised, Gawyn thought.

'We are indeed in the process of fortifying this place,' Olivier said quietly after many minutes of silence. 'We do not anticipate attack this year, nor probably next. Perhaps we shall be left in peace entirely, perhaps we shall be our people's last refuge. We cannot know the future – we can only make intelligent guesses.'

And, Gawyn thought, you have been making those guesses for some time. This fortress has been here for years, and there are probably others.

The Cathars knew this crusade would happen.

'I was wrong,' he muttered.

Olivier looked at him sharply. 'In what way?'

'I didn't understand my enemy. Before, I mean. When I joined the crusade.' He thought back to those days. Thought of himself in Paimpol. The Cathars deserve annihilation, he'd said to Yves. Then, after Lyons, how he'd grown increasingly uneasy at the thought of how soft a target they were facing – decadent and demoralized, he'd judged the people of the Languedoc, too busy with songs and love-poems to come out and fight.

And then had come Béziers. Where heavily-armed knights had fallen on a defenceless town and crushed it like a boot on an anthill.

386

And Carcassonne.

The guilt was overwhelming. For, in addition to his realization that the 'enemy' were not the feeble and degraded people he'd taken them for but instead a far-sighted and astute group who just happened to see the world differently, they were also the people who'd saved his life.

'I won't take up arms against you again,' he said. 'You have my word as a knight.'

Olivier sighed. 'I believe you,' he said.

'But there are two things I would ask.' It was impertinent, and he knew it, as if he were demanding something in return for his promise. But the chance might not come again.

'Ask them,' Olivier said expressionlessly.

'First, that you let me help you with your defences.' He thought he saw Olivier smile briefly. 'Second,' – he hesitated, then plunged on – 'you tell me about the Cathars.'

Twenty

The second part of his request was fulfilled first, for Olivier would not let him get up to inspect the fortress until he was stronger.

For several hours of each day, either Olivier or one of the others who spoke a language Gawyn could understand would sit at his bedside talking to him about the Cathar beliefs and way of life. As if they wanted him to accept what they told him, they began with things he had no difficulty in approving – a man from Brittany told him of the simple hierarchy, fully-committed Perfects at the top, surrounded by a wide group of supporters and sympathizers who were not called upon to take the final step until they wanted to, often not until death approached.

A young woman sat with him one afternoon and told him quite calmly that, to the Cathars, it made no difference if you were male or female, Perfects were of both sexes. While he was still digesting this revolutionary statement, she went on to describe how they were taught medicine, taught to tend wounds and administer drugs. Belatedly, he realized she had a look of Estella, and he asked if she were the elder sister Olivier had mentioned.

'Yes. My name is Esclarma.'

'You sewed me up.'

She repeated the words under her breath, then laughed suddenly. 'Yes. I am sorry, I do not understand your language sometimes. Sewed you up.' She laughed again. He noticed that when her face melted out of its habitual solemnity, she was very pretty.

He said impulsively, 'Won't you ever marry? Have children?' Instantly regretful, he said, 'I'm sorry. I shouldn't have asked you anything so personal.' It's because she nursed me, he thought. Her hands were on my body, even though I didn't know it, and it's made me think I could take liberties.

'I am not upset,' she replied. 'As to marriage, I do not know. Perhaps, perhaps not.' Then, taking him utterly by surprise, she flashed him a look that was blatantly flirtatious. 'If I meet a handsome enough man, perhaps I will marry him.'

Before he could stop himself, he answered her in kind. 'It'd be some poor man's loss if you didn't.'

The small room seemed to thrum with the vibrations of sexual attraction. Then, as if he'd been standing outside and had picked them up, the door opened and Olivier came in.

Gawyn, glancing back at Esclarma, saw her lower her head, eyes fixed on the hands demurely clasped in her lap. Diew, he thought, turning slightly on his side and wincing as the blood surged through his still-tender genitals, I don't know whether to be sorry or relieved.

'Esclarma, your mother requires your help in the kitchen,' Olivier said. 'Now,' he picked up the stool she'd vacated and placed it a little further away from Gawyn's bed, 'what were you discussing?'

The dark eyes bored into Gawyn. He knows, he thought.

'Marriage,' he answered boldly. 'I asked your niece if she thought she would ever marry.'

'Because she is attractive? And you judge it would be a waste if she were not to fulfil her natural function?'

'Something like that,' Gawyn muttered.

'As I have already told you, we look upon matters of the flesh in the same light as we regard all material things: intrinsically evil, made by the evil god – Rex Mundi, we call him, the king of the world – as opposed to the Good God, the God of the spirit. Our life on earth is but a waiting time, until we die and our souls may rejoin our spirits, in heaven. Procreation we cannot approve, since each new conception wrests another soul down here to take up residence in an earthly body.'

'But –'

'How can we hope to continue, unless we propagate? There are two ways of looking at that. The purists among us might say that we do not want to continue, that we prefer to leave our souls in heaven and not make them endure life on earth. Others of us who are perhaps more practical would answer that procreation has a force of its own. That humans continue to unite and reproduce themselves, even if they do come to regret it afterwards.'

'And you have a way of coping with afterwards,' Gawyn said.

'Indeed. When a man or a woman is ready to forswear his or her sexuality, together with all the rest of the animal things of the world, and turn their minds and hearts to the pure spirituality of the Good God, then we administer the Consolamentum.'

Gawyn thought about that. He tried to see a time when he might be ready for such a step. He failed.

As if Olivier read his mind, he said gently, 'I think

that, for a man such as you, the Consolamentum might have to wait until your death bed.' As the tension eased, Gawyn thought he was getting away with it. But Olivier added softly, 'Judging from the way you look at my niece, possibly not even then.'

* * *

Eventually he was well. Well enough, anyway, to get up, to wash and dress – they provided him with a black robe such as they wore themselves – and find his way around the fortress.

It was not big. Very solidly built, the curtain walls enclosed a space that formed a long thin diamond shape, with the only entry in the south face. The living quarters were cramped, with the occupants – he estimated there were about fifty of them – accommodated in simple dormitories. There was a kitchen, off which led a well-stocked food store, and a central courtyard open to the sky. In the middle of this was a narrow well which must, he calculated, be at least a thousand feet deep. He noticed that the roofs sloped steeply, and that there were gutters under the wooden tiles to catch rainwater, which was collected in barrels.

Construction work was being carried out in the form of platforms superimposed on the tops of the walls. The courtyard smelt of cut wood.

He sat by the entry gate one morning, looking out at the faintly-discernible track that led up from the valley below. After some time, Olivier came to join him.

'You never said,' Gawyn remarked, 'how you got me here from Carcassonne.'

'No.'

It was quite a daunting reply. Gawyn was beginning to think it meant, and I'm not going to now, either, when Olivier gave his customary sigh and went on, 'Understandably, you are curious. What exactly do you want me to tell you?'

Gawyn nodded towards the slope in front of them. 'How did you – they – carry me up there?'

'It is not as awesome as it looks, except for the last hundred feet.' He pointed. 'Up this last stretch just below us, your stretcher was hauled with ropes attached to a pulley.' He indicated the apparatus, inside the gate. 'Further down, where the track enters the scrub, it is less steep. It has many twists and turns, to make the ascent easier.'

'And they carried me on a stretcher?'

'Yes.'

He looked down to where the path emerged from the greenery. He still couldn't see how they'd carried a long, heavy, inert body up there. 'How did they negotiate me round the bends?'

'I expect they folded you.' Olivier's tone was almost sharp. 'What else do you wish to know?'

'I'm not going to ask how we got out of Carcassonne, because I'm aware you won't tell me.' Olivier grunted. 'But Carcassonne is some way north of the Pyrenees, even the foothills. With a crusading army thundering after you, how did you manage to escape?'

'The army does not advance as quickly as a small group on the run,' Olivier replied. 'Simon de Montfort pauses at each town or village he reaches, and he does not move on until he has slaughtered all the inhabitants.'

The shame came back. Gawyn could not speak.

'I did not wish to imply a criticism of you,' Olivier said after some time. 'You are no longer a soldier of that army.'

'But I was.'

'Indeed. And I think that you now regret it.'

'I do.'

Clearly eager to move away from the delicate subject of Gawyn's former career, Olivier said, 'Do not forget that, in our journey from Carcassonne, we were travelling through lands still held by the Cathars and their sympathizers. As long as we moved ahead of the crusaders, we were among friends. It was not difficult to obtain food and shelter.'

Nor fresh horses to pull the carts, Gawyn thought. Manpower, even, to help haul an unconscious man up a mountain as steep as a roof.

'What will you do when more people come here to join you?' he asked abruptly. 'You are becoming crowded already, and the crusade – ' He stopped.

'The crusade has only just begun,' Olivier finished. 'We shall expand, as we need to. To the north a small plateau juts out, where we shall build houses. In times of threat, the inhabitants will come inside the walls.'

Gawyn looked up at the half-completed structures overhead. 'Have you weapons?' There was no point in firing platforms with nothing to fire from them.

'We have.'

'What?'

'Bows, arrows. Siege stones, the means to produce boiling pitch or oil, and –'

'Crossbows?'

'Yes.'

'You would be better off with the longbow.'

'It is not a weapon we are familiar with. An English weapon, is it?'

'A Welsh one,' Gawyn corrected him. 'Have you any wood with a long, straight grain to make it flexible? Yew, for example?'

Olivier thought. 'Yes. I believe we could find such.'

'Then I will teach you to become longbowmen.'

'What is wrong with our crossbows?'

The full answer was complex; Gawyn satisfied himself with, 'They're too slow. In skilled hands – and I'll give your archers skilled hands – a longbow can shoot a dozen arrows to the crossbow's three.'

Olivier's mouth dropped open. 'A dozen?'

'Aye.' He stood up, miming the action. 'See?'

Olivier grinned. 'Yes. I see.'

It was a slow and frustrating business, teaching southern archers used to the crossbow how to use the longbow. Especially, Gawyn thought ruefully, for a man whose right hand was still weak. The splints were off and he had been ordered to use it all he could, but, no matter how hard he tried, the former strength wasn't there. Not that he'd ever been a great bowman – he didn't tell his pupils, but a knight's weapon was the sword, not the mundane bow – but he'd at least had the ability to draw the string and hit a fairly demanding target. Now, cursing his pale and floppy right hand and wrist, it was as much as he could do to fit the arrow to the string.

Sometimes he'd see again the moment when the two French knights had relieved him of his sword in the narrow Carcassonne street. I would like, he thought, the chance to direct a hail of arrow fire at them.

It occurred to him that, quite possibly, he might also be put in a position where he was defending the fortress against Yves. Against Cadoc and Barr.

So, do I stop here and now? his pragmatic self would ask. On the vague chance that, in the whole of the Languedoc, the only crusaders I give a fig for happen to besiege this very castle?

He put it out of his mind.

*

As the weeks of September passed, he noticed a mood of excitement growing in the fortress. More people began to arrive, some of them richly dressed and attended by servants, and there were signs that a great deal of food was being prepared in the kitchen. At the end of the third week, Olivier came to find him one morning after he'd been taking his archers through their drill; his wrist was aching fiercely, and he was massaging in some of the ointment Esclarma had given him. She had shown him how to rub it in, and he'd decided that the sensuous, suggestive touch of her graceful fingers was entirely deliberate.

For his own reasons, he'd done it himself there-after.

Olivier came into his room and, going over to the window, stood fiddling with the catch on the shut-ters.

'Yes?' Gawyn prompted him.

Olivier turned to look at him, then turned away again.

'I don't know how to . . .' He trailed off. Then, abruptly, 'You have to be locked in for a day or so. We will bring you food and drink, and sometimes one or other of us will come to talk to you. I'm sorry, but it must be so.'

Gawyn felt first surprised, then slightly hurt. But all he said was, 'Very well.'

Olivier came to stand over him as he sat on the bed. 'Please understand it's not my decision,' he said agitatedly. 'I am only one voice, and we decide mat-ters of weight on a majority vote.' You would, Gawyn thought. Democracy goes hand in hand with your sort of tolerance. 'I told them they could trust you – look at the way he's training the bowmen! I said, and him with a hand only just recovering from a badly-broken bone! – but unfortunately they do not know

395

you as well as I do, and I could not convince them that a former – I am sorry.'

'I understand.' He did, only too well. I'm not sure I would trust me either, he thought. A former crusader, Olivier was about to say, which is exactly how these others he keeps referring to will see me. 'I suppose you can't give me any hint as to why I'm to be locked up?'

Olivier shook his head.

'No, I didn't think you could.'

Olivier said again, 'I'm sorry.' Then he hurried away.

Gawyn's incarceration continued for an evening, a night, all of the following day and night, and half of the day after that. Very early in the morning of the middle day, leaning on his windowsill (which, although looking out to the south, was too far round from the entrance to overlook any comings or goings), he noticed that the sun was directly to his left; to his right, the fortress's shadow extended out from the walls in a perfectly straight line.

It was, he judged, the day of the autumn equinox.

He hardly saw anyone, all day. His food was brought by people he didn't know, who didn't speak. When he spoke to them, they shrugged as if they didn't understand. Probably they didn't – Olivier's 'others' had no doubt ordered that he should be attended by people with whom he didn't have a common language.

In the evening, he thought he heard chanting. Gradually it became louder, rising into a great song of joy.

What was it? Some sort of religious ceremony?

Some secret ceremony, from which outsiders must be excluded.

He lay on his back on his bed, hands clasped behind his head. He felt very lonely.

The next day, as soon as he was released in the early afternoon, he made himself walk around the fortress until he was exhausted; had anyone asked him why, he'd been going to say, because I was cooped up all day yesterday.

But no-one did ask, which, he thought, was probably because he only managed a handful of circuits.

He was, he realized, still very far from fit. Very far from saying, it's time I left and went back to my own people.

Since it was something so clearly beyond him, there was little point in worrying how he'd imagined he might achieve it.

* * *

Autumn turned to winter, and the snows blowing into the fortress made it cold and bleak. There was no repetition of the days he'd been locked up, but, sensitive to his status as he hadn't been before, he knew now that he was an outsider. That, even if he could have overcome his misgivings and seen his way to taking their Consolamentum, it was doubtful the majority of the people in the stronghold would ever forget he was a Breton knight who had come south to kill them.

Why should they? he thought. It's the truth.

He saw little of anyone except Olivier. Esclarma visited him sometimes, usually with her mother, but, although it seemed to him that she went on inspecting the healed scar on the back of his neck for much longer than was necessary, she stopped flirting with him. Once she'd muttered something, giving him a long look from under sweeping eyelashes as she did so, but, when he failed to respond, she shrugged as if to say, I'm not wasting any more time on *you*.

Once her mother came with Estella.

She's a child, he thought, even younger than I'd guessed that day.

He saw her again, eyes wide as he pulled her head back by the hair. The vision sickened him.

He found a piece of wood from beside the hearth and, telling himself it was good exercise for his still-weak hand, carved a little figure for her. A female figure in a long dress, hair flowing down her back as long as Estella's own. He put a cheeky smile on the face, so that the doll had quite a look of Estella.

When he gave it to her, she gasped with pleasure, then put her arms round him and kissed him on the cheek. He felt comforted, as if at least one of the things he carried on his conscience had been lifted off.

The rest was not so easily shifted. In the deep winter, it seemed only natural to be profoundly depressed, but, as the year turned and neared the spring, he found his spirits going down instead of up.

And he still wasn't well.

He sought out Olivier.

'What's going to happen to me?' he asked bluntly. 'Am I free to go?'

Olivier stared at him, shock all over his face. 'But of course!'

'You're not going to keep me here? In case I return to my former ways?'

'You gave me your word you would not take up arms against us again,' Olivier said solemnly. 'That is good enough for me.'

'And the others?'

'And the others. If nothing else, they understand knighthood. They believe you will keep your word.'

I didn't keep my word to the side I started out with, he thought. But he didn't mention it to Olivier.

'What ails you?' Olivier asked kindly. 'You are restless, naturally – we all are, especially in winter when life becomes even more restricted – but there is more, I think.'

'I'm not fit. My wounds have healed, but – but –' He couldn't express what he wanted to say.

'But your mind has not,' Olivier said. 'I know this.' He hesitated, then went on delicately, 'May I say what I think?'

Gawyn shot him a smile. 'You usually do.'

Olivier smiled back. 'Indeed.' He paused, sighed, and said, 'I fear that you are not mending because your mind forbids it. Let me explain,' – he put his hand on Gawyn's arm as Gawyn began to protest – 'and you will see what I mean. You were badly wounded, left for dead, and I believe that, because your conscience is troubled about certain things you have done in the past, a part of you accepted death as a fair punishment. When we came along and saved you, therefore, it was more, you felt, than you deserved. So your mind, believing you ought to be dead, will not let your body recover.'

'Diew,' Gawyn burst out. Then, as the unspoken angry denial faded, he began to wonder if Olivier might not have hit upon the truth.

After a few more moments, he knew that he had.

'What must I do?'

Olivier looked at him with an expression that was almost love. 'You must seek forgiveness for what you have done wrong.'

'Aye.'

Olivier leaned towards him, then said quietly, 'And are you clear as to what these things are?'

He said, 'Oh, yes. Quite clear.'

He tried to pray, but it did no good. I'm not used to praying on my own, he thought, apart from the sort of hasty prayer you shoot off in battle when you're terrified you're about to die.

Without a congregation around him, without a priest at the altar leading the service, he was lost. He could hardly even repeat the words.

Approaching the problem as if it were a military one, he decided there were two alternatives. Either he must join the Cathars, and adopt whatever procedures they had for confession, repentance and absolution, or he must find his way down out of the fortress, out of Cathar-held territory and back to his own people.

'My own people,' he repeated aloud.

As he thought about it, it gained in appeal. Olivier and his immediate family have given me kindness, he thought, in Olivier's case a kindness as great as he'd have given to one of his own. Some of their number carried me here, and someone – I never did find out who – bore my weapons and armour, which have lain in the corner of the room untouched for months.

But, kind though they have been, I am not one of them. Can never be, for, although I have grown to admire them and all they believe in, it's not the way for me.

He saw Esclarma's eyes, lids lowered suggestively. Saw the rounded breasts as she arched her back into an attitude designed to provoke.

For them, it's acceptable to live one life now and another later. For me, it would be impossible – it would have to be all or nothing, and I'm not ready to forswear the things of the flesh. Women. Sex. Marriage and children.

Esclarma's face swam before him again, a questioning look in her eyes.

He smiled. 'No, not you, my lovely,' he whispered.

Later, he thought, I'll go and find Olivier to tell him I'm going to leave. And, assuming I manage to get down the mountain without falling off it and breaking my neck, ask his advice on how I can get myself back into Catholic lands.

Twenty-one

He set out from the Pyrenean stronghold at the end of March. He'd been ready to leave a month earlier, but Olivier had made him wait. He did not know why, although he had his suspicions.

He had gone to Olivier restless and troubled, having persuaded himself into a state where everything about his present whereabouts was wrong, everything outside right. Olivier had talked some sense back into him, made him see the logic of careful preparation.

'To begin with,' he said, eyeing Gawyn with faint amusement, 'where do you want to go?'

'Back into Catholic lands.'

'I appreciate that and, before you start explaining yourself,' – Gawyn shut his mouth again – 'yes, I understand what you mean, and no, I haven't taken offence at your desire to fling yourself into the bosom of the enemy. But Catholic lands are all around us,' – Gawyn wondered if Olivier realized the poignancy of the statement – 'so you must be a little more specific. What is your ultimate destination?'

I don't know, Gawyn thought. But military men never admitted to such failures in long-term strategy: improvising, he said, 'North.'

'North,' Olivier repeated flatly. Then, eyes bright, 'North covers rather a large area.'

'Brittany. I have a castle there.'

'Ah. And you aim to return to your castle and resume your life as a Breton knight? Who went missing, presumed dead, in Carcassonne?'

'Aye.' Gawyn thought it sounded quite good, for something plucked from the air on the spur of the moment.

'And what will your fellow knights think when you return from the dead?'

Gawyn grinned. 'They'll kill the fatted calf and give thanks. Don't worry,' – he caught Olivier's eye – 'I won't say a word about how the Cathars rescued me and cared for me in their mountain fastness.'

'I know you won't.' The moment was intense. Then, as if deliberately lightening the mood, Olivier added, 'Apart from anything else, the Church might be interested to speak to a knight who had consorted with heretics, which appears to me a very good reason for you to keep silent.'

Gawyn had thought of that already. Even before Carcassonne, there had been rumours of a monk called Dominic, who was the leader of a group detailed by the Church to interrogate suspected heretics and encourage them back to orthodoxy. The rumours had been hazy about what constituted encouragement.

'Brittany,' Olivier repeated after reflection. 'Then it's not a good idea for me to suggest, as I was going to, that we send you to Santiago de Compostela.'

'Why would you send me there?'

Olivier looked at him resignedly. 'Because it is a great pilgrimage centre. Catholics go on pilgrimages, I understand, when they feel compelled to be shriven of their sins. Santiago ranks with Jerusalem and

Rome itself, I believe, although since we speak of your faith and not mine, possibly you know better.' The irony was impossible to miss. 'However –' He paused. The pause extended.

'However what?' Gawyn prompted eventually.

'There is another shrine which gains in popularity with every year. They speak of miracles, marvels and incredible events taking place in the presence of a statue of the Virgin Mary.' Olivier's tone suggested he didn't believe a word of what 'they' said. 'The shrine is looked upon as a place to go when all else fails – a place for penitents bearing the heaviest spiritual load.' He glanced sharply at Gawyn. 'They tell me many former soldiers go there.'

'Where is it?' It has to be somewhere within reach and on my route, Gawyn thought eagerly, or else why mention it?

'The shrine is at a place called Rocamadour. The rock of Amadour – Amadour's perfectly preserved body was found, they say, and they claim he was descended from Zacharius.'

'And where is Rocamadour?' Gawyn asked patiently.

Olivier smiled. 'It is on the road north.'

* * *

In the last week of March, when Gawyn had trained himself up to the best level of fitness he could achieve within the fortress walls and was wild to get going, his frustration was increased a hundredfold by another two-day incarceration.

'Why?' he thundered at Olivier, who stood his ground unflinchingly – Gawyn had an instant's admiration for him, since Olivier had come to break the news the morning when Gawyn happened to be

404

trying on his hauberk and weapons. He judged, from the dismayed look in Olivier's eyes as he'd come into the room, that he must present a different picture from the black-clad figure he'd been for so long.

Perhaps I remind him of things he doesn't want to think about, Gawyn thought.

'I cannot tell you why,' Olivier said.

'You couldn't last time either, I remember,' Gawyn said bitterly. Then, going to stand right in front of Olivier, 'Please! Not now, I don't think I can –' In time he heard himself and stopped. Turning sharply away, he went to stand by the window.

'I am very sorry,' Olivier said. 'Believe me, Gawyn, I understand how hard this will be for you. Worse this time than last, for I read in every inch of you how restless you are, how much you want to be away. But there is nothing I can do.'

Quietly he left the room. Gawyn heard the sound of the bolts sliding home.

The next two days followed exactly the same pattern as the last time he'd been locked in. Only the season was different: this time, the day when that joyful evening hymn soared up towards the vast sky was the spring equinox.

They came to release Gawyn, Olivier and three of the other Perfects. He was ordered to prepare for immediate departure.

He didn't ask any questions. Stripping off the black robe, he was dressing in his own garments before they'd finished speaking.

'We have made this for you,' Olivier said as the other two Perfects left, handing him a woollen robe in an unremarkable shade of greyish-beige. 'It will cover your mail and weapons.' Again, Gawyn noticed the swift glance at his sword.

'I can't travel unarmed,' he said gently. 'You must realize that. The Cathars want me because I'm a crusader – I was a crusader,' he corrected himself, 'and the crusaders want me because I deserted them. As you pointed out, the crusaders hang those who change sides. Don't make me feel bad about wanting to be able to defend myself.'

Olivier bowed his head in acknowledgement. 'Very well.' He smiled slightly. 'You are to travel with four others, so possibly you will come in useful in defending them, too.'

Gawyn drew his sword. It still felt heavier than it had done before his wrist had been broken, but the strength was rapidly returning: the hours he'd spent up on the parapets, endlessly repeating sword exercises, had helped.

'I'll do that,' he said shortly. 'Who are they, these others?'

Olivier glanced at him. 'Men whose route lies alongside yours,' he said. 'They will guide you safely on your way, although they will not accompany you as far as Rocamadour.'

Because Rocamadour lies within enemy territory, Gawyn concluded.

He was ready. He moved his limbs experimentally – he'd forgotten how encumbering were the hauberk and the padded garments worn beneath it. I've spent six months in nothing but a single garment, he thought. Reaching for his pack, he took out the wrapped cross, lifting his robe to put the parcel in its old place under his cuirass.

'Have you room there for this?'

Gawyn was startled at Olivier's tone: he sounded quite unlike himself. He sounds nervous! Gawyn realized in surprise. And anxious, as if much depends on my reply.

He looked at the object Olivier was holding out. It, too, was wrapped – in fine soft leather – and appeared roughly spherical. It was about the size of a clasped fist.

He took it from Olivier's hand. It was heavy.

'I'll try it for size.' He slid it beneath his cuirass. It fitted, although he could feel its hard curved edge pressing against the chain mail over his diaphragm. 'Yes, I've room.'

'Will you take it with you?' Again the nervousness.

'Aye. Where am I to take it?'

Olivier hesitated. 'I cannot tell you.'

Gawyn laughed. 'You're not being very helpful!'

Olivier smiled ruefully. 'I cannot tell you because I do not know, either where you must take it or who you must give it to. I can only tell you that, when the time comes, you will know.'

'You trust me that much?' The blunt question was out before Gawyn could stop it.

But Olivier didn't seem to mind. Holding Gawyn's eyes, he said quietly, 'I do.'

After a moment Gawyn said, 'I suppose you won't tell me what it is?'

'I doubt if you would understand – I haven't the time to tell you at sufficient length. Also –' Olivier broke off. Then he muttered, 'Also, it is better that you do not know.'

'Those inquisitive Catholics again?' It was only a guess, but it proved right: Olivier nodded. His face grave, he said, 'What you do not know, you cannot tell. And if you were to speak of this –'

He didn't continue.

Gawyn put his hand on the object. Noticing, Olivier said, 'You may look at it, if you like.' He smiled. 'I know you will do so anyway, as soon as you are able, so it may as well be with my blessing.'

Gawyn drew it out and folded back the covering leather. In his open palm sat a crystal sphere.

He said after a moment, 'It's beautiful!'

Olivier nodded. His eyes were fixed on the sphere, and he seemed to be overcome with some deep emotion.

'What's it made of?'

Recovering the power of speech, Olivier said, 'It is a form of quartz. Very rare, found only in certain places deep in the earth. It is –' Again, he firmly shut his mouth on whatever it was he had been about to say. 'Cover it up,' he whispered. 'Please.' He added something else, but his voice was so low that the words were indistinct. Gawyn thought they sounded like, 'It is too powerful.'

He did as he was told, pushing the sphere back beneath his cuirass. Then he and Olivier went out of his room and descended into the courtyard.

Several of the community were waiting to bid him farewell. Estella and her mother both kissed him, and Esclarma patted his arm.

'Now you look like a soldier,' she said. 'For all that you conceal your mail and your weapons.'

He was amused. 'If you can't see my mail and weapons, why do you say I look like a soldier?'

Despite her smile, he thought she looked sad. 'I was not telling the truth,' she said. 'You always did look like a soldier. It's the way you walk – like all sword bearers, you lean over to compensate for the weight of the sword at your side. Even when you're not wearing it.'

He said softly, for her ears only, 'And it's something to be sorry about, when a man is a soldier?'

Looking up at him, eyes clouded, slowly she nodded.

Olivier walked with him to the entry gate. Four

men stood beside it, dressed for travelling. Olivier introduced them; the leader's name was Armand.

Tactfully, the four went out through the gate, waiting for Gawyn on the rocky shelf immediately beneath it. He and Olivier were alone.

'You saved my life,' Gawyn said. 'I'm forever in your debt.'

Olivier smiled. 'Already I have called in that debt,' he said quietly.

'Why, what have you asked of me? Oh – yes.' The sphere.

'Yes. It is far more important than your life, if you do not take it amiss, so be assured that you have discharged your debt, many times over.'

Or I will have done, Gawyn thought, when I get it to the right hands. Whoever they belong to.

Olivier reached up his arms to hold Gawyn by the shoulders. He stared into Gawyn's eyes, then said, 'Farewell. God be with you.'

It didn't matter whose God: probably, Gawyn thought, one God rules us all. 'Goodbye,' he replied.

They stood like that for some moments. Gawyn knew – and was quite sure Olivier did too – that they would never meet again.

There was nothing more to say. Disengaging himself gently so that Olivier's hands fell by his sides, Gawyn turned, went out through the gate and climbed down to the waiting group below.

The descent was perilous. In places, they had to slide feet-first down bare rock, with nothing to cling on to but more rock. Elsewhere the path appeared to follow an ancient dry stream-bed, where they had to leap from ledge to ledge. When they reached the tree-line the going was a little easier, although the slope was still so steep that the path kept doubling tightly back on itself.

How they got me up there, Gawyn thought, pausing to look back over his shoulder at the fortress high above, God alone knows.

It made him queasy just to think about it.

When at last they were on relatively level ground, Armand put a restraining hand on Gawyn's arm.

'What is it?' He spun round, muscles tensing.

'I am sorry,' Armand said pleasantly, 'but we must blindfold you.'

Gawyn drew his sword halfway from its sheath. Then he put it back.

'Thank you.' He thought there might have been a tinge of relief in Armand's voice. 'You understand, they are afraid, in the fortress, that you might lead others here.'

'Olivier trusted me.'

'Yes. I know. Others too. But the majority –'

'The majority did not. Very well.' He bent down – he was a head taller than all of them – while Armand tied a black cloth over his eyes. Then someone took hold of his hands, binding them behind him.

'I won't take it off,' he said, controlling his voice with an effort. 'You have my word.'

'I believe you.' Armand sounded apologetic. 'However, if you were to stumble, the survival instinct would make you uncover your eyes before you had time to remember that you have given your word not to.'

He was right. Gawyn submitted to being led away.

'You realize, don't you,' he couldn't resist saying as they set off, 'that I can tell from the position of the sun which way we're going?'

'I do,' came the calm reply. 'That's why we're going to stop soon. We shall only go on once darkness has fallen.'

410

Gawyn thought, you think of everything.

They kept him blindfolded throughout the night's journey. When the sun came up, he thought it was to his right, which meant they were going north. Soon after dawn, one of them must have gone off to some pre-arranged rendezvous: he came back with five horses. They got Gawyn mounted – not without difficulty as, perversely, he was refusing to help – untied his hands and bound them in front of him, attaching them to the pommel of the saddle.

At noon, as the sun reached its highest, brightest point, they undid his hands and took the blindfold off. They probably chose their moment deliberately, he reflected, rubbing at his streaming eyes, to pay me back for being awkward when they were trying to get me on the horse.

He glanced at Armand. 'Quits?'

Armand nodded, grinning. 'Quits.'

Soon after midday they stopped to eat, then lay down to sleep. He was so tired he didn't think he'd ever wake up.

The fatigue continued to be a serious problem. He'd been confident that he would steadily build up to full fitness as the days of the journey went by; so confident that, when Olivier had told him he'd be provided with a horse, once the steep descent from the Pyrenees had been accomplished, he'd nonchalantly said he'd probably walk some of the time to put the muscle back in his legs.

Walk! he cried silently, remembering the moment on an afternoon when the pain between his shoulders was all but unbearable. It's as much as I can do to ride.

The others, no doubt picking up the despair that he

fought to keep under control, helped him by their mute support. Armand referred to Gawyn as Le Vieillard, sometimes making a show of offering him the best sleeping place or the only seat: going along with the fun, Gawyn was aware Armand knew as well as he did that it was no joke at all.

* * *

By the end of April they were nearing Minerve. Gawyn could have retraced his steps for much of the journey, but the blindfold had done its job: he knew that, even if his life depended on it, he couldn't have found his way back to the fortress. He knew it was in the Pyrenees, and that the Pyrenees lay to the south-west: that was all.

Along the way they had passed desolate, ruined towns and villages, empty of all inhabitants, some still smouldering. De Montfort's men had ripped up young vines, trampled on the pale green shoots of crops, polluted wells and streams with filth; in one town, where there was no living thing save a ravenous, scavenging cat, they found the well was blocked with decapitated bodies.

Increasingly they found evidence of mass burnings.

'It is his way,' Armand said, white-faced, fierce emotion making his pleasant mouth a thin hard line as he and Gawyn stood together by a huge charred pile of mixed wood and bone; undoubtedly the bones were human. 'We are offered a choice: renounce our faith or burn.'

Gawyn, trying to comprehend, said, 'Why don't you pretend to give up your beliefs, then go back to them when the danger's past?' That's what I'd do, he thought.

Armand looked at him pityingly. 'You do not understand at all, do you?'

'No, I don't,' he said roughly. He wasn't going to be put in the wrong.

'Is there nothing you would die for?'

He paused, thinking. It would have been easy to lie, but he felt that in this matter it would have been dishonourable. 'Aye, there is,' he said eventually.

'What?' Armand looked at him curiously.

Gawyn was picturing the wild dark waters of a river in flood. Seeing a pale arm reaching for him. He thought, I'd have died if I'd known it would have saved her.

He said, 'Someone I once knew.'

'Then perhaps you can understand.' Armand's tone was kinder. 'But I think you do not regard life as we do, as something to be endured while we await the joyful release of death.'

Dear God, no, Gawyn thought. But he'd been among Cathars long enough not to say so. 'No,' he agreed mildly. 'I don't see it quite like that.'

Still, he thought as they both turned back to the grisly pile before them, I wouldn't do that to anyone who thought differently.

He'd known, as they descended into the gorge that lay before Minerve, that he couldn't ride any further. Not until he'd rested. For several days. Armand and the others had some unspecified mission in the town, and he let them go on ahead, flinging himself down in the cool shady grass. Slowly he let the sore, bunched muscles of his legs and thighs relax.

He lay flat on his back in the shade, the afternoon sun filtering through the thick green foliage overhead. Above him, the village up on its plateau was loud with life – as in so many places in the besieged

413

Languedoc, there was the eternal sound of hammering – and he knew he ought to be up there adding his strength to the general effort.

What strength? he thought bitterly. Less than a month on the road, and I'm totally exhausted. After an easy day's ride over the sort of distance I used to cover in a morning, I'm fit for nothing but lying down gasping for breath and waiting for my heart to stop pounding.

Often – too often for comfort – he recalled Olivier's words. You are not mending because your mind forbids it.

He rolled over, easing the collar of his hauberk away from his neck. The six months he'd lived in the fortress up in the Pyrenees had weakened him in more ways than one: the protective calluses at the points on his body where the chain mail rubbed had entirely disappeared. He was now having to break himself in all over again.

He gazed up towards Minerve. It was already a formidable sight – the Cathar resistance had been launching attacks on the crusaders from there all winter – and the additional work now being completed would surely make it virtually impregnable. It'll need to be, Gawyn thought – now that spring was here, de Montfort would no longer have to manage with the token force comprised only of those who hadn't returned home after their forty days: the northern knights were coming back. And not in a trickle, in a flood.

He had learned what had happened over the winter: the Cathars had told him. With admirable restraint, considering they were addressing a former crusader, they described how Simon de Montfort had further refined his tactic of setting ghastly examples: in Montlaur, he hanged every last inhabitant who

414

hadn't the speed to flee him – the very young and the very old weren't very good at fleeing – and in Bram, which he'd taken in March, he put out the eyes of the entire garrison bar one, who was left intact in order to lead the rest away.

They'll fight tooth and nail to take Minerve, he thought, staring at the vast stone walls and the high towers. And the other strongholds.

He wondered, as he had often done over the last month as he learned more and more of de Montfort's atrocities, if he should abandon his plan of returning to his own. If he should stay here and fight it out with the Cathars. A part of him wanted that, badly.

But something was drawing him on. He couldn't have said what it was, beyond the urgent need to find spiritual peace, and if he wanted that, it was no good staying with the Cathars.

There was something beyond that vague but tenacious pull. Gawyn was a realist: no matter how much he admired and sympathized with the Cathars, he didn't underestimate the forces stacked against them. De Montfort and his northern knights in the vanguard, behind them the power of Rome and the might of the French monarchy.

He wanted the Cathars to win. But he knew they weren't going to.

He wondered how long it would be before the others came back. They'll be gone some time, he thought sleepily. Until nightfall, they said. Although they promised to fetch me in time for supper.

He yawned. It'll be bread and vegetables again. Oh, good.

That's the trouble with these Cathars, he reflected as, his drowsiness increasing, the hammering and the shouting voices began to recede. Wonder what they'd be like if they ate the occasional good square meal?

Before he was fully asleep, he was already dreaming. Of young Welsh lamb, the fat sizzling and crisp.

Twenty-two

Two of the party remained at Minerve; travelling on accompanied only by Gawyn and the fourth member of the group – a sad-faced, brooding man who had lost his family at Béziers – Armand set a faster pace.

Gawyn gritted his teeth and stood it for five days. At midday on the sixth, he passed out and fell off his horse.

Responding to cold water splashed on his face, he came to, finding himself lying on the bank of the river they'd been following. Armand was kneeling over him; the silent Louis held the horses.

'We will eat now,' Armand said. 'Then rest until the sun is lower.'

'You eat.' Gawyn was not hungry. 'I'll sit here in the shade.'

Armand put his face up close. 'You *will* eat,' he said with quiet intensity. 'While you are ailing, you hold us up. And if you do not eat, you will have no strength.'

Gawyn struggled to sit up. 'You are accusing me of slowing our progress?'

Armand smiled grimly. 'No. We could not have ridden more swiftly than we have done these past days, that I acknowledge. We must be almost halfway to Rocamadour. But there is danger, unless we continue to move fast.'

There was no need for him to specify what danger.

They shared out nourishing, if unappetizing, rations of flat doughy bread and a sort of cake made of cooked, compressed vegetables; the bean seemed to feature prominently. Gawyn made himself eat all he was given. Afterwards he went down to the river, removing his boots and letting the fast-flowing water cool his feet. When, too soon, Armand called down to say it was time to go, he was ready. As ready, he thought, as I'm likely to be.

He wondered, as the gruelling journey continued, if Armand had deliberately put into his mind the idea that he was the weak link. If so, Armand had achieved the result he wanted: for the next week and a half, Gawyn endured whatever Armand chose to dictate without question or complaint. The going was easy, for as long as they followed the wide river valley they had come across on the fifth day; a day and a half later, the oak-clad hills of Quercy came into view, and the respite came to an end.

They climbed through the foothills and out on to the limestone heights of the *causses*. The terrain became deceptive. What appeared to be an even, scrub-covered plateau would reveal itself to be no such thing: great gorges would suddenly open up, extending out of sight in both directions so that the only way to get across was to descend right down into the depths and climb laboriously up the other side. In the June heat the horses frothed and staggered; Louis and Armand looked exhausted.

Gawyn went beyond exhaustion. As they struggled up out of yet another gorge, he clamped his hands on to the pommel of the saddle, shut his eyes and willed himself to stay upright. Knowing there was no danger that his weary horse would take advantage of his inattention, he let himself lapse into a sort of sleep. He felt sick and light-headed, and the many days' riding had put a severe strain on the neck and back muscles damaged by the wound he had sustained in Carcassonne.

He became aware that his horse's slow steps had ceased. Opening his eyes, trying to straighten up, he saw that, immediately ahead of him, Armand and Louis had dismounted. They were standing on a small mound, staring on down the track that led along the top of the gorge.

Armand turned. Pointing to where he'd been looking, he said, 'Rocamadour.'

Through the sparse trees Gawyn could see a steep cliff dropping almost sheer into the deep gorge below. He said, his voice cracking, 'Where?'

'There!'

He peered harder, trying to focus. He thought he could make out a clump of small buildings crouching under the massive overhang of the cliff. 'There?' He waved his arm vaguely in the right direction.

'Yes. Here we are standing on the *montjoie* – where pilgrims catch their first sight of the sanctuary.' Armand walked back to stand at Gawyn's stirrup. Putting his hand on Gawyn's, he said, 'Louis and I must leave now. We can go no further with you.'

Gawyn, shocked into awareness, said, 'You should not have come as far as this! There was no need for you to risk your lives for my sake.'

Armand laughed shortly. 'I agree.' He punched Gawyn's leg lightly, removing the sting from the words. 'Given the choice, me, I should have left you to your own devices days ago. However, we had our instructions, which were to see you safe to within sight of your goal.' He pointed again towards Rocamadour. 'There it is.'

Olivier, Gawyn thought. It was Olivier who issued those orders.

He felt a moment's warm happiness that Olivier had considered his safety so important. Important enough to have risked the lives of Armand and Louis.

Then he remembered the sphere. No, he amended, it isn't my safety that's so important.

He put out his hand to Armand, who clasped it. 'Thank you,' he said. Armand inclined his head. 'Where do you go now, you and Louis?'

Armand shrugged. 'South,' he said, as if it hardly mattered. 'To whatever the future may hold.' Then he looked up into Gawyn's eyes; there was no need for either of them to say any more.

Gawyn watched as the two of them re-mounted and rode away. Neither turned back.

When they were almost out of sight, he spurred his tired horse and went on to Rocamadour.

At the top of the cliff there was a small settlement of hostels and taverns, whose sole purpose seemed to be to cater for the needs of the pilgrims. The place was thronging with people, carts and horses, the narrow road made even narrower by the stalls selling food and drink. Gawyn's mouth filled with saliva as waves of some strong savoury smell wafted by: a man behind a stall was shouting, 'Cassoulet! Cassoulet!'

He reached for one of his few remaining coins, wondering if it would be acceptable to the stallholder. It was; Gawyn realized that in a place of pilgrimage, traders must be used to all sorts of coins. The man held out to him a steaming pot; dismounting – it was more like falling – Gawyn took it from him. Moving to a small roped-off space immediately behind the stall, he unsheathed his dagger and cut into the baked crust, releasing a fresh surge of the delicious smell. Beneath the crust were layers of beans and vegetables.

And generous hunks of fat spicy pork.

He wolfed down the entire pot-ful, so meat-hungry that he hardly bothered to chew, scarcely noticed how the food burned his throat. Then, his stomach feeling suddenly bloated, he gave back the empty pot and set off to find a place to rest.

A few yards up the road he began to feel sick. Dizzy, he clung on to his horse's neck for support, jostled by the crowds, confused by the shouting voices. Stumbling into a gap between two houses, eyes streaming, heart pounding, he threw up the cassoulet, which he could hear splashing down repeatedly on to the rocks successively far below.

When he had finished and was wiping his face on his sleeve, a kindly voice behind him said, 'Welcome, pilgrim. Are you in need of succour?'

An elderly woman stood there, plump and smiling. Mutely he nodded.

'Yes, I thought so. What a thing to do on reaching Rocamadour, I thought to myself, bring up your dinner all over the Lady Chapel roof!'

He glanced back over the edge: it seemed she was right, for some distance below, he could see a pitched roof made of limestone slabs.

Diew, he thought. 'I'm sorry,' he muttered. 'I –'

'I was teasing!' she cried, laughing delightedly. 'The Lady Chapel's right over there,' – she pointed further down the cliff edge – 'don't you worry!'

He was finding it taxing to stand. 'Is there somewhere I could rest?'

She moved forwards – quickly, for someone of her bulk – and took his arm. 'Yes, yes, come with me. We've many hostels here – this place is called

L'Hospitalet, see? – and the best one is St John the Baptist – my nephew works there, he'll see you're well looked after, and –'

'I haven't much money.'

'Who has?' she said resignedly. 'No matter, some have less than you, I'll warrant.' She eyed him up and down. 'Come far, have you?'

'Aye.'

'Where from?'

He'd prayed, without much hope, that she wouldn't ask that: he was too far gone to make up a plausible lie, and the truth certainly wouldn't do. 'I come from Brittany,' he said evasively.

'Thought so! I can always tell, it's the accent, see? Brittany,' she repeated. 'Brittany. There now! Not that you've come the furthest, oh, dear, no, we've had pilgrims from Paris, from Ireland, from Russia, from Albi, ooh, all over!'

Russia? He wondered if she was right. He doubted it – if her list of places was meant to be in ascending order of distance, he thought, then geography was not her strongest point.

'Here we are.' She was banging her fist against a wooden door set in stout walls. Very quickly, the door opened and a boy stood gawping at them. 'Fetch Dominic,' – Gawyn started at the name, but no, it couldn't be *that* Dominic – 'quickly, we've a sick man here!'

Gawyn's knees were buckling. He leaned against his horse, which stoutly supported him. Sick man, he thought vaguely. Aye.

He couldn't see properly. The old woman was clucking, the boy was shouting, then a man was there too, and he was being lifted, his heels dragging in the dust. Someone called out, 'Father Joseph is visiting nearby – better fetch him to look at this one!'

Then, at last, he was lying down. On a hard plank bed with no covers, but still he was lying down. There was a moment's respite, when they all seemed to vanish and he thought he might be allowed to go to sleep, but then he heard loud footsteps approaching, thumping on the ground as if someone very determined were crossing the yard.

Firm hands pushed him on to his back, and a palm was placed across his forehead.

'Slight fever.' The voice was brusque. 'Dominic, you and the boy strip him and check him for plague sores and leprosy spots. If he has none, wash him and let him sleep. If you have the least suspicion, put him in the cart and get him out of town.'

'Yes, Father Joseph,' a voice answered obediently.

Gawyn put up no resistance as the man and the boy removed his robe and swordbelt. But he was not so far gone that he forgot what he carried under his cuirass: unfastening it, he took it off and put it on the floor, the two parcels concealed beneath it. Dominic was stumped by his hauberk, until silently he indicated how it unlaced. When he was naked, they inspected every inch of him. Then he heard Dominic call out, 'He's clear, Father.'

As they proceeded to wash him – very thoroughly, and in wonderfully cool water – he let himself relax. When they'd finished, they wrapped him in a rough linen sheet. At last he went to sleep.

When he woke, the room was in darkness. Drowsy, slightly confused, he said, 'Olivier?'

No. Not Olivier. 'He's not here,' he muttered, 'he's in the clouds. They fly, Olivier and his people. They watch the sun, and sing hymns of joy.' He could see them, robed in black, the lips of the Perfects forever moving as they recited silent Paternosters. They healed my body, he thought, but they couldn't heal my mind. 'Black,' he whispered, 'robed in black. No light, no light of forgiveness.'

He turned on his side, and a figure crouching by the bed jumped up and ran out: he recognized the silhouette of the young boy.

Almost immediately, someone else came to take the boy's place.

Father Joseph's harsh voice said out of the darkness, 'You have been talking in your sleep, pilgrim. It would appear you are sore in need of Our Lady's grace.' Sitting down by the bed, he struck a flint and lit a candle in the wall-sconce.

'Aye,' Gawyn said. I should be feeling a huge relief, he thought. This is what I've come here for, this is the way back for me.

He wondered why he was registering such disquiet.

'A sickness in the mind, is it?'

Gawyn wondered how he knew. Was he merely making a guess, based on Dominic's report of no visible bodily ill?

Then he remembered the boy. I disturbed him with my ramblings, he thought. And he ran off. To report to Father Joseph.

'I have been sick,' he began carefully. 'I was healed in body, but – ' How do I go on? he wondered. I can't tell him I was tended by a Cathar, who concluded that it was my guilty conscience that was preventing my return to full health. 'But I am uneasy in my mind,' he finished lamely.

'Uneasy,' Father Joseph echoed. 'You feel, shall we say, unlike yourself?'

'Aye,' he agreed tentatively. In that I'm usually strong, and now I'm weak.

'Thinking strange thoughts?'

'I don't –'

'Seeing black where there should be light?' Father Joseph was on his feet now, looming threateningly over Gawyn. 'Haunted by beings who fly through the air?'

'No!' Gawyn shouted. That cursed boy! 'You've misunderstood, you've –'

Suddenly Father Joseph's hand smashed across his mouth, so violently that he felt one of his teeth give way.

'Silence, liar!' he thundered, pushing Gawyn back on to the bed. 'Let not the devils in you speak untruths, for thus they seek to lure the godly away from their suspicions! I am not fooled!'

Face close to Gawyn's, wide pale eyes fierce in their fanaticism, he hissed, 'I say to the man within, if you can still hear me, fear not! I will come to your aid!'

Then, pulling back, in a hollow voice he delivered his judgement:

'Thou art possessed!'

For some time after Father Joseph had at last left him – not before he'd had Gawyn on his knees beside him making the responses to an interminable series of prayers, all uttered at the top of Father Joseph's powerful voice – Gawyn lay stunned, his mental faculties temporarily shocked into inactivity.

Possessed.

The very word horrified him.

Possessed. Unclean spirit. What is thy name? My name is Legion, for we are many.

Those possessed of evil spirits were chained and flogged, to drive the devil out. He shuddered. But wouldn't it be worth it? Worth anything, surely, to be rid of an unclean spirit!

He was repeating the prayers, over and over, the full superstitious dread on him driving him to panic.

Then, as if the sun had come out, he saw Olivier. He was sitting with his eyes closed, the brilliant light of the mountains on his upturned face. Saying, 'When we saved you, you felt it was more than you deserved.' And, 'You must seek forgiveness for what you have done wrong.'

'I'm not possessed,' he said aloud.

The relief was enormous. Logic flooding back, he realized he'd been ensnared by his own background; until Olivier had shown him another way, he'd lived with the faith of his forefathers all his life. Believed in the power of devils, followed without question whatever he'd been taught, obeyed unthinkingly whatever orders he was given.

Even, he thought, when those orders were, go out and kill heretics. Slaughter them all, and God will be pleased. Do your forty days' crusading, earn your remittance.

That was one of the things I did wrong: I followed too blindly, and I was prepared to slaughter people I now know to be good purely because someone else told me to do so.

Olivier sent me here to pray for forgiveness, so that's what I shall do.

Peacefully he turned over and settled down to sleep.

He was awake early, disturbed by a tremendous racket out in the yard; it sounded as if an army were either arriving or departing. No, not an army, they sound too cheerful. He recalled that it was Midsummer Day, and wondered if some party of pilgrims might be going off merrymaking. Dressing, he went to the door to look out.

And found he was locked in.

Anger rose, and for a moment he was about to attack the wooden panels with his shoulder. Then he paused to think, and decided it wouldn't be in his best interests to do so. They'd expect a man possessed of evil to throw himself against his prison door, so it's the last thing I must do.

When Dominic undid the bolts and brought in his breakfast, he was kneeling by the bed, apparently in prayer.

'Good morning,' he said pleasantly, getting to his feet and bowing to Dominic. He tried to give him a reassuring smile, but it hurt his freshly-split lip.

'Morning,' Dominic muttered. Gawyn noticed his eyes slid away. I don't blame him for not wanting to look at me, he thought, waggling the loose tooth in his lower jaw with his tongue, possessed or not, I can't be a pretty sight .

'I wish to go to the chapel,' he announced.

Dominic almost dropped his tray. 'Chapel?' he whispered. 'But –'

Gawyn thought he would have crossed himself if he hadn't still been holding the tray. 'But men possessed of the devil don't go to chapel?' he supplied.

Dumbly Dominic shook his head. 'Well,' Gawyn said, 'you must decide what this means. Does my wish to go and pray indicate that the devil in me is extremely cunning, do you think, lulling you into believing he isn't really there?' Dominic's mouth fell open: Gawyn concluded that he wasn't very bright. 'Or could it,' he continued, 'mean that I'm not really possessed?'

Dominic backed off. 'I'll fetch the Father,' he muttered. And ran off.

He had forgotten to close the door, so Gawyn ate his breakfast bread standing in the doorway. The bread was hard: his tooth loosened a little more. After a while, Father Joseph came pounding into the yard. He was holding up his crucifix like a weapon.

He stopped a couple of paces away from Gawyn, eyeing him intently. 'You have asked to go to the chapel,' he said.

'I have. Straight away.'

Father Joseph frowned. 'You look – different.'

I've slept a long time, Gawyn thought. I'm no longer exhausted, and I think I no longer have a fever. That's why I look different.

'You prayed with me last night,' he said. 'Will you do so again now?'

He watched the doubts chase each other across Father Joseph's face. Eventually he said abruptly, 'Come with me.' Calling Dominic and another man – built, Gawyn noticed, like an ox – he led the way out of the yard and along the road to Rocamadour.

It was a long walk. They left by the Porte de L'Hospitalet, then descended into the gorge by the Vieille Côte. Through another gate – this one sheltered by a huge fig tree – they entered the lower levels of the town. There were even more people here than in L'Hospitalet: after the challenge of the steep descent, having to push and shove through the crowds almost finished Gawyn off. Frustrated with his traitorous body, he thought bitterly, perhaps he's right and I am possessed.

'The Great Stairway,' Father Joseph cried, indicating the long flight of steps ahead. 'Above is the Sacred City!' He plunged on, as if the sanctuary were drawing him. Gawyn followed, Dominic and the ox-like man flanking him.

The steps seemed endless. Sweating, his strength giving out, he noticed that many penitents were going up on their knees. I'll be on my knees anyway soon, he thought. Nudging Dominic, he sank down.

Using his hands for support, at last he emerged into the forecourt in front of the shrine. Collapsing against a cool shaded wall, he closed his eyes.

Sensing someone standing over him, he looked up to see Father Joseph.

'You show a rare devotion,' he said, his face puzzled. Gawyn rubbed at his legs: climbing four long flights of stairs on his knees in a hauberk was not an experience he was keen to repeat. He could feel the blood welling from where the chain links had been driven into his flesh.

Standing up shakily, he said, 'I'm ready.'

Father Joseph's eyes didn't glance away for an instant as, his guards at their stations either side of him, Gawyn walked towards the Chapel of Our Lady. Its entrance crouched under a threatening overhang, as if the cliff were providing a sheltering shoulder. The door was tiny: Gawyn had to stoop.

As he entered the small, dark chapel – it was little more than an oratory – he heard Father Joseph praying.

Hands were on him, restraining him. He resisted the urge to throw them off, instead submitting as he was led forwards. One pace, two, three, and they were standing before the altar.

'Leave him be,' Father Joseph said quietly.

Gawyn stood alone. Still trembling from the climb up the stairway, at first he hardly took in what he was looking at.

Then, slowly, the images got through to his mind.

The altar stood against a wall of bare rock, and it was plain and unadorned. On it stood a statue, carved in dark wood and clad in silver. It was small – about the length of a man's forearm and extended hand. It was the Virgin and Child.

He stared up at the serene face of the Holy Mother.

She was smiling slightly, her expression kind and benevolent. The Child, its face older than its years, held a book in its left hand. Mother and Child had their eyes closed: they seemed to be listening to some inner blissful sounds that only they could hear.

There was an atmosphere of calm as if, oblivious to the crowds in the forecourt, the little chapel was a place apart, distanced in both space and time from everything that was outside. Everything that was in the world. Here, the everyday was left behind: this place belonged to the spirit.

He forgot about the worshippers behind him, forgot Father Joseph and the two guards. Eyes fixed to the little statue, his mind raced back down the long trail that had brought him to that moment.

As he stood there, the midsummer sun found a tiny gap in the chapel walls. A thin, brilliant ray traced a line along the stone floor.

The Virgin seemed to change in the altered light. Transfixed, he watched as her dark, tranquil face took on the features of another. Reddish-fair hair, light eyes, delicate skin with a slight flush of exertion.

As the first shock faded, he realized she wasn't exactly as he remembered her. The short cropped hair was shoulder length, the strain had gone from the face and the eyes were no longer shadowed with dark rings of fatigue. And she was dressed not in boy's clothes but in a dark robe.

Roese, he thought, forgive me. I undertook to get you to safety, and I let you down. You paid me handsomely – he touched her cross, under his cuirass – and I failed to deliver. Wherever you are, I'm sorry.

Blinded by sudden tears, he squeezed his eyes shut.

When he opened them again, he could still see her. She smiled at him, the full summer sunlight on her face. He thought vaguely, Roese in summer.

430

I never saw you in summer, he said to her silently. Never saw you look as you do now, in fact. You were younger then, nervous and uncertain. Now –

With the force of a blow to the head, suddenly he realized what his thoughts meant. It's summer, she's older, her hair's grown. I'm not seeing a memory of her as she was then, I'm seeing – God knows how, but I am – a vision of her. As she is now.

Roese is alive.

Then in a rush he knew what was the matter with him, knew why he was so weak and aimless, knew why he couldn't fix on any purpose: if Roese was alive, then he must get back and find her. There was no other purpose.

She was fading now, and he grinned up at her.

He whispered, 'Wait for me, my lovely. I'm coming home.'

Then she was gone, and once more he stood staring up at the benign face of the Virgin.

* * *

Even before he left Rocamadour, he knew the rumours were spreading. 'A miracle!' people whispered. 'A Breton knight has seen the Blessed Virgin smile on him – he's cured!' 'Sick, he was,' – some reports preferred the more lurid version, that he had been possessed – 'and the Holy Mother took pity on him!' 'Climbed the Great Stairway on his knees, tore his flesh to ribbons, and she was so sorry she showed her face to him!'

Father Joseph, as Gawyn would have expected, regarded his marvellous cure as a personal triumph: in the hastily-arranged service of thanksgiving, Father Joseph wasn't bashful about describing in detail how he had recognized a soul in torment, knelt all night with the poor creature wrestling with the devils inside him, supported him all the way down to Rocamadour and up the Great Stairway, stood shoulder to shoulder with him before the Virgin until at last – he implied strongly that she'd done it as a personal favour to Father Joseph – she'd seen fit to lift her lovely face in a smile of favour.

What did I say to him when I turned round from the altar? Gawyn wondered. I don't believe I said anything, other than that she was smiling at me.

He thought it had probably been less what he said, more how he appeared. Even an idiot would surely have been able to see the change, he concluded – to me, it felt as if I'd just shrugged off a great weight of shackles. Suddenly I could breathe deeply again, and it seemed that, for the first time in months, my heart was beating strongly and my body was responding to what I asked of it.

I could have run out of that chapel and climbed straight up the cliff face without even getting out of breath.

He stood shifting his feet, impatient to be moving – the service seemed to have been going on for hours, and he'd had enough of eulogies and devotional psalms. Looking over the heads of Father Joseph and the gathering of fellow priests he'd convened, Gawyn stared down into the vast crowd that packed the shrine's forecourt: Father Joseph was leading the prayers in the open air, to accommodate the maximum number of worshippers. They're happy, he thought, slightly ashamed of his impatience. Happy because they think they've just witnessed a miracle, and it gives all of them hope that their own prayers are going to be answered, too.

He knew – had known as soon as it happened – that he wasn't going to reveal the truth to anyone.

The prayers and the hymns at last over, Father Joseph was turning to Gawyn for the final act in the drama. 'For such a beneficence,' he'd said to Gawyn, 'such an outpouring of mercy, Our Lady should be given an ex-voto. The very best offering you have to give her.'

I have two treasures, Gawyn had thought. But, since neither belongs to me, I can't give them away. 'My – ' He'd been about to suggest his sword. But, thinking of the hundreds of miles between him and home, he decided he might have more use for his sword than the Blessed Virgin. Saying a rapid, silent prayer – I'm sorry, I hope you'll understand – he suggested, 'My dagger?'

Father Joseph, with the merest hint of a disapproving sniff, had agreed.

Now, at the culmination of the ceremony, Father Joseph was holding out his hands to receive Gawyn's votive offering. Unsheathing the dagger, he looked at it for the last time. The steel blade, though worn thin from countless sharpenings, still bore its inscription. His mother had presented it to him when he was still a boy: the script was in Welsh and he'd had it copied on to his sword. It said, 'Bear me ever at thy side and I shall protect thee from all ills.' There was something else, but he had never known what it meant: his mother had hinted darkly that the words were Celtic, and that they were a magic spell.

Father Joseph took the dagger. Holding it up for the crowd to see, slowly he turned and walked into the chapel. Following him, Gawyn saw him pause in front of the altar, raising the dagger to the statue before placing it reverently among the chains, fetters, redundant crutches, sticks, spurs and swords of other grateful penitents.

Coming out again, he paused by Gawyn.

433

'I have this for you,' he said. He held out a small oval medallion about the length of a little finger. It was made of lead, and on it was depicted the Virgin and Child.

'What is it?'

'It is a sportelle – the badge of Rocamadour. It is what the pilgrims buy to show that they have been here. Like the keys of St Peter of Rome or the scallop shell of Compostela.'

'Thank you.' He hung it round his neck.

Father Joseph was staring up at him, frowning. 'I don't know,' he muttered, 'I am not sure . . .'

His voice trailed off. Abruptly turning away, he strode back to lead his congregation in a closing prayer.

Gawyn knew he should go immediately, before – he didn't know. Something's not quite as it should be, he thought, and I must make my departure while I'm still able to.

Making his way through the press of people, trying to blend into the crowd – not easy, when he stood head and shoulders above most of them – he hurried back to L'Hospitalet. His sword and pack were on the floor of his room, where he'd left them, and his horse was in the hostel's stable, contentedly munching on a hay-bag. Searching for Dominic to pay what he owed, he had no luck – the boy was in the scullery scrubbing at a blackened pot, but he cowered away when Gawyn approached. Haven't you heard, boy? Gawyn thought. I'm no longer dangerous.

He tacked up his horse and tied his pack behind the saddle. Leading the reluctant animal into the yard, he looked out along the road to see if Dominic was returning. There was still no sign of him, nor of

434

anyone else – they must, Gawyn thought, all have gone to the service.

There was a cry from behind him.

'Coooeee! Hello there!' It was the elderly woman. 'Not leaving us, I hope?'

He waited until she had bustled up to him. 'Aye,' he said. 'I am.'

She looked genuinely sorry. 'Ah, that's a pity – we were looking forward to many more joyful celebrations.'

Gawyn was tempted to say yes, that's why I'm leaving. But he said kindly, 'I'm sorry. But I'm sure you'll manage just as well without me.'

She said touchingly, 'I'm glad you're well again.'

'Thank you.'

She launched into a long-winded account of her niece's husband's bellyache, which apparently had been significantly improved by regular appeals to the Blessed Mother of God, although it couldn't be said that the cure was as miraculous as Gawyn's had been, but all the same . . .

He let her drone on, making the occasional comment, wishing she'd stop before everyone else returned. Beside him the horse shifted restlessly.

Then in the distance he saw Father Joseph.

'Excuse me,' he said to her as the priest approached. 'I have to speak to the Father.'

'Yes, of course. I'd better be saying farewell, then.'

'Would you give this to Dominic?' He held out some coins. 'Will that cover what I owe him?'

'Yes,' she said. 'I'll see he gets them.'

She moved away, smiling at him over her shoulder, and he turned to face Father Joseph.

Father Joseph's face was dark with anger.

'You have not been honest with me,' he hissed.

'There was something wrong, something I couldn't put my finger on. I know what it was, now.'

The silence ached between them: Gawyn, aware that anything he said might incriminate him, wasn't going to break it. He raked his memory for what it was he'd done to raise Father Joseph's suspicions.

'You are a fraud,' the priest whispered eventually. The hatred in his voice burned like acid. 'You have been with the enemy. You have consorted with those evil heretics. *Haven't you?*'

Gawyn breathed deeply a couple of times. Then he said calmly, 'What makes you think that?'

Father Joseph's fury exploded. 'Don't act so innocent! You gave yourself away last night. I don't think I'd have realized, only you did it again just now, during our prayers.'

Gawyn was frantically thinking back. Prayers? What does he mean? I got it all right, I made the right responses!

He'd been quite proud of himself for remembering them.

Then an awful suspicion dawned. Responses. The Cathars had a ritual of prayer and response, and he'd been hearing it, many times a day, for six months or more. Pray God to make me a good Christian and lead me to a good end, they'd say to the Perfect. Who would reply, may God be prayed that He make you a good Christian.

Did I get it wrong? Somewhere, in that great welter of prayers, did I slip in a Cathar phrase?

He knew the answer, as if it were written before him.

Yes. I did.

He shook off Father Joseph's fierce restraining grip on his arm, backing away from him and swinging up into the saddle. The horse, startled at the sudden movement, began circling; Gawyn got him under control.

Bending down to Father Joseph, he said, 'God be prayed that He make you a good Christian.'

The pale eyes bulged, the face went dead white and then darkened with a rush of blood so furious that Gawyn was surprised he was still able to stand. The priest raised his arms, calling down curses, threatening retribution, and Gawyn, laughing, said, 'You'd better stop that, before anyone hears you – what will they think, if their precious priest reveals himself to have been mistaken? If the biggest miracle this place has ever known is shown to be no such thing?'

Father Joseph's mouth snapped shut.

'Aye,' Gawyn said, laughing again, the horse prancing under him, 'not furious enough to let that happen, are you?'

Father Joseph called him a name that sounded incongruous on a priest's lips.

'I didn't imagine you'd know what one of those was,' Gawyn said conversationally. Then, tightly reining in his horse's head and spurring him at the same time, he made the animal back towards the priest. There was a loud scream as a large hoof trod squarely on Father Joseph's foot.

'That's for my tooth,' Gawyn shouted.

Then, turning his horse, he kicked him to a gallop and raced away.

Twenty-three

With the return of purpose came a resurgence of strength: he rode hard, full of confidence so that he almost hoped someone would challenge him, for the sheer pleasure of removing them from his path.

His money lasted just over half the way back to Brittany. It was high summer and the weather was hot and dry, which meant he had no need to find accommodation at night; sleeping out under the stars in the gentle hills of Poitou, he dreamt of her. Smiling, he let the dream continue into a fantasy in which she was lying beside him.

'You'd like this better than South Wales,' he said aloud to her. 'For one thing, it's not raining.'

The land was swelling towards an early harvest, and often he lived on what he could filch from the fields. Resurrecting boyhood skills, he tickled trout in streams and snared rabbits. Once he caught a hare, but, after so long without meat, found the flesh too strong to be palatable. He felt sorely the lack of his dagger: after a dismal attempt to gut a rabbit with his sword, he kept an eye out until he spotted a band of chalk, digging out a flint which he knapped into a rough blade.

When his pouch was at last empty, he did a quick tally of his few remaining possessions, wondering if he had anything he could sell. Having eliminated the essentials – sword, hauberk, horse, boots, robe – all he could come up with was the saddle. Like the horse, the harness was plain but sturdy; south-west of Le Mans, he sold it in a village market in exchange for sufficient coins to keep him in bread and cheese till he got home.

Riding bareback for a hundred and fifty miles put the final touches to restoring his muscles to full strength.

* * *

He rode into Paimpol on the last day of August. After some thought, he had decided against making for Brocéliande; tempting though it was to think of being in his own home again after so long on the road and under the roofs of strangers, his need to get on was stronger.

He was banking heavily on Yves not only having survived the crusade, but having had the good sense to quit after his forty days and go home.

It had been causing him increasing anxiety as he rode north. What happened to them all after Carcassonne? Did they suffer any wounds? Did they continue to fight? Both possibilities were, in different ways, grievous.

He wasn't sure what he would do if he found the place closed up and deserted. He thought philosophically, I won't worry about that till it's happened.

He waited outside the town until darkness had fallen. Then, leading his horse, he padded quietly down the road to Yves's house.

439

No light shone out from behind the high walls, and the gates had been secured across the arched entrance. His heart sank.

Then, from within, he heard a soft nicker. Hooves struck stone as a horse turned round in its stall. Going right up to the gates, Gawyn tried to see through the gap between the hinges: there was a faint glow from the stables, and he heard a quiet voice muttering.

A figure emerged from the covered way in front of the stables. He was carrying a lantern in one hand and a pail in the other.

It was Yves.

Gawyn called, 'Yves!', rapping on the gate as he did so.

Yves stopped dead. Then slowly he approached the gate. Gawyn could see his face in the light from the lantern: apprehensive, he thought, grinning, was hardly strong enough. He tapped again and said, 'Come on, open up!'

There was a small shuttered spy-window in the gate. Yves unlatched the shutter and peered out. Gawyn could only see the right side of his face, but he had no doubt that the other side was expressing equal joy.

He shouted, *'Gawyn!'*, throwing open the gates and hurrying out to fling out his arms and hug Gawyn to him. Punching him on the shoulder, stepping back to look at him, then hugging him again, for some time he didn't seem able to speak. When he could, he said, 'We thought you were dead!'

Gawyn said, 'I nearly was.'

'Where have you *been?*' Yves's voice was a squawk. 'It's been months! Did you find your way back to the army? Did you –'

Gawyn interrupted. 'Yves, it's a long story and I've

440

come a very long way to tell it. Do you think we could talk while we eat?'

'Oh, goodness, I'm sorry! Yes, yes, come on – I'll order up the biggest supper you ever had!' He took the horse from Gawyn and led the way into the courtyard. 'I'll call Barr.' He turned to have another look at Gawyn, as if to reassure himself he was really there. 'Dear God, but he'll be pleased to see you.'

'He's safe, then. I'm relieved to hear it. And Cadoc?'

Yves's smile faded. 'Not as lucky as us, I'm sorry to tell you. He was killed at Lastours. Our attack was repelled, and they fell on us as we withdrew. Poor Cadoc got an arrow in the back.'

'God rest him,' Gawyn said. He pictured the boy standing beside him trying to understand the powerful words of de Montfort at Lyons. Before it all began, he thought, before any of us had any real idea of what it would be like. Rest in peace, young Cadoc.

'Lastours,' he said to Yves as they walked into the stables. 'But wasn't – '

What he'd been about to say was driven out of his head. There were six stalls in Yves's stable block, and four were occupied. Yves's bay and Cadoc's sturdy pony, unimpressed by the late visitors, were calmly dozing, backs turned to the entrance. Next to the pony, however, a big grey head was straining out over the half-door. Beyond, Gawyn caught a glimpse of a dainty chestnut nose, very slightly convex.

'You brought them home!' he yelled. 'Both of them!' It was more than he'd dared hope for; running forwards, he tried to pat Arrow and his own grey at the same time.

'All your gear is here too,' Yves said, adding wryly, 'You won't have to ride out of here like a pauper, for all that's how you rode in.'

'I had to sell my saddle.' He was burying his face in the grey's mane. 'Diew, though, it'll be a pleasure to ride you again,' he murmured.

'Come.' Yves touched his arm. 'I'll get Barr to see he's all right,' – he took the bridle off Gawyn's horse, shutting him into the stall – 'you tend to yourself.'

Later, when he'd taken the first edge off his hunger and made himself comfortably muzzy with several mugs of Yves's white wine, he remembered what he'd been going to say earlier.

'You said you were at Lastours,' he reminded Yves. 'That was well into the autumn – surely you should have come home by then? We took the cross at the end of June, so the forty days would have been up by early August.'

'We could have come home, yes. Should have done, really,' – Yves looked sad – 'we'd still have Cadoc if we'd turned for home after Carcassonne. Many did – de Montfort was beside himself, furious with the knights for leaving him and with the pope for putting the importance of the Holy Land above that of the Languedoc.'

'Why didn't you go home?'

Yves stared down at his hands. After a pause, he said, 'We hoped we'd find you. We talked it over, the three of us – I told them we could go if we wanted to, I said it had to be the will of all of us if we opted not to – but they both said they wanted to stay.'

The thought was loud between them that the fruitless search had cost Cadoc his life.

'What made you go in the end?'

Yves shrugged. 'Barr and I sort of gave up, I suppose. After Cadoc, you know.'

Gawyn nodded. 'Aye.'

Some time later he said, 'Yves, do you think we did right? All of us, the crusaders, I mean.'

'I know what you mean.' Yves sighed heavily. 'When I think back, I see things I would rather forget.' Remembering his journey from the Pyrenees to Minerve, Gawyn had no need to ask what those things were. 'We didn't act like knights,' Yves went on, 'we were butchers.' Looking up suddenly, eyes on Gawyn's, he said, 'No. We weren't right. The crusade never should have happened.'

Was I waiting to hear him say that before speaking of my own experiences? Gawyn wondered. Was that why I asked him? He wasn't sure. Either way, he couldn't keep silent any longer; as Yves went to fetch more wine, he put his thoughts in order and prepared to tell him where he'd been since they were last together.

Sometimes over the next couple of days, Gawyn thought he detected a puzzled expression on Yves's face as he looked at him. He was tempted to say, look, Yves! I've lived with heretics and I haven't grown two heads! But, reflecting that Yves was having to do quite a lot of adjustment in a short time, he refrained. A cousin back from the dead, he thought. And via a road that took him deep into the heart of the enemy. Aye, he's entitled to look at me curiously.

When he reckoned he'd stayed with Yves as long as courtesy demanded, he said he was going home.

'I'll ride with you,' Yves said. 'It's many a year since I was in Brocéliande.'

'I'm not going to Brocéliande. I'm going to Wales.'

'You're what? Why, for the sake of God? You quit Wales because Llewelyn ap Iorworth's men were baying for your blood! What sort of folly is it for you to

443

go back and calmly offer yourself to them? Great heavens, Gawyn, haven't you had *enough?*'

Gawyn was surprised at his vehemence. It's hit him hard, all this, he thought. He's weary of excitement – he wants to stay here living the peaceful life of a country knight.

He realized, then, how little appeal it held for him.

And besides, there was another reason for going back.

'I'm not proposing to go into the mountains,' he said, 'not yet, anyway.' He was reluctant to say anything about Roese – knowing that he was racing into danger over a woman who had probably drowned well over a year ago would make Yves even more angry than he was already.

'Not till you see how the land lies?' Yves was calmer now. 'Well, you're talking sense at last.'

But when the morning of departure came, Yves came out to see him off without much enthusiasm.

'Thank you for all you've done,' Gawyn said: in addition to loaning him money, Yves had provided fresh linen, a robe and a cloak. 'And this is for you, Barr.' He flicked the boy a coin. 'My gear hasn't looked so fine since the last time I rode out of this yard.'

Yves said, 'I won't ask you to stay, because you'll refuse. But, for God's sake, take care. Wherever you're going.'

'I will.' Gawyn spurred his horse, and Arrow fell into step behind. 'Farewell, Yves.'

He had arranged his passage to England the previous day. The fraternity of 'independent seamen' down on the quay had greeted his enquiry after Eustace with bland innocence, as if they'd never heard of him, but another master agreed to take him. They sailed with the morning tide, and made landfall on the northern shore of the Severn estuary three days later.

I'm here, he thought as he watched the ship sail away. And I have no idea what I am going to do next.

He'd had the ship drop him the English side of the mouth of the Wye – no point in taking unnecessary risks – and, setting off south-westwards towards Chepstow and the river's steep-sided lower reaches, his task seemed impossible. What do I do? he asked himself. Look into churchyards for recent graves? The land's under an interdict, they don't bury people in sacred ground any more!

Anyway, she's alive.

The conviction remained firm.

For over a week he rode along the bank of the river, investigating every settlement from towns to solitary farms. Sometimes he simply used his eyes, stationing himself for long hours overlooking a busy market, or watching the day's comings and goings in some lively village. Sometimes, stopping to buy food supplies from some isolated housewife, he asked. He spent a day and a half on a foray into the Forest of Dean; an elderly man from whom he'd bought two mutton pies told him that he'd recently seen a forest miner come into market with a bonny young wife. Tracking the miner down, the wife had proved to be not all that young and hardly bonny at all.

He knew he couldn't be covering every possibility, no matter how hard he tried. Although the lower Wye valley was sparsely populated, people there were long used to living in a border land and knew how to keep themselves to themselves: he was well aware that there must be houses, hamlets, whole villages perhaps, which, hidden away, he had no

445

way of checking. If I fail on this first search, he told himself, I'll just have to start all over again. And search more thoroughly.

It was a depressing prospect, and it prompted him to renew his efforts. Everyone he met on the road – not that the total amounted to many – he stopped and questioned.

There was no trace of her.

He followed the east bank as far as the ferry where she'd fallen in. Standing above the landing stage, watching the ferryman calmly hauling the platform across – the water was sufficiently smooth for him to chat to his passengers – his remorse overcame him again and he believed her truly lost.

The ferryman took him across to the river's west bank. His hope all but dead, he resumed the search.

Caught one evening by the onset of hard rain that promised no quick let-up, he found himself far from any habitation and took shelter in a sheep herd's hut. It was small and stank of sheep, but it had been stoutly constructed and kept out the rain. The sheep herd had left bedding in a tidy roll, and there was a bundle of kindling with which to start a fire in the small hearth. The horses were safe enough let loose; the pasture seemed securely fenced with hazel hurdles.

In the morning, the sheep herd found him.

'Good day,' he said – he'd seen the young man approaching, and had gone out to meet him. 'I apologize for commandeering your hut – it is your hut?' The man nodded. 'It was a foul night, and I was glad of a dry nest.'

'You're welcome.' The man was eyeing him suspiciously. 'Where are you headed for?' Gawyn detected the unspoken query: you're off the beaten track here, and I'd like to know why.

Gawyn hesitated. He studied the man's face. Young – about twenty, he guessed – and strong. Tall – not as tall as Gawyn – and his tanned skin indicated a healthy outdoor life. The expression in the eyes was direct.

What have I got to lose? Gawyn thought.

'I'm looking for someone,' he said. 'A woman. She and I were travelling together, and we – I – tried to cross the Wye in flood. I believed her drowned, but now I –' He stopped. Now I'm convinced she's alive after all? 'I've come back to see if I can find word of her.'

The man had turned away as Gawyn began to speak; he appeared to be staring at the flock of sheep that grazed the adjoining pasture.

'A woman, you say.'

The voice was dull. Gawyn thought, he doesn't know, any more than all the dozens of other people I've asked. 'Well, I'll be –' he began.

'I do know of a woman.'

He froze. 'Young? Not yet of age?'

'Yes.' The sheep herd spun round to face him, his expression unreadable. 'She was in the river, and was rescued. Taken there.' He pointed to a distant hillside.

'Where?' Gawyn asked sharply.

'You won't see it from here, it's a small place. Hermits live there – they tended her and brought her back to health.'

Trying to control his joy, Gawyn said, 'Will you take me there?'

'I have to stay with my flock. Find your own way – it's not difficult.'

He started to walk away. Gawyn shouted after him, 'Wait! I have money, I'll pay you to guide me!'

But the man seemed not to hear.

* * *

447

He rode as fast as he could, not taking his eye off the hill the man had indicated. It was tough going, and the hill looked very like its neighbours. Eventually, he thought – hoped – he'd reached the foot of the right one, and began the ascent.

It was easy at first, but then the path grew steeper and more twisting. Dismounting, he led both horses up the tortuous path to the summit.

There's nothing here! he thought, disappointment coursing through him. That man was deliberately misleading me, I'll find him and –

Then, between the thick foliage, he saw the outlines of walls.

Hurrying forwards, dragging the protesting horses, he broke through the shrubbery and came face to face with an open gateway. Beyond it was a small courtyard; standing calmly outside what looked like a chapel was a black-robed man.

For an instant Gawyn thought he was experiencing some shift in time. Then, reassuring himself, he thought, no. It's just the robe. Many monastic orders wear black.

Moving through the gate, he said, 'Greetings, brother. I'm looking for someone, and I believe you may know where she is.'

The monk's deep blue eyes fixed on to his. Then, his face breaking into a smile, he said, 'Greetings. I have been waiting for you a long time.'

The man – he told Gawyn his name was Ranald and not to call him 'brother' – suggested the horses be tethered outside the courtyard. Then he took him into a room furnished with a long, plain table and benches, obviously a refectory, and, asking him to sit down, announced he would fetch refreshments. Returning with two pewter mugs and some thinnish ale, he lifted his mug to Gawyn.

'To your safe return,' he said.

Gawyn thought, where does he think I'm going?
Then realized the man meant the return he'd already
made.

He said tentatively, 'You seem to be unsurprised at
my arrival.'

'As I said, I have been expecting you. I guess that
Aidan told you where to come?'

'The sheep herd?' Ranald nodded. 'Aye.' Unable to
contain himself any longer, he burst out, 'He said
you'd rescued her. She's alive? Well?'

'She is both alive and well.' Was there a touch of
humour in the lightly-accented words?

His heart racing, he said, 'Is she here?'

'No.'

He'd been gearing himself up to seeing her, almost
immediately. The disappointment was so acute it
hurt.

'But she is not far away.' The voice was kind now.
'I will tell you where she is, you have my word, but
first we should talk.'

'Aye, all you want.' But make it quick.

'We will come straight to the point.' Now the
amusement was clear, as if Ranald had heard
Gawyn's unspoken thought.

Gawyn met his eyes, despite himself breaking into
a smile. 'I'd be grateful,' he said ironically.

'I do not wish to keep you from your goal longer
than I have to,' Ranald said. 'You have come far.'

Gawyn was reminded of his initial misgivings – it
was disturbing, that this man so obviously knew
more about Gawyn than Gawyn did about him. 'How
do you know that?' he asked.

'You have come,' Ranald said, 'from the Languedoc,
where you were involved in the slaughter of the

449

Cathars. You set out from England in the late spring of last year, and you were fleeing from some sort of serious trouble in Wales. You undertook to take with you a young woman called Roese, who was also running away – in her case, it was from a marriage she did not welcome – and she paid for your protection with a jewelled cross. In your haste, you crossed the Wye under dangerous conditions, and Roese was swept away. You had to be in France by a certain date, for the muster?' Gawyn nodded – there didn't seem much point in denying anything. 'So you were unable to search for her as thoroughly as you might have wished. Had you had more time, you would have found her, half dead in the shallows.'

'You found her.'

'Aidan did.'

Gawyn stood up, crossing the refectory in a couple of paces and coming to rest by the lectern. Idly he ran his hands over the carvings. An eagle, he thought absently. And something else – a winged being, with blurred outlines. Something crossed his mind, chased out by a more urgent thought.

'She told you who I am?'

'She did.'

And have you passed on the information? he wanted to demand. Is anyone else out there waiting for me to show my face?

'We live apart here,' Ranald said gently. 'We have little contact with the world.'

Gawyn felt the tension run out of him. He dropped his head on to his hands, clasped on top of the lectern.

There was silence in the refectory. After some moments, he raised his head and looked at Ranald: eyes cast down, he was murmuring a prayer.

450

Gawyn didn't need to strain his ears to know it was the Paternoster. The black robe, the figures on the lectern, the instinctive way he'd known instantly he was going to trust this man, had all been shouting the truth at him: the Paternoster merely confirmed what he'd known subconsciously straight away.

He said, 'You're a Cathar.'

And Ranald, smiling, said, 'I am.'

Gawyn resumed his seat on the bench. 'You're all Cathars? How many of you are there? Does the king know? Aren't you afraid?'

Ranald's smile became a laugh. 'Have no fear, we live very quietly here, as I said. Inasmuch as the world ever considers us – which is, I imagine, seldom – we are thought to be simple hermits.'

'You'd be killed if they knew.' He was seeing, too clearly, a devastated village in the Midi.

'I would be killed,' Ranald corrected him. 'I am the sole Cathar.'

'You live with Catholics? But they're your enemy!'

'No. None of us is against his fellows. Each of us worships God as he sees fit.'

'Tolerance,' Gawyn muttered. 'Just like Olivier.'

'Tolerance, yes.' Ranald's voice had an edge. 'In a world where there is so little, we believe it to be important.'

'Aye,' Gawyn said. 'So do I.' Resenting the remonstration, he stood up, resting his hands on the table and leaning over Ranald. 'I've seen sights I hope you never see,' he said forcefully. 'I've hacked my way into a defenceless city, I came close to killing someone who was no more a threat to me than a kitten. I've journeyed through lands where my crusading army went before me, and I've witnessed what happens when there isn't any tolerance.

Believe me,' he sank down again, tired suddenly, 'I believe it's important, too.'

After some time Ranald said, 'I apologize.' Then, his intonation reminding Gawyn powerfully of Olivier, 'You bear a heavy load, I think. You may put it down, if you wish.'

A heavy load. The words echoed in Gawyn's head. He knew what Ranald meant, but there was another interpretation. He heard Olivier's voice. 'I cannot tell you where you must take it or who you must give it to. When the time comes, you will know.'

He gathered up his robe, reaching in under his breastplate for the leather-wrapped parcel.

He placed it on the table. He said, 'This is for you.'

Ranald's gaze on the parcel was unwavering. He put out his hand – Gawyn was moved to see it shook slightly – and touched the soft leather with his fingertips. He started to speak, and his voice broke. Starting again, he said quietly, 'You brought this from the Languedoc.'

It was a statement, not a question.

'From the Pyrenees, aye. I was taken out of Carcassonne – your Cathars saved my life – and tended in a stronghold high up in the mountains.'

'Isolated? Quite small, a lozenge-shaped fortress?'

'Aye.'

'Montségur,' Ranald whispered. Then, raising his eyes for an instant to look at Gawyn, 'You were in Montségur.'

And you wish you had been, too, Gawyn thought.

'They were in good heart when I left them,' he said softly.

'They were?' Ranald looked infinitely sad.

'Aye. But –' He broke off, wondering if there was

truly any call for the absolute truth. This man was strong, certainly, but why tell him what he might otherwise be spared?

Ranald said, 'But what?'

And Gawyn knew he had to know.

'They will last long there,' he said. 'The location is unassailable, the only way the fortress can be taken is by siege. And if de Montfort's short of men, besieging such a place would be difficult.'

'But?'

'But in the end it will fall.' He shut the mental pictures out of his mind, finding them too painful. 'Because this crusade cannot be lost.'

Slowly Ranald nodded. 'You are right, I know it.' Again he lightly touched the parcel. 'They knew it, in Montségur. That is why they gave you this.'

'You know what it is?' Of course he does.

'I do.' The blue eyes locked on to Gawyn's. 'Did they tell you?'

'No.'

'They did tell you, I trust, that you would be killed if it were found on you?'

'They implied it.' Gawyn smiled grimly, remembering: 'What you do not know you cannot tell,' Olivier had said. 'I guessed this was something important.' He hesitated, then said softly, 'To do with your equinox ceremony, perhaps?'

'No! It is not possible that you – '

'No, I didn't see anything. They locked me up.'

'They were brave,' Ranald remarked. There was the ghost of a smile.

'I've carried this right across France for you,' Gawyn said quickly, capitalizing on the moment. 'Risked torture and death, if anyone discovered it. And they came close.' He remembered the little room in Rocamadour, a man and a boy stripping off his clothes when he was all but too weak to foresee and prevent what was about to happen. Wouldn't Father Joseph have enjoyed trying to extract from me what I didn't know, he thought. 'Don't you think you owe me an explanation?'

Ranald appeared to be considering. Then, unexpectedly, he said meekly, 'Yes, you are right and we do.' Reverently, he folded back the fine leather, and for the second time Gawyn looked on the crystal.

'You were quite safe, you know,' Ranald said after a moment. 'You were protected, all the while you bore this.'

Gawyn thought, you don't know Father Joseph.

'Tell me?' he asked.

Ranald's eyes rested on the crystal, the pupils wide. 'Yes,' he murmured. Then, snapping to attention, he covered it up. 'Too powerful,' he said under his breath. The leather covering once more hiding the brilliant thing, he said, 'It is crystal, formed of a naturally-occurring but unusual quartz. When rays of light flow through it, they are altered into a pentagonal shape.'

'Pentagonal,' Gawyn repeated. 'You use the pentagon as a symbol.'

'We do, and this is why. At the special times of the year, when the night and the day are of equal length, the light of the rising and the setting sun is allowed to flow through the sphere, and its power is released.'

Gawyn recalled the great hymn of praise.

'What does that achieve?'

Ranald looked at him. 'It keeps the world in balance,' he said simply. 'This combination of the light, which comes from the heavens, and the crystal, which is of the earth, has an effect far greater than you can comprehend. Than any of us can,' he amended. 'We know only that it has to be. That all the

454

prayer in the world will not help us if these precious treasures are no longer offered up to the sun.'

Gawyn said quietly, 'They won't be when the Languedoc falls.'

'No.' Ranald touched the covered sphere. 'But here, this one will be.'

'One's enough?' He thought of the ravaged lands and all the dead Cathars. Crusaders on the rampage destroyed everything they didn't bear away, and they only bore away things like jewels and gold coins that were easily portable. No other knight, he thought grimly, would carry an object the size of a fist under his cuirass.

Ranald lifted his shoulders slightly. 'We shall see.'

There were silent for some time. Then Gawyn said, 'Are there many secret Cathars in Britain?'

'As far as I know, two.' Ranald's tone was neutral.

'How did you come to be here?'

Ranald studied him, as if trying to decide whether or not he would explain. 'My parents were among a small group of Cathars who crossed to England forty-five years ago,' he said eventually. 'Most of the group were from Germany, my mother included, and my father and his parents were from France. They were young then, my mother and my father.'

'Too young to have taken the Consolamentum?'

'Yes.' Ranald smiled briefly. 'Obviously so, or I should not be here.' His smile faded. 'They were persecuted in England as severely as in the homelands they had left. They were tried – in 1166, at a provincial court in Oxford – and condemned. They were whipped and branded, and turned out to die. Anyone who gave them shelter would himself be punished.'

'Where did they go?'

'Some found their way back to France, and on down to the refuge offered in the Languedoc. A handful stayed here, my parents included. They married – it seemed best, to adopt the lifestyle of the majority – and I was born. Then they both took the Consolamentum.'

'They weren't found out?'

'No. They were discreet.'

'What became of them?'

'They died.' Ranald didn't elaborate.

'And you stayed on alone.'

'Not entirely. Remember, I said there were two Cathars in Britain – the other is a very old woman who was my mother's friend. She lives nearby, in the Welsh hills.'

Gawyn was hardly listening. He was thinking of Ranald, whose life had been blighted by persecution and intolerance, finding the strength to create the hermitage. Create it, and make it work. We believe tolerance to be important, he'd said. The hermitage was the living proof: Gawyn still found it hard to contemplate a place where Cathar and Catholic lived happily side by side, but it was becoming easier.

He looked up at Ranald, about to make some comment to that effect, but saw that Ranald was watching him as if waiting for something.

'You did not take in what I said,' he remarked.

'I did! You were telling me that there was some other Cathar man in England.'

'In Wales. And she is a woman.' Ranald sighed, but his eyes were bright with humour. 'You should have taken more notice.'

Gawyn couldn't see why. 'Should I?'

'Yes. Because it was to the house of this old woman that I sent Roese.'

Twenty-four

Gawyn stood up. When Ranald made no immediate move, he said, 'Come on, then!'

Ranald, amusement in his face, said innocently, 'Where to?'

Gawyn breathed deeply, suppressing his impatience. 'I've been away from her near a year and a half,' he said quietly. 'Will you make me wait longer?'

'No.' Ranald got to his feet, touching Gawyn's sleeve briefly. Struggling again with his laughter, he said, 'May I first be allowed to put this treasure in a place of safety?'

Gawyn grinned. 'Very well. But be quick about it.'

They went out into the courtyard. Ranald said suddenly, 'Perhaps you would give your opinion on a suitable hiding place?'

Gawyn was touched to be asked. 'Aye, gladly.'

'The chapel, I think,' – Ranald led the way inside the tiny building – 'and somewhere no-one is likely to investigate . . .'

'There.' Gawyn pointed to a pair of stone pillars holding up the plain slab of the altar. 'Are they hollow?'

'I don't know.' Ranald tapped one with his sandal. 'It sounds as if they may be.'

'We'll have to disturb the altar,' Gawyn said tentatively. Perhaps even a Cathar, he thought, would hesitate to do that.

'Yes,' Ranald agreed calmly. 'I think it is not as heavy as it looks.'

Together they shifted the altar until the top of one pillar was exposed; its thick circumference enclosed a central space of about a hand and a half. Reverently Ranald placed the sphere inside, and they slid the altar back into place.

'Now we may go,' Ranald said.

As they re-crossed the courtyard, Ranald put his head round the open door of a room on the opposite side from the chapel. 'Benedict?'

A deep voice replied, 'Yes, Ranald?' Its owner, a big man in middle age, came to stand in the doorway, a pot of some fresh-smelling liquid in his hand.

'I am going to see Joanna. I will return tomorrow.'

Gawyn watched as the man's stare moved from Ranald to him, looking him up and down. He knows full well who I am, he thought.

After some moments, Benedict nodded. I pass muster, Gawyn thought. 'Aye, well, she'll be pleased to see you, I warrant,' Benedict said.

Whether he referred to Joanna or Roese, he didn't say.

'Will you ride the mare?' Gawyn asked as they finally left the hermitage – after speaking to Benedict, Ranald had gone into the kitchen and a fat, red-faced man called Matthias had provided them with food for the journey; Gawyn had thought, one more delay and I shall gallop off alone.

Ranald patted Arrow's elegantly arched neck, and she pushed her nose into his belly. 'Does that indicate affection or a rebuff?' he asked.

'It means she likes you.' Gawyn was restraining the grey, who, impatient to be moving, was starting to circle, unwisely for such a big horse on such a narrow path. 'Steady, Lamri.'

'Lamri,' Ranald repeated as they led the horses off down the track. 'You call your horse after King Arthur's.'

'Aye.' He didn't think it required any explanation.

At the foot of the hill, they stopped to mount up. Ranald was a little too tall to sit the mare comfortably, but he was slimly built and his weight did not trouble her.

'It's many years since I rode,' he said.

Gawyn realized resignedly that they'd have to proceed at a beginner's pace. 'How far is it?'

'Half a day's journey on foot, less on horseback.'

Even when one of us hasn't ridden for years? Gawyn thought. But then, with a whoop of delight, Ranald kicked Arrow, almost losing his seat as she broke into a startled trot, then, as her pace settled into her smooth and rhythmic canter, turning to look triumphantly at Gawyn, his face full of laughter. 'I wish you'd keep up!' he shouted.

He let the grey have his head and, putting his weight forward, felt the muscles bunch as the horse accelerated and thundered after the mare. The September sun was warm on his face, the rich green valley was lively with birdsong; he felt like a boy evading his chores and stealing a day's fun.

'Another few miles and we shall be there,' Ranald said when they stopped to eat. 'Here.' He handed Gawyn a hunk of bread and some strong-smelling ewe's milk cheese; he, Gawyn noticed, ate onion and carrots with his bread.

Another few miles, Gawyn thought. Suddenly he wasn't hungry. 'No, thank you.'

Ranald eyed him, but said nothing, for which Gawyn was grateful: he wasn't sure how he'd find an acceptable way to say, I'm so nervous my belly's tied up in knots.

'Beautiful weather,' Ranald said.

'Aye.'

'A lovely month, September.'

'Aye.' Trying to respond with more than monosyllables, suddenly something occurred to him. 'The autumn equinox is this month.'

A look of intense gratification spread over Ranald's face. 'It is.'

'You'll be able to perform your ceremony.'

'Yes. I shall invite Joanna to join me.'

There was a loaded pause. Then Gawyn said, 'They didn't let me witness it, in Montségur.'

'So you said.'

'I regretted that.'

'I imagine you did.'

Gawyn heard the amusement again. 'I suppose it's only for avowed Cathars. Perfects.'

'No, it is for both Perfects and adherents. The unavowed, if by that you understand those as yet unconsoled.'

'What does it take to make an adherent?'

'Simply a sympathy with the Cathar faith.'

I have that all right, Gawyn thought. 'They told me much in Montségur,' he said abruptly. 'I felt the appeal, but I couldn't see a time when I'd want to – be prepared to –' He stopped.

'When you would be ready for the Consolamentum,' Ranald finished for him. 'That is understandable,' – he paused, glanced at Gawyn, and added softly, 'especially in view of your present preoccupation.'

Gawyn bowed his head. 'Aye, well,' he mumbled. 'I – we – ' My present preoccupation, he thought, isn't something I'm able to discuss. Not until I've seen her.

Seen her. His stomach gave another leap.

Ranald said quietly, 'You already have great sympathy with the faith.'

'How do you know that?'

Ranald shrugged but didn't answer.

'I have.' he said. Then he thought, why don't I just ask him? 'Enough to make me want to attend your ceremony, if you'll let me.'

And Ranald replied calmly, 'Yes, I think you should.'

As the surprise faded, Gawyn said, thinking back, 'When I arrived this morning, you seemed to be expecting me. And I keep feeling you know more about me than you possibly can. How is this, when you live like a hermit?'

Ranald said, 'Not entirely like a hermit. The others are content to stay within our four walls, for their own good reasons. I have contact with the world, however, and in our prevailing spirit of tolerance, they do not question my absences.'

'You knew about Montségur,' Gawyn said. 'You were very pleased to receive the sphere, but I don't think you were surprised. It's as if – as if –' He knew what he wanted to say, but it was preposterous. He decided to say it anyway. 'As if you had some way of communicating with other Cathars. And that's impossible, unless Cathars are able to make their thoughts travel over great distances.'

Ranald didn't answer. Gawyn remembered how, months ago, he'd felt a superstitious shiver when he'd wondered for an instant if Cathars could fly. The memory has come, he thought, because I've just had another one.

461

'Well?' he said roughly. 'Can you?'

Ranald said mildly, 'In a way. But that is something reserved for Perfects. You dismiss the possibility of more conventional lines of communication, and I understand why you do, for I know that you have been with the Cathars in their besieged and embattled corner of France. You judge, as well you might, that there is no way they could pass messages out to the rest of us.' Gawyn thought he had finished, but he added, 'You should realize, however, that not every Cathar lives openly in the faith.'

'You mean there's some secret network? Some system by which news is relayed, even from as far away as the Midi?'

'There is.' Ranald smiled as he turned to Gawyn. 'And if I told you of it, it would no longer be secret, so I will not.'

Gawyn was about to press him, but stopped himself: I've got what I most wanted, he thought. I'm to attend the autumn equinox ceremony.

He stood up, knowing that he'd go on with the interrogation if he stayed where he was. While Ranald continued with his interrupted meal, he paced to and fro between the hillock where Ranald was sitting and the tree where they'd tethered the horses: eventually Ranald said, 'We had better get on our way, before you wear all the grass off that pasture.'

* * *

Early in the afternoon, Ranald reined in at the top of a low hill and pointed ahead into the long valley stretching away at their feet.

'You see the group of houses?'

'By there? Near the trees?' There were five or six,

with some barns and what appeared to be a small chapel.

'Yes. Joanna's house is the one set back a little.'

They rode on.

Gawyn's nervousness had trebled. He was finding it difficult to control the questions his mind kept throwing up: what if she can't forgive me? What if she's promised to another? What if living with these hermits has made her decide on a life of devotion? What if she's become a Cathar and taken the Consolamentum?

The voice of reason tried to reply, Ranald would have told you, if any of those things were true.

He was beyond listening to the voice of reason.

Only half a mile to go.

The house was built of stone and roofed in slate. It was well-maintained, and had an enclosed garden. There was a small stand of trees behind it, and a stream ran by.

A couple of hundred yards away – they'd just ridden through the little hamlet, and Ranald had greeted an elderly man leaning on a spade – Ranald said, 'I shall go in to talk to Joanna. Roese often sits down in the copse in the afternoon.'

He couldn't speak: nodding, he turned the grey's head to the left, riding round the side of the house.

His mind was fixed on what was ahead, and he was no longer aware of Ranald, of the small community behind him, of anything. The house had a stout fence and, sliding from Lamri's back, he tied the reins to a post.

He walked on, along what was clearly a well-used path. It led in among the trees, and the sunlight finding its way through the leaves made bright patches on the ground. He could hear running water:

463

presently, he came to the bank of a fast-moving, shallow stream. A willow drooped branches into the current.

The trees had been cut back to make a clearing. Sitting on the grass, face turned up to the sun, was Roese.

She had her eyes closed. Standing back, still in the shadow of the trees, he studied her.

She looked well, far better than he remembered. Her fine skin had a flush of health, and her hair, grown below shoulder length, was thick and glossy. He smiled suddenly, picturing the awful boyish bob, but his amusement turned to pain as the other memories came hurtling back. For so long I thought you dead, he said silently to her. I didn't know I'd come to care for you, but it hurt so much to think I'd lost you that I concluded I must have done.

He stepped forward across the grass. He knew he'd made no sound, but she was aware of his presence. Aware of someone's presence.

'I know I've been here too long,' she said, the remembered smile spreading over her face – her eyes were still shut – 'but it's so lovely in the sun.'

He stood still in front of her, saying nothing.

Her smile faded. He watched as she seemed to stiffen – with fear? No – if she was afraid, he thought, she'd look to see who was here.

She whispered, 'Who is it?'

And at last opened her eyes.

Watching her so closely, he didn't miss a nuance of her reaction. At first she registered nothing, then she went white. Getting to her feet, she walked up to him, stretching out her hand to touch his face.

Then she said quietly, 'Gawyn.'

He didn't know if it was she or himself who made the move, but their arms were around each other and he was hugging her to him so hard that she gasped. He muttered, 'I'm sorry,' just as she whispered, 'I knew you'd come. One day, I knew you would.'

She was pressing her head to his chest and he couldn't see her. Moving his hand to her chin, he held her face so that he could look at her.

She said, 'You look – you're – Oh, Gawyn,' and her eyes filled with tears.

He stroked the tears away. Trying to smile, he said, 'All this way to find you, and the sight of me makes you burst into tears. Fine way to welcome a soldier home.'

She was laughing and crying together, shaking uncontrollably. He didn't know what to do; in the absence of any better ideas, he raised her face to his and kissed her.

He didn't think she minded – she seemed as eager as he was – but after a moment she broke away.

'What's the matter?'

She sniffed. 'I can't breathe. Crying has made my nose run.' She appeared to be searching for a handkerchief; not finding one, she wiped her face on the back of her hand then stood on tiptoe, pulling him down so that she could kiss him again.

When they stopped, holding her very close, he murmured, 'Still the perfect lady, I see.'

He felt her laugh. 'I don't fall in dung-heaps any more.'

He said suddenly, 'Roese, I'm sorry.'

'You said that just now.' Her voice was low. 'I thought you meant you were sorry for squeezing me so hard.'

'No. I'm sorry I nearly lost you. Let you fall in the river. I was wrong to risk it – I should have been more careful with you, only I –'

She stopped him, putting her fingers on his lips.

465

He kissed them, and she smiled. 'I know, you were running away. Ranald and I worked it out. He said you'd come back, if you could.'

He was surprised – Ranald must, he thought, have been very confident, or he wouldn't have raised her hopes. 'He seemed to be expecting me.'

'He was. He told me at midsummer that you were on your way home.'

Midsummer. Rocamadour, he thought, and my vision of her in the Lady Chapel. Sitting in the sun, she was, in a place very like this.

'How did he know?' He tried to keep his tone casual.

She laughed, sounding slightly embarrassed. 'We were down here in the glade together – he'd come to see Joanna for some reason – and he was telling me he'd seen Aidan. Someone who used to be at the hermitage,' she explained. I know Aidan, he thought. 'We started talking about how Aidan rescued me – twice, really, since I might well have been wrapped in my shroud and buried if he hadn't seen me moving – and we got on to you.' Her eyes fell, as if she didn't want to meet his. 'He was trying to comfort me, because I was upset – I'd been worrying in case – oh!' She seemed impatient with herself. 'I couldn't stop thinking about you.' Bless you for your honesty, he thought. 'He said we should think about you together, and we did. I had a sort of dream about you, only I was still awake. At least, I think I was.' She frowned in concentration. 'You were in a dark little chapel, and you looked sick. But then suddenly you stood up and you smiled at me. Afterwards Ranald said, did you see anything? and I said yes, I'd seen you, and he said, I told you he was alive.'

She stopped abruptly.

He said gently, 'Was that what you were worrying about? That I was dead?'

'Yes!' she said spiritedly, wiping her nose again. 'I knew where you'd gone – a few months after you'd left, Ranald told me about the crusade against the Cathars, and we thought it was highly likely that's where you'd raced off to in such a hurry.' She reached up her hand, gently touching his cheek. 'I know what you're like,' she said. 'Remember?' He nodded; he knew she was thinking about the wildness that had lost her a father and a brother. 'I knew you wouldn't stand back and let the others rush into the fray without you. That's why I touched you when you appeared just now.' She laughed shortly, as if ridiculing herself. 'I wanted to make sure you were real and not an apparition.'

She was staring at him, and he saw compassion in her face at the difference in him. 'You were wounded,' she said. It wasn't a question.

'Aye.' There was no point in denying it: he knew it must show. But he didn't elaborate.

She looked at him questioningly, as if expecting more. Her eyes held pity, which he didn't want.

'I got careless,' he said baldly.

As if picking up his mood, she said lightly, 'You shouldn't be so tall. You make too easy a target.' Her fingers ran through his hair. 'You're turning grey,' she said. And her eyes filled with tears again.

It worked before, he thought, bending to kiss her.

Afterwards she said shakily, 'Will you keep doing that every time I threaten to cry all over you?'

And he said, 'Yes. I promise.'

PART SIX

Roese

Early Autumn 1210–Autumn 1211

Twenty-five

When she'd moved forwards to touch him and then thrown herself into his arms, a small part of her had wondered if he would rebuff her. After all, he'd made it quite clear, before, that he regarded her as some sort of a tomboy, dressed up in her brother's clothes, swinging punches and falling off warhorses, a crop-haired freak devoid of femininity and allure.

Then, as his arms closed fiercely round her, she remembered how he'd looked at her.

She'd forgotten how strong he was; he held her so tightly that she couldn't breathe. His chest seemed to be absolutely solid; with a smile, she realized he must be wearing a breastplate.

But, standing so close, she could see the changes in him. There were new lines under the light brown eyes and around the mouth, and the dark hair was streaked with grey; he seemed to have lost a tooth. He'd aged visibly, for all that he'd been away only a year and a half, and that ageing had come about through suffering.

Then, when the pity had made her weep, his face had taken on the expression of embarrassed bewilderment she'd seen in other men when confronted by a woman's tears. But his solution was one she hadn't come across before.

Those few brief moments had set her on fire. Desire rose in her so suddenly that her head swam and, leaning against him, he held her all the tighter, his lean hard body pressed to hers. In swift wonder she thought, I've never known anything like this before!, at the same instant recognizing that it was right, it was what was meant to be.

It had probably been just as well, she thought afterwards, that her blocked nose had stopped the kiss from going on any longer.

When a little later he kissed her again, his hands running across her breasts, her belly, lingering on the curve where her waist went in as if he were mapping out her shape with his palms, it seemed that their two bodies fitted together like the reunited halves of a circle. His mouth on hers, his tongue deep in her mouth where her own eagerly met it, she began to shake.

Eventually, breaking away from her so that she almost fell, he said roughly, 'Come on. We must go.'

'Where?' she asked vaguely, trying to control the trembling.

He took hold of her hand. 'Diew, I don't know – somewhere there are people. Ranald and what's her name.'

'Joanna?'

'Aye.' He had started to walk fast, pulling her along with him, and he glanced down at her. He looked different, some strong emotion darkening his expression, and for a moment she was anxious. Then he said, almost to himself, 'You don't understand, do you?'

She shook her head, although she was beginning to think she did.

He stopped, sliding his hand round her neck under her hair, his thumb brushing her lips. Staring first at her lips then straight into her eyes, he said, 'I want you. More than any woman I've ever met, I want you.' She felt her heart give a strange shuddering leap, deciding nervously that must mean she wanted him too. 'And,' his voice a murmur, he leaned down to speak right into her ear so that his warm breath set her quivering, 'if we stay here in this copse of yours that hides us so nicely from the rest of the world, I might find I can't wait.'

Striding off again for Joanna's house, he was moving so fast she had to run to keep up.

* * *

It was a long time before he kissed her again. As if they knew – they probably do, she thought, they both used to live in the world of men and women, even if they don't any more – Ranald and Joanna seemed to go out of their way to make sure she and Gawyn weren't left alone together. Not even for a moment.

Sometimes, catching his eyes on her and a look in them that held both amusement and frustration – much more frustration than humour – she would ache for him. And, now that she knew what she was missing, for herself too.

Once, when presumably he imagined she was out of earshot, she overheard Ranald say vehemently to Gawyn, 'If you stare at her with all that heat, the poor child will melt.'

She saw Gawyn's eyebrows go up but she didn't catch all of the reply. He seemed to be questioning, somewhat forcefully, Ranald's use of the word 'child'.

There came a morning when Gawyn and Ranald were absent when she went to breakfast.

Hearing the edge of panic in her voice, she said to Joanna, 'Where is he?'

Joanna patted her hand. 'Not far away,' she said kindly. 'Ranald wanted to visit the hermitage to ensure all goes well in his absence, and he suggested Gawyn went with him.'

'But –'

'Gawyn didn't want to go,' she continued, giving Roese a reassuring smile. 'He said, if I recall aright, that he had better things to do than go traipsing through the hills, to which Ranald replied that was exactly why he was taking him along.'

Roese sat down abruptly. She felt elated and embarrassed at the same time. 'When's he – when are they coming back?'

'Tomorrow or the next day,' Joanna said blithely.

Two days.

Joanna came to sit beside her, putting an arm round her shoulders. 'I know, child, believe me.' Her voice was soothing. You don't, Roese thought rebelliously, you're much too old! Then, instantly repentant, she leaned across and kissed the dry cheek. Joanna chuckled. 'Nobody gets to be old without first having been young,' she went on with inarguable logic, 'and I remember quite clearly how it feels to fall for a handsome young man.' She eyed Roese ruefully. 'Not, perhaps, to fall as hard and fast as you seem to have done, but then the circumstances are somewhat unique.'

She paused, and Roese thought she had finished. But then she said, 'Ranald has taken Gawyn away because he and I both feel strongly that the two of you need time to think, and you don't seem to be able to do that when you're together.'

474

'Think about what?'

'Your future!' Joanna's tone was slightly abrasive.

They're right, Roese acknowledged, we can't think when we're together; she hadn't given one single thought to anything beyond the wonders of *now*.

But he had, obviously; shocking Roese to the core, Joanna said quietly, 'Your Gawyn has told Ranald he wants to *marry* you.'

She squeaked, '*Marry* me?'

And Joanna, laughing, said, 'Does it come as such a surprise?'

She almost said, we hardly know each other! But she didn't, because she didn't believe it. She thought of making the sensible points: where would we live? *How* would we live? How do we know we'd make each other happy?

None of that mattered, and she knew it. What mattered was that fierce mutual hunger which would be assuaged, within or without the sanctity of marriage. What mattered was what had caused it: an encounter with a laughing stranger who'd turned into a saviour, only to lose her through his own haste-born carelessness. And the loss had weighed so heavily on him that he'd come back, as she'd known he would. Over the months and the miles, he'd been unable to forget. And so had she.

She said, knowing she would never change her mind, 'I want to marry him, too.'

Joanna looked at her for a long moment. 'I should warn you that Ranald intends to place before him every objection he can think of.'

'Why?'

She smiled slightly. 'He doesn't entirely trust Gawyn's motives. He, too, remembers what it is like to be young – it is not so long ago, in his case. And,' she added simply, 'he is a man.'

475

Roese wished she understood more thoroughly. Then she realized she didn't need to. She said, 'Whatever he says, it won't make any difference.'

Joanna sighed. 'Yes. I quite agree. You are too young to be wise, he is too singleminded.'

'Wise?' Roese repeated apprehensively.

Joanna looked away. After a moment she said, 'Never mind.'

When Gawyn and Ranald returned, they were a day later than Joanna's estimate and they didn't come from the direction of the hermitage. In addition, Roese saw as she stood watching them approach, they had a third rider with them.

As they came closer, she heard a voice grumbling through a familiar list of complaints. '. . . saddle like the point of a roof and rain all down my neck, it'll be as much as I can do to walk, never mind –'

Then, the tone changing to delight, Ismay cried, 'Roese!' and, sliding off her stout pony and abandoning him entirely as if she had no further use for him, she bustled the last few steps to where Roese stood waiting.

As she and Ismay hugged, she looked up and caught Gawyn's eye. She mouthed to him, 'How?', but before he could answer, Ismay said, clucking her disapproval as if Roese had just dirtied her shoes or let the dinner burn, 'I never heard the like, rushing off to foreign shores without so much as a thought for who's going to look after you, let alone what everyone's going to think, you being a young girl with no chaperone and no ring on your finger, I don't know what the world's coming to, I –'

'Who's rushing off to foreign shores?' Roese demanded. 'Ismay, what are you talking about?'

'She is referring to Gawyn's suggestion that you –'

476

Ranald began, but he got no further. Swinging down from the big grey, in two paces Gawyn was by her side, disentangling her from Ismay and taking hold of her arm.

'Gawyn,' Ranald said warningly.

Gawyn turned to look at him. For a brief instant they stared at one another – Roese could feel the silent battle between them – then Gawyn said, 'I have to talk to her. Alone.'

And Ranald said, 'Very well.'

Gawyn marched her off across the grass to the edge of the copse. Then, glancing over his shoulder with a slight smile, he said, 'They can still see us here, so Ranald won't be tormenting himself with thoughts of what I might be doing to you.' He bent to kiss her, briefly but hard, on the lips. 'Stop looking at me like that and listen.' He swung away from her, putting a couple of paces between them. 'We have to get married, but we can't marry in England because of the interdict. Ranald doesn't know how things are in Wales – there may be priests who will perform the ceremony, but I'm not willing to take the risk.' He turned to look at her. 'I have reasons for keeping out of Wales.'

'Yes, I know.' He looked surprised, and she said, 'I don't mean I know what they are, I just mean I know you were running away. I told you that.'

'Aye, you did.' He frowned, then said softly, 'What are you doing, Roese my lovely, agreeing to marry me when I have –'

'I haven't agreed.'

'What?' His expression was incredulous. 'But –'

'You haven't asked me,' she pointed out.

'Haven't I?' She shook her head. 'Will you, then?'

'Of course.'

He muttered something about wasting time, then,

as if he'd suddenly been hit by the full import, said abruptly, 'You're sure, now?'

'I'm sure.'

He made as if to move towards her, then stopped. From two steps distant, she could read in his face what was going through his mind – she'd been discovering it was usually quite easy to work it out, he was a direct sort of man – and she wanted to laugh and cry at the same time. She said gently, 'I don't think Ranald would excommunicate you if we had a very quick hug.'

'He can't anyway, he's a –' He stopped, starting to grin. 'A *very* quick one?'

'Why not?'

But it was different this time, as if he was honouring whatever promise he'd made to Ranald; it was, she thought, impossible to think of Gawyn making him any promise and *not* honouring it. The powerful desire was there – she could sense it, like some great force kept under tight control – but he held her as if she'd been Joanna, or Ismay.

The thought leading on to another, she said, 'You brought Ismay back.'

'Aye. She was happy enough where she was, she told me, but she feels her place is with you. She wants to come with us.'

Feeling that she already knew the answer, she said, 'Where are we going?'

'Brittany.'

It became apparent very soon that Ismay interpreted the chaperone role even more stringently than Ranald and Joanna had done. From never being allowed to be alone with Gawyn, now Roese found she was scarcely allowed to see him at all. Ismay seemed to think Roese had compromised herself –

478

whatever that meant – by riding off with him when she'd fled from the arranged marriage, and Roese found herself protesting again and again that Gawyn had hardly noticed her except when she did things like falling in the river that slowed his progress.

'In that case, my girl,' Ismay said darkly, 'why did he race back halfway round the world to find you? Answer me that!'

'It wasn't halfway round the world, it was from the south of France.'

'There you are, then!' Ismay was triumphant.

It was impossible to argue with her.

She insisted on making Roese something new to wear – black, she said, wasn't at all appropriate for a bride. Roese had to agree with her, although, after so long in borrowed black robes, it was going to seem wildly flamboyant to dress in bright colours again. Joanna took them to market and let Roese choose what she wanted, and Ismay made the lengths of fine cloth up into a kirtle and a heavy, lined cloak with an interlining of padded wool.

She was walking up and down the long hall of Joanna's house, getting used to a trailing train again, when Ranald came to find her.

For some moments he watched her without speaking. Then he said, 'You look very different from the boy Aidan fished out of the Wye.'

She smiled, lifting the full, deep red folds of the skirt. 'In this, I doubt if I'd have survived to be fished out.' Picturing Aidan's earnest face, her smile deepened. I'll never see him again, she thought suddenly. She asked quietly, 'Is he well?'

'He is. He has a fine touch with living creatures, and makes a good sheep herd. He spends much time with Benedict, too; Benedict is passing on to him all

479

he knows of medicine, and reports that Aidan is an apt pupil.'

'He's a natural healer,' she said absently, remembering.

'He is.'

'When you see him,' she began impulsively, 'would you –'

But she didn't have time to complete the request: Gawyn came into the hall, and his presence drove everything else from her head.

Towards the end of the month, Gawyn accompanied Ranald on another trip to the hermitage, and this time Joanna went with them. Ismay relaxed her vigil to allow Roese to bid him goodbye – perhaps, Roese thought, she intends to make me pay by nagging me solidly for the next two days on how to be a good wife – and in the precious few moments alone, she asked him why they were making the trip.

He said awkwardly, 'Something we have to do.'

'What?'

He stared down at her, honesty struggling with anguish. 'Roese, I can't tell you.'

And it hurts you that you can't, she thought. She made herself smile, so that he would think she didn't mind. 'Ah, well, you men always have your mysteries.' Then she remembered that Joanna was going too. 'I mean – '

'I won't, not after this.' He kissed her swiftly. 'When we're in Brocéliande, I'll be there at your side every day, and you'll share my every thought and deed.'

Somehow, she thought as she watched him ride away, that doesn't sound very likely.

* * *

They returned on the evening of the second day, not a moment too soon for Roese, who had endured the full force of Ismay trying to teach her how to bake a loaf that didn't sit on the stomach like a rock.

Gawyn wasn't with them, but Ranald reassured her that he'd be back in the morning – he had gone to arrange their passage across to Brittany. 'You sail from a place on the coast this side of the Wye,' he told her. 'He says the risk of him being recognized is more acceptable than the risk of taking you over the river again.'

'Will he be all right?' she asked anxiously.

'He will.' Ranald gave her an amused look. 'At present, I don't think anyone could stop him doing anything.'

True to his word, Gawyn arrived early the next day, and they were packed and on the road by midday; he was, she remembered, always impatient to be gone once everything was ready.

Ranald was to ride with them to the coast, but Joanna bade them farewell at her house. Standing with her in the hall, Roese searched for a way to express her gratitude: you took me in, she thought, looking at the wise old face, someone you knew next to nothing about, who no doubt disrupted your calm routine, simply because Ranald asked you to. And, even if you've remained something of an enigma, you've been kind to me.

She put her arms round Joanna and hugged her, and the hug was reciprocated.

'Take care, child,' Joanna said. Then, releasing her but keeping hold of her hands, 'Be tolerant.'

'Tolerant?' It seemed a strange thing to say.

'Some men aren't born to be husbands,' Joanna said enigmatically. She looked out at Gawyn who, already mounted, was trying to control the eager grey with one hand while he held on to the reins of three other horses; Arrow had taken it into her head that she didn't care for Ismay's pony, and was trying to put as much distance between them as she could. 'Remember, he's a knight first, a husband second.'

It sounded like a warning. 'What do you mean?'

Joanna smiled at her kindly, stroking the hair away from her forehead. 'Don't look so alarmed, child. I'm sorry, I meant no harm.' She stared out again at Gawyn, who at that moment turned to call out to Roese.

'He cares for you, that's plain to see,' she whispered. 'And, God willing, that will be enough.' Kissing Roese, she pushed her gently out through the door.

In a small inlet concealed by low cliffs, a boat was waiting for them, tied up to a makeshift jetty. Pulling up on the edge of the shingle, Gawyn said, 'Best not to come any further, Ranald.'

For some reason she couldn't explain, she wanted the moment to pass quickly. There was something in the air, some sense of sadness that sat ill against her joy. Ismay watched her, then, turning away, rode on towards the jetty. She hissed, 'Come on!'

Ranald held her eyes for a moment. He seemed to be trying to impart something to her, but she didn't know what it was. He said, 'Good luck, Roese.'

Was this what was making her sad, the poignancy of parting? She didn't know. There was much she could have said to him, but either she must say it all or none of it – in the end, she just said, 'Thank you.'

She began to ride slowly off along the shore. But, as if drawn round by strings, she found herself looking back over her shoulder.

Gawyn and Ranald had both dismounted and were

facing each other; Gawyn said something, and Ranald made a reply. She couldn't hear the words, but somehow there was a formality about the exchange – at one point she thought Gawyn bowed. As the two of them stood together, suddenly she saw that they were alike – not to look at, for their colouring was different and Gawyn was bigger, but in some less obvious way.

Power, she thought suddenly. They're strong men, both of them, and they each recognize and respect the power of the other. That's why it feels sometimes as if the air between them is bristling with drawn swords – they're meeting each other head on. If they were stags, they'd be clashing antlers.

Then, confounding her theory, abruptly the two men embraced.

Then Gawyn mounted and, without looking back, came down the beach after her.

Sailors were waiting to lead the horses below, and, as soon as the gangway was raised, they untied the ship. Moving slowly at first, then more quickly as they came out from the shelter of land and the wind filled the sails, steadily they pulled away from the shore.

Roese stood holding Ismay's hand, Gawyn behind them. Ranald was a dark figure on the headland, almost swallowed up by the land mass rising behind him. Goodbye, she thought, goodbye.

There was a lump in her throat and she had to blink fast to keep the tears at bay. Why am I crying, she wondered, when I'm doing exactly what I want? She sniffed, hoping Gawyn wouldn't hear – he wouldn't understand, he'd probably made this trip dozens of times and would laugh at her for her ridiculous sentimentality. What was there to lament?

England had hardly treated her well, and the only people she was leaving behind were monks who were probably much happier since she'd left their hermitage.

But she was still crying.

She felt his hand on her shoulder. Turning to look up at him, she saw his eyes were fixed on the all but invisible figure on the headland.

When they couldn't see him any more, silently Gawyn put his arms round both Ismay and Roese and led them below.

Twenty-six

It wasn't until they got to Brocéliande that Roese realized she was about to marry a rich man.

She'd suspected his family might be wealthy when they reached Paimpol and, escorted by a young man called Barr, were taken to the house of Gawyn's cousin Yves. Yves's house was about the most comfortable she'd ever been in – not that she'd been in many – and Yves clearly didn't want for anything; coming from a wealthy family, however, wasn't the same thing as being wealthy yourself.

Yves was quite obviously amazed that Gawyn had brought a bride back with him, but courteously disguised his amazement in front of Roese. He treated her with a careful politeness she'd never encountered before, and at first it made her feel awkward. Gawyn, observing, whispered, 'Shall I tell him what you're really like?' and, before she realized how she was implicating herself, she flashed back, 'Don't you dare!'

Yves made the arrangements for their marriage. Gawyn said he didn't want any great fuss, and she hastily agreed – I just want to be married, she thought. Yves got hold of the priest, who hummed and hawed about it being rather sudden and they really should make a public proclamation first and have the ceremony later, but his objections faded to nothing when Yves gave him a bag of gold.

'It can be my wedding gift to you, Lady Roese,' he said gallantly.

'It's very generous,' she said.

Gawyn remarked that it was only a small bag.

On the morning of her wedding day, Roese suffered herself to be fussed over for at least two hours by Ismay, who made her bathe in milk (she didn't like the feel on her skin and washed afterwards in cold water when Ismay wasn't looking), provided scented oil to rub into her limbs, and brushed her hair with two hundred strokes till it gleamed like amber. We'd better stop soon, she thought, or Gawyn won't recognize me.

At the appointed time, Ismay took her into the hall where Yves, dressed in what looked like a new silk surcoat over shining mail, was waiting to escort her to the church. It wasn't far from the house, and, to her amusement, he lifted her up in front of him on his horse. She heard Ismay clucking again, but she didn't care.

'Hurry up!' she called to Ismay as Yves spurred his horse, 'I'm not starting without you!'

The church seemed to be full; only having seen Gawyn on his own or as the master of a deserted castle, it was quite a surprise to see that so many people knew him.

But, when she saw him, she ceased to notice anyone else.

It was a long time since she'd seen him fully accoutred, the hauberk not hidden beneath some shabby outer garment. Now, tall and broad-shouldered, the black of his surcoat making him loom even bigger than he really was, he made her feel weak.

On his breast the scarlet bear's head seemed to shine.

Walking up the aisle with what Ismay later told her was quite indecent haste, she joined him in front of the altar.

She didn't remember much of the interminable ceremony; it took twice as long because she and the priest had no common language, so everything had to be repeated for her by Yves and Gawyn, and often their two translations were slightly different. She did notice that Gawyn seemed ill at ease sometimes, rattling off the responses as if he was in a hurry to be done. She concluded that soldiers and churches probably didn't go together very well. Afterwards Yves threw open his house to anyone who cared to come along, and as the day wore on everyone seemed to be laughing or singing or both.

Gawyn said quietly to her, 'If you're ready, we could get going.'

She thought, perhaps when he gets used to having a wife, he'll start telling me in advance what we're doing. She said, 'I hadn't realized we were going anywhere.'

'Of course we are!' He looked surprised. 'We can't stay here, this will go on for ages yet, and we'll never have any peace.' He glanced across at a particularly ribald group. 'Just as well you don't understand what they're laughing at.'

She had an idea; the men seemed to look at her with a speculative sort of expression.

'I'll tell Ismay, then.'

'No, don't do that.' He put his hand on her arm. 'Yves will bring her down in a day or two – I want to travel just with you.'

She met his eyes. 'Like we did before?' she whispered.

And he said, 'Exactly.' Then, as if deliberately breaking the romantic mood, added, 'Except that it's not raining.'

The lack of rain wasn't the only difference: instead of sleeping out in the open, he took her to an inn. It was late by the time they stopped, almost fully dark, and there was a fire blazing in the chamber to which the landlord led them. They refused his offer of food, but he brought them a jug of spicy-smelling mulled wine.

She looked around her. 'Where's everyone else?'

He smiled. 'Who were you expecting?' He was standing by the hearth unbuckling his swordbelt.

'Oh, no-one in particular – I thought the sleeping accommodation in inns was communal, that's all.'

'It is in England. You're in civilized Brittany now, where you can have privacy if you pay for it.' He glanced up, meeting her eyes. 'Do you honestly think I'd have brought you to a place where we had to share a bed with other people?'

There was something in his look that seemed to catch her heart, making the beat irregular. She said softly, 'No.'

He was stripping off his surcoat, laying it on top of the chest at the foot of the bed. Reaching up to un-buckle his cuirass, he said, 'I've something here be-longs to you.'

'What?'

'Close your eyes.' She did so, and felt him move to stand behind her, fastening something round her neck. 'This isn't a wedding gift,' he said, 'for all that it goes so well with your gown.'

She opened her eyes and saw her mother's cross hanging on its chain on her breast.

'It's yours!' she cried, spinning round to look at him. 'It was your payment!'

'Payment for a task I didn't complete.' His voice was almost harsh. Then, softening, he added, 'Besides, it looks better on you.'

He went on looking at her, and gradually his face grew serious again. He put out his hand and touched her cheek, and said, so quietly that she had to strain to hear, 'I almost lost you.'

She stood up, moving into his arms. Still mail-clad, he smiled and evaded her. 'Wait. I've still got far too many garments on.'

She watched as deftly he unlaced the sides of the hauberk and slid it off, removing his boots and mail leggings. Clad only in linen breeches, he reached for the fastenings of her gown.

She was so occupied with staring at him that she was naked before she realized it. Slowly his eyes ran down and up again. His face changed; putting his arms round her, lifting her off her feet, he carried her to the bed.

Lying beside her, he began to kiss her. She wondered why she was not nervous – wasn't a girl meant to be, the first time she was bedded? Kissing him with growing passion, she felt him move to lie above her, his hands sliding down over her, fingers playing with her nipples, hands circling her breasts. His lips were forcing hers apart, his tongue stroking hers with a rhythm that she found fiercely exciting; she reached up to touch his skin as he was touching hers.

He took hold of her hand, guiding it down across his chest and his flat belly, down into his groin to the hard bulge of his erect penis. She gasped in surprise; she knew what was to happen – you couldn't live in the country and not know, especially if your father bred horses – and for a moment she was fearful.

He said huskily, 'Not yet. It's all right.' Then she felt his hand push in between her legs, exploring her with a touch so slow and gentle that she wanted to urge him to go faster, for he was making her feel so strange, so wonderful, yet she knew there was more.

After what seemed a long time, he put his hand on her thigh and firmly parted her legs. Then, lifting up and positioning himself between them, he started to put himself inside her.

It hurt, and then it didn't – then she was pushing up towards him, wanting more of him, and he held off, taking her at his pace and not hers. She heard him whisper, 'Roese, oh, Roese,' and then he was kissing her again, drawing her into him as she was drawing him into her. There was so much of him – she felt full, as if she couldn't contain any more, then somehow her body altered to accommodate him and she could.

Deep inside her, he paused. Chest pressed down on to hers, he wound his arms right round her, hugging her to him with such strength that she felt he was trying to absorb her into himself. Lifting her legs, she clasped her feet behind his back; she thought dreamily, we couldn't be closer.

It was the moment of unity.

Then, almost imperceptibly at first, he began to move. Rhythmically, keeping pace with him, her breathing accelerating as his did, the tension and the thrilling new feelings grew until she was almost sobbing. Then, when she was beginning to think it was too good, that she couldn't bear such pleasure any more, something else began. He seemed to know, for he reached down to stroke where he'd been stroking before, making the great surging swell of ecstasy rise rapidly to such a peak that, when at last it broke, she felt tears of mixed relief and joy flood her cheeks. He didn't seem to notice, for he was moving faster now, and there was sweat on his body as the muscles tensed and hardened. As the throbbing in the heart of her own body subsided, she felt the same thing begin in him; with the beginnings of a muted cry, he took her face between his hands and muffled the cry in a kiss.

For some time afterwards they lay quite still, clasped together, their own sweat and each others' drying on their bodies. Then, pulling out of her with great tenderness, he reached down for the discarded bedclothes and covered them both up.

She didn't know what to say. Perhaps you don't speak, she thought, perhaps you just lie quiet while you recover.

Lying on their backs, he had one arm round her shoulder, the hand resting on her breast. His other hand was low on her belly. She felt cherished.

Suddenly his drowsy voice said, 'Are you all right?' Although he didn't exactly shout, still he made her jump.

'Yes!' she said. It seemed a little inadequate: 'I feel wonderful,' she added. 'Do you?'

'Mmm.'

'Is that how it always is?'

She heard him laugh softly. 'No, my lovely, that's how it hardly ever is, especially the first time a man and woman lie together and when she's never lain with a man before.'

'I haven't,' she said earnestly. She didn't know why, except that she'd been led to believe that it mattered to men.

He laughed again. 'You don't have to tell me, I know.'

'How?'

'I could tell.' He yawned hugely.

491

'How?' she repeated. 'Did I do it wrong? Like someone who doesn't know how?'

Now he laughed so loudly – right in her ear – that she had to move away. 'No, Roese,' he said through the laughter. 'On the contrary, you did it like someone who's been doing it all her life.'

He raised himself on an elbow to look at her; in the firelight his brown eyes looked reddish. 'I can't believe my luck,' he went on, staring down at her very tenderly. 'The only woman I've ever come across whom I wanted to marry, and she enjoys it as much as I do.'

She was delighted by his remark, but it implied a familiarity with the activity that she felt she might question. 'Have you bedded lots of women, then?'

'Hundreds.'

'Really?'

He grinned. 'Not really. Some. Enough.'

'And how did you –'

He closed her mouth by putting his own on to it. Then he said, 'Roese, if you were more experienced – which I should go down on my knees in gratitude that you're not – you'd realize that such things aren't a matter for discussion.'

'I'm sorry. I don't know what the rules are.'

He was kissing her neck, slowly tracing his mouth down over her collarbone towards her breast. Closing his lips round her nipple, he stroked it with his tongue. 'The rules,' he said between strokes, 'are that we lie here doing this for a while, then, when we both want to, we make love again.'

Sighing, lying back against the pillow, she said, 'Oh, *good*.'

* * *

When they entered the forest, she imagined they were nearly there; he'd told her his castle was in woodland. But this forest was vast: all day they rode – far too long, she thought ruefully, for someone who'd had her first bedding the night before – and still the soaring trees continued without a break. She would have found it oppressive alone – and even with Gawyn beside her, increasingly cheerful as the day went on, the dim light was beginning to get her down.

Towards evening, she noticed a creamy mist beginning to creep around the horses' feet, as if the earth were sighing, exhaling as it prepared for sleep. Abruptly the trees cleared, the path opened out and she found herself on the shore of a lake.

He turned, smiling. 'Almost home.'

They drew rein, standing side by side looking out over the still black water. The mist was denser here – it seemed to be growing out of the water – and she thought that she saw the vague shape of an island rising up like a hump. There wasn't a sound: it was a magical place.

If we stay here much longer, she thought, a great shiver running up her spine, I shall start imagining things.

Perhaps he felt the same, for suddenly he said, his voice loud in the silence, 'Come on. I'm starving,' and, wheeling the grey away from the water, he trotted off along the firm sand.

At the western edge of the lake a track led though the thinning trees into a village – hamlet, she thought, would be more appropriate – it was little more than a collection of dwellings huddled in a vague square; they were stoutly made, she noticed, with roofs of dark grey slate. Rounding a corner, they forded a shallow stream that led off towards the lake.

There was a forge, deserted now as evening drew on, but a radiating warmth from the walls suggested it had been in use not long ago.

They passed a chapel and a standing stone. Entering a copse, they emerged on the other side and Gawyn's castle rose up in front of them.

The curtain wall was solid, stretching away on either side, with nothing to break the impenetrable surface except for arrow slits some way off the ground. At either end were thick round towers, their tops crenellated. Beneath the wall was a broad ditch, its lower slopes already filling with the onset of the autumn rains.

A wide drawbridge led to open gates; although it was now almost fully dark, nobody seemed about to secure the castle for the night.

Inevitably, she thought of that other castle, hundreds of miles away in the Black Mountains.

They rode across the drawbridge side by side.

At the inner end a small guard room was set into the massive wall. Dismounting, Gawyn put his head round the door and shouted something in a language she didn't know – presumably it was Breton.

His voice seemed to echo in the quiet. She had a sudden fear that this place, too, was going to be deserted. That she'd been too headstrong, not waiting to find out what sort of life he considered normal, and had let him bear her off to some crude existence with no comforts and no servants. The sort of existence he'd led when last she stayed under his roof.

The silence extended, and she felt her happy optimism drain away.

Then suddenly there were shouting voices, and the courtyard was lit with flares as what seemed a huge crowd of people poured out of various doorways.

Men and women, young and not so young, jostled each other as they tried to touch Gawyn and get a glimpse of her, and cheerful faces, full of undisguised curiosity, seemed to flash before her. People asked her questions and, not understanding, she could only laugh and shake her head.

Then someone at the back of the crush was shouting, trying to push a way through; word of his presence spreading, they all stood back and made a path. A short, thickset man with grey hair approached, dressed, as were many of the men, in a distinctive black-and-red livery. Going down on one knee, his face serious, he said something which she guessed was a formal greeting, a welcome home. Then, responding to Gawyn's outstretched hand, he stood up and took it; Gawyn leaned down from the saddle and put his arms round him, thumping him so hard on the back that the man coughed.

Roese became aware of someone tugging at her sleeve. Looking down, she saw a woman and a girl of about her own age. Pointing at Gawyn, indicating her damp cloak, they seemed to be inviting her to dismount.

She shook her head again. 'I'm sorry. I don't understand.'

In the midst of a loud conversation punctuated by a lot of laughter, Gawyn must have heard. He spun round to look at her, his face full of happiness. 'Are you all right?'

It was what he'd said when they'd made love. For a second some uncontrollable part of her gave a shudder of memory. She smiled.

'Oh, yes!' He's not referring to *that*. 'But I can't understand them – what are they saying?'

He turned to the two women, who repeated whatever it was to him. 'They say you look tired, cold and wet, and what am I thinking of, keeping you standing out here.' He grinned.

'They didn't say all that! Did they?'

'They say you must go with them and they'll sit you down in front of a roaring fire, feed you spiced wine and cakes while they heat enough water to fill a tub, then they'll put you to bed.'

His eyes rested on hers; the smile had changed to a different expression.

Knowing – hoping – that no-one else understood, she said, 'Will it be your bed they put me in?'

And slowly he nodded.

Some time later, she was lying between hastily aired sheets – they were still warm from being held in front of the fire – in a huge bed that was built into the wall, almost like a cupboard. It was wonderfully cosy, and, when the older woman demonstrated how the doors closed, quite free from draughts.

I like her, Roese thought, I wonder what she's called? And the younger one. They'd had a lot of fun while she'd been fed, warmed and bathed, and the two women had kept up a constant stream of chatter which, judging from their amazed tones, must have concerned the shock of the lord and master turning up without any warning and accompanied by a new wife.

Lying there, she could hear male voices not far away, in the hall, presumably. Gawyn would have a lot to talk about, she didn't doubt, and the grey-haired man – his steward? – would probably want to tell him everything that had happened in the time he'd been away.

How long *had* he been away? Had he been here on his way to or from the south? What does he do here, what sort of a life to they all lead deep in this forest?

I don't know, she thought. So much about him I don't know.

The thought made her nervous suddenly. She wished the women were still there – once she was in bed, they'd wished her goodnight (managing to invest the simple valediction with a certain amount of suggestion) and left her alone. Without them, there was nothing to take her mind off her anxiety.

She gazed out into the room. It was a good size, with a huge hearth in which a fire blazed in an iron firebasket. There were hangings on the walls – it was difficult to make out the details in the light of the torches, but she thought they were tapestries of hunting scenes – and fur rugs on the stone floor. The wooden tub they'd brought in was still in front of the fire, steam rising from the water, and a big earthenware jug for topping up stood in the chimneybreast, keeping hot for Gawyn. The cloth with which she'd dried herself had been soft, and the bedclothes were of fine quality.

She thought suddenly of her own home. What must he have thought of our arrangements? How did he like standing in the yard at the communal washing trough, pigs rooting at his feet? The thought made her smile.

It was here that he was bringing me. When we fled and I fell in the river, he was taking me to his castle in Brittany.

This castle.

He hardly knew me, didn't even like me much, yet, because he accepted his responsibility for my plight, he was prepared to put all this luxury, all these nice people, at my disposal for as long as I needed to be here.

A wave of deep satisfaction swept through her. I might know nothing of the details, she thought, but it's not important, because I know him. He'll look after me, he'll always be there.

Something flashed across her mind – she thought she saw the hermitage, and Aidan standing beside her, supporting her. Someone else was there, a young woman who looked like her – and Gawyn was sitting on the ground, long legs bent up in front of him, weariness in the curve of his back.

For an instant, she felt piercingly sad.

Then it was gone.

I'm more tired than I thought, she realized, I was beginning to dream. Propping herself up on the bolsters, she strained to hear, from the sounds coming from the hall, if the party might be nearing its close.

She was asleep when he finally came. Vaguely aware of a soft splashing – as if he were washing, but trying not to wake her – she opened her eyes and saw him, naked, dry himself with the cloth she'd used. She studied him, the heavily developed shoulders and upper arms, the long legs, slightly bowed – did all men who spent much of their lives in the saddle have legs like that? – He looked, she thought, exactly what he was. Joanna's words flitted through her head: 'He's a knight first, a husband second.' She banished them.

She watched as he tiptoed across the room – he looks absurd, she thought, trying not to laugh, he's far too big to tiptoe – then he pulled back the covers and slid into bed.

She inched towards him, and he put his arms round her. 'Don't wake up,' he whispered, his hand stroking down across her shoulder and cupping her breast, 'You were worn out, you need your sleep.'

She kissed him, opening his mouth with hers, running her tongue around his lips. As she broke away, moving down to kiss his chest, licking the warm, slightly damp skin, he muttered, 'Well, if you insist,' and then he was responding, kissing, touching, sucking with so much enthusiasm that she was touched he'd been prepared to restrain it if she really had been worn out.

Her hands round his neck as he lay on her, her fingers found a long scar, a deep, straight furrow though the thick muscles of his back. About to question him, she felt him tense, and knew, with a brand-new instinct born of their physical closeness, that he didn't want her to.

But the discovery added something else to her passion for him. Older than her, vastly more experienced, bigger and more powerful, she had imagined that he was the strong partner, she the vulnerable one. Now, the memory of that fearsome scar still in her fingertips – whatever sort of injury could have caused it? – a different light shone on him.

He'd suffered, she'd known that the moment she saw him in Joanna's copse. But she hadn't known then how much.

Looking up at him, she saw he had his eyes closed, lost in sensation as, gently, he began to penetrate her. Pleasure was taking over her body and her mind, but now something else was there as well, intensifying the pleasure, making her the more eager to hold him, meld with him.

Tenderness overwhelming her, she realized that she loved him.

Twenty-seven

Through the weeks of the autumn, she lived in a world of discovery and delight. Riding out with Gawyn on mornings when the early mists were breathed in by the strengthening sun, its bright golden light drawing a last flamboyant show from the dying leaves, she thought she'd never seen anywhere more beautiful than Brocéliande in October.

She understood almost immediately his love of his home, and it crossed her mind to wonder how he could ever bear to leave. Everywhere they went people welcomed him, greeting him with respect and affection, turning to her as he presented her with open expressions that seemed to say, we're glad to meet you, happy for him that he has taken a wife.

The steward Pierre clearly had everything under control – Gawyn told her he was well aware that his own role was that of figurehead, the whole place ran equally smoothly whether he was there or not. She observed for herself that he didn't seem to know all that much about some aspects of the husbandry of his lands. Well, she thought lovingly, no-one's good at everything. And it was presumably the money earned from Gawyn doing what he was good at that kept the estate running.

But she didn't want to think about that.

There seemed to be a constant supply of visitors, knights and their ladies coming to renew acquaintance, lesser landowners coming to swear fealty. Yves, true to his word, had arrived a few days after herself and Gawyn, accompanied by Barr and Ismay; after several weeks he was showing no signs of being about to leave. There was a holiday air, as if everyone was too busy catching up on news and the precious demands of friendship to think about doing anything more productive.

She tried to think if it had been like this in her father's home, concluding that, in essence if not in actuality, it had.

It was lovely having Ismay with her, especially since Ismay's Welsh mother tongue proved to be fairly close to the Breton spoken by the other serving women. Close enough, anyway, for understanding. Roese listened and attempted to join in; her efforts caused hoots of laughter, but she perceived that the women warmed to her for bothering to try.

To her joy, Gawyn seemed to need time alone together as much as she did. There were the rides – on most mornings he managed to dissuade anyone else from going with them – and in addition he sometimes took her out in the afternoons to a woodland clearing overlooking a lake. She would sit and sew – Ismay had virtually ordered her to, implying that no man would respect a wife who could not embroider a pretty panel. When she told Gawyn why she was struggling with it, he'd remarked that skill with a needle wasn't an attribute he rated very highly. She was feeling smugly pleased with his reply when he added, glancing over her shoulder at the posy of pansies that looked more like a lurid purple and yellow cloud, that it was just as well.

He would lie on his back on the grass at her side, talking in a rambling sort of way about whatever entered his head. She would join in, and slowly they filled in the gaps in their knowledge of one another.

He never spoke of the crusade in the south.

Autumn gave in to winter, and the castle developed chilly corners. Everyone took to lingering in the great hall, where the fire was kept stoked up all day and well into the night. The stream of visitors trailed off, Yves and Barr went home. December brought a spell of bitter weather; the lakes froze over and the snow was so deep that it made riding out a challenge.

She'd have gone on accompanying Gawyn, except that she'd begun to feel sick in the mornings. Ismay, handing her a cloth to bathe her face after one bad session, suggested she might be with child.

'I can't be!' They were alone, Gawyn having set out with Pierre to see if the mill stream was still frozen.

Ismay gave her a look.

'If I'm pregnant, I won't be able to ride for ages!' she cried, feeling that her instinctive negative reaction required explanation. 'And I'm sure I'm not. We've only been married three months.'

Ismay sat her down on the bed and said bluntly, 'Three minutes would have been long enough for you two.'

'What do you mean?'

Ismay laughed briefly. 'Did you think others wouldn't notice? Diew, child, he doesn't take his eyes off you. And you're as bad! How often does he bed you? Every night?'

Roese nodded. It hadn't occurred to her that there was anything unusual in the frequency with which she and Gawyn made love, but then, she thought, I've no yardstick. Dear God, have they all been nudging each other and laughing at us? She felt deeply embarrassed.

Ismay regarded her kindly. 'Don't look like that, Roese, we're all mad with envy.'

Roese hugged her, hiding her flaming face in the crisp white apron.

'Feeling better now?' Ismay enquired.

'Yes.'

'Then lie down for a moment, and let me have a look at you.'

She did as she was told, feeling slightly apprehensive. But Ismay's hands on her belly were gentle, and she let herself relax.

'Hm. Quite a bump, when you're lying flat,' she commented. 'When did you last have your courses?'

Roese thought. It had been soon after they'd come to Brocéliande. 'The beginning of October.'

'Hm.' Ismay lifted Roese's shift and touched her breasts. 'Do they feel tender?'

'Yes.'

Ismay folded the shift right back to look. 'Roese, there's no doubt about it. No woman's breasts swell like this unless she's pregnant. Didn't you know?'

'No.' Then, angry frightened tears rising up, 'How could I know? Nobody's told me *anything!*'

Ismay covered her up and put her arms round her, shushing and soothing. 'There, child, don't take on so! There's no need to be afraid, it's natural, and I'll be here to look after you.'

But she couldn't stop. 'I'm not afraid,' she sobbed. 'It's not that.'

'What is it, then?' Ismay's voice was concerned.

Roese hesitated. Didn't it make something more real, more threatening, when you put it into words? Then, feeling Ismay's kindness and warmth enveloping her, she longed only to have her anxiety out in

503

the open, to share the burden with someone who cared.

'I'm scared he'll be different, if I'm with child,' she whispered.

'No "if" about it, my lovely.' Ismay kissed the top of her head. 'How do you mean, different?'

She tried to explain. 'He's – I – He used to think of me as a boy, and he likes me being able to ride with him and keep up with him.'

Ismay snorted. 'He doesn't think of you as a boy any more, Roese, take my word for it.'

She had to laugh. It helped to stop the tears. 'I didn't mean it quite like that. I meant –'

'Yes, I know what you meant.' Ismay paused, then said, 'Roese, I could say to you now, don't worry, you're bothering yourself about nothing, he'll be a splendid husband, here whenever you need him, sitting patiently by your side when you're too vast to do anything but lie groaning.' Thanks, Roese thought. 'But I won't tell you lies, and anyway I believe in facing up to things.' She lifted Roese's head so that she could look into her face. 'Child, he's a fine man, a man to be proud of. But he's no stop-at-home, and you're right to expect that things will change. They will.'

Roese felt her heart plunge. A knight first, a husband second. Had everyone except herself realized?

'Now then, don't start crying again!' Ismay put out a gentle finger to catch the tears. 'Shall I tell you what you should do?' She nodded, sniffing. 'Tell him, watch how pleased he is – he'll be pleased, mark my words – then give him his freedom.'

'What? But I –'

'Listen! Don't keep interrupting! Roese, if you throw a net over that man of yours you'll keep him by your side, perhaps, but you'll kill this strong thing you have between you. Do you want to do that?' She gave her a shake, and Roese muttered, 'No.'

'Of course you don't. There's a wildness in him, and, like all wild things, he needs to run free. But he'll come back, believe me. Because he'll know you have the strength to let him go again.'

It was a depressing picture to contemplate on the day she'd discovered she was with child. There's no escaping it, though, Roese thought. Ismay has confirmed my fears exactly, and I trust her judgement even more than my own.

She straightened up, wiping her sleeve across her face. 'I'll tell him tonight,' she said starkly.

'Good girl.' There was admiration in Ismay's eyes. Then, smiling wryly, she added, 'Perhaps you'll manage to be a mite more enthusiastic by then.'

He was as pleased as Ismay had predicted, and even more so when Roese reported that Ismay said it was all right to go on making love, provided there was no sign of bleeding. He took her to bed early that night, making her lie naked on the covers, the roaring fire both warming the room and providing light, while he inspected her body.

'Here?' he asked, hands on her belly where Ismay had felt the bump.

'Yes.' She guided him. 'Have you got it?'

He frowned, pressing his hand down further over her pubis. 'I don't know what I'm looking for.'

'A little higher – there!' She watched as a delighted grin spread over his face.

'Aye! I can feel a bulge, just above the bone – is that it?' She nodded. 'Roese, clever Roese, you're pregnant.' He bent to kiss her, one hand still on the bump, the other moving to her swollen breasts. Then, pulling away, he studied her.

'What?'

He looked as if he was finding it hard to believe. 'Nothing. I just want to take care of you.' He kissed her. 'Keep you safe.' He kissed her again. 'Make love to you.' She could hear the laughter in his voice. 'If you feel we should,' he added solicitously.

'Oh, I don't know,' she said cautiously, trying to watch his face, 'I do feel tired, and I think I'd rather just go to sleep.'

He looked aghast. Then, not quite quickly enough, smiled and said, 'Of course.'

She put her hand on his thigh, stroking upwards till she could feel his hardness – what did I expect, she thought, amused, lying here with no clothes on while he examines me minutely – and then said, 'Silly. I was teasing.'

He said gruffly, 'Well, don't.' Then, smiling, 'You're sure?'

'Yes. Let's do it while we may – you won't want me when I'm big.'

Stripping off more quickly than she'd ever seen him manage before, he said, 'Oh yes I will.'

Her pregnancy continued to be a source of wonder to him. She was surprised at his pride in her, until she recalled that he was a landowner and a knight with an ancient and noble name – of course he'd be proud, he wants children, probably sees them as one of the main reasons for marriage.

But, watching his face as he stared at her growing belly then, with a tender expression, looked up into her eyes, she thought, I'm doing him an injustice.

The first time the baby moved, he was more affected than she was. After that, he took to standing behind her with his arms round her, palms spread across the bump, waiting for it to happen again. As she grew larger and more cumbersome, he often asked her to lie as she'd done when she'd first told him, naked, secure in the warm seclusion of their bed, so that he could watch the tiny limbs pushing against the stretched skin.

She asked him once why it fascinated him so. Looking away, he'd shrugged, then said, 'I don't know. It's just something I want to do. I suppose I don't want to miss a moment.'

I love you, she thought. I love you so much.

She didn't tell him. Partly because it might be construed as putting a net over him, partly because she imagined he already knew.

When it came, his urge for freedom took an unexpected form, so much so that it was a little while before she recognized it.

He said, without any leading up to it, 'I have to go home to put things straight in the Black Mountains.'

After a shocked silence, she said carefully, 'Your castle, you mean?'

'Aye. The castle and the land. I don't know what's been going on, the whole place may be in ruins.' He was staring at her, but she had the impression his eyes didn't see her. 'It isn't only mine, it belongs to him.' He indicated her stomach.

Him. The child is a boy, he kept saying. She didn't know if it was some form of second sight or just wishful thinking.

It made sense, this sudden desire to see to his Welsh estate. It was a waste, apart from anything else, to possess land and not utilize it; she was the daughter of a landowner, even if his acreage had been modest compared with Gawyn's, and she understood.

But understanding didn't prevent the cold shiver that ran through her.

She said, knowing it was hopeless, 'Brocéliande is a great inheritance. Is there truly the need for more, especially when it lies a long journey distant?'

He said simply, 'It's mine.'

Yes, she thought, and whatever it takes, whatever the risk – unable to help herself, she was remembering the unknown threat that had made him flee before – you will take back what is yours.

There was no point in protesting, but she tried. 'Will you not leave it until the summer?' When the crossing to Britain is safer?

He was on his feet, pacing the length of the hall. She could feel his pent-up energy, frustrated by the long winter months of inactivity.

'No, it's best I go now.'

When no-one will expect you, she added silently. Out of the blue she remembered her father explaining how the Lionheart had changed the rules of warfare, refusing to abide by the tacit and gentlemanly agreement not to attack in the early spring, when men were busy sowing their crops. Some of his most audacious victories, according to her father, had come because no-one had been expecting him.

Sensing her disquiet, he came to stand in front of her.

'I need to discover how the land lies,' he explained. 'That's all. I'm not proposing an attack, not at this stage. For one thing, I would require time to amass an assault force, for another, attack may not be necessary – I may just walk in and resume occupation.'

'Then you'd send for me?' It was out before she could stop it.

'Aye, if all's well. You and the child, when you're fit to travel.'

Me and the child? But the birth was still more than

three months away! How long an absence did he envisage?

She said desperately, 'I thought you'd be here, when the baby comes.'

He crouched down, putting his arms round her. 'What could I do?' he asked softly. 'You have Ismay. You don't need me.'

I do, I do, she wailed silently.

If you throw a net over him, Ismay's voice said in her head, you'll kill this thing you have between you.

So that he wouldn't see the tears she leaned towards him – awkwardly, for the bump was growing – and hid her face against his chest. 'Take care,' she muttered.

He said, 'Aye. I promise.'

He set off in mid-March, accompanied by a tough young man she knew only by sight. It was a comfort, if only a small one, to know he wasn't going alone.

Ismay had impressed upon her again and again the need to be brave. To show him she could manage. It was hard, when every bit of her wanted to cry out to him to stay.

On the morning of his departure, he came to her in their room, dressed and fully armed, a joy in his face she had never seen before.

Then she knew.

The castle in the Welsh mountains was merely the excuse; if it hadn't been that, it would have been something else. Perhaps, she tried to console herself, something even worse, like announcing he was off to Outremer to rid the Holy City of the infidel single-handed.

She couldn't prevent the tears – they were flowing as if they had a mind of their own, faster than she could mop them up. When he kissed her goodbye, her nose was blocked and she had to break away.

He said, 'Will you borrow my sleeve or use your own?'

She couldn't summon a smile, and, as if he acknowledged it, he wrapped his arms round her, holding her with the same strong intensity of the moment when, making love, he entered her. He whispered, 'I'll be back. I'll be there for you, Roese, I promise. I'll never leave you.'

Safe in his arms for a precious last moment, she couldn't speak, only hugged him the tighter.

He broke away, holding out to her something he'd been concealing in his hand. It was a lead medallion, on it the image of the Virgin and Child. 'Give it to my son, when he's born,' he said. 'For protection.'

'But – ' She wanted to say, but what of you? Shall you not keep it, so that Our Lady may go on protecting you?

The moment was gone; already, with a jingle of his spurs, he was crossing to the door. His sword bashed against the wall as he turned to look at her.

She'd never said it, for her own good reasons. But it didn't matter, not now. Now that he was going anyway. Choking, she said, 'I love you.'

For an instant his face fell into anguish. Staring into her eyes, he said, 'I love you too.'

Then the door slammed behind him and he was gone.

Twenty-eight

She managed to wait for a little over a month, then she went after him.

It was folly, she knew it, when she was six weeks from bearing her first child and already always worn out by evening. It caused a ferocious row with Ismay, and a marginally more frightening one with Pierre, who apparently saw his stewardship as extending to a responsibility for the wellbeing of the master's lady.

But she shouted them both down, finding a strength she didn't know she had, an authority that came partly from her long line of aristocratic fore-bears – they might have been minor landowners, she thought, but it still counts – and partly from her unwavering conviction that she *had* to go. Something was wrong, she knew it, and she couldn't rest until she found out what it was.

It was this that finally made them give way. Ismay said despairingly, worn out with the arguing and the drama, 'If you carry on like this, my girl, you'll lose that baby anyway, so you might as well do what you're set on.' Pushing her face up close to Roese's, she said, 'But don't blame me if it all goes wrong!'

'I won't,' Roese said mildly. Now that she had won, she felt strangely calm.

Pierre apparently washed his hands of her. He detailed another young man from the estate to go with them – Ismay refused to be left behind, for which Roese was secretly more grateful than she'd imagined, even though she knew full well Ismay wouldn't pass up one single opportunity to nag her – and sent word via a fast rider to Yves, telling him to expect her and requesting every assistance.

It'll do no more good Yves trying to persuade me against going, she thought. Even if he is Gawyn's cousin, he has no power over me. She touched the purse of gold coins she carried under her cloak: *I have power*, she thought, *the power of money*. She sent a silent prayer of thanks for a husband who, understanding how vulnerable were those without means, had left her a private supply.

Pierre prepared a covered cart for her, and Ismay made it as comfortable as she could with a straw palliasse and blankets. Roese couldn't help remembering how different it had been when she'd first ridden into Brocéliande.

Some of the women came out to see her off. They were quiet, subdued even – she wondered if they, too, disapproved. Or perhaps – the thought was chilling – *they understand. Perhaps they sense as strongly as I do that something's wrong.*

It was no mood in which to start out.

She was increasingly tormented by her memories as the journey wore on. Perhaps there was only the one route from Brocéliande to Paimpol, but, to her dismay, the youth took them over what looked like exactly the same ground she'd covered with Gawyn. On top of her anxiety and misery was the physical discomfort: the growing baby must, she thought, be practising turning cartwheels, and besides, his weight was giving her backache; towards the end of each day's travel, she couldn't find a position that didn't hurt.

With Ismay's disapproving presence ever by her side, she couldn't even have a good moan.

Predictably, in addition to offering the remembered generous hospitality, Yves tried to dissuade her. He pointed out that Gawyn was an experienced soldier, that he didn't take unnecessary risks – she noticed his eyes slid away from hers as he said this, and realized he didn't believe it any more than she did – and that, especially in her condition, wouldn't she do better to return to Brocéliande and quietly wait for his return?

She didn't answer him at first; he was gazing into the fireplace, and she waited till his eyes returned to hers. Then she said, 'I can't do that.' After a pause, she added softly, 'Could you?'

He began to protest, but stopped. Slowly he shook his head. Then abruptly he was on his feet. 'Rest here tonight and tomorrow, let us look after you while you recover your strength,' he said authoritatively. 'I will find a good man to take you over the sea.'

'Thank you.' With the removal of the last stumbling block, she felt a surge of relief, closely followed by a stab of apprehension. 'I have gold,' she hurried on, fighting the fear, 'I can pay.'

He gave her a very sweet smile. 'I won't take your money.' His hand closed over hers offering the purse, and gently he pushed it back at her. 'You may need it for other things.'

He didn't specify. Her apprehension increased.

Late the following day, he escorted her down to the quay. What appeared to be a very small boat was tied up to the jetty; the youth went with a couple of sailors to trundle the horse and wagon into the hold. Ismay gave a sniff.

Yves presented the ship's master to her. 'This is Eustace,' he said. 'He took Gawyn and Denys across six weeks ago.'

She looked at Eustace. 'Will you take me to the same place?'

'I will, lady.' He was staring at her. She was wrapped in a thick fur-lined cloak that Gawyn had given her, but she imagined he detected her condition. She was wondering if he was about to make some remark about disclaiming responsibility for fool-hardy women who chose to sail the seas when they were far gone in pregnancy, but he didn't. Perhaps it happened all the time, perhaps – much more likely – he didn't care provided he was well paid.

When Yves had gone – they were sailing straight away with the evening tide – Eustace showed her to a small cabin which, although furnished only with ru-dimentary fittings, was adequately comfortable. She'd expected him to go straight away, but he lingered as if he had something to say.

'Shall we have a calm crossing, do you think?' she asked.

'Nay, lady. There's bad weather blowing up,' he said dauntingly. 'We get these storms, leading up to the solstice. We'll try to run before it – the *Kermaria*'s built light, she'll fly like a diving kestrel, given a following wind.' He smiled grimly. 'You'll be in the Severn estuary before you know it.'

She said, 'I'd rather be beside it than in it,' and his smile turned into a snort of laughter.

'Aye, God willing.' Then, unexpectedly, 'You know where he's bound, do you?'

'Yes.' How I shall find it, she added to herself, is another matter.

Eustace crossed himself. 'I don't. I never ask. But I tell you, lady, I'm praying for him.'

She didn't sleep that night. Once out of the lee of the peninsula, they were exposed to the full force of the rising south-west wind; as the hours went on, the gale steadily increased.

Ismay began to be sick almost immediately. Roese found her a pail, then, as the heaving and moaning showed no signs of ceasing, made her lie down with a basin under her cheek; she had brought up all she had to bring up by then, and the dry retching didn't produce much. Roese made her take sips of water – it was easier being sick if you had something to be sick with.

As the dawn broke, the ship's motion changed; just as she was trying to work out how, the cabin door opened and Eustace looked in.

'How goes it?' he asked. His face was wet and strained. He glanced at Ismay, sleeping at last, her mouth open and vomit on the pillow. 'Ah. And you, my lady?'

Roese was feeling the first signs of queasiness. 'I was all right. But . . . '

'We've changed course. We were running north-east, but we're being taken too far eastwards. We'll be blown up to the Isle of Wight unless we veer out of the wind's path.'

She felt sweat on her face. Her mouth was watering. She said shakily, 'How long?'

He shrugged. 'We'll aim for a landfall on the south coast of Devon. We can go on to the Severn when the storm has blown out.'

It was only when he'd gone – she heard his urgent steps pounding up some companionway – that she realized he hadn't answered the question.

Then she started to throw up, and could think of nothing at all.

She didn't know how long the torment went on. It was light, then dark, then another dawn broke. Eustace brought them fresh water, and at one point she heard Ismay praying. Her whole body ached from her ribs to her groin, muscles crying out from the effort of endlessly being sick.

At last, Eustace came down to tell them land was in sight. Lifting her head, she was hit by another wave of nausea.

'Will you try to come up on deck?' he asked. 'With the eyes fixed on a target that stays steady, the sickness often goes away.'

I'm not sure I can move, she thought. She glanced across at Ismay, sitting white-faced leaning against a folded blanket.

'I'll try.' The words croaked in a throat that felt as if it had been sandpapered.

Ismay came over to her, clinging on to every handhold that offered, and Roese sat up, pulling her cloak around her. Together Ismay and Eustace helped her to stand, and they inched out of the cabin and up a wooden stair to the deck.

At first she felt worse – the dark grey sea tortured into vast rearing white-topped waves wasn't a reassuring sight – but then, perceiving that the little ship was rising with each surge and refusing to let herself be swamped, her courage returned. After a few moments she picked up the *Kermaria*'s rhythm; moving with it, her eyes on the long black line of the distant coast, slowly the nausea subsided.

The storm had all but blown itself out by the time they were approaching the shore, and Eustace proposed that he sail on round the tip of the Cornish peninsula and up towards their final destination. Roese, imagining that if they went ashore she might have to go through the ghastly process of acquiring her sea-legs all over again, agreed.

Towards evening, she began to feel hungry. With the excitement over, so, apparently, did everyone else; appetizing smells wafted up from the galley, and Eustace said something about the ladies joining him for a meal.

But, in the middle of a discussion with Ismay about what was likely to constitute dinner on board a small ship, she was assaulted by a sudden sharp pain. It grew in intensity, then faded. Rubbing at her belly, she resumed the conversation.

A little while later, it happened again.

Ismay eyed her intently. 'What is it?'

'A pain,' she said brusquely. She didn't even want to think about what it might mean.

'Dear God,' Ismay muttered. 'Where?'

Roese said, 'Everywhere.'

Ismay took her arm and helped her down to the cabin. She made her lie down, covering her with her cloak. After some time she said anxiously, 'How is it now? Any more pains?'

Roese shook her head, and Ismay looked relieved.

I won't tell her the rest, she thought. There's no point – there's nothing she can do.

So she lay waiting for the crossing to be over, keeping to herself the frightening realization that she hadn't felt the baby move since she'd stopped being sick.

She slept for a long time; when she woke, it was full daylight and a warm ray of sunshine was coming in through the skylight.

Around what had once been her waist was a steady ache.

Ismay said cheerfully, 'You'll have to stir yourself, child, we're nearly there. I've been talking to the lad – Jean, he's called – and to Eustace, and we think the best thing to do is make for – Roese, are you all right?'

The smile faded, and Ismay came to bend over her.

She tried to speak, but had to wait while the pain rose to a peak and subsided again. 'I don't think I can go very far,' she whispered.

'It's begun, then.' Ismay touched Roese's belly with a gentle hand. 'I was afraid of this, last night.' Her expression anguished, she said, 'What shall we do, Roese?'

'Where are we to be put ashore?'

'To the west of the Wye mouth. Eustace says that's where he dropped Gawyn.'

Gawyn, oh, Gawyn, I wish you were here, she thought desperately. Wish you'd stayed with me to care for me, to make decisions for me, to support me so that I didn't have to come racing after you, terrified something's happened to you, out of my mind with worry.

You would hold me and make it all right, she thought, feeling herself drifting. If only I could get to you, I could . . .

The thought trailed away, driven out by the memory of other hands holding her, other people making it all right. Not Gawyn: these people were dressed in black.

They saved me before. She smiled, feeling her dry lips crack. Perhaps they'd appreciate the irony of bringing me back to life, only to have me return needing their care all over again.

She saw Aidan's face, the earnest expression reproduced in her mind with total clarity.

With a guilty disloyalty, she realized it was far more comforting to think of Aidan looking after her than Gawyn.

She was aware of being helped off the ship, of Eustace, having done his duty and delivered her where she wanted to go, bidding her God's speed with obvious relief. She held on to consciousness long enough to tell Ismay the way they must go – she was surprised when Ismay nodded and said she knew of the place, until she remembered that Ismay was not only a local woman but an incorrigible gossip to boot – then, the jolting of the cart making the pain all but unbearable, she closed her eyes and gave in to the blackness growing across her mind.

Often she was disturbed – once it seemed that the boy Jean had required help to haul them out of a deep rut in the road, once she heard Ismay shouting at him – but always the darkness claimed her back. She wondered, with a detachment that surprised her, if she were dying.

Then she was lifted from the wagon, carried on some sort of hard flat surface. Quiet male voices were giving directions. Over her someone with dark blue eyes – with an effort, she remembered it was Ranald – said, 'Can you hold on a little longer? We are almost there.'

Time had gone backwards. The infirmary looked and smelt exactly the same, they had laid her on the bed by the fire she'd had before, Benedict's voice was deep and comforting as it had always been. Eyes closed, she felt hands on her, lifting her gown and her shift, a palm placed on her convulsing belly with a sure touch that, amid the fear, the apprehension and the pain, still managed to reassure her.

She heard voices. Ismay was obviously arguing

again, for all that she tried to do it in a whisper. Who with this time? 'I should look after her!' Ismay hissed. But she sounded some way off – in the doorway, perhaps? 'It's not fitting, not fitting at all, to have a lady tended by some monk! I don't know what the world's coming to, really I don't!'

There was a sob in her voice – poor Ismay, Roese thought, what a lot she's been through. She must be exhausted.

Echoing her thought, Ranald's calm voice said, 'You must rest, madam. You are past being of any help until you have regained your strength. Put anxiety away for a spell, eat, and then sleep. Be assured, the lady is in good hands. The very best.'

Roese smiled. The very best. Yes, Benedict nursed me before, and it's rather like coming home, to have him tend me again.

And there, now, that's him speaking. Agreeing with Ranald, offering to escort dear old Ismay to the refectory, find her something heartening to eat. And to drink, I don't doubt.

She felt another pain gathering itself for the attack, and, whimpering, braced herself. The palm on her belly pressed down, against the straining muscles, and somehow it helped.

As it faded, it occurred to her to wonder who, if Benedict was taking Ismay across the courtyard, was there looking after her?

With a huge effort she opened her eyes. He looked very different – he had filled out, and appeared to be taller, and was no longer dressed in black – but there was no doubt who it was. As he smiled down at her, reaching out his free hand to wipe the sweat-soaked hair from her forehead, she murmured, 'Hello, Aidan.'

* * *

It got far worse. In a nightmare of pain that seemed to go on and on, achieving nothing but a fatigue that felt like death, she laboured on into the night, screaming, crying for Gawyn if she had breath left to cry with. Whenever she reached out a strong hand was there, and she held on as if it were a lifeline, gripping so hard she felt his bones crunch together. She heard him grunt with pain, and, shocked into a moment of clarity, said, 'I'm sorry,' trying to put the injured hand to her lips to kiss it better.

Sometimes Benedict came to her bedside to speak to him – their roles have reversed, she thought at one point, Benedict defers to him now. But perhaps it's only in matters of birth that the pupil has outrun his master. She wondered vaguely how he had come to gain his experience, and thought she remembered that he'd been a sheep herd. It seemed funny, for a moment, to be tended in childbirth by a sheep herd.

Hours later – it was late afternoon, judging by the long shadows – Aidan finally delivered her child. She was barely conscious, so weak that the last great effort to do as he said and push had all but finished her. She was aware of a different sort of pain, and felt herself tearing as he helped the baby out.

She saw Benedict by the fire, a tiny bundle on his knees, rubbing gently at the wet, bloodstained skin, big hand supporting the tiny head as he repeated something, over and over again. One word: 'Breathe.'

Aidan, leaning over her, was pushing hard on her stomach, pulling at something that issued from inside her. Noticing her eyes on him, he said, 'It's the afterbirth. Don't worry, I just have to make sure it all comes out.'

She said, the words barely audible, 'The baby?'

He glanced at Benedict. 'He's alive, but reluctant to breathe.'

Him. The child is a boy. Gawyn had been quite right.

Gawyn, oh, Gawyn. Your son is struggling for his life.

She heard a tiny sound, hardly worthy of being called a cry. Benedict said, pain in his voice, 'I don't think he's going to live. He's a bad colour.'

Roese reached out and touched Aidan's hand. 'Hold?' she managed.

He nodded. He said, 'Benedict, let her hold him.'

Benedict got up, treading carefully across the room and tenderly laying the baby beside her. She stared at it, the sense of waste – all that effort for nothing – and the grief growing till she couldn't control it. Lifting her arm with a huge effort, she laid her fingers on the pale cheek. It felt chilly to the touch, and had a blueish tinge.

She heard Benedict begin to speak, and realized he was praying. 'Take, Lord, the soul of this innocent child and let him look upon Thy face. Roese, what is his name?'

Without thinking she said, 'Gawyn.'

There was a stoup of holy water by the door, and Benedict went over and dipped his fingers in it. Making the sign of the cross on the baby's forehead, he said, 'I baptize thee, in the name of God the Father, and His beloved son Jesus Christ. Lord, receive Gawyn here departed into thy care. Amen.'

Aidan muttered, 'Amen.'

He reached down and gently removed the little body from under her hand. He wrapped it in a cloth which he put over its face.

She realized that her child was dead.

Twenty-nine

She slept for a long time, then, when they stopped giving her the bitter-tasting drink, wished she could go on sleeping for ever.

She pleaded with Aidan – *'I want to die!'* she screamed, punching him so hard that he bore a bruise for days – and his response was to hold her tight against him. In the nightmare, sometimes she thought he was Gawyn.

A morning came when she awoke without instantly descending into despair. Aidan was there – she guessed he never left her – and she said, 'I have to look for him.'

He came to sit by her, taking her hand. 'Not you,' he said gently. 'Others have already gone.'

'But –'

'Ismay knew where William is. She has gone off with Ranald and your lad –'

'Jean.'

'Jean. They will –'

But she wasn't listening. She was trying to remember who William was. The name brought to mind a long-limbed boy, voice breaking as he struggled with his emotions . . .

'William! But he went away, Gawyn found a new

place for him just like he did for Ismay.'

'Yes. It was the same place.'

She tried to make herself concentrate. 'Ismay will take them to William, and William will take them to Gawyn's castle. Is that right?'

'Yes. Then, when they have gathered what news they can, they will collect Ismay and come back.'

They were out there now, William, Ranald, Jean. Searching for Gawyn, perhaps already knowing where he was, if he was all right.

She said sharply, 'How long have they been gone?'

'Three days.'

Three days. Unless they flew, they couldn't possibly be back for ages yet. Even if finding news of him – finding him – proved to be a straightforward matter.

She whispered, 'How will I wait?'

His face sombre with compassion, he said, 'Roese, I don't know.'

There was no sign of the little cloth-wrapped bundle. When she nerved herself to ask, Aidan said he was in the chapel. Seeing the question in her eyes, he said, 'We thought it best to give his father the chance to be here for his burial.'

Four days later, the party came back.

She knew from the way they sat their horses – and from the fact that there were only the three who had set out – that they hadn't found him.

But it was worse than that.

Ranald came to see her. She was aware of Aidan hovering nearby, muttering something to Benedict, then they left.

She said to Ranald, 'You have something to tell me.'

He stood over her. His back to the light, she couldn't see his face.

'The castle had obviously been recently occupied,' he said expressionlessly. 'But not by Gawyn – whoever lived there destroyed whatever they couldn't carry away with them.'

'Then he's not –'

'Roese, it's almost certain that forces hostile to him had taken the castle,' Ranald said urgently.

'He'll have gone away, then,' she said. She wished she could make herself sound more confident. 'Seeing them there, I mean. He said he was only going to find out how the land lay, and that if it was going to mean a fight, he'd go off and recruit some soldiers.'

Why wasn't Ranald agreeing with her?

'That must be what's happened!' she cried. 'Mustn't it? He wouldn't have tried to go in alone, just with Denys, he wouldn't be so foolhardy!'

But suddenly she could see him, buoyed up with excitement, spoiling for a fight. Finding his castle occupied by his enemies. Losing control.

She was no longer sure *what* he'd do.

'It's possible he retreated and is now off somewhere gathering together a band of knights,' Ranald said. 'That would take time, of course, and since he wouldn't be able to do it openly, would account for why we have been unable to find word of him.'

She could tell by his tone he didn't believe it.

'But?'

He sat down on the edge of her bed, and reached out to touch her arm.

'You must know, Roese, that there had been fighting there. There were signs that whoever was inside the castle had been defending themselves –'

'What signs?' She had to know, wasn't going to let him get away with skating over the truth.

'Spent arrows,' he said bluntly. 'Three dead bodies piled up at the end of the drawbridge.'

Not his. Ranald would have told her immediately.

'Well, perhaps he made an attack, then, finding the resistance too strong, retreated to find reinforcements.'

'Perhaps.' Ranald sighed. 'We found a sword, sticking into the ground that falls away beneath the drawbridge. Jean wasn't sure, but he thought it was Gawyn's.'

Dear God.

'Let me see.'

He turned and nodded to Benedict, who stepped outside and returned bearing a long wrapped shape. He handed it to Ranald. Touching it as if it hurt, Ranald folded back the cloth.

Gawyn's sword lay across his lap.

She stared at it. Putting out her hand, she tried to close her fingers round the handpiece. It was too big – he had large hands.

Piercingly, she felt him there. His sword, that rarely left his side, seemed to carry something of him. She shivered, falling back against the pillows.

Ranald covered the sword, and Gawyn's vibrant presence went away.

'We found a pair of boots,' Ranald said neutrally. 'Perhaps someone tried them on then, finding them too big, threw them away.'

He had large feet as well.

Ranald unwrapped another bundle. 'Were these his spurs?'

She looked. Nodded.

'You're sure?'

'Yes.' She added, proud of her knowledge, 'These are rowel spurs. They're a new design – most men still wear spurs with a point.'

His sword. His boots. He couldn't function without either. What happened, Gawyn? she cried silently. Where are you?

She tried to picture him swordless, bootless, fleeing. It was impossible.

'Did you search everywhere?' she asked desperately.

Ranald seemed to know what she meant. 'Everywhere.'

Where are you?

He took her hand. 'There was no point in going over the ground again,' he said. 'Had I thought it would have done any good, I would have done. And there were the boys to consider. William is squire to a good man, and I had undertaken not to take him into unnecessary danger. Jean, too, is young.'

She picked up his unspoken words. Too young to risk being killed, if Gawyn's enemies came back and found us there.

'If you didn't find his body, surely it means he's still alive?' The thought that he might be dead had appeared on the very edge of her mind. She couldn't let it come any closer.

Ranald said nothing.

Again, she wished he would agree with her.

Eventually he stood up, still holding the sword and the spurs.

'We will bury your child,' he said quietly. 'Tomorrow. Will you be strong enough to come out to the graveyard?'

She nodded. 'I will.' Aidan, somewhere beyond Ranald, muttered something.

'Before we do, there is something I must tell you,' Ranald was turning away. 'I will return this evening, and we will speak alone.'

527

As he left the infirmary, he laid the sword and the spurs on Benedict's workbench.

He came back in the evening. Aidan had been with her throughout the intervening hours, making her eat, making her walk a few steps up and down the room, telling her that she must get up and start to move about if there was to be any possibility of her attending the burial the next day.

She couldn't manage more food than a few mouthfuls.

When, on Ranald's arrival, Aidan quietly disappeared, she felt strangely bereft.

'He'll be back.' Ranald, watching her face, gave a half-smile.

'He looked after me before, didn't he?' Ranald nodded. 'I –' She felt she should explain herself, but didn't know how.

'You trust him,' Ranald supplied for her. She looked at him gratefully. 'It's hardly surprising. And your trust is well-founded.'

She wondered what he meant, but he didn't explain. Pulling up a stool, he sat down.

'Roese,' he said after a long pause, 'what do you know of the Cathars?'

It was the last thing she'd expected. 'Not very much. They're heretics, I know that much, and they live in the south of France.'

'The Languedoc.'

'Yes. There's a crusade against them because the Church says they're evil, and that's where Gawyn went.' She glanced at Ranald. 'He never spoke of it, it's no use you – '

Ranald shook his head. 'It's all right, I'm not asking you for information. I would not have expected that he would have discussed it with you,' he muttered.

He paused again, and she had the clear impression he was searching for the words to say something he found difficult. 'Roese, are you a devout woman?'

Am I? she wondered. 'I say my prayers,' she said defensively. 'I used to attend mass regularly, before the interdict.'

But I'm not sure I really miss it now I can't go any more, she added to herself.

Bewilderingly, he seemed relieved. 'Don't look so guilty,' he said – the half-smile was back – 'I'm not taking you to task. I wondered – ' He stopped. Then, in what for him was quite a rush, said, 'I have to ask you if you have in mind what I should do by way of a burial service for your child. The Church decrees a form of words which I will use if you so wish, but . . .' He trailed off.

'But what?' She couldn't think what he was trying to say.

Looking straight at her, he said softly, 'Gawyn was an adherent.'

'A what?'

'An adherent. In the Languedoc, he came to realize that the Church was wrong. He was wounded,' – I know, she thought, the memory of that dreadful scar hitting her forcefully – 'and cared for by the very people he'd been fighting. He lived with them for some time, and they trusted him with – they impressed him with their beliefs.'

She couldn't take it in. 'What does it mean?' she whispered. 'Are you saying he might be in danger from the Church?'

'No, I doubt that very much. I'm trying to tell you, Roese, that, unless you have strong feelings in the matter, I would like to bury your child – Gawyn's child – as a Cathar.'

529

Bury my child. She thought, I don't care how you bury him.

Ranald put his arm round her, and she felt that he was trying to comfort her. But she sensed he found the contact awkward, and as soon as she felt able, broke away.

'I'm sorry,' she said.

'Don't be.' His voice was quiet. 'I am sorry, that I have to speak of these things to you. But it is your right to choose.'

In the absence of Gawyn, he could have added.

Suddenly she thought of something. 'Did he tell you how they do it, then? The burial, I mean?'

It was as if he'd been waiting for the question. He said, 'He didn't need to. I am a Cathar. It was I who accepted him as an adherent.'

'You! But – yes, it was when you came here with Joanna, wasn't it?' It was obvious. 'In September, before we left for Brittany.' Don't think of that. 'Is she one too?'

She'd meant it as a joke, but he said, 'Yes. She is.'

'Why didn't he tell me?' she whispered. It hurt, that he hadn't.

Ranald regarded her kindly. 'I don't think it mattered all that much to him,' he said. 'He was the sort of man not given to long introspection on anything – having made his decision, I would imagine he put it out of his mind.'

It was exactly what he would have done, and she smiled. It was good, realizing that Ranald had understood him so well.

'Yes, he was –' She stopped. Mouth dry, couldn't go on.

She'd just noticed they were both speaking of him in the past tense.

* * *

They buried her child at sunset.

Aidan had sat with her since she woke – much too early – and without him she didn't know how she'd have got through the day. He helped her over to the chapel at one point – Ranald was praying, and apparently had suggested she should be there, but she couldn't take it in and worried that she was letting him down. Perceiving her distress, Aidan took her out into the sunshine, sitting down with her on the hillside just outside the walls of the hermitage and talking about nice normal things like sheep and flowers.

She said as they'd gone back inside, 'You lent me a black robe before. Will you do so again?'

He said, 'I no longer have a black robe. But I'll find you one.'

She wondered why he wasn't dressed like the others. But before she could ask him her mind slid off and she forgot about it.

Late in the evening, as the last of the light was fading, Aidan guided her out into the courtyard. Ranald was standing there holding the figure of the baby, made to look bigger than she remembered by the layers of bindings. There was a sweet spicy smell, underneath it something more sinister. Behind him, Benedict carrying Gawyn's sword and his spurs, wrapped in their cloth.

She was about to ask Aidan what they were doing, but the answer came to her: where else would they put Gawyn's things but with his son?

Ranald started walking slowly out through the gate, Benedict behind him followed by another pair of monks, one red-faced and stout, the other pale and thin. The thin one was carrying a large processional cross. They were chanting, and it sounded like something she vaguely recognized. Confused, she thought, do Cathars sing our psalms, then? Carry crosses just like we do?

She and Aidan fell into step at the back. She felt as if she were in a dream, and that she might float away over the hills. Aidan held her hand but, as if he sensed her frailty, let go and instead put his arm round her waist. She found it was comfortable to lean against him.

Out through the gate, along a path that led away round the curve of the hill. Not far away, they went into a small graveyard. A few long thin humps marked earlier interments.

Someone had dug a little grave. For an instant she thought he was still there, perhaps waiting to fill it in again afterwards, for she thought she saw a tall man sitting on the ground, hunched over, long legs bent up in front of him.

But it was only a trick of the waning light.

Ranald was saying a prayer, over and over. To her surprise, she could join in: it was the Paternoster.

Benedict moved forwards and, with the fat monk kneeling beside him, stretched down into the grave and placed Gawyn's sword and spurs deep in the ground. Grunting with effort, the two of them together placed four squares of rock in a rectangle above the wrapped parcels, leaving a small space in the middle.

She realized what they were doing – they were making a place for the baby, to protect him from the force of the earth when the grave was filled in.

She thought of his tiny body there under the silent earth. Unable to stop herself, she sobbed aloud.

There was an echo, each sob followed by another, softer one. Perhaps the sounds were reverberating from the enclosing hills.

She turned to Aidan, and he took her in his arms.

532

She noticed fleetingly he was looking over her shoulder, his face, although marked with strain and sorrow, showing surprise. She spun round to see what he was looking at, and saw a young woman about her own age standing there. As she watched, the woman sank to her knees.

The figure grew faint then came back into focus. It was almost as if a wisp of mist were rising from the damp earth, obscuring hard edges so that everything became blurred. Roese screwed up her eyes, and when she opened them again, the woman had gone.

Ranald was holding her child, cradling him tenderly as if he were sleeping and Ranald didn't want to wake him. Then he knelt down beside Benedict and placed the little bundle in the grave.

She stepped forward, falling to her knees beside them. Unfastening the chain round her neck, she held out the medallion, letting it drop into the grave. She heard Gawyn's voice in her head. *Give it to my son, when he's born. For protection.*

'I have,' she whispered to him. 'See?'

She stumbled as she tried to stand, and Aidan moved to her side to support her. Her sense of unreality growing, the scene seemed to shimmer and grow vague. Her eyes were wet, and shapes were distorted. Ranald's prayer went on, endlessly repeated, and the others were still chanting. Benedict and the stout monk began to fill in the grave.

At last they turned and started to walk away.

At the entrance to the graveyard she turned for one last look. It was him! He was standing by the grave, head bowed – he knows, then, she thought with relief, they must have told him – and as she watched he sank down to the ground.

In her distress, her vision blurred by the tears, she thought he was really there.

'Come on!' she called softly. 'Come with us, we'll –'

Then she noticed he was strangely transparent: she could see the hillside and the trees through him.

She broke away from Aidan, running forward a few steps, then stopping. She couldn't see him any more.

'Where is he?' she cried. 'He was there, but now he isn't. Where's he gone?'

Aidan hadn't made any move to follow her. He said quietly, 'Roese, come away.'

'But –'

'Leave him there.' His voice gentle, he added, so softly that she could hardly hear, 'Wouldn't he want to be with his son?'

She knew then.

He'd kept his word, was there for her. Wouldn't leave her.

The howl of grief rising up in her, she thought, what use is that, when he's dead?

* * *

Without either her child or Gawyn, she could think of no reason for being alive. Deranged by grief, she lashed out, throwing a proffered bowl of hot soup in Benedict's face, kicking out at Ranald when he held her to prevent her dashing her head against the walls of the infirmary. At first she clung to Aidan – Aidan who had also seen his long shade out there in the graveyard, Aidan who seemed to understand – but then, waking from a troubled sleep one night and believing the arms around her to be Gawyn's, the disappointment on finding they weren't was so awful that she pushed him violently away.

A deep voice – Benedict's – was saying soothing words, his strong hand holding her jaws apart while he made her drink, then, holding her mouth closed, stroking her throat so that she had to swallow.

He must have made it strong: almost immediately she was falling into a sleep so deep that it felt like death.

In the end, the will to live was stronger than the wish to die. Life was black and without hope, but she seemed to be stuck with it.

When she was sufficiently recovered to look around and take notice, she realized Aidan wasn't there.

'Has he gone back to his sheep?' she asked Benedict, who huffed and didn't answer. Later, when he came in the evening to visit her, she asked the same question of Ranald.

He didn't answer either, at first. Then, the severe expression melting as he looked at her, he said, 'You have noticed he has gone, then.'

'Of course! Why wouldn't I?'

He shrugged slightly. 'Because –' He stopped. 'No. You were not to blame. Poor child, you were beside yourself.'

'What did I do?' Her eyes flew from him to Benedict, standing behind him looking disapproving, then back again. 'Why do you and Benedict look at me like that?'

'Because he –' Benedict began angrily.

Ranald put a hand on his arm. 'Benedict,' he said warningly.

'Why should she not know?' he responded, rounding on Ranald. 'What does it matter, now?'

'Very well. But I shall do it.' The authority in him reminded her suddenly of Gawyn, and the memory seemed to kick her in the pit of her stomach.

'You were wild with grief, Roese,' Ranald was saying, 'and I think that you did not realize what you did or said. I cannot think that you would deliberately have done what you did.'

'Tell me.'

'He – Aidan – was tending you day and night. Had been doing so, in effect, since you came back to us.' I remember, she thought, a surge of affection spreading through her as she thought of him. As if picking it up, Ranald said, his face softening, 'Did you not realize how much he cares about you?'

'I – ' She thought she was going to say she didn't, but as the words formed she knew they weren't right. Yes, I knew, she thought. While it was happening, all that awful time, I was aware, somehow, that I'd have given up and died, without him. He held on to me, wouldn't let me go.

Yes. I realized.

Silently she nodded.

'He loved you from the start, Roese,' Ranald said gently. 'From the first time you came to us, when he dragged you out of the river. He was confused, then – too young and too inexperienced to understand his own nature, he thought that what he felt for you meant his life here was a lie, and he ran away.'

Is that why he no longer wears the black robe? she wondered. Because he's no longer a monk?

For the first time in what seemed like months, she felt a faint happiness.

But they'd been accusing her of something. Something she'd done – to Aidan?

'What did I do?'

Ranald stood up, as if preparing to leave.

'You pushed him away.' There was an unmistakable reproof in his voice, as if he was saying, how could you be so ungrateful!

I thought he was Gawyn, she wanted to say. Can't you understand? He wasn't, and when I knew that, it didn't matter who he was.

'I didn't mean to hurt him,' she muttered.

'No. And I expect he knows that.' Now Ranald was crossing to the door, and Benedict was opening it for him. In the entrance, he turned. 'Perhaps, though, you might like to make sure.'

'Where is he? Here?'

'No. But he hasn't gone far.'

She felt she knew what he was suggesting. It was an appealing idea, and a part of her wanted to say yes, tell me where to go.

He loved you from the start, Ranald had said. A greater part of her, aware of what it would mean if she took up his suggestion, knew that she wasn't ready. Might never be ready.

He was still standing there, a questioning look on his face.

Meeting his eyes, she said, 'Not yet.'

July 1994

Down in the village of Montségur they found a small archaeological museum displaying pieces found in recent excavations of the site. There were also books and posters for sale. Nina was standing in front of a display of arrow heads and fist-sized rocks which, according to the explanatory notice, were catapult shot.

Mark came to stand behind her, looking over her shoulder into the cabinet. Suddenly he drew a sharp breath.

'Good God. That's a surprise.'

'What?'

He pointed to an object propped up at the back of the display. 'That. It's part of a longbow.'

She tried to think why he should find its presence so amazing. Wouldn't you expect to find weapons in a fortress? She searched for a label, but there wasn't one other than the group description: OBJETS TROUVÉS AU DESSOUS DE LA TOUR DE L'OUEST: ARCS, FLÈCHES, BOULETS DE LANCE-PIERRE. The English translation said BOWS, ARROWS AND SHOT FOUND BENEATH THE WESTERN TOWER. The other fragments were obviously from crossbows; her memory duly jogged, she said, 'We won the battle of Crécy because the longbow could outshoot the crossbow.'

'Yes?'

He seemed to be waiting for more. Proud of dredging up the one fact, she hadn't expected to have to go on. 'That's it,' she said tersely.

'Crécy was 1346,' he said. 'The first major English victory of the Hundred Years War and, as you say, won largely on account of the discipline and deadliness of the English archers. More properly, the Welsh archers – the longbow was originally a weapon of the men of Gwent, who used it maybe two hundred years before it won the English the battle of Crécy.'

'What's a longbow doing here?'

He said with some agitation, 'Another bloody impossible question! God, Nina, doesn't it make you wild? It's as if the whole pattern's there waiting for us, if only we know how to uncover it.'

She thought of the treasure hunt analogy. 'We're warm,' she said. She believed it.

'Yes, I know.' He leaned forwards to inspect the bow more closely. 'It wouldn't have been very big,' he said. 'Not as long as the traditional longbow. I've seen something similar dug up in a castle in Dyfed.'

There was a silence between them. She thought, one of us has got to say it. 'If he was here, perhaps that's his bow.'

'He was a knight. Knights fought with a sword, PBI used the bow.'

'What's PBI?'

He grinned. 'Poor bloody infantry.'

She shook her head in frustration. 'Well, perhaps he'd mislaid his sword.' Mark laughed. 'Okay! But perhaps he needed a bow as well – perhaps he had someone with him who didn't have a weapon, and he said, wait a minute, I'll make you a bow.'

Mark sighed. 'It's as likely as anything else.' He turned to look around the rest of the room. 'There are some books over there – I'm going to see if there's anything useful.'

She wandered around the remaining display cabinets, then went to join him. 'This is interesting,' he said. He was studying a huge academic-looking tome. 'It's in French, so I'm not a hundred per cent sure I've got it right, but there's something here about the Cathars being great astrologers. The bloke who wrote this seems to think they held the clue to keeping the world in balance – or harmony, I'm not sure – which was something to do with some magical prism they held up to the sunrise. The Cathar symbol of the pentagon derived from the fact that this prism was a form of quartz with a five-sided crystal structure. And apparently the fortress of Montségur is constructed so as to help in astrological orientation.'

'Like Stonehenge.'

'Yes. And countless other edifices dating from ancient times. This chap says you can fix the directions of the sunrise and sunset on the equinoxes and the solstices by reference to the fortress.'

She felt a shiver of recognition, as if some atavistic knowledge she carried without her awareness were saying, that's right.

And, in a subliminal flash, she thought she saw him smiling at her; bareheaded, the long rays of a pale sunrise caught the golden lights in his brown eyes.

Mark was still reading. 'He thinks he knows why the Cathars asked the besiegers for a fortnight to come to their decision. He says the two weeks covered the time of the spring solstice, in March, and hypothesizes that the Cathars used their magic prism for some secret ceremony, then smuggled it out so that when the end inevitably came, it was in safe hands outside.'

'Hm. As you said in another context, it's as likely as anything else.'

He looked up from the book towards the cash desk. 'I'm going to ask if they have this in English. I may have got it all wrong, and I'd like to check.'

He crossed over and engaged the young woman behind the till in rather halting conversation. She looked at the tome, then shrugged.

'*C'est vieux,*' she said dismissively. '*Il n'y a aucune édition anglaise.*' She raised her eyes to stare at Mark, then, flicking the book with a long-nailed fore-finger, added, '*On ne le croit pas aujourd'hui. C'est uniquement pour les touristes, pas pour les historiens sérieux.*'

He thanked the woman, then went to put the book back on its shelf. He said to her as they left, 'That's put us in our place!'

'Why, what was she saying?'

'She was implying that it's all claptrap for gullible sensation-seeking tourists.'

'Huh!' She felt affronted – bet *she's* not in touch with a medieval knight! 'That's all *she* knows.'

Mark put a companionable arm round her shoulders. 'Quite. But I didn't know how to say that in French.'

* * *

After Montségur the trail went cold. They went to other Cathar castles, but there were neither tangible clues nor, for Nina, frissons of sudden awareness. Back on the autoroute on the long journey home, Mark summarized what they'd found out.

'We think he was in Rocamadour, Carcassonne and Montségur,' he said.

'And Minerve and by that river where we had the lovely goat's milk cheese.'

'With the Corbières,' he said reminiscently. 'How could I forget? It's not much, Nina.'

'Sorry! I was doing my best.'

She saw him smile. 'Yes, I know. Let's try to put it together. We have a knight from Wales or Brittany, or both, going off in 1209 on the Albigensian Crusade. He's at the siege of Carcassonne, involved in some way in the rape and slaughter of a group of Cathar women.' She was only a girl, Nina thought, remembering. 'Then he's transported to a fortress deep in Cathar country, so deep that it was the last place to fall when the crusade was finally victorious in 1244. There he spends his time whittling longbows as, at that time, only a Welshman could. When whittling begins to pall, he rides off to Rocamadour, donates his dagger to the Virgin to thank her for curing whatever he had wrong with him –'

'He was wounded,' she reminded him. A deep cut between his shoulders and something wrong with his wrist. She felt the hairs lift on the back of her neck as a faint shiver of pain ran down her spine.

'Right. Then he buys his sportelle to prove he's been there, and – and what?'

'Goes home,' she supplied.

'What do you base that on?'

'He must have gone home eventually, because we found the sportelle up at the monastery.'

'All right, then, he goes home. Of course, we don't know when he went home or if he went straight home. And I don't see how we can find out.'

She said suddenly, 'His sword and spurs are there too. Oh, Mark!'

He glanced at her briefly. 'Don't cry out like that when I'm in the fast lane! What's up?'

'We've got to have another look up there.'

'Yes, that's the conclusion I'm coming to. We –'

'You don't see, do you?' She didn't wait for him to answer. 'A knight might be able to do without his dagger, and be prepared to give it away for a good reason. But the other day you laughed when I said he might have mislaid his sword and you were right – I only meant it as a joke. Mark, he wouldn't have buried his sword unless he had no further use for it. Unless he was dead.'

'He could have become a monk.' He didn't sound as if he thought it likely.

'No, he couldn't.' All that vigour and virility confined within in a habit and walled away from the world? No! 'And if the sword was buried under the baby, it means he was dead when the body was put in the ground.'

Mark was silent for so long that, had she not known better, she might have thought he wasn't going to answer. But eventually he said, as if as the conclusion to a very lengthy thought process, 'We've got to get Peter to put a date on the baby's bones.' He reached out for her hand, as if he knew how much the thought of the little skeleton upset her. 'If it's anywhere around the first decade of the thirteenth century, we'll know you're right.'

I already know I am, she thought. But it seemed arrogant to say so.

* * *

Bryn greeted them with the news that the baby's skeleton was to be reburied before the university term started in October: he told them that, according

543

to Peter, the university's powers-that-be had decided the concept of a department full of young adults all picking up eight-hundred-year-old vibes was too awful to contemplate, and they'd panicked themselves into shutting down the entire operation.

'There's been a lot about it in the press,' he said, tossing an edition of the local newspaper across his desk towards Mark. 'They're comparing our monastery with a Jewish cemetery in York, where insistent lay objections similarly put a stop to the scientists' work. We actually made the regional TV news one night – your friend the bishop, Mark, spoke out against disturbing the dead, and very publicly gave his permission for the bones to be reinterred up at the monastery.'

'I thought they'd already re-buried the two monks there,' Nina said. 'Did they have permission for that?'

'In fact they were acting within the terms of the relevant burial legislation anyway. Still, having involved himself, the bishop's promised to say a few words over the remains himself.' He smiled at her expectantly. 'Nina? Did you hear what I said? I thought you'd be pleased!'

'I am,' she said distantly. 'It's great.'

She was seeing a small procession of black-clad figures. And a tall man, stooped with grief, who stayed behind when everyone else had gone.

'What happens in the meantime?' Mark asked.

Bryn shrugged. 'They've locked the skeleton away – Peter says they've done most of what they wanted to do, and he's taken bone samples to work on if he needs to do anything more. The bones and the grave goods are just waiting now to be buried again, I suppose.'

Nina said, trying to sound casual, 'Do you happen

to know if they've put a date on him? The baby, I mean?'

'There's a supplementary report somewhere.' He rummaged through a tray of papers on his desk. 'Can't find it – I'll have a proper look later. It said the child was male, and the calibrated radiocarbon date is 1200 plus or minus fifteen AD.'

'What does that mean?'

'He died between 1185 and 1215.'

'Can't they be more exact?' She was aware of the urgency in her voice; out of the corner of her eye she saw Mark looking at her sympathetically.

'There's some suggestion that because the burial was up there on the hillside rather than in a church-yard, it might have taken place during the interdict. You know, when King John was excommunicated and no conventional marriage or burial services could take place.'

'When was the interdict?'

'1208 to 1214.'

She glanced at Mark. He said, 'Well, I must get on. I'm going to look through my post.'

She followed him out of the office. 'I'll make some coffee,' she said. 'Bryn?'

'Yes, please.' He was already returning to what-ever it was he'd been working on when they came in.

She caught up with Mark in the corridor. Hearing her steps, he turned. The look he gave her made her heart jump in surprise.

The tenderness giving way to an amused smile, he said, 'Pity you didn't put money on it.'

'I only bet on certainties.' Then, unable to contain herself, she cried, 'Oh, Mark! We're getting warmer!'

He said instantly, 'But there's a long way to go yet.'

'Oh.'

He must have noticed the effect of his words; he

put his arms round her in a brief intense hug. 'Chin up,' he whispered. 'I'll make a deal with you – if you promise to put this whole business out of your mind and devote yourself all day to helping me deal with my post, I'll take you out to dinner tonight.'

'Tonight?' she squeaked. She didn't know why she should be so surprised and, judging by his smile, he didn't either.

'Yes. Unless you're washing your hair.'

'That would be lovely,' she said more calmly. Then she heard the echo of his words that night outside Rocamadour: wait till I get you home. The calmness disappeared.

She gave a nervous cough. 'You don't have to,' she said. 'I'll help you with your post anyway.' That's what you pay me for, she might have added.

She wasn't sure, but she thought she felt his lips brush the top of her head. 'I know I don't have to. I want to.'

Then he went into his office, leaving her alone in the corridor.

She went dreamily along to the kitchen and put the kettle on.

He collected her at eight. It felt strange getting into the camper again: the same vehicle – the same man – but everything was subtly different. Somehow being taken out to dinner now, here in their own home town, was far more significant than all the meals they'd eaten together when they were away. Then we were eating just because we had to, she thought as they drove off. Now, it's something else.

She wasn't prepared to think about what the something else might be.

They managed to keep off the subject of the monastery site until coffee. Then, after a long pause (the first gap in the conversation they'd had all evening), he said, 'We'll attend the reburial. If you want to, that is?'

'Of course!' After all the fuss I've made, she thought, I should think I do! 'Why wouldn't I?'

He looked discomfited. 'Oh, I don't know.' He was staring down at the tablecloth, which he was decorating with swirly patterns with an unused fork. 'Yes, I do.' He raised his head and stared into her eyes. 'Because the thought of the baby unnerves you so much. You don't have to answer this, Nina, and you probably won't, but I've always wondered why that is.'

'It unnerves everyone,' she mumbled, feeling shaky and sweaty suddenly. 'Doesn't it?'

'Yes. But not the way it does you. I've watched you, seen how you look when you're confronted with that little body. And he knew, too.'

'What do you mean?' She didn't really need to ask.

He reached for her hand. 'God, you're hot,' he remarked. Then, softly: 'Your knight knew which one of us to come through to. It could have been any of us – no disrespect to you, but he might have achieved his purpose a lot more quickly if he'd made an ally of Peter, for example – but he knew what he was doing.' He paused, then said, even more quietly, 'He came to the one who would understand best. The one who knew instinctively how important it was to let the child rest. Because that's what you do, for someone you've loved.'

'I'm a woman,' she said baldly.

'I'm aware of that.' She heard the amusement in his tone. 'But not all of us males are totally devoid of sensitivity. Your knight, for example, up there for centuries guarding that little baby.' He hesitated,

547

then said, so softly she wasn't sure she'd heard right, 'Me.'

He held her eyes with his own. Sensitive, she thought. Yes, I know you are. And kind. And not *quite* so thoroughly preoccupied with work as you used to be.

Do you know, kind sensitive Mark, how I feel about you?

I expect you do.

'I got pregnant,' she said quietly, dropping her eyes. 'It was ages ago, before I came to Earthworks. The man never knew – he'd gone off to Rio de Janiero before I found out.'

'What happened?' His voice was kind, the judgemental tone she'd dreaded totally absent. Looking up, she saw that same expression of tenderness on his face.

'I had a miscarriage.'

'Would you have had the baby?'

She'd always told herself the miscarriage had been a good thing. It had saved her having to face an abortion.

Now, for the first time, she looked beyond that convenient, consoling platitude. And recognized it for the lie it was.

She whispered, 'Yes.' And, to her distress, felt the tears pricking beneath her eyelids.

He gave her his car keys. 'Go out and wait in the camper – I'll settle up, then come and find you.'

Grateful for his consideration, she hurried out of the restaurant. She got into the camper and unthinkingly locked the doors, so that he had to bang on the window to be let in. He drove her home, going up to the flat with her and sitting down beside her on the sofa.

He put his arms around her.

548

'I'm sorry I brought this on,' he said against her hair.

She shook her head. She wasn't entirely sure it had been him – it was everything that had happened recently.

He whispered, 'It's okay to grieve, Nina.'

The images raced through her head. Her baby. The tiny child up at the monastery. Babies crying, mothers comforting them. The Virgin at Rocamadour, child on her knee. Fathers standing guard, strong and protecting. The way it ought to be, only it so seldom was.

Crying for herself, for him, for all the world, she put her face against Mark's chest and howled.

* * *

The intervening time before the reburial was, for Nina, spent in a sort of limbo. No reference was made at work to the monastery site – the three of them were pouring all their energies into supporting a local community attempting to stop a waste tip being set up in their own back yard; success was imminent, and there wasn't much time to think about anything else.

Sometimes Mark took her out – they went to the cinema, and for a Sunday walk up Symond's Yat so that she could meet the falcon people. He was obviously happy in her company, but made no move to increase the intimacy of their relationship. She felt almost that he was waiting for something.

Earthworks were invited to the party thrown one Friday night to celebrate victory over the council. The evening developed into raucousness – inevitably, she supposed – which might have been a matter for concern had the party been held in someone's private house. Just as well, she thought, watching two couples dancing on the tables, it was held in the rugby club.

Mark took her home. As she was getting out of the camper he said, 'Peter phoned this afternoon.'

'Oh yes?' She knew what was coming; had it been anything else, he'd have told her earlier.

'It's tomorrow. At five o'clock.'

She couldn't answer. Nodding to indicate she'd heard, she hurried away.

She wondered what one wore to a reburial.

Mark phoned at lunchtime and said he'd pick her up at four thirty, and she asked him.

'Since the bishop's officiating, I suppose we should go in something slightly up-market,' he said. 'Not jeans, in other words.'

'Will it be a big do?' She fervently hoped not.

'No. Don't be worried,' – Nice, that he'd picked up the fact that she was – 'Peter says just the bishop and his aide, him and the head of the archaeology department, and us. Nobody's told the press.'

'Is Bryn going?'

'No. He's gone to Cardiff.'

Six of them. Unless you counted the knight, the same number that attended the first time.

The bishop was late – his aide murmured something about a meeting of the ecumenical council having gone on longer than anticipated, but he didn't look very upset, Nina thought, about the great man keeping them waiting nearly an hour. It probably wasn't done for aides to apologize on behalf of their bishops.

But as she watched him lead them in a simple opening prayer, she revised her opinion. The bishop's face was calm, and she sensed kindness and true sincerity in his surprisingly undramatic voice.

She realized suddenly that he was doing this because he cared – had it been any sort of self-aggrandizement exercise he would, she thought, have ensured a bigger audience.

He was saying something about the soul of this little child, asking God to receive him now as He had done before.

'Extend Thy merciful arms and receive this . . .'

She missed the next words. He was beside her, between her and Mark, taller than Mark, standing straight and unbowed. She tried to focus, to see him clearly, but he was strangely transparent – she could make out the trees and the hillside beyond him.

He seemed to be wearing chain mail, covered in something dark. There was a bright red device on his chest. He was bareheaded, his dark hair turning grey.

As she stared up at him, for a moment he turned to her. The light brown eyes were wet.

They were putting the sword, the spurs and the coffined bones into the ground, into the same spot from which they'd been taken. Peter and Mark stepped forward to throw in handfuls of earth, and, after a moment, she did the same.

When she returned to her place, he was gone.

The bishop and his aide were escorted out of the graveyard by Peter and his departmental head. She could hear their quiet voices – 'Lovely service . . . Good to have done the deed at last . . . Invaluable information, taught us a lot . . .'

Peter turned to them in the entrance. 'Are you coming? We should secure the site for the night.' The area was still marked off by the temporary fence, a portion of which they'd removed for access.

Mark looked at her. 'Ready to go?'

'Not quite.' There was one more thing she had to do.

'We'll be along in a minute,' he said to Peter. 'Don't worry about the fence, we'll deal with it.'

'Okay. Be seeing you, then.'

In a few minutes it was as if the others hadn't been there at all. Alone on the hillside, Mark and Nina slowly circled the graveyard.

After a while he said, 'You've got it with you, then?'

'Yes.' She reached in her pocket. On the end of its chain, the sportelle swung gently.

'They'll fill in the grave tomorrow, I expect,' he said. 'We can easily slip the medallion in under the cover.'

'That's how we got it out,' she said.

As they knelt down she said, 'Was this all, do you think?'

He didn't seem to understand. 'Was what all?'

He wouldn't, she realized, have the same memory at this moment. Of a strong hand pushing hers into the earth. Leading her to the sportelle. The first clue that had taken her and Mark off on their inconclusive treasure hunt. 'Was this what he wanted? For us not to give up till we'd got this child reburied?'

She thrust the sportelle deep in the soft soil where no-one would find it. Sitting back, she looked at Mark. 'Well?'

'It seems pretty important to me,' he said. 'Especially since all the time the skeleton was down there in the university lab, the poor knight had to be there too. Instead of up here.' He glanced around and she had to agree that the glorious view and the wide, lonely sky was an improvement on a provincial campus. In the late September sunset, the colours and the contours were particularly beautiful.

'Yes, I agree, but why were we so important? Peter and his admin made the decision anyway – there was nothing for us to do when we got back from France, they'd already announced they were abandoning the site and reburying the child.'

He shrugged. 'I don't know.'

They stood up and began walking slowly towards the entrance. As they emerged on to the path he said, 'Let's go and have a last look inside the monastery.'

'Okay.'

They made their way in through the ruined walls to stand in the middle of the courtyard. She caught her tights on a bramble and wished that, bishops notwithstanding, she'd worn jeans after all, especially since she'd got her best skirt dirty kneeling by the grave.

Mark said, 'I'm trying to remember which bit's which. He told us, didn't he – Peter – when we first came up here?'

'Refectory and dormitories, infirmary, chapel.' She turned slowly, pointing as she spoke. 'Look how the chapel roof seems to grow out of the hillside behind it.'

'Mm. There's a sort of tower on the top – a turret, I suppose – look, there.' She followed the direction of his arm. 'Do you suppose there was a bell?'

It was a curious construction. Rising up from the western end of the chapel, it seemed to have been stuck on to the apex of the roof as an afterthought. 'I'm not sure,' she said. 'There doesn't seem to be anywhere a bell could have hung.'

He was crossing the yard, grabbing hold of tree branches and hauling himself up the sloping bank behind the chapel. She wondered briefly if he too was wishing he'd worn jeans. 'What are you doing?'

'Having a closer look,' he called. 'Coming up?'

I'll have to have the skirt cleaned anyway, she thought. She ran after him.

A huge beech overhung the chapel, and, by edging out along one of the stout branches, they were able to get right over the mysterious tower.

'Not a bell tower,' he said, his voice strangely hushed. 'But there's something under there. What is it?'

Reaching out, he pushed back the brittle ends of the branch, sweeping away the dead leaves which had settled on every surface of the turret. Under the single elegant arch had been set a chunk of iron, wrought into a rough circle: its centre was made of a different material. The surface was dingy with centuries of neglect, but she thought it might be glass.

'Here.' She took a handkerchief out of her pocket – she'd brought it in case the emotion of the occasion had proved too much. 'Give it a wipe.'

He leaned out but couldn't reach. 'Hold my legs.' She did so, and he stretched further. Her damp handkerchief made little impression at first, but then suddenly the green coating yielded to his scrubbing and gradually disappeared.

The glass began to sparkle.

'It's beautiful,' she said. She felt breathless, as if the air was being gathered up. She glanced into the sky, half expecting to see thunderclouds. But it was clear; in the west the sun was descending behind the Black Mountains, sending out last long rays that reached out towards her like yearning arms.

'I can't do any better with a sodden hankie,' Mark was saying, 'it'll –'

He didn't get any further. As the setting sun sent out its final vivid burst, the light reached the monastery and touched against the very edge of the object in the tower. And simultaneously a humming began, a low thrum which at first was barely detectable, then, growing fast, rose to something more.

It was like a choir, a huge choir, yet it was not human. Something was singing, though, something was lifting its voice in joy, in thankfulness, in an emotion so profound that she felt the hairs along her spine stand up in response.

The sun's last beam hit the object square on. And, as if the glass were a double-sided, vastly powerful magnifying mirror, it shot out its response. On either side of it light burst forth like a hundred suns, leaping away to the east and into the west in a dead straight line as far as the eye could see, flying above the hills and the valleys, across the patient earth which sang her ecstasy in a sound that was all but deafening.

The song of the earth.

Time stopped, she was aware only of feeling healed, of bathing in a precious sacred light so beneficial, so *good* that surely nothing unsound or malevolent could have survived its triumphant advance. In blissful delight she looked down into the courtyard, and he was there – of course he was! – standing with others, a man and a woman, lifting his arms to the sky, his face full of the same joy. As if he knew she was there, he turned and for a moment looked straight at her; the years of strain seemed to have fallen off him, and he was young again, lighthearted as if she had set him free. She tried to find words, something to say that would reach him, but swiftly he shook his head, smiling, and she knew words weren't necessary.

Still looking at her, he put his hand on his heart and then extended it towards her. Then he turned back to the others.

Then – a minute, an hour later, she had no idea – the incredible light began to fade, dimming as the sun disappeared, and the great euphoric hymn slowly ebbed to a soft chant, then to nothing.

She was in Mark's arms, held so tight that it felt like they were part of each other. He said shakily, 'What on earth was that?'

It *was* the earth.

But, 'I don't know,' she mumbled.

They sat clutching each other for some time. Then, the mists beginning to swirl around below making them shiver, carefully they climbed down.

She stopped at the very spot where he had stood. Into her head he said, *Now you know.*

What do I know?

Why nothing must be touched.

'Yes,' she said. It's a powerhouse, she thought, a solar temple. And it's this that he's guarding, this that mustn't change. Mustn't be probed and investigated, irrevocably disturbed.

The child was personal – his son, of course he was – but this, this is for the earth.

Aye.

She knew he'd gone. And, because there was no further need, knew too that she wouldn't see him again.

Mark took her hand. She jumped slightly at his touch, and, as if he understood, he pulled her close and hugged her. 'All right?' he said quietly.

'Yes. Think so.'

He waited for a few moments, not speaking, then gently began to nudge her in the direction of the path.

It was time to go.

* * *

She thought it was greatly to his credit that he never asked her about those last moments in the courtyard.

556

Perhaps he knows, she thought, or at least senses – he's the sort of man who would. And perhaps he, too, feels it's not something to talk about.

It was a warming thought, that they might have shared it.

When all the fuss had died down, the grave had been sealed and a last couple of trenches dug and filled in again, she and Mark went up to the grave-yard. She had a posy of flowers to put on the baby's grave.

It's quiet now, she thought. Safe.

No-one would disturb the site again; they were going to put a permanent fence around the whole of the monastery for the transparently false reason that it was dangerous – the ruined buildings had been judged unsound and likely to fall on anyone explor-ing them. For once in her life Nina was thankful for good old British red tape – with the beech branch allowed to swing back across the magical glass, with any luck the secret would be safe for another eight hundred years.

She wondered what was the real reason for secur-ing the monastery from prying eyes. Had someone else seen that incredible beam of light, heard the earth's song? Someone who, like herself and Mark, knew the legend of the Cathars and their magic crys-tal and, putting two and two together, now knew it wasn't just a legend after all?

It didn't seem likely. Much more likely it was sour grapes – if we can't do a thorough excavation, Peter and his band would have said, no-one else is going to.

Either way, the monastery and what was hidden there were safe.

Standing over the grave, she and Mark were silent; she guessed that, like her, he was deep in his own thoughts. After a while he said, 'I wish we knew how it got here.'

They'd had the conversation before; as she'd done then, she said blithely, '*He* brought it.'

'But how? Tell me how a knight crusading against the Cathars could possibly have acquired one of the prisms that were their greatest treasure. Not only acquired it, but smuggled it halfway across Europe and delivered it here.'

She knew he was seeing the knight as unvaryingly opposed to the heretics: it could never have occurred to him that the knight might have been *given* the crystal. But then, she thought charitably, he hasn't been permitted the knowledge I've been given.

'Perhaps he nicked it.' Sorry, she said silently to him. 'Then got on his horse and galloped away before they'd noticed it was gone.'

He smiled faintly. 'Keep working on it,' he said.

But she knew she wouldn't. Didn't need to. She thought it would probably fade to the back of his mind, too. When the next problem cropped up.

As they left she whispered, 'Goodbye.'

He heard, and put his arm round her. 'He's been dead a very long time,' he said gently. 'They did die then, babies. People probably half expected it.'

It was kind of him to try to comfort her.

As they set off back to the camper he said, 'If I married, I'd like to have children.'

Not really paying attention, she said, 'Me too.'

'Oh, good.'

A few yards further on, she replayed the exchange in her head.

And stopped.

'Mark?'

He was a couple of paces ahead. Turning, he said, 'What?'

She didn't know what to say. If it hadn't been what she thought, she was going to look pretty stupid saying, 'Yes, I will marry you.' On the other hand, if it had and she ignored it . . .

He, too, didn't seem able to find words. Coming back up the path to her, he put his arms round her and kissed her.

The kiss went on for a long time.

Afterwards, resuming the descent hand in hand, she realized she didn't need to reply. Given his track record, he wouldn't bother to press her for an answer; he'd either assume she'd tacitly agreed or else hadn't understood. In which case, he'd probably mention it again some time.

The sun came out from behind a cloud and, the beauty of the peaceful land augmenting her happiness, she decided it didn't matter either way.

Epilogue

The Hermitage

SPRING 1212

Ranald had sent her back to Joanna as soon as she could travel. It was better, living in Joanna's quiet household. She could pretend none of it had happened, that she was back where she'd been a year ago. Living an undramatic life, waiting to see if he was ever coming back.

But as she grew stronger, denying his existence and his love began to seem like a betrayal.

In the long dark winter evenings Joanna would leave her alone, and gradually she came to terms with what had happened.

She relived it all, from the moment he'd laughed himself silly when she fell in the dung-heap right up to their final parting. When, at long last, she'd told him she loved him and he'd said he loved her too.

You did, Gawyn, she thought as she gazed out at the first snowdrops incongruous against the frost-hard ground. I don't doubt you, and I know that, if it had been within your power, you'd have come back to me. Like you did before.

Not knowing what had happened to him was a

torment she'd just had to learn to live with. In her prayers for him, she begged that his end had been swift.

He was a fighter, the thought seemed to say in her mind. Fighters hit as hard as they can and are hit with equal force in return.

It seemed to be an obscure way of affirming that it *had* been quick. The fearful visions of him lingering somewhere, in pain that grew to agony before death released him, ceased to haunt her.

When she knew she could do so without breaking down, she talked of him to Joanna.

'I told you, child, that he would ever be a knight first and a husband second,' Joanna reminded her. But there was compassion in her face.

'You did.' So did Ismay, she added silently. Ismay had returned to the household Gawyn had found for her, since Joanna had no need of a servant; for once, Roese was quite glad she wasn't there.

Despite the uncompromising reply, Joanna went on, 'You would never have had all of him, you know. He might have lived with you for months, perhaps even years, at a time, but sooner or later the other life would have called him.' She leaned forward. 'Men are summoned by God to be knights,' she said. 'Or so they believe. The whole chivalric code is binding. Unto death. For a man like Gawyn, domesticity could not have competed.' Perhaps thinking she had been too harsh, she said more kindly, 'No matter how much he loved you.'

Thank you for that, Roese thought.

Joanna was right. She knew it, had always known it. But, she thought, I was prepared to take however much of him he offered. It would have been enough. I *know* it would.

* * *

Gradually, so gradually that she only became aware of it after many months, her grief became controllable. The worst that she could possibly imagine had happened to her, yet she was still breathing, still walking around. Still, sometimes, laughing. And winter was nearly over: the earth was stirring, coming back to life.

When spring came, she was restless. Joanna lent her a horse and she started riding out, a little further each day.

She waited to see if Ranald would come to visit. When he didn't, she went to find him.

* * *

Aidan had had a hard February and a worse March. In April the weather improved and he began to think he was going to be left with a viable flock after all.

Lonely, he took to visiting the hermitage more frequently. The rough winter had found holes in roofs and the spring rains had burst blocked-up gutters; there was plenty for him to do.

Sometimes he was tempted to ask Ranald to admit him to the community. But he didn't.

He thought of her constantly. To have lost her a second time had been almost more than he could bear, although compassion for her had overridden pity for himself. He didn't know how she'd survived the successive blows of a dreadful childbirth – however much she'd thanked him afterwards, he knew full well he was no fit midwife for a woman, he was much better with his ewes – only to lose the baby and, almost immediately, realize that her man was dead.

He thought, she'll never risk her heart again.

Perhaps she would find a convent and shut herself away. Live out her days in silent prayer, mourning the knight who didn't come back. Marry herself to Jesus, who wouldn't let her down.

What a waste that would be.

Struck by the blasphemy of the thought, he tried to take it back.

But couldn't. Angry suddenly, he thought, if she did that, I might as well take my vows too.

It was May, and the dog roses were beginning to bloom. Their effect on him was stronger than it had been the previous spring.

He avoided them if he could.

Sitting on a grassy bank mending a hurdle, he saw a figure in the distance. Ranald? He hoped so, he could do with some good company to lift him out of his thoughts.

He stood up, beginning to walk down the hillside towards whoever was approaching.

At first he didn't let himself believe it. It's my imagination, he thought wildly, I'm seeing what I want to see.

But he was wrong.

Closer now, so close he could see the light dancing on the bright hair. The smile spreading across the face.

'I owe you an apology,' she said. She was breathless, whether from the climb or the tension, he didn't know.

'What for?'

'I pushed you away. When you were caring for me.' She hesitated, and he thought the pink cheeks grew slightly pinker. He smiled to himself: he'd forgotten her tendency to say exactly what was uppermost in her mind. 'It was very silly of me,' she plunged on. 'I would probably have died without you.'

'No, you wouldn't.'

'Perhaps not from anything physical, sheep herd,' – a brilliant smile flashed across her face, as if she were on the verge of laughter – 'but I wanted to die, and you refused to let go.'

He bowed his head. There was a swish of grass as she came right up to him, and he felt her warmth. 'Aidan?'

He met her eyes. As he'd seen them so often in his mind, they were clear grey. 'What is it?'

But she seemed to be unable to go on. Mutely she stood before him, her eyes on his. He thought, I love you. I've always loved you. And it's frightening, thinking what I'm thinking. That, perhaps, you're here because you could just be discovering you feel the same.

Why else, he wondered, have you come?

Still she didn't speak. But she put out her hand and took his.

She said very quietly, 'Nobody grieves for ever. But I won't forget.'

He nodded. 'I know.'

'Can you bear that? To have him there in my memory? In my heart?'

She looked as if she were in pain. As if her honesty was hurting her.

Does she fear, then, that if she speaks her mind, tells me what to expect, I'll turn her away?

'Roese –' His voice sounded strange. He began again. 'Roese, I understand. I –' Should I go on? he wondered. *She* did, she managed to get out what she felt she must say. Frankness should be repaid in kind.

'I love you, Roese,' he said gently. The grey eyes

filled with tears. 'I would rather live with you and your memories than suffer life without you.'

'You would?'

He nodded. Her emotion was catching, and he didn't trust himself to speak.

He remembered Gwynhwyfar. Sometimes words won't do.

Feeling that he had been given what he'd waited for all his life, he took her in his arms. Her face turned up to his, he met her lips with his own.

The scent of the wild roses blew softly across the pasture and, high above, a skylark began to sing.

Postscript

Extract from *Today's Archaeology*, Spring 1995

*Concluding the Investigation of the Wye
Monastery Site*

Further to the report in last quarter's journal concerning the winding-down of this investigation, the following discoveries, made during the last few days of
the dig, have been added to the record:

Prior to the permanent fence being erected to dissuade trespass into an ancient site whose buildings
have been designated unstable, a last survey was
made. In the graveyard where, in the summer of last
year, two adult and one child skeletons were discovered and subsequently reinterred, another large
grave was found near the entrance. If indeed this was
a monastic community (this is in dispute; see
Today's Archaeology, Vol. 7 no.3), then, it was
hypothesized, this grave might be that of outsiders to
the community, buried apart from the brothers.

The hypothesis was borne out. A brief inspection
of the grave uncovered two adult skeletons, a man
and a woman; the calibrated radiocarbon determination gives a date of 1260 +/- 20 AD for their deaths.
Both had lived to a good age, not only for their
century but for any other: it is estimated that both
were over 75.

Interestingly, their interment followed the pattern
of the others on this site in that they were buried with
grave goods. Alongside the man was an iron-tipped,

ivory-handled shepherd's crook, and on the breast of the woman, beneath her left hand, was a gold Celtic cross set with garnets and amethysts. It was originally intended that both objects should be donated to the Wye Valley Archaeological Museum, but pressure was brought to bear and the goods were reburied with the bodies, which for security reasons were sealed into a lead-lined coffin.

It is concluded that the man and the woman died at the same time; those present at the unearthing of the two bodies recorded that they had been buried hand in hand.